LIGHT BEARERS

BOOK TWO

MINDY HITE

Visit Mindy online at https://mindyhite.com

The Deliverance

Light Bearers Series, Book 2

© 2025 by Mindy Hite

e-Book ISBN: 978-1-953419-76-7

Paperback ISBN: 978-1-953419-77-4

Hardback ISBN: 978-1-953419-78-1

Published by Fayette Press https://www.fayettepress.com

The persons and events portrayed in this work of fiction are the creations of the author, and any resemblance to persons living or dead is purely coincidental.

Printed in the United States of America.

* * *

In Loving Memory of Rebeccah Glass Lowe
Your love, laughter and life shone brightly and
you are greatly missed.
I'll see you in Heaven, dear friend.

* * *

Contents

PROLOGUE

SARAH

THE WIND WHIPPED THROUGH my hair as I ran through the dense woods, hoping with every beat of my racing heart I would finally find her. It had been four years since the night we were separated. Four years since I was forced to leave my sister behind, and four years of coming to terms with that sobering fact. I knew when I left it was my only choice but knowing that didn't make me miss or worry about her any less. The last four years were spent in The Light, training, getting stronger, doing everything I could do to ready myself for whatever it was going to take to find her and rescue her.

I will find you, Amelia.

The words went through my mind, as much a promise to myself as they were a promise to her.

Despite the cold night air, sweat dripped off my forehead and rolled down my spine. My breathing was labored, but I could tell my training was paying off. Running the last 10 miles had been easy and I felt like I could run 10 more. I knelt and pulled the small pack off my back, grabbing the water bottle I had tucked next to the burner phone Nyiah insisted I carry. It was a risk, but we determined we should all carry a burner anytime we worked alone. Nyiah had wanted to come with me this time, but we had learned the more of us that gathered together, the easier it was for the Terrobah to trace us. And tonight, I wasn't taking any chances. This was the best lead we'd had in a while. I chugged some water and shoved the bottle back into my pack, swinging it onto my back as I took off down the trail I was following.

I slowed my pace as I reached a clearing. They weren't far away now; I could feel their presence in a way that caused the hair on the back of my neck to stand up. I had a small light guard up. It wasn't bright, and certainly not anything the Terrobah would notice, but I needed it to see more clearly in the dark. Off in the distance, not too far up ahead, I saw what looked like the opening of a cave.

My heart and my mind raced. I had searched tirelessly for the last week, combing cave after cave, only to be disappointed each time. Was this it? Could this be the cave I had seen so clearly in my dreams? I reached the mouth of the cave. The Light had guided me here; I felt it deep in the recesses of my soul. Raising my arm, I extended a beam of light into the cavern. No need for a flashlight when you have the ability to emit light.

The cave was deep, which made me feel like it had promise, but at the same time made me think it could be a trap. I risked moving farther into the darkness until something caught my eye.

The remnants of a campfire were spread across the cave floor as if it had been kicked out in a rush, but that wasn't what made my stomach hitch into my throat. No, that was the blood-red stains that had been smeared on one of the cave walls.

I had no time to dwell on what might have happened here as I felt the hairs rise on the back of my neck. I generated a stronger light guard in response and a bright glow was emanating from me as I turned around quickly to face the threat.

Three men that looked like hikers stood at the mouth of the cave, quite at home in the inky blackness of the night. They didn't fool me for a second though; they were Terrobah, and weak ones at that. Disappointment sliced through me as I saw no sign of Amelia anywhere.

I did not lower my guard even a fraction because I had no idea who else was lurking in the cave or in the forest waiting for me to do just that.

"Where is she?" I asked, feeling my anger and power grow. If these weak Terrobah were the only enemies present, then I had wasted my time. Amelia wouldn't be here under such a small guard.

"Oh, she had to step out," one of the would-be hikers hissed with sarcasm. He was a little bigger than the other two on either side of him; clearly, he was the leader.

"Where is she?" I asked again, slowly dragging out each word, filling them with light and power. The smallest Terrobah dropped to his knees from the pain of my spoken words. I had learned early in my training that my voice, and The Light that pushed through it, was toxic to the Terrobah. The other two cringed but seemed to recover quickly. They, of course, had no concern for their "brother" who was writhing on the ground.

"Whoa, easy there, little girl, we're just here to have a nice chat," the leader said slowly. I could sense his words trying to come up against my guard, but they were nothing to me.

The smallest Terrobah stood again. I turned my head and raised my eyebrow at him, evidently the weakest of the three.

"Where?" As I spoke, I allowed the full force of The Light to come forth.

He cringed, crying out, "Stop... stop... stop... she's not here." He immediately suffered a blow from the leader for his weakness.

"Fool!" the leader spat at him. "We'll never get a better assignment with you in our midst." He sneered at the form on the ground and then kicked him, hard.

"Not enjoying guarding empty caves?" I taunted, still feeling my anger at being thwarted again.

"Not particularly," the leader growled, leaning away from me, attempting to lessen the force of my words.

"Where is she?" I asked again, tasting the anger on my tongue.

The power in my voice brought down the other Terrobah next to him who had been silent the whole time.

"Like they tell me anything. She was gone before we got here," the leader said, clearly feeling the pain but still strong enough to stand against it.

"So, she's okay," I said, almost to myself and with no power behind it.

"I wouldn't say she's okay," he commented with a sneer. I blasted him with a light pulse out of each hand, knocking him backwards.

"What do you know?" I reared back for another blast.

"Stop!" he screamed. "I only know...what...I saw before," he gasped out, trying to prevent my next attack.

"Which was?" I asked, causing him to scream in pain.

"With what she was enduring, she's going to wish she was dead," he snarled, clearly enjoying the anguish his words caused me.

With one large burst of light from my hand, I knocked him unconscious. I wanted to kill them all right then and there, but I knew I couldn't do that. I couldn't let any darkness in if I wanted to stay pure in The Light. I blasted them one more time for good measure, I'm only human after all, then walked out of the cave and into the night.

This wasn't over, not by a long shot.

Chapter 1

MITCH

There I sat, a grown, twenty-six-year-old man with my sister sitting beside me in the waiting room. She might as well have been holding my hand and spit-washing my face with all she was having to do for me lately. But as foolish as I felt, I was also grateful to her for coming to help me during and after my surgery.

I had gone with some of my buddies to blow off some steam by hitting the slopes, but instead of coming home rested and ready to go, I came home with a torn ACL, a ligament in my knee I needed to be 100% if I was going to keep enjoying my active lifestyle. I hated having to sit still for anything, so this kind of injury was pretty much torture. And the length of rehab I knew I had ahead of me did nothing to improve my mood.

Unable to drive myself to my appointment, I sat in the waiting room with Sharon, about to have my first outpatient physical therapy session. I picked up an outdated magazine and thumbed through it without really seeing the pages before giving up and setting it on the table next to my chair. My eyes roamed around the office, taking in the fact that it was clean and tidy. There wasn't much to it, just some chairs lined up across from the reception desk, a fake tree, and some framed pictures of famous athletes.

I was rarely sick, so all these doctor's visits and now physical therapy were new to me. Too many doctors in my opinion. Too much time that I could be doing something else. But my new reality was doctors and physical therapy until my knee was back to 100%, and then I would be back to the life I enjoyed.

This office was supposed to be one of the best outpatient sports medicine PT clinics in my area and that's why my doctor sent me to it. He knew how active I was and that I would be pushing myself to heal quickly. I'm sure the physical therapist already had a note in my chart from the doctor to reign me in so that my ACL graft wouldn't fail.

"Are you alright, Mitch?" Sharon asked.

"Yeah, why?" I answered, swallowing, not meeting her gaze. She placed her hand on my arm until I looked at her.

"Well, your good leg is bouncing all over the place, and I can hear you grinding your teeth," she said with a playful smirk.

I took a deep breath in and released it slowly, rolling my shoulders and my neck around as I tried to relax.

"Are you in pain?" she questioned me softly, trying not to embarrass me.

"Not physical pain," I paused, "well it's not all physical pain," I said, managing a smile to try to ease her worry.

She raised one eyebrow as if asking me what I meant by that cryptic comment.

"I'm feeling sorry for myself over here, sis, just ignore me," I tried to soften my tone a little.

"Sorry bud, I'm your sister and here to help you get back on your feet. I'm afraid you get all of me and that includes my worry."

"Well, don't let my surly mood fool you, I'm really thankful for your help. I couldn't have done this without you. Can you imagine Troy having to help me like you've been?" Troy was my roommate and not what you would call a caretaker. I faked a shudder and said, "I'd probably be lying on the floor passed out from the pain because he forgot to feed me and give me my meds."

She laughed, "Poor Troy, he almost seems afraid of your leg."

"Yeah, that's because he was behind me on the slopes when my leg twisted under me, and I rolled like a frigin' snowball down the run. I think the sight of my leg and the string of cuss words that flew out of my mouth pretty much scared him off." My knee ached all the more as I remembered the accident.

"Ugh, don't even mention it. It's bad enough to know I'm going to have to change your dressings. I don't want to think about your leg twisted in the wrong direction," she made a face.

"Oh, come on, sis, I know you like the gory details," I teased, knowing she was pretty squeamish.

"Not!" she glared at me.

"Seriously, I'm super grateful to have you here taking care of me."

"Mitchell James Wright, there's no place I would rather be."

"What are you middle-naming me for?!" I feigned annoyance.

"Sisterly right," she said, going back to her phone.

It was a running joke between us. She called me Mitchell, or my full name, even though everyone else called me Mitch. It was a term of endearment coming from her. I cleared my throat and said, "I'm sure there's gonna be places you'd rather be when it comes time to change my dressings."

She lifted her head to look at me. "You know, it's funny, I'm not really afraid of what's under the dressings. It's the thought of hurting you that makes me nervous and a little queasy."

"Well, I'm glad my knee doesn't totally gross you out."

"Not yet, anyway," she quipped. "Let's try to keep that swelling down, though." She pretended like she was about to vomit, which made me smile. She'd already talked about how my "fat knee" weirded her out.

"Swelling kept at a minimum, got it," I gave her a small salute. "Hopefully, they'll ice me down after my session. I have a feeling it's not gonna be pretty when I'm done here."

"True, just be sure . . ." she continued, but was cut off by my name being called.

"Mitchell Wright?" A man standing at the door to the PT gym called my name with a chart in his hands.

I worked to get myself up to standing, and then Sharon handed my crutches to me one at a time. Once I had my crutches underneath me, Sharon asked, "You want me to come back with you?"

"Nah, go take a break at the Starbucks across the parking lot. I'll let you know when I'm done here."

"Okay," she said as she rose. "Don't overdo it."

"Never," I responded, as I made my way toward the physical therapist waiting at the door. I didn't turn to look, but I heard Sharon laughing at me. Okay, so I was the king of overdoing it, but she didn't have to laugh so hard.

"Sorry for the delay," I said as I crutched through the doorway.

"No problem, those crutches are tricky to navigate even if you're not full of pain medicine that can make you dizzy." He chuckled as he led me across the room. "Here we are," he said, gesturing to a flat, padded table. "Go ahead and slip your shoes off and have a seat on this end of the table with your back against the wall."

I turned myself so that my back was facing the table. The physical therapist took my crutches, and then I used my arms to push myself backwards onto the table. He helped me swing around by lifting my surgical-repaired leg and the bulky brace, setting it gently on the table. I leaned against the half wall that the table was set up against.

I was in one of the three rows of tables in the middle of the room. There were some people working out on tables like the one

I was sitting on, some with workout equipment, and some were on the floor.

It's like a gym in here, I thought, and then remembered the sign on the door had said, "Physical Therapy Gym." *Brilliant observation there, Bro.* I made a mental note to maybe back off the pain meds a bit.

"Now that we have those crutches out of the way," the PT said, bringing my attention back to him. He was holding out his hand for an obvious handshake that I returned as he said, "I'm Ethan Hernandez. I'm a physical therapist, and I'll be doing your evaluation today."

"Nice to meet you, Ethan."

"You too, Mitchell."

"Call me Mitch," I quickly corrected, as he moved to stand behind a little rolling table that had a laptop on it.

"Mitch it is, then," he said with a friendly smile. "Mitch, I need to gather some information from you first, and then we'll see if we can get that knee moving a little better."

"Okay," I responded, even though I felt more than slightly nauseous at the fact that he would be touching and moving my knee. My leg had been in a brace since the surgery three days before. I only took it out for my range of motion exercises the physical therapist had taught me at the hospital. Just removing the brace hurt and bending it made me feel like I would pass out.

"That must have been pretty traumatic," I heard Ethan say.

"Uh, what? Sorry." I apologized, knowing I had missed something he'd just said.

"Your ski accident. It had to have been pretty traumatic."

"Yeah, it's not something I want to repeat, that's for sure."

"I hear that. Not to worry, though, we'll get this knee as good as new," he assured me.

"And exactly how long will that take?" I asked, bracing myself for his reply.

"Around nine months." Ethan replied, seeming unphased by the fact that he just quoted me three quarters of a year.

"Nine months?" I asked in disbelief.

"You'll be back to a lot of activities before then. That's just how long it'll take if you want to hit the slopes again."

"I'm not sure I'll be hitting the slopes again even at nine months; that was a brutal fall, I'm not keen on repeating it."

"I completely understand." He looked at the computer and back at me. "Did the doctor tell you that he also had to repair your meniscus?"

"Yeah, I think he said something about the cartilage. That's the meniscus, right?"

"Yes. When they have to repair that, it slows down our rehab schedule." I sighed a noticeably heavy sigh, but he continued. "We have to work within a limited range of motion and limited weight bearing for six weeks."

"O-kay," I dragged out the word, feeling like the bad news just kept coming.

"I have some paperwork that will outline all of that, step-by-step. The better you follow these guidelines, the faster we can progress."

"Did the doctor tell you to say that?" I questioned him.

"What do you mean?" Ethan asked, looking puzzled.

"Vernhoffer already warned me against pushing too hard, so I figured there was a sticky note in my chart warning you about it as well."

"I have the notes from your MRI and surgery, but no, Dr. Vernhoffer did not put an extra sticky note in here warning me about you." He smiled, then added with a smirk, "You just have 'pushes self too hard' written all over you."

"Seriously?" I chuckled, a little offended, but mostly proud.

"I'm just giving you a hard time, but yes, I can read my patients like that. First off, you're a guy, and we stink at being patient with the process and being told what to do. And then I can see that you're fit, which means you don't spend a lot of time lying around on the couch."

"Well, I can't really argue with any of that."

"Don't worry, Mitch." Ethan had moved out from behind the laptop to lean against the table at my feet. "I work with ACL reconstructions every day, and I have a tremendous success rate. I will push you as hard as I can while still allowing for the necessary healing. The best way for you to get back to all the things that you love is to follow my instructions, exactly," he raised one eyebrow at me, pausing for effect at that last word.

"Well, I will certainly try," I conceded.

"And I'll be right here to reign you in or give you a push in the right direction. Although, I'm guessing I'll be reigning you in." I chuckled. *I'm gonna like this guy.*

Ethan moved back behind his laptop to finish up his questions, and before I was ready, he was helping me remove my knee brace. I wasn't going to say it out loud, but just the thought of having to bend my knee made my stomach roll.

"You okay there?" Ethan asked.

At his words, I realized I had closed my eyes. "Ugh, yeah, I guess so." I opened my eyes to see that he was putting on latex gloves.

"Don't pass out on me there, I haven't actually touched your knee yet."

That was enough to make me grit my teeth and keep my eyes open as he unwound the ace bandage that went from my calf to my thigh. He pulled off the surgical gauze pad that had been on my knee since I left the hospital. There was some brown, dried blood that I tried to ignore.

My knee stayed bent, even though now, without the brace, it should have been flat on the table like my other leg. Ethan tucked a rolled towel under my knee which brought relief I hadn't even known I was seeking. Without missing a beat, he was looking at my knee, gently touching here and there. He looked over my whole leg and gave my calf a firm squeeze and then another.

"Any pain with that?" he asked.

"No," I could say without lying. He continued to ask about pain as he squeezed his way down to my ankle. He moved my ankle up and down and then asked me to do the same thing on my own. The movement was stiff and slower than normal, but Ethan didn't seem concerned.

He brought out a very specialized looking ruler and said, "Okay, now we're just going to take some measurements so we can know where we're starting from." He was using the royal 'we' because we both knew I wouldn't be taking the measurements, and he wouldn't be feeling the pain.

Ethan removed the towel and gently let go of my knee so it could lower on its own. It didn't really move. My knee was definitely swollen, and that was probably getting in the way. I said as much to Ethan and he agreed, but also said my soft tissue had tightened up as well.

"But I had full motion before the surgery, I did what the doctor said to do," I commented, trying to keep the annoyance out of my voice.

"That's good, that will help you overall."

"But I lost the motion." I felt my frustration rise.

"Unfortunately, yes, because the surgery is a trauma as well. Your knee responded just like it did after the accident. With swelling and tightening. It doesn't know the difference between the injury and the surgery. Pain and injury signal the body for 'all hands on deck' which includes swelling. The good thing is, since you had full motion before the surgery, we'll get there faster."

"So, I have to get my motion back first?"

"That's exactly right." He was crouched down with his ruler, one end in line with my thigh, the other headed down to my calf, with the circular measurement hinge right beside my knee.

He stood up and grabbed a strap from the half wall behind us. He hooked a loop around my foot and then handed me the two ends of the strap, slipping a flat towel under my heel.

"Okay, Mitch, let's see you bend that knee. You're going to gently pull on the strap to bring your heel along the table surface as far as you can." Before I could respond to tell him that seemed impossible, he continued, "Don't worry, I'm gonna help."

With the strap gripped tight, I began to pull. The towel under my heel allowed me to move it easily at first, for about an inch or two, but then my knee just stopped. It was barely bent at all, and I was stuck. Ethan had his hand on my foot but was using his other hand to hold the ruler to measure the bend in my knee. I pulled harder and my pain shot through the roof.

"That's enough, Mitch. Let off the straps." Ethan helped lower my leg slowly back to the table. It didn't take long. I had barely lifted it before the pain caused me to break out in a sweat.

"Are we done for the day, then?" I asked, only half joking and trying to ignore the pain as it was still present but beginning to fade away.

"Not quite," Ethan returned, smiling. He moved around me on the table, taking what seemed like a million small measurements.

Is he measuring me for a suit?

"Almost done here, Mitch, hang in there."

He made notes on his computer and then came back to my injured knee, instructing me to flex my thigh while he was tapping it gently with his fingers. It should have been easy. But my thigh did nothing. Ethan encouraged me to keep trying. That felt like a joke since literally nothing was happening. I tried it on my other leg just to make sure my brain was still working, and my thigh muscles popped right up on that leg.

"It's alright, Mitch, we just have to wake those quad muscles back up. With all this swelling, they've checked out for a bit. The more you practice this, the more they'll remember their job."

"I'll take your word for it." I stared intently at my thigh, mentally willing my knee to go down. On rep nine or ten, I saw a flicker of movement in my thigh, which was strangely exciting for such a small accomplishment.

"Okay, one more, and then I'll get another measurement."

I finished my last rep and breathed a sigh of relief. I felt like I had just run three miles, when in reality I had only done like 12 of those "quad sets," as Ethan called them.

My relief was short lived as he handed me the strap to bend my knee again. Fear must have shown on my face because Ethan said, "We're gonna take it nice and easy, man, moving in the range that's available to us without pain."

A few minutes later, I was exhausted and covered in sweat, but I had completed the exercise. Ethan took another measurement and said, "You've already gained 24 degrees back." I didn't know what that meant exactly, but gain was good.

"Really?" I asked.

"Yep, that work you did before is paying off." He was documenting something on the computer. I couldn't believe I'd made that much progress with a few exercises.

Ethan took me through a few more exercises, giving me reminders along the way. When he mentioned sleeping in the brace, I gave him a disgruntled look. He continued, acknowledging my frustration, "I know it's not comfortable to sleep in, but it keeps you from messing up what the surgeon did in there."

"Wait, you said you know it's not comfortable, have you had a knee injury?" I asked, now curious about this guy that I was trusting with my healing.

"Yep, sophomore year of high school," he said from behind his computer.

"How did you do it?"

"Playing soccer," he answered with a small smile.

"What did you do to your knee?"

"Same thing you did. Torn ACL, torn meniscus."

"And that happened with soccer?" I asked, doubting in a way because my fall seemed a bit more traumatic than anything that could happen in soccer.

"Yeah," he came to lean on the end of my table again. He continued, "It's a pretty common injury with soccer. I did a pullback turn for a drop pass to my defender and was hit from behind. My cleat stuck in the grass and then all the torque of the twist went through my knee. I heard a loud popping sound and felt extreme pain, and that was that."

"And you came back full strength?" I asked, even more impressed with this guy.

"Sure did," he returned. "I have arthritis in that knee now since I lost a lot of cartilage in my injury and even more with the clean up during surgery."

"Arthritis?" I questioned with barely veiled disgust. That was an old person problem, and Ethan couldn't be more than a few years older than me.

"Yes, osteoarthritis. It's when you have less cartilage and get some bone-on-bone contact in the joint," he answered casually, like he wasn't bothered by it at all.

"How long after your surgery did you get that?"

"Six to seven years. I take some supplements, and I keep active. I don't really notice it unless a cold front comes through. I keep my knee strong and keep going with all that I want to do."

He moved me on to the next exercise that involved the belt again, but thankfully it was a calf stretch, which felt surprisingly good. We did two more exercises, and then I got to feel the sweet relief of the ice machine.

I texted Sharon to let her know I was almost done, and five minutes later, she was walking into the gym. Ethan had said it was fine to invite her on back since we were finishing up.

"How'd it go?" she asked, looking me over.

"It was a lot tougher than a few simple exercises should be," I replied, still a little annoyed at how weak I had felt. Ethan chuckled from behind his computer table, causing Sharon to turn her attention to him.

"Did he give you a lot of trouble?" she asked Ethan and turned a teasing eye back to me.

"Nah, he's gonna be a great patient. Right, Mitch?" he asked with a smile. He moved around his computer and extended his hand to Sharon, "I'm Ethan Hernandez, Mitch's PT."

"Sharon Wright, Mitch's sister." She returned his handshake, blushing slightly.

Ethan didn't seem to notice as he moved to check the dressing on my knee.

"I know you're a little discouraged with how hard everything seemed to be today," Ethan said as he finished helping me get my brace back on. I didn't have to respond to Ethan's comment; it was true, and he knew it. He continued, "It's supposed to be really hard right now. You're only three days out from surgery, and your whole body is involved in all of this. I'm not saying you won't have bad days, but if you follow your home exercise program and post-op care instructions, you'll get progressively better and better."

"Thanks, Ethan," I replied as he handed me my crutches.

"My pleasure," he returned. "Now let's get you out of here, and I'll see you on Wednesday."

"Looking forward to it." I muttered, which caused Ethan to laugh as I crutched my way through the door that Sharon was holding open for me.

Once I was settled into the passenger side of my blue sports car with the seat all the way back, Sharon drove us away from the clinic, my second home for the next few months. I was supposed to come three times a week. That wouldn't be a problem for this week and the next as I had those off from work, but it would be more of a hassle once I returned to the office.

Sharon broke into my thoughts, "You want some food on the way home?"

"I wouldn't pass up some Chick-Fil-A," I said, letting my eyes drift closed and feeling so tired I wasn't sure if eating was a priority or if I should just sleep.

"I think I can handle that," she replied. "I could really go for a frozen lemonade right about now."

"I was thinking about some nuggets, but a cookies and cream shake might be good, too," I said with my eyes closed.

I heard her chuckle, "I thought you said you were really going to watch what you ate since you can't work out right now."

I opened one eye to look at her, "That was the most grueling workout I've ever done. Five simple exercises, and I'm the most tired I've ever been after a workout."

She laughed.

"Don't laugh; you should pity me."

"Poor Mitchy, let's go get you your shake to make you feel better."

"That's more like it," I said with my eyes closed once again. I felt like I could fall asleep right there and, apparently, I did, because the next thing I knew Sharon was nudging me to tell me we were home.

"I thought we were going to stop at Chick-Fil-A." I asked as she bent to help me get my leg out of the car.

Sharon laughed. "We did! You just slept through it. But don't worry, I got your milkshake for you." I pushed myself up to standing.

"Aww, thanks sis, you're the best," I said as she handed me my crutches at my door.

"And don't you forget it, Mitchell James."

"Race ya," I said, acting like I was going to race her on my crutches.

"Don't even think about it," she scolded "or I'll drink your milkshake."

I dropped all joking; I really wanted that milkshake.

CHAPTER 2

MITCH

"Mitch! Mitch! Mitch, wake up!" My name was pulling me back from a black fog, and I clung to that as I tried to wake up and find my bearings.

"Mitch!" Sharon's voice called out to me in a panic. *Sharon!* My eyes shot open.

"What?! What's wrong, are you okay?" I bolted upright in bed, immediately wincing from the pain in my leg.

"Me? You're asking me if I'm okay?!" she questioned, practically shouting, her eyes opened wide in fear.

"Well, you're screaming at me and shaking me, and every light is on in the apartment. Is someone trying to break in or something?"

"No," she said firmly, still looking at me with wide, panicked eyes.

"Well, what then?" I asked in total confusion.

"You were screaming like someone was killing you in here." She was still in a panic. I pushed myself to a more comfortable position leaning against the headboard.

"What?" I was still confused. "I was the one screaming?"

"Yes," she continued quickly. "I thought someone was torturing you in here."

A chill ran through me as flashes of my dream came back to me. Sharon was saying something about me scaring her to death, but already my mind was trying to grasp onto bits of the nightmare that were slipping away. My eyes were darting around the room to make sure the monsters hadn't escaped my dreams and entered reality with me. Pushing the fear down, I tried to focus my attention back on what Sharon was saying.

"I haven't heard you scream like that since we were little." The look on her face made me wonder what memory she was seeing from our difficult childhood.

"Hey." I had to clear my throat. "It's okay, I'm okay. I think those pain meds are giving me bad dreams," I said to reassure her, but I wasn't sure that was it. Normally, the meds knocked me out, and I didn't remember a single dream.

"Oh, that might be it, I hadn't thought about how those might be affecting your sleep," she said quietly, but seemed to be processing what I was saying.

"I was probably dreaming about falling down that mountain," I said, chuckling a bit and trying to dispel her fears even further.

"Maybe," she said quietly, clearly not buying my explanation.

"What? You don't believe me?" I asked, patting a spot on the mattress next to me for her to sit.

"Well, you were screaming in pain and begging someone or something to stop," she said as she sat down next to me. Fear gripped me as a flash of my dream came back, and I saw Sharon being tortured. I sucked in a breath.

"What?" she asked, looking at me with frightened eyes.

"Just got a twinge of pain," I covered, "I, uh, forgot about moving my leg carefully."

"Oh, I'm sorry you're in pain."

"Not your fault." Another fragment of my dream flashed, and I shuddered involuntarily.

"Are you cold?" Sharon asked in concern.

"A little." I lied, as my eyes darted around the room. Why did it feel like someone was watching me? Clearly, no one else was in my room, and I needed to get a grip, or I would freak Sharon out more than she already was.

"Let me turn off this fan." She seemed to be coming back to herself now that she had something to do to help me.

"Could you also hand me my water?" I asked.

She handed it to me and sat down at the foot of the bed, drawing her knees up under her arms, a self-protective move that I saw a lot from her growing up.

"Are you okay?"

"No," she said simply.

"Okay, I guess that was a silly question. But hey, for real, it was just a dream, we're okay."

"You don't get it, Mitch. I really thought someone was killing you in here. I had a kitchen knife in one hand and my other hand was ready to push the button to call 911. It was absolutely terrifying." Her voice tapered off.

I swung my leg off the bed and pushed my way down next to her, wrapping my arm around her for comfort.

"Well, I'm completely fine, except for a bum leg. Nobody was trying to kill me. Plus, I had my sister on guard duty; she would have taken them down," I said, joking with her.

She elbowed me. "It's not funny, Mitch; you're all I have left."

I gave her another squeeze around her shoulders. Knowing my sister, I couldn't let her stay in this dark place.

"Shari," I said gently. I heard her sniff, but I couldn't see her face because she'd tucked it down into her folded arms. "Shari," I said in a singsong voice. "Don't make me sing."

She lifted her head at the memories and covered her ears in protest. "No! My ears can't take it."

"I don't mean to change the subject, but I have to use the facilities, my dear sister," I said, the last part in a thick British accent, which made a small smile peek through.

As she handed me my crutches, I said, "Good thing Troy wasn't here this weekend. I'm sure my screams would've freaked him out too."

"Probably so," Sharon replied as she followed me to the bathroom. "It would've been fun to see him scared though. It'd serve him right for always scaring and creeping me out."

"He's not that bad," I replied.

"He's not that good either," she said, as I closed the door for some privacy.

Troy was just Troy. He was really cocky, thinking he was invincible and perfect. But I suffered from that same disillusion on some level. He made fun of almost everyone for something. He was getting a big kick out of my injury and the fact that I needed Sharon's help to do almost everything. I had to agree with Sharon, Troy wasn't that good, but he was just being a guy. All of us could be tools from time to time.

Sharon was cordial to Troy, but I knew she didn't like him, and she definitely would have been in no shape to put up with him right now.

I came out of the restroom and was startled to find Sharon still standing right there.

"You okay?" I asked in concern.

"Uh yeah, I just wanted to make sure you were okay in there. You don't need a fall now after the hard work you put in this past week."

I let her explanation go. Clearly, she was still scared and probably just wanted to stick close.

"Well, hey, since I woke you up, why don't I tuck you in," I offered.

"I'm fine, Mitch," she replied, not looking me in the eyes.

"I know you are; I just want to make it up to you."

"But I need to help you get back into bed," she tried once more.

"Nope, I'm good. Plus, in two days, I have to do this without you anyway."

"I know," she said, "I have to get back to work." I nudged her leg with one crutch and nodded toward her room. We headed down the hallway, me crutching along behind her.

Once she was settled under her covers, I sat on her bed, still bothered by something she'd said earlier.

"Sharon?"

"Yeah?" she ended with a yawn.

"What did you mean earlier when you said I'm all you have left? What about Slater?" I asked, referring to her fiancé. Tears immediately filled Sharon's eyes.

"What happened?" I was instantly worried and wishing I hadn't brought it up when she was already having a rough night.

"We broke up," she said softly, tears filling her eyes and making my heart break.

"You broke up? Why?" I was stunned.

"He was cheating on me," she whispered as the tears continued to flow.

"What?! Why didn't you tell me?" A protective anger roared to life inside me as I questioned her.

"Because I knew you'd freak and wanna kill him, and it happened not long before your accident." She blurted the words out as a tear made a trail down her cheek.

"But you've been here for almost two weeks, and you haven't said anything to me," I saw red as my anger at him reached its peak. There was also anger at myself for not seeing her pain sooner. "I thought I asked you about him, didn't I?" I asked, as much to myself as I was asking her.

"Yes, you did, but I lied. I didn't want you to know."

"Why would you not want me to know?"

"I was so ashamed," she was still crying and looking extremely miserable.

"What do you have to be ashamed about? Slater's the one that should be ashamed," I practically spit out his name. I felt so enraged I could have crutched to D.C. to kill the man.

"Well, you warned me that guys only really want one thing. And I guess he no longer wanted it from me." I almost couldn't hear the end of her sentence as she trailed off.

"Aww, Shari," I pulled her in close, feeling her pain wash over me.

"I really didn't think it was a big deal to have sex before we were married, we were engaged after all, but I guess I was a lot more invested in our relationship than he ever was," she said softly, continuing to break my heart. "He promised me forever, but he wasn't even that upset at having been caught. He said his tastes had changed, and he wasn't into me anymore. He said he wasn't even sure if he'd ever loved me."

"I'm gonna kill him," I growled out.

"See, this is why I didn't tell you." She started to pull away from me.

"I can see why, but that doesn't change the fact that that jerk needs to answer to someone about his blatant disrespect of my sister." I was seething with anger.

"No, Mitch, seriously. I would be even more humiliated if my little brother chewed out my ex-fiancé." Her tears had stopped, but the sadness in her eyes stopped my angry tirade and I pulled her back into a hug.

It still took us going back and forth a few more times for me to finally say I wouldn't hunt him down, even though I had no intention of honoring that promise. Slater would answer for what he'd done to my sister, but she didn't need to worry about that right now.

The emotions and the arguing had taken it out of both of us, so after she was settled into bed again, I told her goodnight.

As I made my way back down the hallway, I could feel the exhaustion weigh heavily on me. I stopped to hit the hallway light switch before I made my way back to my room. As I turned in at my doorway, that same chill from before ran through me, and I just knew that someone was there. I could feel it; someone was watching me.

My heart pounded in my ears, and it felt as though the darkness in my room had immediately surrounded me. Ever so slowly, I reached my crutch out to the hallway light and flipped it back on. With more light, the feeling already seemed to be lessening, but I wasn't taking any chances with my sister down the hall.

My crutches made a slight click and creak with every movement as I looked around the entire apartment, even in Troy's room, a place that was typically off-limits. Troy and I were very good about respecting each other's space. Surely, he'd be okay with the fact that I was checking for an intruder . . . then again, he probably wouldn't. He was a jerk about his stuff. He'd either be a jerk about the fact that I was in his room, or he'd be making fun of me for being jumpy.

I was about to hit the light switch on the way out of his room when my eyes fell on his desk. I had no idea what on earth urged me forward, but the next thing I knew, I was opening a binder on top of his desk. I jolted back at what I saw. I was expecting to see pictures of people, but instead it was a picture of a knife that had blood on the blade.

What a freak show.

Creeped out, but strangely curious, I flipped the page to find another knife picture, this one was even more bloody than the first. As I continued to turn the pages, I discovered more knives, each bloodied to some extent.

Man, this guy is one weird dude.

I knew he liked to hunt, but this was intense, even for Troy. The hairs stood up on the back of my neck. I glanced up quickly, expecting Troy to be standing in his doorway when I turned around, but no one was there.

What kind of sick dude am I living with?

I slammed the binder shut and made my way out of the room.

As quickly as my crutches would allow, I flipped off the hall light and made my way into my room, moving faster than before.

I pulled up short, just stopping myself from screaming. Right in front of me on my dresser was a knife.

After my moment of panic, I remembered that Sharon had brought it in when she thought it was necessary to save my life. It was my kitchen knife, clearly not a bloody trophy from Troy's book of knives. Nonetheless, I quickly hid it in my top drawer so I wouldn't have to look at it.

Sharon's phone was still there too. I should probably take it to her, but I could admit to myself that I was too freaked out to make another pass down that hallway. I liked the comfort of my own room at the moment, and I wasn't too proud to admit it. I'd make sure Sharon got her phone... in the morning.

My knee was throbbing, and the pain was increasing, a fact I became aware of as soon as I sat down on the edge of my bed. I needed to get it elevated. I carefully got myself situated in my bed and tried to calm my heart rate and my mind.

I don't know why I had been nosey in Troy's room, but the only thing I could hear in my head was, *curiosity killed the cat.* Whatever that meant. It was totally creeping me out, so I put in my earbuds and played some loud music on my phone to drown out my thoughts as the phrase kept repeating in my mind.

Curiosity killed the cat.

Curiosity killed the cat.

I reached over to the nightstand and grabbed the bottle of pain meds, shaking two pills into my hand. I looked at the pills, shook my head, and said aloud, "What a weird night."

As the effect of the medication washed over me, the throbbing pain in my knee lessened and I drifted off to sleep, the voice inside my head whispering one more time, *curiosity killed the cat.*

* * *

I was jolted awake by loud music blasting me and a stabbing pain in my left ear. Fear sat me up like a shot, and I immediately regretted it as pain seared through my knee and up my leg. As I became more alert, I realized it had only been my earbud still playing loud music in my ear and making it hurt. My ear hadn't been sliced off by a knife-wielding roommate. And the pain in my knee was normal because I had surgery on it nine days ago. I smiled at the absurdity of my thoughts as morning peeked through the curtains in my room.

Okay, heart, you can stop pounding now.

Just then, a loud clang came from the kitchen, sending my heart racing again. I tried to listen to what other sounds I could hear, but realized my earbuds were still blaring and shut off the music on my phone. There was a commotion coming from the kitchen, but it was hard to hear over the pounding in my ears.

Probably just Sharon making breakfast. Get a grip there, Mitch.

Taking some deep breaths seemed to help, but I still felt agitated, and my knee was killing me. I knew I needed to take some pain meds, and there was also an increasingly pressing need to visit the bathroom. I slowly got out of bed and reached for my crutches. My knee ached as I made my way slowly to the window where I opened the curtains. Just letting the light hit my face helped me breathe easier. I made my way to the bathroom as the smell of breakfast wafted down the hallway.

Shortly after, I made it to the kitchen where I discovered Sharon making pancakes. The smell of bacon was also in the air, which meant she had some in the oven. My stomach let out a loud rumble as I made my way to a bar stool.

"Hey, sleepy head," she greeted me with a smile as I slid onto the stool.

"Hey," I replied. "Were you able to go back to sleep last night?"

"Surprisingly, yes. Maybe it was good to get scared out of my wits, have a good cry, and spill my guts," she made a silly face.

"Yeah, who knew that was the secret? Ouch," I grimaced in pain.

"What?" Concern for me immediately taking her joy.

"My knee is pretty ticked this morning," I downplayed the pain.

"Maybe you should move to the couch," she suggested.

"I think you're right."

Sharon left her pancakes to follow me to the couch. I didn't really need her help anymore, but with the pain I was in, I wasn't going to stop her. She helped me lift my leg onto the couch, putting two pillows under it as I laid down flat. She was feeling around on my knee. "Mitch . . ." she paused, "It's really warm, even through the ace bandage. Let me flip my pancakes, and then I'll get you some ice."

"As long as pain meds are on the menu, and I get to eat some of those pancakes, you can do whatever you like!" I commented to her back.

"Those are both on the menu, right alongside the ice and the bacon I have in the oven."

"Sounds great, thanks."

"Somebody has to take care of you, or you'd be a mess."

"Ain't that the truth!" I couldn't see her face over the back of the couch, but I knew her smile had returned.

I pushed myself up to sitting and started to take off my brace to assess the damage of last night. My whole leg was screaming, even from just taking off the brace. Sharon returned with my ice in time to help me remove the brace from underneath and then she began to unroll my ace bandage like a professional.

"Oh Mitch," she whispered in pain, and I didn't even need to ask what. I was staring at my knee as well, and it was very swollen with purple indents from the ace bandage. The swelling was even pressing out on my stitches. It seemed my busy night had taken its toll on my knee.

"Well, let's get the ice on before my knee makes both of us throw up," I joked.

I raised my leg with my hands while she wrapped the blue cryo-cuff around my knee and hooked it up to the tube from the canister. Once she had the canister raised, she remarked, "You know, I didn't even feel queasy when I saw it. I just hurt for you."

"Wow. Look at you. That's growth," I said with authority.

"I know, right?!" she exclaimed, setting the jug down and unhooking the valve. "I'm going to get the other ice pack to put on the back. You lay back down and get some ankle pumps in," she said as she was walking away.

"Yes, doctor," I answered sarcastically.

"That's right, you'd better show some respect," she commented while slipping the ice pack behind my knee.

I let out a sigh of relief as the cold started doing its work. My leg was elevated above my heart, and I pumped my foot up and down, over and over. Ethan had told me the swelling was fluid in my knee and I had to assist it in leaving. Since I wasn't moving around as much, and I wasn't bearing weight on my left leg, my veins weren't getting the assistance of my muscles to return all the fluid back to my heart to be pumped elsewhere. I never thought I'd enjoy learning about the body, but lying back pumping my foot, I was able to picture exactly why I was doing what I was doing, and I liked that.

Between the ice and the pain meds, my knee was feeling a lot better. I was even dozing off and on as Sharon kept up with my schedule for icing, twenty minutes on, twenty minutes off. With a full belly, the right meds, and some rest, I was back in my right mind. I turned my head to see Sharon reading in the chair next to the couch.

"Whatcha' reading?"

She blushed a little at my question.

"What?" I asked.

"It's a little embarrassing; it's a romance novel."

"Why's that embarrassing? Just because I don't like them doesn't mean you can't," I said, not really understanding why she was upset.

"Have you ever even read one?"

"Can't say that I have," I replied.

"Well then, you don't know if you like them or not."

"You're embarrassed just to be caught reading them, so why would I want to?"

"Oh, I wasn't embarrassed about that; it's more because of my situation with Slater." A wave of sadness crossed her face, and she lowered her eyes back to her book.

"Oh, yeah, sorry," I muttered, remembering what she had told me the previous night and feeling the burn of anger churning in my gut.

"Yeah, I guess I should just give up on romance."

I didn't know how to respond to that as I wasn't really a romance kind of a guy.

"I just can't help but hope for someone better," she whispered.

"Well, I've never cheated on a woman, so there are at least halfway decent guys out there."

"But I know it's probably too soon," she said quietly, not looking at me.

"Too soon for what?"

"To hope."

"Don't let him kill your hopeful sparkle along with your love for him. It's never too soon to hope," I said gently but firmly.

She looked back at me with a small smile. "How'd you get so wise Mitchell Wright?"

CHAPTER 3

MITCH

THE NEXT FEW DAYS flew by. Troy returned in a foul mood. He was such a jerk that I had sent Sharon to the spa on her last evening with me just so she could avoid him. I asked him what his problem was, and he got in my face telling me he could behave however he wanted and that if I had a problem with it, I could move out. If I hadn't had a bad knee that made moving impossible, I would have taken him up on that. He mellowed out over the week, and by Thursday when he got home from work, I felt safe asking him how hunting went.

"It was lame. We didn't catch anything," he grumbled, zoning out on the movie playing on TV.

"Don't you mean you didn't shoot anything?" I clarified.

"Either way, I came home empty handed," he said, not even looking at me. He drained his beer and got up to get another one.

I almost asked him if he used knives when he hunted, but I heard that phrase *curiosity killed the cat*, and the question died in my throat. Nope, I wasn't curious enough to set off a guy with pictures of bloody knives in his room.

In fact, I had almost cut myself on the knife that was in my top drawer when I reached in for socks, but thankfully my hand hit the handle first. I hadn't removed the knife from the drawer. That was probably unsafe, but somehow knowing it was there helped me sleep. I was a grown man, and yet the darkness suddenly seemed to hold something that scared me. Ever since the dream Sharon awakened me from, it was like I couldn't completely relax.

The thought of my sister reminded me of our last conversation before she got on her plane Wednesday morning.

* * *

"I'm fine, Mitch, seriously," she tried to assure me.

"I know, but you moved to D.C. for him, so what's left for you there?"

"I don't know, my job and friends."

"I thought you said most of your friends were his friends," I reminded her gently.

"Most of them were, but some have sided with me, saying they knew he was a jerk all along. Man, I sure wish they had clued me in on that before," she said, trying to make a joke.

"Well, just think about moving back here, okay?" I coaxed. "Like you said, we're all each other has left, and I think we need to stick together."

"It actually sounds like a good idea, Mitch, but I need my job, and I don't want to feel like I'm just giving up."

"Don't think of it as giving up, think of it as making a fresh start," I countered.

"Where would I even live?" she asked, but it sounded like she was considering what I was saying.

"With me, of course!" I flashed her a cheesy grin.

"Living with Troy full time? Uh, no thanks," she scoffed.

"If you move back, we'd find our own place that is completely Troy-free," I assured her. She looked at me with one eyebrow raised.

"Come on, Shari, say you'll save me from Troy," I teased, as I poked at her with my finger.

She smiled. "Okay, okay, I'll think about it." I gave her one more poke in her ribs. "Cut it out, or I won't think about it," she protested, but with a good-natured smile that told me she was already on board.

"Okay, I'll put this away then," I said, making a big show of tucking my finger into my pocket.

She laughed, and then leaned toward me saying, "I need one more hug." The crutches definitely made hugs harder. I had to move both crutches under one arm and then hug her with the free arm. I gave her a nice long hug and kissed the top of her head before she moved away.

"Take care of that knee," she said as she started moving in the direction of the security line.

"Yes, doctor," I said with a smile. "You call me if you need anything, even if it's just to talk."

"I will. Love you, Mitchell."

"Love you, too." She gave me a forced smile and then turned to go.

* * *

I came back to the present to see Troy finish his next beer. I would have loved to join him, but alcohol doesn't mix well with pain meds, and I had no desire to end up in another delusional, terror-filled dream. So, instead, I was just a witness to his nightly check out ritual of downing a few beers and binge-watching murder shows.

I looked at him a little harder. I couldn't shake the feeling that maybe I was on high alert because I needed to be. What if I was in danger? My heart started to speed up as someone onscreen was being chased through the woods; I felt like I was being chased.

Wow, dude, you seriously need to get off these pain meds.

I was in my head way more than normal and paranoid on top of that. Maybe I should call my doctor and ask him about the pain meds, since I wouldn't be seeing him for another two weeks. I'd already had my stitches removed, and the doc said I was in great shape. Sharon and I had shared a quick glance at his pronouncement of my great progress. Thanks to Sharon's vigilant care and nagging for me to take it easy, the swelling had gone down. If he'd seen me the day after the dream incident, he probably wouldn't have been as enthusiastic.

I had the creeps just thinking about that night again and shuddered. "Hey man, I'm gonna call it a night. See you in the morning," I moved to get up, but Troy was too engrossed in his show and his beer to respond. Good thing I could take care of myself now. Once I was in the relative safety of my bedroom, I couldn't help but crack open the top drawer of my dresser to be sure the knife was still there. There was little doubt in my mind that despite the pain meds and my overall exhaustion, I would not sleep easily tonight.

*   *   *

The next day, I was at my physical therapy appointment getting warmed up on the bike and mentally replaying the phone conversation I had with my doctor that morning. He said the meds I was on were not known to cause dreams or hallucinations, but he was happy to back me off to an over-the-counter medication with higher frequency. That would also help me get back to driving and help with returning to work on Monday.

I was so caught up in my own thoughts and the half circle I was making with the pedals, that I was surprised when movement from the back door caught my attention. The stationary bike gave me a good view of the entire clinic, so I saw her walk in from the door that only the therapists used.

It was like she was moving in slow motion. Her honey brown hair caught the light from the windows as her ponytail swung with each step she took. She was being greeted by the other PTs with shouts of "Sarah!", "Welcome back.", "Hey, long time, no see." But my eyes were riveted on her beautiful face and radiant smile. She was absolutely gorgeous.

She took time to say something to each of her co-workers and some of the patients as she embraced them with either a hug or a high-five. The whole atmosphere in the room seemed to change, and I was helpless to look away.

As she unpacked her bag, someone said something to make her laugh. Her laugh, her smile, the easy way she moved, I was instantly wrecked by her and had the feeling I would never be the same again.

"You okay, man?" Ethan, my PT, asked, which brought me back to earth. I'd stopped pedaling completely as I watched her.

"Oh yeah, I'm," I had to clear my throat, "fine. I uh, thought I knew that woman over there." I could feel my ears heating at having been caught so blatantly staring, possibly with my mouth hanging open.

"Oh, okay, I was worried your knee was bothering you," he responded. That would've been a much better excuse than admitting I was staring.

"Uh yeah, but the bike is loosening it up for me."

"Are you talking about Sarah?" Ethan asked, turning to look in her direction.

Thankfully, he hadn't noticed me staring.

"Is that the woman that just walked in and you guys said hi to?" I asked, trying to appear like I didn't really care.

"Yep, that's Sarah. She's another PT here. Did you say you knew her?" he asked, making it seem like he found that hard to believe.

"Oh no, she just seemed familiar, but I don't think I know her." I said, trying to cover my tracks.

"She's been gone for a week, but you should have seen her when you were here your first week. Maybe that's why she seems familiar to you. Only, you saw her through the haze of prescription medication," he smirked.

Had I missed her? Maybe she'd been out to lunch on my first day, but there was no way I could have overlooked her.

"This place just isn't the same without her," Ethan commented.

"Why's that?" I asked, still trying to seem like I didn't care, but I really did want to know more about this woman.

"She's awesome, both as a PT and a friend. Always willing to help anyone out. She makes the rest of us better," he said with a smile in her direction, and for some reason, my jaw clinched.

I had a hard time focusing on my exercises during the rest of the session. Ethan kept asking me what rep number I was on, and I would have to confess yet again that I had no clue. It got worse after he invited her over to meet me. She was working with another patient and said she would be over in a minute.

I felt a lump in my throat that I couldn't swallow, and my palms grew sweaty. I wasn't normally one to lose my head over a pretty girl, so I wasn't sure what this was about. I dried my hands again, trying not to drop the strap I was using as I did my straight leg raises. I closed my eyes and prepared to do another set.

"Hey guys." I heard a woman say and opened my eyes to find her standing next to my table. Even her voice was beautiful, and my throat immediately went dry. I pushed myself up to sitting so quickly she chuckled.

"Easy there," she said with a smile, moving to help me get settled.

"I'm," my voice broke like it hadn't done since I was a teenager, so I cleared my throat. "I'm fine," I said, feeling my ears heat again and hoping she either didn't notice or chalked it up to exertion.

"Mitch, this is Sarah Jones," Ethan added, "Sarah, Mitch."

Almost in unison we said, "Nice to meet you." She laughed and offered me her hand. I wiped my hand once again before I shook her extended one. Warmth immediately shot up my arm, and all too quickly the handshake ended.

"Mitch, I wanted you to meet Sarah because I looked at the schedule, and you'll be with her some starting next week since your schedule is changing for work."

"Oh, uh okay, sounds good," I looked at Ethan, not trusting myself to look at Sarah.

"Well, Mitch, I'm looking forward to working with you. It seems like your knee is coming along great!"

"It should, he's working with one of the best," Ethan added with a smirk, causing her to give a quick laugh and a small shove on his arm.

"So true, my friend, one of the best," she joked. I felt a pang of jealousy at the warmth in her eyes as she looked at Ethan.

"Seriously though, Mitch, you'll be in great hands. Sarah is *also* one of the best." He returned her warm glance.

"I don't know about all of that, but we'll work hard together." She smiled, looking at me as she spoke. It may have just been wishful thinking, but it seemed like her eyes held the same warmth for me.

"You bet, we will," I replied, immediately regretting my enthusiasm.

"I'll see you Monday, Mitch, keep up the good work." Sarah gave my shoulder a pat and walked back over to her patient.

"Okay, how many straight legs raises did you get?" Ethan asked me.

"Huh? Oh . . . what's a straight leg raise again?" We both laughed. "Just kidding man, I think I did like eight."

While I tried to focus on what Ethan was saying and asking me to do, my gaze kept drifting over to Sarah. As my body went through the motions at Ethan's command, my mind was completely captivated by her every movement. It felt like an out-of-body experience, and while I wanted to blame the pain meds, I felt certain the effect was coming from Sarah.

Sarah seemed to move so gracefully, and she was so full of, well I wasn't sure what to call it . . . life? She had three patients at one time and didn't seem at all frazzled by the different people needing her or the fact that she had to keep leaving her laptop. Where the other PTs at times seemed like they were almost hiding behind their rolling desks, she was barely ever behind hers. I was still in my physical therapy session, and already I felt excited about having a session with her on Monday. I couldn't believe I was excited for more PT, just so I could see a girl.

I smiled to myself. *Well, it wouldn't be the first time you did something stupid for a girl.*

Then, Sarah was headed for the waiting room door. On her way, she looked back at Ethan with a beaming smile that he returned. I felt another pang of jealousy. Were they together? He wore a ring, but she didn't. They also didn't have the same last name.

As I sat icing my knee, I watched her work with what seemed to be a very difficult patient. I wondered what Ethan meant when he said she made the rest of them better. Did she cheer them on? Write their notes for them? What? Sarah almost glowed with ... who knows what it was, but what I did know was I was excited to find out more about her when we worked together on Monday.

* * *

SARAH

I was glad to be back at work, back to a more normal routine than what I'd been doing. Trying to search for Amelia without being hunted by the Terrobah myself was challenging, not just physically, but mentally. Often, after weekends like the one I'd just experienced, I had to remind myself who I was, and who I was called to be in this world.

I was Sarah Joy, a Light Bearer from a very powerful line of Light Bearers, each gifted with certain supernatural abilities that allowed us to war against the Terrobah and their powers on this earth. My parents died fighting the Terrobah and the Darkness when Amelia and I were young. And I, too, had been called into that same fight.

A man we thought was our uncle claimed us as family and raised us, sparing no expense for anything and everything he thought would give us pleasure. While we thought he loved us and cared only for our well-being, he turned out to be a very high-ranking Terrobah. And, like all Terrobah, he was a creature of pure evil, loyal only to the Darkness, and bent on destroying us and our lineage as Light Bearers.

For the past four years, my sister had been in his clutches. For four years, I had neither seen her face nor heard her voice. But for every second of those four years, I'd carried on in the hope that The Light could still save her.

Looking around the PT clinic as I settled in, I couldn't help but smile. One of the reasons I chose to work at this clinic was the lack of Terrobah, not that there were many in my line of work. They tended to stick to professions that didn't have to do with directly helping people on a daily basis. The other reason I chose it was the four weeks of vacation they offered and every other Friday off. I didn't mind working the early or late shifts while I was there, but those vacation weeks and long weekends were crucial to the other part of my life.

It wasn't necessarily that I led a double life. I was the same person whether in the field or in the clinic, but so many around me didn't know the power of The Light that I possessed, a power I could bring forth at any time. The enemies I encountered on my travels knew my power, though, and had felt the sting of it if they tried to harm or capture me.

Here at the clinic, I kept a low-level light guard up. There was no glow or light emitted at this level, so there was no risk of detection, but I felt more comfortable feeling the constant hum of The Light running through me. I had put the same light guard into the walls surrounding the clinic to repel any Terrobah or Terrobists (humans that partnered with the Terrobah) who might inadvertently stumble upon the clinic and discover me.

On more than one occasion, I had witnessed people pulling into the parking lot, getting out of their cars, then immediately reversing course and leaving. The first time it happened the receptionist said, "Man, that patient really didn't want to do PT." While some of my coworkers thought these people might be lost, I knew they were repelled by The Light, even if they themselves didn't know why they were leaving.

The Light here didn't just come from me; it was starting to emanate from Ethan as well. I smiled as I thought about him. I had liked him from the very beginning of my interview. Pneuma, a being of The Light and my source of wisdom and comfort, told me that people I immediately connected with were most likely people who could come to know The Light and maybe even bear The Light. Four years ago, when I was rescued and taken to Ganheela, Pneuma had helped me discover my true identity as a Light Bearer and find my place in The Light.

I liked Ethan and was fortunate that he was the director of the clinic. But I learned quickly that he was very observant, especially of me. He couldn't figure out why I was so successful with my patients. They got better faster, seemed happier, and recommended me to their friends.

Each time he complimented me, I laughed it off or thanked him and moved on to help the next patient. But he persisted in asking why I was so successful. I tried to just pass it off as a fluke, but he wouldn't let it go. It had started from a place of jealousy for him but then moved to a humble inquiry. He was watching me more and more, and I knew eventually he would catch on about my trips as well. When he came to me almost desperate to understand, I asked him if he could stay late. That was three months ago...

* * *

The clinic had just closed, and Ethan had stayed to help me lock up. Once we were sure the building was clear, I moved around the room adding extra light barriers, to not only keep away unwanted guests, but to also keep them from hearing us.

When I finished, I turned back to Ethan and saw that he sat on top of one of the PT tables and pointed to the one across from him.

"Talk," Ethan said firmly, crossing his tan arms in front of his chest.

I knew because of his interest and his humble curiosity that he was ready to hear some of my story. He was ready to hear about The Light. I popped myself onto the table across from him and began.

"Well, Ethan, I'm different from most people," I started.

"Yeah, I kinda got that part on my own," he said with a grin and motioned with his hands and arms, mimicking what I had just done around the clinic.

"I was trying to make sure we weren't overheard."

"That statement just brings on even more questions," he frowned at me.

"I wasn't always like this." I repeated my hand gestures, "but now The Light has become a part of me and affects everything I do." His frown deepened and his eyebrows drew together.

"You mean like kindness?" he questioned.

"No, like actual light, although kindness does come from The Light," I paused, watching him.

"Continue," he said with his brow still furrowed; but he didn't call me crazy outright, so I elaborated.

"The Light is the good in this world, and it can be tangible. I've learned how to harness The Light within me. For example, when I work with my patients, through my words and my touch, they receive light." I paused, but he didn't interject, so I kept going. "The Light has some healing properties, that's why they heal better, faster. Through my words, they receive life, and they feel hope and happiness."

Inhaling and exhaling a deep breath, I waited to see his response. I'd brought seven others into The Light before, all of whom had become Light Bearers. I had seen others awakened that were not Light Bearers. What would Ethan end up being? He was looking at me strangely, but not repulsed, which was always a good sign. He hadn't even leaned back away from me. I raised my eyebrows at him as I waited for his response.

"Sarah, that all sounds crazy," Ethan said, shaking his head. "But I've seen what you can do. I've tried to mimic all of your techniques without success. Watching you has helped me become more personable, but I'm still not seeing your results." I waited as he continued to process and gave him a small smile.

"This seems ridiculous to say, but I believe you," he stated, a smile stretching across his face.

"I thought you might; you seemed ready to hear." My smile matched his.

"See, even your smile. I can't help but smile back. Is there light or whatever in that too?"

"Yes," I answered, still beaming at him.

"Can I feel it?" he asked softly.

"You already have," I informed him, still smiling, "but sure." I reached across the gap between the two tables as he reached for me. I gave his hand a squeeze and purposely passed more Light to him than I normally would. Peace crossed his face as his hand slipped away from mine.

"It was warm," he marveled. "I could feel it in my hand and then moving up my arm."

I nodded my head as he seemed to need reassurance that what he felt was in fact The Light coming from me.

"Can you see The Light too, or is it just the feelings?" Ethan asked.

I extended my arm out to my side and pushed out a gentle ball of light toward the wall of full-length mirrors. The orb moved slowly toward the mirror and bounced off, coming back at us.

"Should I duck?" he asked with a hesitant laugh.

"No, it won't hurt you," I assured him as the orb passed in front of me. I squashed the ball between my hands and light sparks flickered out around us, causing me to laugh in delight which caused Ethan to laugh as well.

"Were you always like this? I mean, able to do this?"

"No."

"Can you please explain? Were you bitten by a radioactive spider or dumped in a vat of toxic waste?" he joked. I liked his easy and open manner.

"Yes," I responded, laughing when his eyes got big. "Not about the toxic waste or spider, but I can explain more." He made a rolling motion with his hand for me to go on. "Four years ago, The Light rescued me. I learned all about it, including how to harness it."

"So, you have to be rescued by The Light in order to be able to do what you do?"

"Not necessarily."

"Is being vague also part of harnessing The Light?" he asked sarcastically.

I laughed, "No, it's just a lot to take in, and I don't want to overwhelm you."

"I'm not, I'm amazed. I'll let you know if I get overwhelmed."

Over the next two hours, I told him about meeting Lucas and going to Ganheela. I explained more about the life I now lived and some of what that looked like. I left out my background with Uncle and Amelia, not ready to share those details with him yet. He asked insightful questions and seemed only more and more amazed.

"Don't you need to go?" I asked, taking a breath and letting him absorb the fact that my trips involved battling Terrobah.

"No? Why would you ask that? Are you tired of all my questions?" He seemed energized by all I was telling him, which was a good sign that he was likely going to be a Light Bearer.

"No. I just assumed that your wife would want you home soon. It's almost 10pm."

"Wife?" he asked, confused. "Oh, the ring, yeah, uh. I guess I should tell you since you've told me your secrets." He paused as he gazed down and spun the ring on his finger. "My wife was killed two years ago."

"I'm so sorry, Ethan," I said with genuine sorrow. "Why did I not know that already?"

"Most people don't. I tried to take my ring off, but I got asked out by my patients. One of the women was really forward and kept pressing for a date; I was half a second away from telling her off," he grimaced slightly in embarrassment. "Now, I keep my ring on and let people make their own assumptions."

"Well, I definitely assumed you were married, but I did wonder why you never talked about her."

"It's not a pleasant story."

"I battle Terrobah on a regular basis; I'm very used to dealing with unpleasant things," I replied softly, letting him decide how much he wanted to tell me.

"Elizabeth was murdered for her purse," he paused. I sensed he would go on, so I didn't speak. It seemed like he hadn't talked to anyone about this in a while, and I wanted to give him the space to do just that.

"She was such a beautiful person, both inside and out. Knowing what you've just shared with me about The Light, she may have had some of that as well." He paused again, breathing deeply, probably trying not to cry. I moved to the table beside him and put my hand on his arm. He lifted his head to look at me, his eyes shining with tears. As a tear slipped down his cheek, I wrapped my arm around him.

His head dipped forward, and his shoulders shook gently as he cried silently. I leaned my head onto his shoulder and wrapped both my arms around him as far as they could go. Not exactly appropriate behavior with the boss, but this was about so much more than that. Also, when I had a feeling in The Light, I tended to go with it. He needed comfort, and I was the form in which The Light was giving it to him.

The shaking settled. "She would have given that thief her purse and the jacket off her back if he had only asked," his voice was thick with emotion. He lifted his head; his eyes were glazed over as if he was back in that time instead of there with me. I let myself release more light into him. "Instead, he shot her and got $5 and some worthless credit cards."

"Do they know who did it?" I asked, my voice barely above a whisper.

"No, they never caught him. He never even tried to use the credit cards. None of it made any sense."

With all the pain and tragedy I had witnessed over the last four years, I knew there was probably more to this than just a thief. While Ethan saw no meaning, I couldn't help but start to connect the dots. Who was Elizabeth to the Terrobah? Why had she been silenced? I knew not to bring any of this up at that moment. Ethan couldn't choose The Light out of vengeance or revenge. He had to choose it from a pure heart.

"I'm so sorry that you lost Elizabeth," I said, knowing from experience there was little I could do to lessen his grief.

"Thank you, Sarah." Ethan's voice was more normal, so I released my arms from around him. "And thanks for the light." He looked at me and gave me a small smile. "I could feel it coming through me right when it seemed like I would break from the pain. It felt like warm honey flowing through me." His description made me smile, because I, too, had experienced the warm-honey flow that came from the comfort of The Light.

"My pleasure," I said in return as I got off the table and grabbed a hand towel for him to dry his face. I hopped back on my table to give him some space. It didn't last long. Ethan moved to shoot the towel into the dirty linens bin like a basketball and then sat beside me on my table.

"So..." Ethan started but trailed off.

"So?" I asked in return.

"So how can I get The Light, how can I be a part of this?" he asked timidly. My heart nearly burst; it was so sweet.

"It's simple, but not easy," I said slowly.

When I didn't continue, he gave me a wide-eyed expression, "Well, what are you waiting for?"

"You make a decision to follow The Light instead of the Darkness."

"Okay, done. You've already told me about the terro-whatevers, and I don't want anything to do with them." His humor fell away, and he continued more softly, "I want to help people." He looked up at me. "I want The Light."

I knew beyond a shadow of a doubt that what he was saying was true. And so, I helped welcome Ethan into The Light.

CHAPTER 4

SARAH

THAT AMAZING NIGHT FROM three months ago was still in the back of my mind as the physical therapy tech brought me the folder for my new patient – a female with a partially torn rotator cuff. *Lovely*, I thought to myself, and I meant it. I loved to meet new patients and give them the first taste of healing and hope.

I looked over to see Ethan looking at me. We smiled at each other; he gave me a head nod and went back to his patient. His patient was looking at me too. *Mitch*, I recalled. He would be my patient on Monday. His gaze was often on me, but he seemed harmless.

As I walked to the gym door, I thought about how incredible it was to have a teammate in Ethan, not just a nice co-worker. We were on the same side, saw things the same way, and had each other's back. Now that he knew about my mission for The Light, he was even more understanding and helpful regarding my vacation time. Over the past few months, we'd been training regularly, and I'd shared with him about Amelia. I knew he would ask me about my latest trip once we were alone.

Just as I had that thought, a chill went down my back. I immediately raised my light guard as I looked around the reception area. I felt another chill, but after a quick look around the room, I confirmed there were no Terrobah present.

What is going on?

The receptionist asked me if I needed something as I was just standing there with the gym door held open.

"No, I'm good," I said more brightly than I felt. "Just got lost in my thoughts there for a second."

"Okay, well…" she cut her eyes to the left toward the chairs that were lined up on the wall. "Good luck," she said with a conspiratorial whisper. I was barely able to make out what she said.

Interesting.

"Letta Frank?" I called out to those waiting in the chairs.

"About time," a lady grumbled to me as she wiggled herself out of a chair.

Remembering she had a torn rotator cuff muscle, I moved toward her and asked, "May I help you?"

"Oh, you leave me out here for an hour, but now you want to help me?" she asked angrily, as she finally got herself to her feet.

"An hour, ma'am?" I asked, raising my eyebrows at the receptionist. She shook her head at me and rolled her eyes.

"Yes, an hour," the patient retorted. "And my shoulder felt every minute of it."

"Well, I'm so sorry that you had a long wait," I apologized, even though it wasn't true. "Let me get the door for you."

"You'd better; it's not like I can use my lame arm. You might as well do your job."

"I'm happy to help, Ms. Frank," I replied as I held the door for her.

"It's Mrs. Frank to you." I felt bad, but my first thought was, *Poor man.*

"Of course, Mrs. Frank. We'll be at this table right over here." I gestured to a table off to the side of the room. I wasn't going to put her at a table in the middle of everyone with how rude she was already being to me.

"Well, how do you expect me to get up on this thing?" she practically yelled. She was loud enough that Ethan turned to look at us. He raised his eyebrows at me.

"I have a stool for you to step on to get up there, but why don't you have a seat in this chair while we talk through what's going on with your arm." I purposefully kept my voice bright and cheerful.

I looked over at Ethan, but he had moved on to help a patient at the exercise bands. He knew this wasn't my first difficult patient, and I could handle Mrs. Frank just fine. She didn't know it yet, but I was sure her bad day and bad mood were about to turn around.

I couldn't have been more wrong. My voice, my touch, nothing seemed to have any effect on her, none that she acknowledged anyway. She complained about everything. The heat was too hot. The stretching too painful, but to be fair, most shoulder patients in PT complained about that. The towels were too scratchy, the table too hard, the lights too bright, and we ended with the ice being too cold.

As grouchy as she was, I had such compassion for her pain. Her body was impaired with fibromyalgia and rheumatoid arthritis, and she was doing very little to keep it moving. She was taking medication, but it didn't have a chance to work with how sedentary she was.

Her shoulder pain had started six months ago, but she had refused to see a doctor about it. Over time, she'd lost motion and strength, what little she may have had in the first place. She slept on her bad shoulder with her arm stretched above her head, and she told me in no uncertain terms that she wouldn't be changing that.

Normally, patients didn't faze me at all. The things the Terrobah said and did were much worse than a grumbling patient. But by the end of her evaluation session, I was worn out. After I got her set up for her future appointments at the front desk, I walked through the clinic and headed for the back door. I stepped outside into the sunshine, letting it hit my face. I closed my eyes and just breathed in its warmth and comfort. I felt The Light humming under my skin. It was weird that I hadn't noticed that while I was with Mrs. Frank.

"You okay?" Ethan asked as he stepped out beside me.

"Yeah, but that was a weird one," I responded with my eyes still closed.

"How so?" he questioned. I could tell by how he asked that he knew this wasn't just a typical patient problem.

I opened my eyes to look at his serious face. "When I opened the door into the reception area, I had a feeling. I thought one of 'them' was in the room," I said cautiously. We were outside, and I couldn't take any chances.

"One of *them*, them?" He drew out the word in suspicion, which made me laugh.

"Yes," I said through my laughter. "I thought there was one in the reception area, but I didn't see one."

"So, what was it?" he asked, completely serious after I had shared that there could have been a possible Terrobah sighting in our lobby.

"I'm not exactly sure. I've never met a human that has this much 'stink' on her before." I used air quotes when I said stink since I wasn't even sure what else to call the way I sensed Terrobah.

"They stink?" he asked so humorously that I had to laugh again.

"We've talked about this before, remember? I can sense them because I've had so much experience with them. It's not that I really smell them. It's more of a sixth sense that I've gained with The Light."

"Oh yeah, you just threw me off with saying your patient had that stink on her. So, you don't know what caused that with the lady today?" His face was very serious.

"No, I don't," I was baffled. "I may need to call Pnu, uh, a helper, later to ask. If I don't hear from her first," I trailed off with a whisper.

Just then the door swung open from the clinic. We'd been standing in view of the glass doorway and windows so everyone could see where we were. Jess, one of our PT techs was standing there. "Hey Ethan, Mrs. Sawyer just came off the heat."

"Thanks, Jess," he said cheerily, "I'll be right in." She turned and let the door close behind her.

Ethan immediately turned serious eyes back on me. "Are you okay?" he asked quietly, and I knew he was asking as more than just my boss, making sure I was safe. He also gave me a "friendly" pat on my shoulder, passing some light into me as well.

"I'm good. Thanks for checking on me and making me laugh," I said with a smile. "That helped me to slough off some of the stink."

"That's a new one," Ethan said with a smile. "I'm happy to help you slough off stink anytime, Sarah." He gave my shoulder another squeeze before he turned and went in the door.

"Thank you," I said with a gentle breath that was caught up in the breeze. I was so thankful for Ethan and my thankfulness just came out in a breath to The Light beyond. To have someone at work that understood and was trying to help me was such a wonderful gift. And his sense of humor was just icing on the cake, sourced from The Light as well.

Ethan had a sense of humor before, but more in a self-deprecating way. Now it was as if his humor came from The Light within. He walked around now with an easy smile and a ready laugh. I had even heard one of his patients say they thought he was in love. Which was sort of true. He had a deep love with The Light;

he'd found his place, and now The Light was starting to overflow out of him. Those same traits he saw in me as a PT, that *special something* he thought I had, now he had it too.

* * *

MITCH

It was finally Monday, my first day back to work in weeks, and I was more than ready to get out of the apartment. Troy had been home all weekend, in another one of his moods, giving me plenty of motivation to want to be anywhere else. People always talked about women having mood swings, but Troy could rival anyone in that department. He was either really on or really off. It wasn't just Troy's mood or getting back to work that had me anxious for the weekend to be over; it was the anticipation of seeing Sarah again.

Normally, on most weekends, I would have been hiking, biking or something active. In fact, one of my ski buddies had even called to see if I could be their fifth in a pick-up game of basketball.

"Are you serious, man?" I asked, jarring his memory.

"Dude, I'm so sorry. I'm an idiot," he apologized for having forgotten I'd just had major surgery. "You're still welcome to come and watch though," he offered, letting himself off the hook. But having to watch my friends play while I just sat there had even less appeal to me than hanging out with Troy, which was saying something.

Sharon had called me the night before to wish me well on my first day back, and to be sure I wasn't overdoing it. I mentioned her moving in with me again, and she said she'd been looking into different job options in my area to make that happen.

By the end of the workday, I was exhausted but feeling a little more like myself. It was nice to be back crunching numbers and in my normal routine. There was, of course, a mountain of work that I knew would take me a lot of time to catch up on. Work though, I knew I could handle.

But as I drove to the physical therapy clinic with my stomach churning in anticipation of seeing Sarah, I suddenly wasn't so sure of my ability to handle anything.

Pulling into the parking lot, I found a spot fairly close to the door. I opened my door, pulled my crutches across from the passenger side, and stepped out with ease. It was amazing how much easier it already was to balance on one leg and move around confidently. I had already changed into my workout clothes at the office, so I was ready to go. Thankful for the handicap button that kept me from making a fool of myself trying to get the heavy glass doors open, I crutched through and checked in with the receptionist.

I took some deep breaths, trying to calm my heartrate and my anxiety. Less than a minute later, the PT tech called me back and got me warming up on the bike. I didn't see Sarah; was she sick? Shouldn't the receptionist have told me if I had a different PT? I was starting to grow angry when Sarah walked out of what seemed like the supply room.

I let out a breath of relief, and then realized I was staring. I tried to focus on the half-circles I'd been shown on the bike and not watch her cross the gym to hand her patient the exercise sheet as well as the band she'd cut for them.

Half-circles, Mitch, half circles.

She was still giving some instructions to her patient, so I tried to focus on what I was doing instead. I didn't want to be caught staring at her; she didn't need to know what her mere presence seemed to do to me.

Half-circles, half-circles.

"Hey Mitch, how's that knee today?" My head jerked up to see her standing right in front of me.

"Umm," I stopped and cleared my throat. "It's okay," I responded, staring at her eyes.

She must have thought I had forgotten her, because she extended her hand and said, "Sarah Jones, I'll be working with you today."

"Mitch Wr..." I started to say my name back as I shook her hand but remembered quickly she had already said it. "It's, uh, good to see you again," I said instead.

"Today was your first day back at work, right?" she asked, staring right into my eyes. I almost forgot her question but then remembered she said "work."

"Yeah," I had to clear my throat again. "Sorry, my throat's a little dry," I said, trying to cover the fact that my voice was cracking like an adolescent boy.

"Let me grab you some water then. Be right back." She smiled and headed for the water cooler.

Get a grip, Mitch. You're acting like . . .

She was back before I had a chance to finish my pep talk to myself.

"Here you go," she offered me the water.

"Thank you," I replied, and drank the whole cup, framing my next response.

"So, work today?" she asked again.

"Yeah, it was good to be back in the normal routine."

"I'm glad. And how did your knee do with it?"

Of course, she'd want to know how my knee was doing, not how the work itself went.

"My knee did alright. I had to prop it up throughout the day when it throbbed."

"Were you able to ice at all?"

"Yeah, I took my Cryo Cuff and iced my knee like three or four times throughout the day."

"That's good, I'm glad it was a good first day back. Are you feeling a little stiff?"

"Uh, no, not really."

"You've just been on the bike for almost 15 minutes," she pointed to the screen, "so I thought maybe you needed a little more time on there to loosen up." Sure enough, my timer was now counting up past five minutes, when it had been set to 10 minutes counting down.

Clearly, I couldn't admit I'd been distracted by her. "The bike was just feeling good today, so I thought I would hang out a little longer on here," I covered.

"Okay, well let's get you over to your table and get started on some other exercises," she instructed, handing me my crutches.

Get a grip Mitch, I silently coached myself again. I normally didn't feel like I was going to make a fool of myself with women. I was usually very confident and at ease around them. Where was that Mitch when I needed him?

Once I was up on the table and had taken off my brace and ace bandage, Sarah had me start with my normal exercises to continue working on what Ethan had me doing. I managed to stay focused until she took a measurement which required her to touch my leg.

When she touched me, I felt a jolt go through me. Mind you, she was barely touching my leg to lift it and put the towel roll under my ankle, but it was quite a shock to my system. Sarah was, of course, completely unphased by my reaction and continued like she hadn't felt a thing.

Before I had recovered, she was moving me on to my next exercise.

"When do I get to go farther in my range of motion again?" I asked, continuing the heel slides she had me doing.

"At your four-week mark, we'll move you to 120 degrees, which is..." she was behind her computer, and she paused to look at something, "...next week," she said with a smile.

"Okay, good." I said. "These slides are just feeling pretty pointless now."

"I know it's hard to only go to 90 when you got back there quickly. We do the slides to maintain your motion and to push any excess swelling out of the joint."

I felt like saying her exercise was pointless was probably not the best move, but she didn't seem to mind. I almost started to apologize anyway, but then she spoke again.

"I know it's hard to be so inactive when that's not your norm."

"It is hard. But I know you, I mean, you guys know what you're doing."

"Just wait until you get past the meniscus healing, then we can push you and you may not like us as much," she said with a smile. It was breathtaking. I mean it literally took my breath away. If I had seen her somewhere outside the PT clinic, she definitely would have caught my eye.

"Oh, is that a threat?" I joked.

"Of course," she replied, her smile changing to a smirk. She got me started on the next exercise and turned to help her other patient with something on the next table.

We worked through the rest of the exercises, and thankfully, there was no more voice cracking or forgetting my own name. That is, until she sat on a stool beside the table and started to touch my knee again. My knee felt foreign; there were numb spots, sore spots, and scab spots. She had put on gloves, but I was still aware of the heat in her hands. The sensation of her touching my knee and gently moving my kneecap was something else entirely. It wasn't like I got charged by it to where my heart would race. It was the opposite. Her touch calmed me.

She was only moving my kneecap around, and it felt better than the best massage I'd ever had. It seemed like she was done quickly, even though she'd probably worked with it for five minutes. When she finished, I felt relaxed and calm, almost sleepy. Then, the tech hooked me up to the ice machine, and before I knew it, Sarah was saying goodbye until Wednesday.

I left the clinic almost in a daze but found my way to the car and drove home. I had meant to stop and grab some food on the way home, but I spaced out, mentally replaying my PT session, and drove straight home.

I pulled into my designated space, seemingly on autopilot, turned off my car and realized my mistake. I put my head down on the steering wheel and mentally wrestled with the decision to drive back out and grab food. In the end, my exhaustion won the debate, and I decided I'd just throw something together for dinner.

Once inside my apartment, I realized there wasn't much to eat. Frozen pizza seemed to be my only option. I warmed up the oven, put the pizza in, and laid down on the couch to rest for a minute.

The next thing I knew I was jolted awake by a horrible screeching sound. I sat straight up as my mind registered the sound of the smoke alarm and the smell of something burning, but I was still partially focused on the voice in my head that had been saying, "You'll never have her; she's ours," and Sarah's voice screaming, "No!"

Beeping, burning, "My pizza!" I shouted out loud.

It took me a minute to get myself off the couch and crutch to the oven. I turned the oven off and turned on the microwave fan to help clear the smoke, opening the oven to find a very dark, very crispy meat-lovers pizza.

Well, this is awesome.

Mercifully, the smoke alarm stopped blaring. But I was starving, and now my only dinner option had gone from frozen to beyond burnt. I looked at the blackened crust and tried to decide if I was hungry enough to eat burnt cardboard when I heard keys in the door.

"I've got wings." Troy shouted, opening the door to our apartment. "What the?" he said with a wrinkled face as he walked in the kitchen.

"I fell asleep and burned my pizza. I'm surprised you couldn't smell it as soon as you walked in."

"Yeah, I could, just didn't have a chance to ask before I saw your charcoal pizza. Uh, I'm going to open a window because that smell is awful. Good thing I got wings for the both of us, huh man?"

"You're a lifesaver, seriously dude. I'm starving and wings sound amazing."

"Okay, well, go get your gimp leg up, and I'll bring you your food."

"Thanks." I didn't even care about the gimp comment because it was true, and I was starving. Troy was being nice for the first time in two weeks. Who was I to turn down a meal right now?

He brought my wings to me in a Styrofoam container and tossed some napkins next to me. "You want a Coke or something, man?".

"Uh yeah, a Coke would be great, thanks." Would wonders never cease?

He brought me a cold one from the fridge and sat down with his wings and beer and turned on Monday Night Football. I was stuck staring at him for a minute, and then my stomach growled, reminding me I needed to eat. I took a big bite of my first buffalo wing and said, "Thanks, man. You're a stud!" before devouring the rest.

Troy was great for the rest of the week. He did the grocery shopping the next day and brought dinner home again on Wednesday night. He even asked me how physical therapy was going. I told him it was great but spared him the details about my new PT. I wasn't embarrassed about working with a girl. I just knew Troy would want all the details, especially her measurements, and for the first time, I didn't want to talk about a woman like that. It was better if he thought my PT was still a guy.

I was so thankful to have a cool roommate again that I had almost forgotten about the knife binder. Almost.

CHAPTER 5

MITCH

FRIDAY TOOK ITS SWEET time arriving and the end of the workday seemed to take even longer. I had some big projects that helped time move faster at the office, but two days had been too long to go without seeing Sarah.

Thankfully, Friday evening was a little slower in the clinic, so she hung out by me, working on her notes while I did my normal exercises. I was her only patient, and I had just asked if she had ever done any other type of PT work.

"Only on my internships," she replied. "This is the only job I've had since I graduated from PT school."

"But you liked sports medicine best out of your internships?" I prompted, wanting her to continue.

"Yeah, I especially loved working with children," Sarah paused. "Their cases were more difficult and emotional, but I loved helping them reach even the smallest of milestones," she said with a smile. Since we had made it to Friday, I'd calmed myself enough to be able to have a more normal conversation with Sarah. And she seemed to enjoy our discussions as well, or maybe that was just wishful thinking on my part.

"Well then, what are you doing here with all of us broken adults?" I teased.

"The little ones are so pure, so they don't need me as much as the adults here do," she responded in an absentminded way. It seemed like her mind was focused more on the note she was working on than her answer.

"What?" *Pure* was a weird word to use in relation to physical therapy. And why would kids not need her as much as adults?

She looked over her computer at me. "What?" she asked in return.

"You said that they're 'pure' and don't need you as much. What did you mean by that?"

She came around her computer before she replied, "Children have fewer distractions, and they follow instructions much better than adults." She looked at me purposefully, then chuckled.

"I can believe that. I know I'm a terrible patient," I said in an exaggerated way to make her laugh again.

She smiled but replied, "You're a great patient, Mitch. You do your rehab at home and follow whatever instructions we PTs give you here in the clinic." I tried not to let the compliment go to my head.

"Not without complaining, that's for sure."

"We're used to it. They don't call us *Physical Torturers* for no reason," she smiled again. "How many is that?" she asked, checking on my reps.

I was caught, yet again, having no clue, so I said twelve.

"That range looks good; let's do some quad sets and then move into straight leg raises."

I had to hold the quad sets for five seconds and count my reps, so I was stuck focusing on that instead of talking to her. Then, I moved on to my straight leg raises. I was thinking about what to say to her next when she spoke.

"Okay, those are looking a little too easy for you. I'm going to add a one-pound weight to the next set." One pound? Was she serious? My leg had to weigh 50 pounds by itself! How would I even notice one more pound?

Boy, was I wrong. Sarah quickly strapped the weight to my leg, and it felt like I was lifting a mountain. "Easy, Mitch, make sure you flex your quad muscle before you lift your leg. You want your leg perfectly straight before you raise it."

I retried doing the quad set, first, which seemed to help. But by the sixth rep, I wanted to scream uncle. One pound, ridiculous! I was even sweating!

"Good work, Mitch," she encouraged, touching my quad in between reps. "Rest a little longer in between, and let's try for two more."

I wasn't about to wimp out in front of her, so I made it through the next two reps, but it was tough. "One hundred," I joked out loud after gritting my teeth. Sarah laughed.

"Good job, I know that was hard. Go ahead and roll onto your side, and we'll do your side leg raises next with the weight."

I did as she said, but she had to adjust my hip once again. I never seemed to keep my leg in the right position with this exercise. Once she "corrected" my leg position, the raises were definitely harder.

"Make sure you tighten your thigh muscle with these as well. We want that knee locked out before you raise your leg," she instructed as she assisted me with the first one. "Good, let's keep going." She ended up taking the weight off before I finished the second set because my leg was shaking so badly.

"That was pretty sad, wasn't it?" I asked after I finished the set.

"No," she replied easily. I gave her a look to let her know I didn't believe her.

"We're still trying to wake up some of those muscle fibers that checked out after your injury." She continued, "It's great that you've already moved to one pound."

I raised one eyebrow at her in disbelief.

"Seriously, Mitch, you're doing great," she encouraged with a smile that made me believe her this time. "We'll help your muscles remember where they were before your injury, and you'll be back to leg pressing 300 pounds before you know it."

"Thanks, coach, what's next?" Her encouragement made me want to keep working.

We finished up the exercises, and she got me on ice. The rest of the clinic had cleared out, and even the tech had gone home. Sarah stood behind the computer doing her documentation, while she chatted with me.

"Have you ever had to do physical therapy yourself?" I asked her.

"Yes, lots of times, actually," she peered at me over the computer.

"What did you injure?"

"I broke my ankle in high school playing soccer, so I needed PT for that. I also had many different injuries in grad school, like sprained ankles, shoulder issues, back pain. I had to rehab those as well."

"You came to a PT clinic for all of those things?" I questioned.

"No, just the broken ankle in high school. The other injuries ended up being fun class practice in grad school since we were all learning how to rehab injuries."

"Oh, you were like the rescue dummy in CPR, but for PTs."

"I'm not sure if you just called me a dummy, but yeah, something like that." We both laughed.

"Definitely not calling you a dummy; you have your master's, right?"

"Actually, I have my doctorate," she responded with a fake prideful look on her face.

"Hold up. So, I should be calling you Dr. Sarah whenever I address you?"

"Yes, Mitch, you've been very rude," she said sarcastically. "In truth, I actually prefer to be on a first-name basis with my patients since we're working together to get them healthy and whole."

"I'll still call you Sarah, but I won't make the mistake of forgetting how highly educated you are."

"You'd better not," she smirked as she removed the ice from my leg. She'd already worked on my knee, but I almost asked her some crazy question about my kneecap just to get her to work on it again.

Turns out, I didn't have to ask. She touched my kneecap as she was inspecting something on it, but thanks to the ice, I was too numb to feel anything. I chuckled at the sensation, which made her look at me with a question on her face.

"Sorry, it's just so weird to see you touching my knee when I can't feel a thing." Good cover, since it was partly the truth. I wanted to feel her touch, but it just wasn't the same when my knee was completely numb.

"I know, it's a weird feeling," she agreed, making a funny face. "Okay, Mitch," she said in a voice that told me we were wrapping up. "You can get your brace on, and then you'll be good to go."

"I can't wait to be done with this thing," I commented as I strapped my leg back into the brace that went from mid-thigh to mid-calf.

"You just need more strength in your leg and then that brace will be gone for good," she reminded me, giving the brace a pat.

"Thanks, Sarah." I didn't want our time to end, but I also didn't want to hold her up. As I finished getting on my brace, I asked her if she had plans for the weekend.

"No, it's pretty low key, just hanging with my roommate and maybe having dinner with some friends on Saturday."

"All my weekends are low key right now," I complained.

"They'd better be," she tried to sound stern. She followed me to the door because the receptionist had left as well.

"Have a good night, Mitch."

"You too, Sarah." Our gazes locked for a second, and then she gave me another small smile. I took her cue and turned to go.

At my car, I watched as she locked the door securely and then made her way through the reception area, turning off lights as she went. She'd already been turning off different machines during our session, a routine I assumed was part of closing the clinic. I climbed slowly into my car, just wanting to be around her a bit longer. A few minutes later, I realized how awkward it would be if she caught me still in the parking lot, so I backed out quickly to head home.

As I turned the corner out of the parking lot, a text popped up from Troy on my dash. "You want me to grab dinner?"

I told my car to text back, "Sure, I'll pay you for this one."

"Chinese sound good?" came Troy's reply.

"Chinese sounds great," I responded with a smile. My night was looking up.

✳ ✳ ✳

SARAH

As I closed up the clinic, I was caught up in thought about my conversations with Mitch. He seemed a lot more relaxed during the session we had just finished. He was talkative and asked quite a few questions. He hadn't seemed that talkative with Ethan, so I could only assume it was me. He seemed like a nice guy and would probably make a great friend, but it seemed like maybe he was interested in more.

I was completely on board with being his friend; I even felt like he had potential as a Light Bearer. Obviously, I didn't know him that well yet, but I had liked him right away, just like with Ethan.

The only downside seemed to be his romantic interest in me. He wasn't the first one to show this interest; it actually happened fairly frequently because of The Light. These guys usually took it as a physical attraction. If they were my patients, it was easy to deal with; I didn't date patients.

The truth was, I didn't really have strong convictions about dating patients because of work; it was just an easy excuse. My excuse with friends was my focus on being a Light Bearer. The truth in my heart was Lucas.

I met Lucas four years ago, when he rescued me and led me to The Light. I was a Light Bearer, a human who carried and wielded the power of The Light, and Lucas was a Mythreal, a non-human being *of* The Light with gifts and strengths given only to those like him. Though I knew Lucas wasn't human, my heart had a hard time coming to terms with that fact. I loved Lucas, so it wasn't fair to anyone else to pretend that my heart was available.

In The Light, I had a great capacity to love, and I knew that I could love another. But my heart wasn't ready to let go of Lucas, even though it had been four years. I was also very focused on finding Amelia; that left very little time for any relationship. Many of my weekends and all of my vacations were tied up in trying to find my precious sister and fighting the Terrobah.

I finished my patient notes for the day so I could wrap things up and head home. The last note I came across was Letta Frank. She was still a puzzle. I'd asked a few of my Light Bearer friends as to why they thought her presence made my skin crawl even though she wasn't a Terrobah or Terrobist. One of them had suggested that maybe she spent a lot of her time around Terrobah and that's why I got those sensations.

It didn't seem to matter what I did or said, she never seemed happy. I even tried to emit more light when I touched her, but she said I was hurting her. I had never hurt a human with The Light before and it greatly disturbed me that my touch was painful to her. I'd come across humans that were less receptive to The Light and not as drawn to it as others. If someone were extremely self-focused, they often didn't even notice any light I tried to impart to them.

Even Nyiah, my roommate who had grown up knowing about The Light, was unsure of how to proceed with Letta and suggested I talk with Pneuma. She was concerned that Letta was a scout for the Terrobah, and that Ethan and I would be compromised. I didn't feel that same level of concern, but at the same time, Letta was very tough for me to be around. I felt drained each time I saw her. I wore as much of my light guard as I was able to, but some of her comments and negativity still made their way through.

I took Nyiah's advice and decided I would talk to Pneuma about Letta. I felt confident, if I were in danger, Pneuma would have already told me as much. She could see everything, but she only revealed things to me in her timing. That's how it worked with Amelia, as well. Pneuma gave me brief glimpses or visions of Amelia, and I chased down those leads and locations. So far, Amelia was always gone when I arrived. Sometimes, I'd missed her by just a few minutes. On my last excursion, I arrived to see her fire still smoldering. I knew the Terrobah loved this game and thrived on my discouragement and defeat. Even in that moment, I felt the despair creeping in.

Help, I thought in my head.

She is alive. She will have life, came the reply.

That voice was not my own; it was Pneuma encouraging me and reminding me of the promise she had shown to me. It was a promise I could rest in. I took a deep breath and saved Letta's note to the server.

There was one more thing I had to do before I walked out the door. I walked around the clinic touching the walls, the tables, my co-worker's computers, the reception desk, giving them all some light. I made sure to check that the light boundary I had created in the clinic walls still stood.

As I did this, my thoughts returned to Mitch. He was very handsome and full of life. I'm sure he had not often been rejected, so I didn't look forward to the inevitable day when he would ask, and I would have to refuse him. Maybe I could make subtle comments about how I didn't date patients. That might be enough to discourage him. Most guys wouldn't ask if they weren't sure of a positive answer.

A small laugh came out of me; in reality, I was no dating expert. Actually, I'd never dated. It was only what I had observed in others over the last four years. And since I would never date, it didn't matter whether I was an expert. As I finished that thought, I heard, *Never say never.*

"Pneuma?" I asked out loud. "What does that mean?"

There was no answer to my question. I knew from experience that she would talk to me more about it later, so I didn't need to dwell on it. I grabbed my stuff, set the alarm, and locked the door behind me. I walked to my car, enjoying a deep breath of the cool night air. The clinic closed at seven, so it wasn't terribly late, but I was hungry and ready to get home.

I climbed into my silver Jeep, a great vehicle for off-roading if one has need to traverse rough terrain, as I often did. I started the engine and rolled down my windows. I had the hard top on but still wanted to feel the breeze on my face. My stomach growled, and I smiled, knowing my roommate would have dinner ready.

After parking in the garage of our ranch-style home, I made my way into the house and was greeted by a tantalizing aroma. Nyiah called a greeting to me that I returned.

"Whatcha making?" I asked as I came into the kitchen to see her busy at the stove with multiple pots going.

"Sweet and sour chicken, brown rice, and sugar snap peas," she turned to smile at me as she said it.

"Oh, my favorite!" I exclaimed, making her laugh.

"Pretty much everything I cook is your favorite."

"Well, this meal is one of my most favorites," I said truthfully.

Nyiah loved to cook and bake and made us gourmet food all the time. I enjoyed cooking as well, but Nyiah was definitely the more accomplished of the two of us. Her mother had taught her well; she'd been cooking since she was young.

"I know," she returned. "I made it because I knew you would be seeing Mrs. Frank again today and would need a pick-me-up."

"And you were right. Even just writing her note was difficult," I responded softly, feeling a little defeated.

"Have you talked to Pneuma?" I knew she didn't mean how all of us heard from and talked to Pneuma in our minds.

"Not in person, but I plan to tomorrow, at first light."

"That's good; I don't think you'll make much progress until you do," she said, adding the red sweet and sour sauce to the chicken and vegetables.

I kind of zoned out thinking about my future conversation with Pneuma.

Nyiah brought me back by saying, "This is almost ready if you want to wash up and get comfy."

"Thank you," I said with a smile and headed toward my room to change.

Nyiah was such a gift. I'd met her when I was just beginning my grad school work. She was in the business school at the same university. We'd met in the atrium where we were both having lunch. I was eating a salad with one of my classmates, and Nyiah had noticed me.

She told me later she had noticed me right away but wasn't sure if I was an Awakened, someone whose eyes had been opened to The Light, or a Light Bearer. Both were a part of the Eklesi, but only Light Bearers partnered with Mythreal, like Lucas and Owen, to battle the Terrobah. The Awakened still took a stand in their everyday lives against the Darkness.

Nyiah had moved to the table next to me to see if she could figure it out. When she moved closer to me, she was able to tell I was a Light Bearer. When my classmate left to go meet with our professor, Nyiah quickly joined me at my table, startling me just a bit.

I smiled, thinking back to that moment.

*   *   *

Nyiah's dark brown eyes were surrounded by the longest black lashes and set deeply into the most beautiful, caramel-skinned face. She looked at me so intently, then said, "Ego eimi to fos," Although I was still new to The Light, I recognized it for what it was, a greeting of the Eklesi. My heart started to race, but I tried to play it cool.

"Excuse me?" I asked, hoping she would repeat those beautiful words.

"Kalos," she said, giving me a lovely smile, which I returned. She seemed completely at ease interacting with me, but I still wasn't sure of the protocol. Was I supposed to wait until she said, "Hi, Pneuma sent me"?

I remained silent, with what I'm sure was a deer-in-the-headlights expression on my face.

Nyiah laughed. "What's your name?" she asked so kindly, I found myself answering before I'd really decided if that was the best thing to do.

"Sarah."

Before I could ask for her name, she blurted out, "Are you, *the* Sarah?" her eyes going wide and her voice dropping to a whisper.

"*The* Sarah?" I asked, not sure what she meant.

"*The* Sarah that defeated over fifteen hostiles at one time?"

I was surprised she knew anything about that. It's not like there was a Light Bearer group on social media. I could sense she was of The Light. Instead of answering, I reached out to her, and she gave me her hand. I looked down and a blue light sparked between us. The spark, called a nee-tote, was a spark of life that let us know when we were with one of our kind. Like a secret handshake, but much cooler.

Beaming at her, I dropped my voice to a whisper, "I have no idea how you heard that story, and I had a lot of help, but yes, I'm that Sarah."

"She told me to come here today." I instinctively knew Nyiah was referring to Pneuma. "I had no idea why, but I don't ever question when she tells me to do something. I was excited to meet another one of us, but I had no idea it would be you." In her excitement, she was talking rapidly.

My joy was inexpressible at having been found by another Light Bearer. I'd seen some people before who I thought might be Light Bearers, but because Pneuma told me simply to wait, I had no idea how to make contact. Besides that, I had only been at school for the summer and was so focused on my classwork and making it through my first two summer sessions that I'd really had little time for anything else. Even so, I still longed for others who understood the life I was living in The Light.

Nyiah grabbed my hand again and squeezed. "I'm sorry, I'm just so excited!" She smiled so brightly I thought she would burst.

"I'm excited too!" I responded. *And a bit overwhelmed.*

I continued, "Pneuma told me to wait, but I wasn't sure what I was waiting on. I'm so thankful you spoke first."

"Sarah, we aren't just meeting; we're going to be roommates," she stated with a dazzling smile.

"Really?" I asked, taken aback. We'd just met, and yet, she wanted me to move in with her?

"Yes, I have a house, and Pneuma made it clear I would be taking in whoever I was meeting." She smiled like she knew a secret. "I just had no idea it would be you, *the* Sarah."

"How do you even know about me?" I chuckled, still confused by that part of her introduction.

"You don't think we share battle stories as well?" she hinted with a cheeky smile.

"I haven't really interacted with others like us," I whispered.

"Well, that's about to change. Let's talk logistics." She took charge of the conversation, and I listened intently.

I glanced at my watch and realized I was going to be late for class. We quickly exchanged phone numbers, and I promised her I would call after class. How could I not? I had just been handed a lifeline.

✳ ✳ ✳

The memory faded away as I changed into sweats and a hoodie. It was still such a sweet memory, and my smile remained as I took off what little make-up that I wore.

When I made it back to the kitchen, Nyiah had already set the table. She was setting down our drinks as I plopped into my seat.

"How could I live without you?" I asked, meaning every word.

"Let's just be thankful you don't have to," she sassed, smiling back at me.

"Seriously, I couldn't do any of this without you." The conviction in my voice let her know I wasn't joking.

"That feeling is mutual, Sarah Joy," Nyiah said, smiling. We both closed our eyes and thanked The Light for all he had done for us. I added in a special thank you for Nyiah and then dug into my food.

"Now, what brought on this gush of emotion?" Nyiah questioned, watching me eat.

After I had taken a couple of bites, I paused to say, "I was thinking earlier about how we met."

"I love that story." Nyiah beamed as we ate our dinner and talked about our first days together.

CHAPTER 6

SARAH

I WOKE UP EARLY on Saturday morning to meet the dawn and to see Pneuma. I only called her at first light when the world was just awakening. I quickly washed my face, got dressed in some sweats, and pulled my hair back. I turned off the house alarm, slipped on my shoes, and slid the backdoor open to the chilly morning.

Pneuma could not be summoned in our realm the way she could in Ganheela. I could not just call her name and have her come to me in person. She didn't even always respond when I spoke to her in my mind. Pneuma wasn't one to be ordered about by my wants or wishes.

In Ganheela, Pneuma was ever-present, available to us in person with just a thought. But life in Ganheela was not the same as life outside its borders. While not wholly separated from Earth, but more adjacent to it, Ganheela was a realm unto itself. On Earth, time moves as we travel around the sun, but not so in Ganheela. Though we share the same sun, in Ganheela, time stands still. It is a place completely free of the Darkness, where The Light flows freely without the depravity of the world to hinder it.

Outside the realm of Ganheela, I was given a way to bring her to me in human form for a few minutes. I didn't know it at the time, but Lucas had given me my necklace in Ganheela, not just in remembrance of him, but as a way to call Pneuma. She was always with me, in my heart and mind, but when she came to me in human form and I was in her presence, I was restored to complete peace and understanding.

The pond behind our house was still dark as the sunlight had not made it through the trees that filled our large backyard. There was a fence surrounding our property that had the protection of The Light embedded into it, the same way the walls at the clinic were protected. The Light barrier concealed any light Nyiah and I gave off as Light Bearers, and it also repelled any Terrobah that might pass by.

I arrived at the edge of the pond as the first beams of sunlight reached the water, sending sparkles of light glistening across the surface. I reached for my necklace, finding its clasp and removing it, feeling the chain as I allowed the stone pendant to slide through my fingers. This necklace had become such a part of me. The only time I ever removed it was in this place and for this purpose, to ask Pneuma to come forth.

Bending forward, I dipped the necklace into the pond, letting the stone sink just below the surface. A brilliant light burst out from around the stone, delighting me with colors I'd only ever seen in Ganheela. I laughed at the merriment it created in my heart. Each time I called for Pneuma in this way, I felt the most childlike joy making me want to run and laugh and splash, much in the same way I had done when I visited Ganheela. And as quickly as the spectacle of color came, it was replaced with a glittery gold prism of light, as though flecks of gold itself floated across the beams. I released the necklace, and it stayed suspended in the presence of The Light, its stone still just below the surface of the sunlit water.

"Pneuma, ahoova-te lah geh shay," I uttered. It was the phrase that was inscribed on my locket. In the language of The Light, it meant, "My love, draw near." As the last syllable left my lips, I sensed her already there. I looked behind me to see Pneuma sitting on a bench by the water, shimmering with light and at peace, like she'd been there all the time.

"Pneuma!" I exclaimed, as if seeing her for the first time, and fell into her arms. It was such a relief to feel that sense of home so strongly, like I had reached my ultimate place of belonging.

"Sarah Joy, my beloved," she affirmed me as we continued to embrace for many minutes.

"I have drawn near, Sarah, what is it you wish to speak with me about?" Pneuma knew all, and therefore, already knew why I had called. This question was to draw me back to the present, back to what I was facing in the world. If I could, I would have stayed forever in her arms because it was everything I needed. But for the time being, I was called to remain a part of this world and to fulfill the purpose The Light had for me in it.

I drew back to look at her glorious face. Her beauty and light were such a stark contrast to the world around me, even in its most glorious state at dawn. In Ganheela, everything was pure, and I was cleansed of the world, making it easier to look upon her. But not so in this place, where my humanness and the darkness within the world itself prevented me from staring too long at her glory.

"Pneuma," I thought the first thing that would come out was my concern about Letta, but instead, I said, "She wasn't there." A sob escaped my lips and tears rolled down my cheeks. The emotions were so unexpected. I hadn't even realized they were pent up inside of me.

"I know, my love, your waiting has stretched on far longer than you anticipated. I am so saddened by what this looks like and what it does to you." She pulled me close to her once again.

"Do you still see her in The Light?" I whispered, as another tear trailed down my cheek.

"Yes, my love, but it may not be in a way that will bring you peace."

"I would take any way of getting her back at this point," I cried, "even if I never have peace again."

"Take care, my dear one. Do not utter things that you are not prepared to face and that, truthfully, you would not be able to bear." She spoke with compassion in her voice.

"I'm sorry, Pneuma, you're right; it just hurts so much. I want Amelia back by my side."

"What Amelia are you seeing beside you?" she asked, gently stroking my hair.

"The Amelia from my childhood. My big sister." I was picturing her as the sister that comforted me after we lost our parents.

"She is no longer that Amelia." Pneuma paused, "I have seen her very much changed."

"But she could change back, couldn't she?" I asked, pleading for hope.

"Humans cannot 'change back,' as you say."

"What do you mean?" In my mind, the idea had always been to change Amelia back to the girl she was before she had been deceived into choosing the Darkness.

"You know that each of you changes with the things that happen to you." I nodded as she had explained before that every event in our lives shaped us into who we are in the present. How we react to each event either brings us closer to The Light or closer to the Darkness.

"When those changes occur, they cannot be undone. Only new changes can occur, moving one forward. There is no going back. Change is only forward."

"So, she won't ever be that big sister I remember from our childhood? But she could still move forward to The Light?" I asked, looking for confirmation and the comfort it would bring.

"In some cases, it is possible, but Amelia seems to have reacted in a way that has driven her very deep into the Darkness."

"You just said that forward is the way for her, though." I commented, confused.

"Yes, but she must endure many changes to move forward to reach The Light."

"Pneuma, what are you saying? Is Amelia beyond the reach of The Light?" I drew back from her, and fear gripped me in a way I had never known in Pneuma's presence.

"That is impossible. No person is ever beyond the reach of The Light," she stated firmly, helping my fear dissipate.

"Of course," I breathed in and out deeply. I knew that truth. I let myself relax back into Pneuma again.

"Doesn't that bring us to the reason for your call, my love?" Pneuma gently prodded, and in her gentleness, I was able to release my thoughts of Amelia.

"Yes, I have this patient who presents like a servant of the Darkness. She's cruel and my touch hurts her, but she isn't a Terrobist."

"No, she isn't," Pneuma confirmed.

"What is she then?"

"The wife of a Terrobah."

"What?" I asked in disgust. "I didn't know Terrobah could marry humans."

"Yes, unfortunately, it happens."

"Why?" I questioned. "They can't love, so why would they want to marry a human?"

"Because, in that way, they can control the human." She stated. "They have more influence over them in close proximity."

"Why would they endure that torture though?" I still didn't understand.

"It's not torture to them if the human doesn't wield The Light."

"Oh right," I said, having momentarily forgotten that not everyone operates in The Light.

"In this case, though, it is torture for the Terrobah, just as it is torture for poor Letta."

"Are you saying that she's Awakened in The Light?" I was shocked. That did not fit at all with the woman I'd been treating at the clinic.

"Yes, and not just Awakened, she is a Light Bearer." Her gaze locked with mine.

"Then, how could she not see that her husband was a Ter-robah?" The more information I got, the more lost I felt.

"They have manipulated her with their schemes. Letta was a strong Light Bearer, though, so they are most likely using other means to sedate her and keep her with a Terrobah. It seems she's in a trance of sorts that blinds her to her spiritual surroundings."

"Can she still be saved?"

"Yes, but it won't be easy."

"Pneuma, when is something you have given me to do ever easy?" I joked.

"I know, Love, I do ask much of you because you are capable of great tasks." She knew I was joking, and yet she chose to be serious.

"I would rather be with The Light and doing the hard tasks than be without it," I said, meaning every word.

"Sarah, you do The Light great honor by saying that." Her voice trailed off, and she turned her eyes to gaze at the water.

Another thought occurred to me, "Does Letta have any family that are missing her?"

"She has no one missing her, but she does have family." With each of her responses, I felt like Pneuma was drawing me to an-swers of my own.

"Who are they?" I asked, but before I even finished the ques-tion, I knew from the look in her eyes that, somehow, she meant me. "We're related?!" I exclaimed in disbelief. Not all of my talks with Pneuma were this dramatic.

"Yes, she is your great aunt. Your maternal grandfather's sister."

"So, of course, since she's part of our line, she would have to be either killed or tortured." I responded, growing angry and feeling weary of hearing of the pain that my family endured. Pneuma knew it would hurt to hear.

"The Terrobah do not marry just any beings of The Light. They pick strategic people."

"Then why…" I stopped midsentence not wanting to offend Pneuma.

"I do not mind your questions, Sarah, go ahead," she prompted.

I hesitated another moment, which was silly since she knew all of my words before they were even on my lips. "Why doesn't The Light protect its people better?"

"How you see the world and how The Light sees the world is very different. The Light has always been and will always be, for now and forevermore. There is a great tapestry woven throughout time, but only The Light can see its true picture. As a human, you only see the back of the tapestry; a bunch of messy knots and threads that don't make any sense."

She paused, letting the word picture settle in my mind.

"Humans create chaos by trying to set themselves up in the place of The Light, making their own picture out of the knots and the mess. In doing so, they partner with the Darkness. Those humans who partner with the Darkness wreak severe havoc on other humans and the world around them."

She paused once more, allowing the weight of her words to press into me.

I knew all of this already. I'd asked about the state of the world many times before and why it was the way it was. It just felt like if The Light expected my family to do great things, it would help us out once in a while. I was immediately embarrassed at the thought, already knowing The Light had helped me out tremendously.

With grace, Pneuma did not pursue my thoughts but went in a new direction. "Letta's blindness appears as if she had chosen the Darkness, all but extinguishing her light."

I grabbed onto that, "But it's not extinguished, so there's still hope."

"Yes, there is always hope, dear one," Pneuma confirmed.

"Well, obviously, I can't just tell her who I am or who she is; she'd never believe me," I said, thinking strategically.

"No," Pneuma said slowly, turning my attention away from my own strategies and back to her. Why would I strategize when I had all the wisdom in the universe sitting right next to me? She continued, "This may take a more visible demonstration of The Light within you."

Pneuma had used this phrase before. I knew she meant warring with the Darkness, most likely to rescue Letta. Aunt Letta. "Well, I'm getting enough practice with all of these weekend trips," I quipped.

"You are a fierce warrior for The Light, Sarah Joy. Many are your rewards in the Land of The Light." She spoke with such power in her words that I fully felt the honor of them.

"Thank you, Pneuma." I knew she would go shortly. She had given me both comfort and wisdom, and I would walk it out with the strength of The Light and her voice in my head.

"Go ahead and ask your last question," Pneuma prompted, smiling cheekily at me and raising one eyebrow.

I didn't think I had another question for her but was surprised when one came into my mind at that moment. "Is Mitch a significant person to me?"

"I think you already know the answer to that question," she said, that same playful smile filling her words.

"I am to encourage him to The Light," I stated matter-of-factly, as that was usually my role with those who were significant to me.

"Yes, but that is just the beginning."

"Just the beginning? The Light is everything," I responded with confusion.

"That is true as well," she responded with a breathtaking laugh.

"Are we going to end our time with a riddle?" I asked, somewhat jokingly.

"No, beloved, I do not want you to be confused. I just want you to be aware that encouraging Mitch in The Light is just the beginning of the journey that you two will take. Do not close yourself off to different possibilities." She spoke this out loud, and then I heard her whisper inside of me, *Never say Never.*

I didn't know what to say to that, but she spoke again before I could say anything.

"Our time has ended."

I looked out at the pond and saw that The Light from the necklace was dimming and retreating back across the water. When Pneuma came, time, as the world measures it, slowed greatly. The earth still moved, but it was so slow that, to my eye, the sun hadn't changed positions since she arrived. And she was leaving.

"I love you." I told her, my voice thick with emotion. There were so many other things that I said with that simple phrase, and I knew she understood them all.

"And I love you with an everlasting love, Sarah Joy." Pneuma rose and retrieved the necklace from the pond. I followed, and she fastened it back around my neck. I hugged her fiercely one last time, then she disappeared as The Light from my necklace went dark.

Going back to the bench, I sat for a few minutes more, looking out over the sun's reflection on the pond. I needed to get moving or I would be late for work, but my whole being yearned to stay in that place a little longer. I took another deep breath as I noticed yet again how dim the sun seemed after I was exposed to the pure light of Pneuma. I closed my eyes and exhaled slowly. I learned so much each time I sat with Pneuma and this encounter was no exception.

With the inhale of another deep breath, my thoughts moved to when Pneuma had told me that Amelia would return to The Light, just not in a way I was picturing. I wasn't sure what that meant, but I felt a strong urgency to find Amelia fast. When the next dream came, I would move as fast as I could, no waiting for weekends or vacation.

Not only had I learned that news about Amelia, but Pneuma had revealed to me that I had another family member, one who was also being tortured by the Terrobah. I would see Letta for therapy again on Wednesday, and I would be seeing her from a whole new perspective. And Mitch, well, I didn't even have the brain power to think about that relationship at the moment. I would see him Monday evening and treat him as I did every other patient in the clinic.

"Sarah?" Nyiah called from the house.

"Yeah." I said, but I didn't turn.

I heard her making her way toward me. "Are you okay?" she asked.

"No," I said, shaking my head. "This is the most unsettled I have ever felt after meeting with Pneuma."

"What happened?" she asked, sitting next to me.

"Well, Amelia has gone so far into the Darkness," I paused, trying to push back the sobs that threatened to strangle me, "that... um, that Pneuma couldn't guarantee me an easy way out for her."

"Oh Sarah, I'm sorry," she consoled, reaching her hand out to grab ahold of mine.

We sat for a moment, then Nyiah continued. "Did she say anything about Letta?"

"Yes!" I looked at Nyiah, grateful for a change of subject. "Letta is actually a Light Bearer!"

"What?!" she asked in disbelief, just like I had with Pneuma.

"Yes, she's in some sort of trance under the influence of her Terrobah husband," I answered, still feeling the disgust on my tongue.

"My brain can't even keep up with this information," she said, releasing my hand and rubbing her temples, drawing my gaze to her.

"Oh, it gets worse ...or better, I'm not quite sure yet." That's really how I felt.

"What is it?" she asked, as she lowered her hands slowly.

"Letta's my great aunt," I mumbled.

"You shut your mouth right now!" Nyiah exclaimed.

I didn't even tell her about Mitch. She knew he was my patient and that he had potential in The Light. We shared almost everything with each other, but I wanted to work through more of what Pneuma had said before I shared that little piece of information with her. It was a lot to process anyway.

"Well, now I see why you're still sitting out here instead of getting ready for work," she soothed, reaching for my hand once more.

"What time is it?" I asked, giving her hand a squeeze back.

"Six."

"I'd better go in and get ready, then," I responded, not moving from my spot on the bench.

"Okay, well give me a hug first." I knew she was passing me some of The Light to counteract my other thoughts and feelings. I felt the warm honey and breathed deeply. I should have been full up with light after meeting with Pneuma, but my worries and anxieties made me leak like a sieve, unable to hold onto Pneuma's peace. In Nyiah's embrace, I tried to let the worries go.

"Thank you," I said, as we released our hug.

"Anytime." She smiled, as she offered me a hand up from the bench. We walked to the house arm in arm, Nyiah continuing to give me that connection with The Light.

While my dark thoughts weren't gone, I was feeling much better by the time we reached the house. As I finished in the shower, I tried to focus on the good things happening around me and with The Light. I wanted to be thankful and not stuck in a mood when I saw my patients. If I wasn't carrying hope, then I couldn't pass it to them. Pneuma had taught me that early on, saying "You cannot give away something that you do not already carry inside you."

As I got ready, I thought through my day. Since it was Saturday, I only worked a half day. We were only asked to work one Saturday a month, and this one was mine. It would have been nice if Ethan was going to be at the clinic with me, but at the same time, I knew he would be able to tell something was up right away, wanting to know everything. I would get to talk with him soon enough as he was coming to dinner at our house that evening. Nyiah wouldn't mind a recap and would want to hear more about my time with Pneuma, as it was uplifting to all of us to hear about experiences with The Light.

On my drive to work, I thanked The Light for the privilege of being able to see Pneuma every few weeks. As far as I knew, I was the only Light Bearer that was given access to Pneuma in this way. Other Light Bearers would love to share in the privilege I had. Nyiah had even said as much. In her delight in Pneuma, Nyiah would probably ask fewer questions and just enjoy the time. I always seemed to have an agenda when I talked to Pneuma. When I pulled into the clinic parking lot, I put my Jeep in park and resolved that the next time I sat with Pneuma, I would just be with her and enjoy the gift I had been given.

* * *

Slipping into my jammies later that night, I thought back on how incredible it felt to have friends like Nyiah and Ethan, friends I could talk to about anything. My connection with Pneuma was vital, but she had also emphasized the importance of having human friends who could say, "I know how you feel." They were such a joy and dinner had really lifted my spirits.

I thought again about how Ethan and Nyiah would make a great couple, but just like Ethan and I, they seemed to be great friends instead. I couldn't help but wonder if Ethan hadn't opened his heart again to the possibility of a relationship, just like I hadn't. I didn't sense anything in Nyiah toward him either. She'd told me before that she felt a sisterly bond to him in The Light, but nothing more, and that was okay.

Normally, I spent the time before bed reading, but I quickly turned off my light, extremely tired from the day. I was just drifting off when a vision from Pneuma filled my mind. Her voice accompanied the vision, almost like a narrator.

Sarah Joy, Amelia calls, you must go now. Do not go alone, take Nyiah and Ethan and any other Light Bearers you can reach quickly. You must go now.

As I woke up with my heart pounding, I could still clearly see the abandoned warehouse with its broken-out windows. Pneuma didn't need to tell me what I was seeing; she had imparted the location of the warehouse to me through the vision. I needed to get to a shipping port in Miami, so I quickly got up, dressed, and started packing a bag.

As I was packing, I felt the need to go wake Nyiah and have her get ready too, but I pushed it away. This was the first time I was deliberately disobeying Pneuma, but I was so afraid that if I brought too much light, the Terrobah would flee with Amelia before I even arrived. Pneuma's words from that morning had continued to linger with me, and I felt like this was my last chance to save her.

I grabbed my keys, then threw some snacks into my bag. If I'd learned anything from my escape from Camp Tuano, it was that I didn't want to be stuck out in the middle of nowhere with nothing to eat.

I pushed down another urge to at least tell Nyiah where I was going and quietly slipped out the door. I was determined to do this alone.

CHAPTER 7

MITCH

"Where's Sarah?" I asked the PT working with me. I think he said his name was Tim when he was getting me on the bike. I hadn't wanted to ask about her right away, but I had felt anxious from the moment the receptionist told me I wouldn't be working with Sarah that day.

"Vacation day," he responded, not looking up from his laptop where he was entering notes on my pain, exercises, and whatever else.

Why wouldn't she have told me on Friday that she was going on vacation? "Does she take a lot of those?" I asked, while I was doing my heel slides. It felt so great to be able to go past 90 degrees.

"No more than the rest of us," he answered, glancing up at me and shrugging his shoulders, thankfully not picking up on my anxiety at not seeing her. He dropped his gaze back down to his computer.

"Well, she didn't tell me she was going on vacation," I mumbled. He didn't respond as he kept typing on his computer. I was glad he didn't sense my worry, but I was starting to feel angry at his indifference about Sarah being gone, so I spoke out of my frustration. "I actually think she said something on Friday about seeing me on Monday, so that seems a little unprofessional to just take off on a vacation without warning her patients."

Tim looked up at me in surprise, realizing he may need to calm down an angry patient. "I'm sorry that the schedule had to change. She had to go out of town suddenly, so the director asked me to cover her patients for her. I was only working a half day today since I'll be working on Saturday, so I was able to make it work."

"Why did she have to go out of town suddenly?" I almost interrupted him, barely hearing the rest of what he said in my concern for Sarah.

"I can't say, I'm sorry," he apologized, narrowing his eyes at me.

"Oh yeah, of course," I said like I understood his need to keep things confidential, but really, I couldn't care less. I just wanted to know about Sarah. "I was just concerned for her," I assured him.

He seemed to relax a little. "I get it, man, Sarah is as nice as they come."

"Yeah." I responded, not liking how Tim was talking about Sarah.

"Just a heads-up, though, she doesn't date patients." I felt the anger in me rise immediately. Apparently, he was a little more aware of my feelings than I thought.

"What about co-workers?" I shot back.

"Not those, either," Tim said with a smirk. And with that, it was clear, he had tried to ask her out and had gotten turned down.

"I'm done with the leg raises," I informed him.

"Okay, I'll get your ice on you." He apparently didn't do any of the soft tissue work or moving my kneecap. Just as well, I'm sure I wouldn't have enjoyed it anyway.

While I was the last patient in the clinic again, this time I didn't linger after I came off the ice machine. I headed for my car as soon as my brace was back in place and my crutches were under my arms. I was in a terrible mood. Tim wasn't a bad guy but not getting to see Sarah and then to hear that she didn't date patients, had really set me off. I was already getting rejected, and I hadn't even asked her out.

There was a bright side to it. I would only be her patient for a few months, but Tim would be her co-worker for a lot longer. I had almost said that to him to rub it in but realized how cocky that would make me look. There was no guarantee that once I was no longer her patient, she would say yes to me when I asked. She seemed nice to everyone, maybe that's all it was with me as well. My terrible mood was still going strong when I walked into the apartment.

The place was dark. Troy had been home so much lately that his absence took me by surprise. A chill crept down my back, making me shiver, and I quickly flipped on the overhead light to dispel the darkness.

I crutched my way into the kitchen to find Troy had left a scribbled note on the counter, "*Gone huntin' -T.*" Immediately, I pictured the binder with the pictures of bloody knives. And with that one image, I went from bummed he was gone to being relieved that he was no longer there.

Once I shook that thought off, I considered what I would do with myself for the evening. Watching football and playing video games with Troy had become my norm. The week stretched before me, suddenly seeming much longer than it had before. I pulled out some leftovers and heated them up. While they were in the microwave, I texted Sharon to see how she was. When she texted back, "Not great," I asked if she wanted to have dinner with me via FaceTime. She sent a smiley face back, and with that, I had plans.

"Hey Shari," I greeted, once I could see her smiling face on my iPad.

"Hey baby brother, thanks for calling." She was sitting at her kitchen table just like me. We both had our iPads propped up, so it almost felt like we were sitting at the same table together.

"Anytime, sis. How was your weekend?"

"It was rough after the work week I had. They made me let someone else go, and I missed out on the promotion I was hoping for." She continued quickly before I could respond, "And I ran into Slater at the dry cleaners on Saturday."

"Why didn't you switch dry cleaners?" I asked, going with that train of thought first.

"I did, but apparently so did he. It must be closer to his new girlfriend's apartment." I could hear her getting choked up, but she had her eyes down on her food.

"I'm sorry, Shari. You don't deserve any of that; not how he treated you and not how your work is treating you." I still wanted to fly to D.C. and bring serious hurt to my sister's ex-fiancé, but she needed me to be empathetic and not angry for the time being.

She sniffled a bit. "I know, this is definitely not how I expected my life to turn out." She looked up at me and attempted a smile. "Aren't you glad you asked me to dinner?"

"Yes," I assured her quickly and without hesitation.

"I'm sure you are," she said with a laugh.

"I'm serious. I'm always glad to talk to you whether you're happy or sad."

"Yeah, right," she muttered, looking away.

"I'm being serious, Sharon. It still tears me up that you didn't want to tell me about Slater breaking up with you." I paused. "Like you said, we're all each other has. I'm here for you, no matter what."

"Thanks, Mitch," she said. "Same goes to you."

"You proved that while you were on gimp duty."

"How's your knee doing, anyway?"

"I'll answer that quickly, but then we're going to talk more about your work and when you plan on moving here."

"It's sounding more tempting all the time," she agreed.

"Then, let's make it happen," I clapped my hands together, ready to rent a moving truck on the spot.

"You said we could talk about your knee first," she pointed out.

"Oh, right, fine." I gave her a quick rundown of my progress in PT and quickly mentioned that I had switched from Ethan to a physical therapist named Sarah.

"Did I meet Sarah when I was there?" she asked curiously. Out of all the information I had given her, of course, Sarah was the piece she latched onto. Just hearing her name made my heart jump in my chest.

Trying to appear casual, I responded, "Uh, I don't think so," thankful for the pixelated connection we had at the moment.

"Yeah, I didn't remember meeting anyone named Sarah. Was she gone or something?"

"Yeah, uh, she said something about being on a vacation when I started doing PT." I was trying to act casual and unaffected.

"Okay," she said, and thankfully moved on to talking about my weight-bearing progress.

An hour later, we wrapped up the call, our conversation outlasting our dinner. Sharon promised me she would look harder into jobs near me while I did the same thing from my end. I told her I would look at different apartments for us as well.

"And hey," Sharon added right before we ended our call. "Next time we talk, I want to hear more about this Sarah. Don't think I didn't pick up on that, baby brother."

I laughed and responded quickly, "Gotta go, I think we have a bad connection. I didn't hear that last part. Bye."

I ended the FaceTime call to Sharon's laughter and turned off my iPad. My reflection was the only thing staring back at me and my thoughts immediately switched to Sarah.

"Sarah, I hope you're okay, wherever you are."

* * *

SARAH

This building hadn't been used in years. Most of the windows were gone and no one had even bothered to lock the side door I came in through. I made my way down a hallway that looked like it used to contain offices for the warehouse. The few remaining florescent lights left on were buzzing with a loud hum and flickering to eerily illuminate the filthy hallway. All were signs that I should not be there, but a creepy hallway wasn't going to stop me.

In my dream, I had seen Amelia in an open part of the warehouse – a large expanse of concrete with trash littered throughout the room, and the floors covered in years of dust and dirt.

Still being as quiet as possible, I continued down the hallway in what seemed like the direction I would find Amelia. I already had my guards up, my light shield and sword in hand. A chill raced down my back, making my whole body shiver. I turned quickly, extending The Light behind me to see if I was being followed.

Very real fear came over me now. It had been a long time since I felt truly afraid. I think it came from the fact that I'd come by myself even though I had heard Pneuma's voice clearly telling me not to go alone. But I was so scared any extra presence of The Light would be what would cause the enemy to run again that I didn't call my friends for help or even tell my roommate where I was going, which we had promised we would always do. As I progressed, I was emitting enough light that if any Terrobah were nearby, I'm sure they could sense me. This thought occurred to me as I was pushing open a heavy, rusted door that gave a terrible metallic screech, letting anyone in the building know my exact location.

I'm strong. I'll be able to stand against whoever comes at me, I reassured myself. I moved more confidently into the room as the door slammed shut behind me.

The familiar chills that I always had in the presence of Terrobah started racing across my skin and down my spine. They were in the room with me.

I sent out a wave of light to the shadows they were most likely lurking in, causing a few grumbles as the light reached its target. The Light in any form hurt the Terrobah. One by one, they slunk forward into the scattered light of the large fluorescent dome lights hanging above. It was like someone was shining a spotlight on the worst horrors imaginable. They were shape shifting from their shadow forms to the things that I only saw in my nightmares.

The Terrobah didn't even bother to remain in their human forms with me anymore. There were at least ten of them that I could see, and they were surrounding me. I heard, *Foolish choice,* in my head, and I completely agreed with Pneuma. I had been so foolish to come alone when Pneuma had counseled me otherwise. She told me I would need others with me, but I had been too focused on my emotions of losing Amelia to the Darkness forever.

I had also forgotten about the fact that I was very valuable to The Light. If I was taken out in this battle, The Light would lose a great warrior. I didn't think that in pride, but with deep responsibility. The Light had entrusted me with much, and here I was squandering it in disobedience.

"I'm sorry, Pneuma, so very sorry. Please help me," I whispered in humility, hoping for her gracious aid.

I didn't hear her voice or see anything in my circumstances change, but I knew she was with me. Though my choices had placed me here without my friends, I had reached the point where I could no longer back out. I would have to fight. I took a deep breath and called forth as much of The Light in myself as I could manage. I was glowing, and I heard some grumbles starting around me.

"Where is she?" I questioned the monsters, and the very air seemed to vibrate with my words. The groans got a little louder, but it was clear I was dealing with more mature Terrobah who didn't cower at The Light in my voice.

No answer came, so I tried again. "Tell me where Amelia is!" At that, one shriek broke out. I was hurting one of them with just my voice, but this would still be a battle I could not win alone.

I started pushing even more light into my words, "Tell me..."

"I'm here, sister," said a voice I hadn't been sure I would ever hear again. My head turned toward the sound to my right.

"Amelia!" I said in shock, joy, and relief. She was still in the shadows, but I knew it was her. My precious sister I'd searched for years to find. She was in front of me, and I was overcome with emotion; first joy, then worry at why the Terrobah were letting her talk to me, and finally turning to despair as she stepped farther into the fluorescent light shining down from overhead. The outline of her figure was all wrong. She looked nothing like I'd been picturing over these last four years.

Amelia took one more step forward and was centered under one of the overhead lights that shone down on her like a spotlight. I was helpless to stifle the gasp that came out of me. Amelia looked like a cross between the sister I remembered and something from the pit of Darkness.

She looked menacing while, at the same time, still appearing beautiful with her human features. Her hair was darker than ever, almost black, and hanging down to her waist, much longer than she'd ever worn it. She had new scars on her face, four lines in a row, like she'd been clawed on her cheek. Her skin was whiter than I had ever seen it, and her features stuck out all the more against it. Her lips were blood red and her eye make-up, if it was make-up, was very dark. She had markings of some sort on her neck that I couldn't make out. I extended out my light as I looked more closely at her neck. Brands – they had branded her on her neck and who knows where else. She was much more muscular than I had ever seen her and thicker too. She had on sturdy, black leather boots that laced up to her knees.

But it was her eyes that were the most haunting. They changed back and forth from her normal beautiful brown color to blazing red, like the fire inside her just had to show itself.

"Get a good look, sis," she sneered at me with the Darkness lacing her words.

"Oh Amelia," I uttered her name, feeling terrible at what she had endured during the years we'd been apart. "I'm so sorry they hurt you."

"*They* hurt me? Oh, that's rich coming from you, Sarah. That's really rich." Her voice dripped with contempt.

I felt her words hit my shield.

"Amelia, I'm so sorry I left you. I wasn't strong enough to stay." I spoke with as much love and light as I could. Her angry hiss told me of the depth of darkness she was ensnared in as she reacted just like the Terrobah to The Light. Now she, like them, hated the things of The Light; they were painful to her.

I took some of the force out of what I said next. "Amelia, come with me, I want to show you all I've learned." Without the power of The Light in my words, many of the Terrobah laughed at what I'd said.

"I, too, have learned much, Sarah." Her voice went deeper and more menacing when she spoke, and I knew she was trying to hurt me with her words.

"Amelia, my precious sister, I've searched for you for years." A tear escaped down my cheek. I saw a softening in the anger she had etched on her face.

"No! That's a lie! You left me and never looked back!" She said each word with such a mix of anger, hurt, and confusion that it shook me.

"That's not true. I've never stopped searching for you. I have missed you so much." I pleaded with her to understand me.

"You're a liar, Sarah! You've never cared for me. All you ever did was judge me!"

"No, that's not true. I have always loved you." In my emotion, more light came forth than I intended. Her posture immediately became more defensive, and I knew I had hurt her again.

She growled at me in response.

I could hardly bear the fact that the powers of The Light that I used to help so many were of no help to me in convincing her of my intentions.

The look on her face toward me was pure hatred. Not a bit of her was happy to see me anymore. My eyes tracked around the room, noticing that every Terrobah was focused on Amelia. They were clearly imparting lies to her, lies that made her want to kill me, if the look on her face was any indication. I strengthened my light guard in that moment. My words of love caused her pain, while their messages of death only strengthened her in her pursuit to hurt me, the one she thought was her worst enemy. It suddenly became clear to me. I wouldn't be rescuing her; I would be fighting her.

My light dimmed ever so slightly. How could I hurt my precious sister when it was clear she'd been through so much already? Even just the brands on her neck spoke of her distress. I lowered my guard even more as tears streamed down my cheeks. This caused a slight shift in her features and the confusion returned. I knew then that I couldn't hurt her.

She'd been fed a steady diet of lies and pure evil, while I knew the truth. And that flicker of confusion in her meant there was still good in there somewhere. There was no way I would harm her and add fuel to the Terrobah's fire. I lowered my guard even more, to the point that most likely she couldn't see it anymore.

A mysterious black tar started oozing out from under her feet and creeping its way toward me. No Terrobah I had ever encountered before had used this dark substance against me, so I had no clue what it was. The tar moved slower than my light did when I extended it, but I was guessing that it would be poison to me just like my light was poison to the Terrobah.

I was frozen with indecision. I knew my defeat would come if I didn't raise my defenses to full strength and fight back, but how could I? I couldn't hurt my sister who had already endured so much. My sister whom I had left behind in the darkness of Camp Tuano.

Before I could react, it was already too late as the tar wrapped around my ankles and climbed my legs. In that moment, I felt hopelessness, pain, fear, shame, and death. I tried to make my shield stronger, and I could feel the effects lessen slightly. I called forth any light that I could, begging The Light to help me. The poison that had latched onto me was already affecting me physically. My body started spasming. It felt like the raging battle between The Light and the Darkness was now fully inside me. As my spasms grew more severe and my vision started to fade out, my shield slipped, and the poison came through undeterred. I knew I was done for; I couldn't even restore my shield as the convulsions racked my body, and I began to heave. "Help," I groaned.

A bright light filled the room as I shook, my body still trying to reject the Darkness it had received.

I looked up through burning, tear-filled eyes; someone was taking a defensive position in front of me. Someone had come to save me. I could see his back. I would know that back anywhere. "Lucas," I managed to croak out as I dropped to my knees.

Don't hurt her. Was my last thought as the blackness overtook me.

CHAPTER 8

SARAH

I WAS DYING.

Not at the hands of Uncle or the Terrobah, and certainly not at the hands of an enemy. I was dying at the hands of my sister. For four years, I had searched tirelessly for her, nearly losing my life on more than one occasion. I had endured dark caves, blistering heat, blinding rain, and freezing temperatures, all while battling countless Terrobah in the process. And once I had gotten close enough to physically touch her, she was the one who would end me.

My heartrate slowed, and I began breathing easier. The air tasted almost sweet, and the blackness was becoming a dim memory. Even with my eyes closed, I could sense warmth coming toward me. I was sure I was on my way to the Land of The Light. What a disappointment I would be there. A Light Bearer of my caliber being brought down because I didn't heed the words of Pneuma.

They might very well cast me out.

"That is utter nonsense," I heard.

"Pneuma." I breathed out her name, opening my eyes to the warm glow.

"Yes, my love," she answered.

My eyes focused on her face, which looked even more beautiful than when I had seen her last.

Pneuma was leaning over me, stroking my hair with a look in her eyes that made me immediately burst into tears and say, "I'm so sorry I didn't listen to you."

Her eyes softened. "It is forgiven, my love."

I slowly pushed myself to sitting, and she immediately took me in her arms.

"Do you see why I counseled you to take someone with you?" She spoke kindly and without condemnation.

"Yes. I can see it all so clearly now. I was not ready to face her on my own." She didn't respond, so I continued. "I was just so afraid that if there was too much light present, the Terrobah would sense it, and they would take her again."

"You let your fear dictate your actions," she concluded, still holding me.

"Yes," I agreed, feeling ashamed that I had both ignored her and believed I was smarter than her eternal and infinite wisdom.

"No more of that lie now. Sarah Joy, you will never be cast out. You have The Light in you, and you will remain in The Light. You made a mistake, and it is forgiven."

I felt sick to my stomach at the realization that I had grown so little. I used to let my fear of people and Uncle dictate my every action. And I was still doing it.

"That is not true," Pneuma broke into my thoughts.

"What?" I asked.

"You do not let fear dictate your every action, and you have grown tremendously."

"I have?"

"Yes," she responded with such conviction I felt it to my very core.

I closed my eyes, savoring the feeling, and started to see image after image of how I had grown. From my decision to save Lucas, then my training in Ganheela, my battle against Uncle, and so many Terrobah encounters since, I saw firsthand the measure of my growth. As the images continued, I saw my studies of The Light, my strength in everyday activities, and recruiting new Light Bearers. But as quickly as the images moved across my mind, another alarming thought hit me.

I might have grown a lot but trying to do things on my own had led to my early demise. *In the end, I failed.*

"You are not dead," Pneuma spoke over my thoughts.

"I'm not?" I asked in disbelief at the realization that I was still alive. I opened my eyes to see the truth on her face.

"No," she said simply, offering no explanation as she continued, "Neither have you failed."

"Then, how am I with you?" I didn't understand. I had not used my stone, yet here Pneuma was before me.

"I came to you, my love. I knew after seeing Amelia you would need my touch as well as my voice."

"Lucas," I whispered.

"He is still in the room with you, binding Terrobah, but Amelia was taken. She is strong, but not strong enough to fight both of you, and they know that."

"They took her again?" I asked, feeling great pain roll over me.

"Yes." At her reply, I began to cry in earnest.

"I've lost her again," I wept. "I have failed."

"You, Sarah Joy, did not lose her, nor have you failed. She has made many choices leading toward the Darkness, and now it has a great hold on her. I, too, am eager to see her return to The Light."

"But I did fail. If I had only listened to you, my friends and I would be leaving here with her," I cried.

"That is not the story that unfolded, and so you do not know the outcome that would have actually happened."

"But..."

"I knew even when I gave you that vision that you would disobey me." She spoke the words in kindness, but I physically ached from my poor decision. "We can only go forward, and today that does not include you walking out of here with Amelia."

"With what she's been through, how can we expect to ever get her back?" I whispered, acknowledging that it seemed almost impossible now after witnessing the extent of my sister's suffering.

"She may never come back in the way you want her to, but she made those choices, not you."

"I don't think she chose to be branded by them," I pointed out.

"I agree; she would not have outright chosen to be tortured or branded, but she has made numerous choices to follow the Darkness." Pneuma spoke calmly and evenly, helping me to settle and focus.

"But she doesn't know the truth; she doesn't know about The Light and the Darkness. Please, we have to…"

"She does know," Pneuma interrupted my plea.

"What? How could she? We never knew, and for the past four years, she's been fed a steady diet of lies," the pitch of my voice rising in hysteria.

"Sarah, breathe."

This was the first time that I'd ever grown more anxious in Pneuma's arms. I did what she said and took a few deep breaths, welcoming the calm that returned. My anxious thoughts retreated somewhat in the loving comfort of Pneuma's embrace.

"It is not an easy thing for a human to understand, but each of you are responsible for your own choices, no matter what happens to you." As she spoke, I just kept breathing. "You lost your parents in a tragic accident as well, and yet you still made choices for The Light. Amelia even knew about The Light before Camp Tuano."

Pulling back to look at her, I whispered, "How?"

"Your mother taught her. The bedtime stories you heard as fairy tales were true stories of your ancestors and Mythreals. While you thought they were make-believe, Amelia knew them as truth. She even knew your mother was a Light Bearer."

"How can that be?" I wasn't questioning Pneuma, as I knew she only spoke truth. But with the new revelation, I leaned back into her as questions started to swirl in my mind once more.

"Amelia preferred what the world offered. In her grief, she buried what she knew about The Light deep down, choosing temporary pleasures instead."

"Why have I been searching for her then, if she already made her choice?" My throat constricted with emotion.

"No one is ever truly lost until their final breath."

"So, there is still hope for her to choose The Light?"

"There is always hope, my love. Where there is Light, there is hope." She spoke with such authority, that I felt the truth of it. Amelia wasn't as lost as I had thought only moments before. I could still bring her back. Plans started swirling as I subconsciously sat up.

"Sarah," Pneuma broke into my thoughts, causing me to look her in the eyes. I had done it again.

"I'm so sorry, Pneuma. I was trying to do it on my own again, wasn't I?"

She smiled with understanding. "Remaining in The Light is more important than finding Amelia. Can you understand that?"

"Yes," I said aloud, but my inner voice resounded, *but I still want to save her*. "So do I have to give up the search for her now that I know what she is?"

"Sarah, I long for Amelia to return to The Light just as you do. It is always deeply grievous for me when someone walks into the Darkness. Just as you never stop thinking of Amelia, nor do I. For now, breathe again, Beloved. You will need strength when Lucas awakens you."

"Is it almost time?" I asked, not wanting to leave her so soon.

"Yes."

"I don't want you to go, Pneuma. I'm afraid I won't know what to do and fear will overtake me, and I'll try to do it on my own, and fail completely." I spoke quickly before she could stop me.

"If you learn from today, you will not fail," Pneuma spoke the words with such assurance I felt her confidence inside of me.

"Sarah Joy, you are a *fierce* warrior. They used Amelia to sow doubt in you. They chose Amelia purposefully to get to you because they knew it would work. But, as long as you stand in their way, The Light will prevail. Remember, I am always with you. Always!"

I could feel her moving away, "Wait!" I called out.

"Lucas is waiting," she responded as she slipped away.

Lucas is waiting. She said the one thing that would make me want to go back, not that I had a choice. In the next instant, I was awake, cradled in Lucas's arms instead of in Pneuma's embrace.

"Lucas!" I exclaimed, filled with joy. But his face did not reflect the same joy. His eyes were filled with tears and pain.

"Lucas, what is it?" I raised my hand to touch his cheek. There were a lot of ways I pictured a reunion with Lucas, but this was certainly not one of them.

"I just witnessed you dying at the hands of your sister. And to see Amelia like that . . . to know the suffering she's endured at their hands. . ." A tear escaped his eye.

"Lucas. I'm so sorry," I said, immediately understanding what he must have gone through while I was with Pneuma. "I was with Pneuma," I explained, "so I was okay."

His eyes still roamed over my face, checking me over, as another tear ran down his other cheek.

With understanding, I said, "It was awful for me to see her like that as well." I paused. "That's why I let my guard down."

"You shouldn't have been here alone in the first place, Sarah," the frustration he felt evident in his voice. I had not been on this end of Lucas's anger before, and I knew I never wanted to be again.

"I know. It was stupid. I was overconfident in my own plan and in my ability to control the situation." I shifted my gaze from his wonderful face to say the next part. "I disobeyed Pneuma. I'm so sorry that my actions hurt you as well."

"Sarah, you know you're forgiven… by Pneuma… and by me," he said simply, the pain still in his eyes. I was freed by his forgiveness, but the impact of my actions still lingered.

His pain was almost too much for me to bear, and I moved out of his arms to sit facing him. I had to focus on the positive. Lucas was here with me, and this was the first time I'd seen his face in four years.

"The circumstances are less than ideal, but I'm still so glad to see you." I was unable to contain the smile that spread across my face.

He returned a small smile. "I would have rather seen you under any other circumstance, but I'm very glad to see you as well, sweet Sarah Joy."

Tears instantly filled my eyes. His voice and his smile still had such a strong effect on me. He was pure light itself.

Lucas grabbed my hand and brought me back to reality by saying, "We'd better go; more Terrobah are most likely on their way."

With his help, I stood up slowly, grabbing my backpack and swinging it over my shoulder. I was dizzy and felt a little off. I'd been with Pneuma, and then in Lucas's arms, but I still had some residual effects from the black tar. It had done a number on me, for sure, and wasn't something I wanted to repeat anytime soon.

Lucas took the backpack from me, smiling as he slung it over his own shoulder. "Always prepared, I see," he said, then grabbed my hand, leading me toward the exit at a quick pace.

Lucas opened the rusty metal door without it making a sound, and we quickly exited the building.

There was cloud cover in the sky, but it was still bright as we exited the old warehouse and moved quickly into the morning light.

"Great. Just great," I muttered, stopping short as I saw my car. The tires had been slashed, and the car had been graffitied with curse words. I walked toward it, reaching for the driver's side handle.

"Stop!" Lucas shouted, as he grabbed my shoulder and pulled me back.

"What?" Unsure why he didn't want me to touch the car.

"There is most likely something in or on the car that will harm you," he answered as he looked around.

Immediately, I realized my mistake. In my haste, I had forgotten to put a light guard around my car. Blinded by my need to get to Amelia quickly, I had made one mistake after another and almost gotten myself killed because of it.

"Sarah, I'm baffled." Lucas's voice seemed to have an edge to it. "You thought to bring a backpack, but you didn't think it wise to come with others?"

"I know, it was really stupid, and Pneuma told me not to come alone," I responded, my voice breaking as my gaze fell to the ground again.

He used his fingers to gently lift my chin so that I had to look at him. He had done this many times in the past, and I wanted to weep at his touch. I had missed him so much.

"Sarah, this doesn't change how I feel about you. We all make mistakes." The edge in his voice was completely gone.

"Not you," I said, turning away in embarrassment.

"Oh yeah?" he asked, turning me gently and pulling me into a hug. "Who was the one who lit a fire when the Terrobah were chasing us through the woods?" That made me smile. Lucas had been shocked at his mistake as well.

"Well, you don't make nearly as many as I do," I retorted, enjoying the hug and breathing deeply. I felt the last of the effects of the black tar leave me.

"Well, I shouldn't make any. I am a being of The Light, whereas you are human."

"I guess that's true." I still felt foolish, but tried to give in to his attempt to make me feel better.

"Oh, you guess, huh?" he teased.

"I just know a lot is expected of me, and I feel like I am letting everyone down." My voice was weighted with conviction.

"You're not expected to do any of it on your own, Sarah." He pulled back and lifted my chin once more. "You're one of the best students of The Light we've ever seen, but that does not mean we expect you to be perfect."

I smiled at him, garnering a warm smile in return. "That's quite a relief. I just feel like because I've been given such an amazing gift, I need to use it to do great things."

"You already are." He stated.

I felt humbled by his words.

"Our ride is here," he said, looking past me.

"Our ride?" I asked, turning to look as a cab pulled to a stop on the other side of my car.

"You called a cab out here?" I asked Lucas in shock.

"I sure did," he said with a chuckle, which I didn't quite understand until a familiar head came over the top of the car.

"Are you two going to stand out here and hug all day, or are we gonna get going?"

"Owen!" I exclaimed and ran to hug him.

He smiled at me as I jumped into his arms, but when I pulled back, he was regarding me with a serious face. "Are you okay?" he asked.

"It was really tough, but I'm okay," I said, tearing up instantly as I thought back to Amelia.

"We can talk more about it in the car," Lucas reminded us. "We need to leave now."

Owen turned to me and said, "Your chariot awaits!" He ended his sentence with a flourish, extending his arm out to the side as he bowed to me.

"Thank you, kind sir," I returned with a smile, fully enjoying his attempt to make me feel better as I slid into the backseat.

"Don't forget my backpack, I've got some snacks in there," I said sheepishly, attempting to diffuse Lucas's intensity now that I knew we were okay. He shook his head, grinning, and followed me into the car, sending memories flooding through my mind.

The last time we all climbed into a car together, we were headed back to Camp Tuano to save Amelia. As the memories returned, so did my emotions. My eyes started stinging at the thought of Amelia and what she'd become. I was devastated that I hadn't gotten to her sooner.

I was lost in my thoughts about Amelia and didn't realize we'd already reached the highway until Owen said, "So, black tar, huh?"

Wiping the tears from my cheeks, I answered with a quiet, "Yes."

"I haven't seen that before," Owen said out loud, more to himself, it seemed, than to us.

"It was pretty much my worst nightmare, and unfortunately, I lowered my guard when I saw Amelia." I paused, thinking back to the awful feeling of death working its way through my body. "Without my shield all the way up, the tar dropped me in seconds." I still couldn't believe I'd found my sister, but wasn't able to save her, and my heart ached in my chest at that thought.

My precious sister. In all the time I had searched for her and thought about what I'd find, the picture that I ended up seeing was so much worse. I had pictured her as emaciated or bruised and bloody, but seeing her as one of them, so far gone to the Darkness, it was more than I could take. I didn't even realize I was sobbing until Lucas pulled me to him.

I hated the Terrobah for what they had done to her. I hated myself for what I had allowed them to do to her. I even felt anger at The Light and the Eklesi for not helping me get to her sooner. Why couldn't we have made it back to the camp in time to save her? Her choices had shadowed her in darkness for four years, and now she was a monster of their making. I continued to sob as I felt the letdown from four years of searching with no success. I had never stopped searching; I had never given up hope. But seeing Amelia as she was now, it was hard to see how there was a way out for her.

CHAPTER 9

SARAH

IT WAS LATE MORNING when we left the warehouse. An hour later, when I was all cried out and quietly resting with my thoughts, we stopped for gas. Even being held by Lucas hadn't fully healed all the pain. This type of hurt ran much deeper than physical pain and would take longer to heal. In fact, I didn't want to heal completely. I wanted to hold on to some of the sadness and some of the pain, maybe out of guilt, and maybe because I felt connected to Amelia in some way through it. The Light would've taken the pain from me, but I refused to allow it.

Our next stop was the airport. I had flown in and then rented a car to drive to the warehouse in Miami. Unfortunately, I no longer had a car to return to the rental car company, but we still needed to make it right. Owen joked he would take the money for the rental car out of his taxicab fares. We had a good laugh about that. Owen didn't really drive a cab for a living, but he always seemed to have a car available anytime someone needed a ride.

The lady at the rental counter just stared at Owen when he set a stack of cash in front of her to cover the cost of the damage to the car. He winked back at us as he did so.

I need to ask him about all that money later.

He showed her the picture on his phone of the vandalism. She looked from his phone to me and back to the stack of money on the counter, then insisted she needed to call her manager to accept that amount of cash. But in his very convincing way, Owen assured her that wasn't necessary. His words were very persuasive, as all Mythreal's could be.

Unsure of how close the Terrobah might be to our trail, we decided my safest option was to be transported home with Lucas and Owen as my security detail. Once we were back on the road, they must have sensed I was in a better place and started asking me questions about what had happened at the warehouse.

Their questions were pretty basic in the beginning: how many Terrobah were there, and did I recognize any of them. Most of the Terrobah had fled at Lucas's arrival, like rats jumping off a sinking ship. When I told them I had counted at least ten before I saw Amelia and that none of them had cowered at my voice, Lucas interrupted me, "I still don't understand why you didn't take anyone with you." His voice was filled with the agony he still seemed to be feeling.

I started to speak but he stopped me, "And don't repeat the same answer about you being afraid of too much of The Light being present."

"Well, it's true," I responded, feeling angry at him and myself. Before he could speak, I rushed on, "You keep asking why I didn't take anyone with me. Well, where've you been? You haven't come to help me in four years!"

His gaze no longer held the penetrating intensity. Instead, it was filled with sadness, such sadness that I was compelled to apologize. "I'm sorry."

"You don't need to be sorry, Sarah. It's true that I have not come when you've called to me, but I was not permitted by The Light to draw near to you. Though I have wanted to see you many times, I'm not my own to come and go as I please." In the next breath, he continued, "I am honored to serve The Light; it is my very essence. And though it hurt me not to return to you, my allegiance is to The Light first."

My heart ached at his admission, even though I knew it to be true. Mythreals, like Lucas and Owen, were pure beings of The Light, able to do only what The Light asked them to do. They were so much a part of The Light that they wouldn't go unless they were sent, and they wouldn't resist any orders given to them. It was confusing to think about, especially when I was around them, and they looked so human.

"I was pulled from another assignment to come here," he said, looking out the window.

"So, you're not staying?" I questioned.

"No. Once Owen arrived, I was to entrust you into his care and return to my mission," he confirmed.

"Oh," a wave of sadness and hurt washed over me now that I knew my time with him was so short. Perhaps Pneuma had shortened our time together because she knew my feelings for him remained strong. Embarrassment washed over me, knowing that my feelings for him could be what kept us apart.

"Are you disobeying Pneuma?" I asked, all the while thinking that it couldn't be the truth since I was sure that Lucas wouldn't do that.

"No, I merely asked her for more time to help you through what you had seen and to determine where you were to go from here. She agreed that you needed that." As he spoke, his eyes came back to rest on me, but they were unreadable.

"Of course, you wouldn't disobey her," I muttered, annoyed at myself for thinking otherwise and feeling a renewed disappointment in myself for having disobeyed her.

"It's not the same for me, Sarah, as it is for you. I can see truth more clearly. I know that obedience is better. And Pneuma forgave you, so now you need to release your shame over that as well."

"That's easier said than done."

"I know it is, but...," he started

"No, you don't know!" I interrupted, the anger returning to my voice.

He didn't respond with words, but he looked at me intently, not at all angry. When I didn't continue, he said, "Sarah, I stayed so that we could talk and work through this. What is it you need to say?"

I turned my gaze out the window, embarrassed now at my outburst. Of course, he didn't know. He was a Mythreal, and while they often worked with humans, they didn't see and feel things the way we did.

"Pneuma said they were using Amelia to hurt me. They did this to Amelia just to get to me. That's a terrible burden to bear."

"That's not your fault."

"But it is. I chose The Light, and Amelia is the one that's had to suffer the consequences."

"That's your pride talking, Sarah. I'm not trying to hurt you, but saying your choices have led Amelia down the path of the Darkness is saying you have power over her. We had to flee in order to save you from her same fate. She made choices, even that very night, to move more toward the Darkness."

He was right, and it did sting and even angered me a bit. I argued, "But if she really knew what the Darkness was, I doubt she would have chosen it."

"Each time she chose to put people down to make herself feel better, each time she shopped away her troubles, she chose the Darkness. Amelia heard The Light whispering to her, but she remained on the same path of destruction. She even refused my help at the bonfire that night, choosing the Darkness over The Light. When I spoke to her, if she was leaning at all toward The Light, she would have come with me."

"She had The Light from you while she recovered," I pointed out.

"She did; I infused her with light while I was trying to heal her. But if she continued to make choices for the Darkness, it would have diffused very quickly. The Light does not remain where the Darkness is welcomed."

"You told me she was safe to stay there," I accused him. Four years of feelings came out with my words.

Lucas looked a bit taken aback by what I said, but I knew he hadn't been harmed, which made what he said next surprising.

"That had a little darkness in it, Sarah."

"What?" I asked in disbelief.

"What you just said to me had darkness in it...it wasn't just light that you emitted."

"How can I emit darkness?" I questioned, not quite believing him, but also feeling fear that it was true. Before he could answer, I continued, "Did I hurt you?"

"I'll answer your second question first. It stung a little, which was very strange coming from you, but it was mostly diluted with the light around it."

"I'm sorry," I whispered, feeling quite humbled at the realization that some darkness had both entered and escaped me. Somehow, I had allowed the Darkness in. Otherwise, I wouldn't have been able to emit it.

"It's okay, I'm fine, but this is why I stayed."

"What do you mean?"

"You're angry with me, and I think you're angry with The Light as well. If you continue to hang onto this anger, the Darkness in you will only grow."

There was a part of me that wanted to hold onto that little bit of anger. I felt more powerful when it surged through me, like I could even take on Lucas. But I didn't want to hurt Lucas; I loved him. I didn't want any harm to ever come to him. I quickly said, "Okay, what do I need to do to get rid of it?"

"Talk to me. We must get what you're feeling out in the open and shed light upon it. Darkness will flee from The Light."

Owen drove on as Lucas and I talked. As my anger slowly subsided, I shared with Lucas about the hurts I carried. I understood in my heart and in my head that he'd not been permitted to come help me. It wasn't him rejecting me; he was just obeying the truth of The Light.

At one point, I looked up and caught Owen's eye in the rearview mirror. I smiled thinking about how *he'd* been the one who was always there for me.

There was a period after Lucas left that I traveled with Owen. He taught me about what life would look like for me as a Light Bearer in the real world, how I would need to be careful about using my powers around humans and how I could guard myself and my surroundings from the Terrobah on a daily basis. I learned that I had to be careful who I spoke to and what we spoke about until I knew which side they were on. I couldn't just go around talking about The Light as though everyone knew about it and could understand it. After all, it had taken me some time to accept the reality of The Light, and I had been ready to hear it.

Owen also taught me about bringing others to The Light, just like I'd done with Ethan. He was like the best big brother ever, helping me get everything I needed for school and making sure I was settled before taking off to his next mission.

Waiting for school to start had been extremely lonely. I tried to see some of the local sights around my university, but I was still getting used to "sensing" the Terrobah and they were often in public places. I began to fear being found out and started to stick to safer places, mostly my house and campus. I practiced using The Light frequently in my apartment, which Owen had protected with a light guard. Pneuma visited me in my dreams, but it wasn't quite the same as having been with her in person while in Ganheela. I had never been alone in my life, and it was hard.

Eventually, cabin fever set in to the point that I had to get out.

I had decided to try out the international farmers market my classmate had suggested, but it was a mistake. There were Terrobah and Terrobists working there, and it freaked me out. In my fear, I put up an exterior light shield, low enough that humans couldn't see, but the Terrobah sure could.

When two of them started moving toward me, I raced back outside to my car, and they followed me. I knew I shouldn't go home with them behind me, so I went to a park. As it was becoming dusk, I knew they would engage me, but I didn't know how many there would be. With all my heart, I had wished Lucas would show up to help me. But much to my disappointment, he never came.

The Light was very strong in me and the three Terrobah that followed me to the park that day were very weak, so I was able to stun them quickly using my weapons in The Light. Owen had taught me that a very carefully aimed light pulse at their heads could erase some of their memory, so I gave it a try, hoping I had done it long enough to be effective. The last thing I needed was them showing up at my house.

Still, I wondered why Lucas hadn't come.

"You didn't need me," Lucas said, bringing me back to the present and smiling at me.

"It felt like a need to me. I thought that you would come whenever I felt the need," I explained.

"No, I only show up when Pneuma sees the need. That is a very different thing indeed."

"And this was more of a want," I whispered, afraid to meet his eyes.

"Yes, Sarah," Lucas continued. "By fighting that battle on your own, you learned that you could fight a battle by yourself. That one experience gave you the freedom and the courage to leave your house and venture out into the world."

"I guess I get that."

"Sarah Joy, we've been through a lot together; we are noorha."

"What was that word?" I knew it was from the language of The Light, but I wasn't sure I had heard that one before.

"It means we are connected by The Light, bound together for eternity, and so it hurts me that you're hurting. I don't like that you thought I wouldn't come for you if ever you were in a real need like you were today."

I started to speak, but he stopped me by squeezing my hand and saying, "I don't want you to apologize again. There's nothing left to forgive. You're safe and Pneuma will send me anytime I'm truly needed. I hope you'll trust her judgment."

"I do, and I will."

"What about me?" Owen piped in from the front seat. Both our heads swung toward him. He continued, "I want in on this action next time too; don't leave me out of the fun."

"Okay, Owen, we won't," I replied, catching his eyes in the rearview mirror.

"And did I hear someone say there were snacks in that back-pack?" he asked.

Owen, ever the comic relief. We all started laughing as the last of the tension melted away.

*　*　*

MITCH

"Mitch, your knee is looking great!" Sarah said with such joy that I wanted to pick her up in a big bear hug. I didn't, of course. I could still hear Tim warning me that she didn't date patients. So, I was biding my time as her patient and, hopefully, her friend, until I was done with my rehab.

In my adult life, I'd never had to wait for something I wanted, and I wasn't sure I had ever wanted something this much.

There was a small part of me that was concerned that even after I wasn't Sarah's patient, she still wouldn't want to go out with me, but I couldn't imagine my feelings were all one-sided. My pride wouldn't let me. It was bad enough that I thought of our Friday evening sessions as a date. Since we were regularly alone by the end of the session, I thought of it as "our time."

Oh man, I have it bad.

I returned Sarah's high-five with enthusiasm. I really was excited about my knee's progress, and it was better to think on that instead of my non-existent love life. The doctor had cleared me for all motion and weight-bearing last week, and I already had my full bend or flexion, as Sarah called it, back in my knee. I was finally able to walk without pain, most of the time. I still struggled with soreness at the end of a long day, but it was nothing that a little RICE couldn't help.

Sarah had given me that acronym, RICE: Rest, Ice, Compression, and Elevation. Throw some Advil in there, and I was as good as new. Well sort of. I couldn't run, jump, twist, etcetera, but I was on my way.

Sarah hooked up the NMES machine to my thigh to work on stimulating the muscle fibers in my quad. I was regaining my strength, but my left quad still seemed like it was half the size of my right. I said as much to Sarah.

She chuckled, "Mitch, that's far from the truth, and your strength is coming back quickly." She turned on the machine, and I contracted with the electrical pulses I felt. Five seconds on, three seconds rest. "Now that you have full range of motion, we can really focus more on strength. We wanted your muscle fibers to be at their optimal length before we worked on strength too hard."

"Optimal length tension, right?" I asked with a smile, remembering how she had explained it to me before.

"Oh, so you *have* been listening," Sarah smiled.

"I try," I said, play acting like I was a big deal. "Sometimes good ideas make it through this thick skull of mine."

She smiled as she looked back down at my leg. Her smile could still make my mind go blank, and unfortunately, it did, causing me to miss the start of my next contraction. I managed to come in at the end, but her eyebrows drew together as she watched my quad muscle. I made sure to do the next one on cue and with everything I had. With my effort, her eyebrows relaxed as she continued to observe my quad muscles.

It suddenly struck me as ironic that I was "flexing for her," but it wasn't my biceps or abs, how a guy would typically show off. I couldn't help but chuckle aloud at that thought.

"What?" she asked, looking at me curiously.

"Oh," I responded, embarrassed at my thoughts. I didn't want to make her uncomfortable by telling her why I was actually laughing. "I was just thinking about something funny that happened at work." I covered quickly with a lie.

"Oh yeah?" she asked, inviting me to continue. And unfortunately, I couldn't even make something up that would have been that funny. My work was a serious place. If you weren't a borderline workaholic, then you got passed by, fired, or you quit. Luckily, I remembered something just then from a few weeks before.

"Well, this guy at my office, he's kind of a jerk. Actually, 'jerk' is a very mild name compared to what most people call him. He takes credit for other people's work and gets away with it, and he seems to thrive on making people feel small."

"He sounds like a treat," she interjected.

"Yeah, no one really likes him." I paused, trying to frame how to tell the story since I'd just jumped into it.

Sarah was curious. "So, what happened?"

"Well, he has a bad habit of eating other people's lunches or snacks from the fridge even if they're marked." Sarah made a face at that; she didn't like him already. "Somehow, no one ever seems to catch him, but there has often been evidence in his trash can. I mean this guy has plenty of money to buy his own food or even have it delivered, but he takes other people's food just to be an ..." I cleared my throat, "just to be a jerk."

Sarah smirked at me catching myself. I used my fair share of curse words, but I had noticed that Sarah never cussed, so I tried to be careful how I said things around her. "So anyway, last week, one of my co-workers, who will remain nameless for his or her own safety," Sarah smiled and returned my conspiratorial look. "They brought in some leftovers from home that they might have had in the fridge for way too long. The 'label'" I used air quotes, "on the fancy take-out container may have mentioned pesto and blue cheese, but that's not what was in the container..." I trailed off.

"Eww," Sarah responded with a wrinkled face. "Mold?" she asked, still cringing.

"Yep, mold, but the jerk couldn't resist such fancy leftovers and as a reward for his selfishness, he was out with food poisoning for two days." Sarah's face was still wrinkled up. "I know I probably shouldn't be laughing, but..." I trailed off again, trying to read her face.

"That's awful, but he kind of deserved what came to him," she remarked with a grimace.

"Absolutely." I agreed. "Normally, I wouldn't wish food poisoning on anyone, but there was some satisfaction seeing him running for the restroom after only a few bites and not coming out for a while."

"Mitch, are you the employee to remain nameless?" she asked, stifling a laugh.

"No, no, it wasn't me." I held up my hands in self-defense. "But I have to admit, every time I see him eating a lunch he brought himself, it makes me chuckle. He won't even put his lunch in the fridge. He keeps it in his office, just in case."

She let out a laugh and joy washed over me. "Well, that turned my stomach, but I guess guys do love a good vomit story." She took off the sticky pads on my knee from the machine and we continued with the rest of my exercises.

As I finished up my last rep, she commented, "You're all done here. Let's get you iced."

As she wrapped the attachment for the ice machine around my leg, I asked, "Any big plans for the weekend?" It was Friday evening, so it was just the two of us in the clinic finishing up as usual.

"Nothing too big, some plans with my roommate, but nothing major," she answered.

"No traveling?" I asked out of nowhere, while she said, "How about you?" at the same time.

She smiled and tried again, "No, no traveling this weekend. How about you?"

"No traveling for me either," I returned, but the look on her face told me she knew I was being goofy, so I continued, "I actually do have plans for this weekend. I'm moving in with a new roommate."

"Oh yeah?" she said, even though she was now focused on her computer, closing out her notes.

"Yeah, it'll be my first time living with a woman, so that'll be different," I commented, waiting for her response. I was not disappointed as Sarah's eyes grew big as she quickly looked up from her computer at me.

"Oh, okay," she tried to cover her reaction by dropping her gaze back down to her computer. I could feel her disappointment.

I wasn't sure whether it was in me or in the situation, but I couldn't take it, so I quickly said, "It's my sister. I'm moving in with my sister."

"Oh," her eyes came back up to mine. "I thought your sister lived in D.C.?"

"She did, but she's moving back here." I wanted Sarah to know what Sharon had been through. Sharon could use a friend right now, and I knew Sarah would be sympathetic. "Her fiancé cheated on her and kind of took all their friends when they broke up."

"That's terrible." She crossed her arm and came to stand against the table next to me.

"Yeah, it was, and if she'd let me, that lame excuse for a man would be in a world of pain." Sarah looked like she was tracking with me, so I continued. "She was really getting lonely there. I could only convince her to move back here if she had a job and a place to live. So, she worked on the job side of things, and I found us a place."

"You're a great brother to let your grown sister live with you."

"Even though Sharon is my older sister, I still feel very protective of her. I don't want that poor excuse for a man to have control over her anymore." At that, Sarah's face fell.

"You okay?"

"Yeah, uh, yeah, I'm fine. I just feel bad for Sharon," she returned to her computer.

"How's your sister?" We'd never talked about her sister before, but Tim had told me that was who she may have gone to visit when she had left so suddenly a few weeks before. For some reason, her sister came to my mind when the shadow of pain had crossed her face.

Her face turned pale, and her eyes glistened with unshed tears. But just as quickly as it'd come, it was gone. "My sister?" she asked, seeming very guarded.

"Oh yeah, uh, I think Tim had mentioned that you went to see her a few weeks back, family emergency or something. I was just wondering if she was okay." I wished I could just take it all back to break down the wall that had clearly formed between us.

"I didn't know you knew about that." Sarah was the most closed off I'd ever seen her.

"I'm sorry I brought her up. I was just thinking it was cool we both had a sister." I wanted to know why mentioning her sister had her so shaken, but I didn't press any further.

"No, it's okay. I just don't really talk about her much." It became clear to me that Sarah wasn't as close to her sister as I had assumed when she dropped everything to go to her.

"Well, again, I'm sorry for bringing her up."

She managed a smile. "Mitch, it's really okay; we all have a history, right?" I could tell she was just trying to move past this conversation. My ice machine beeped right then signaling we were finished.

As she was taking off the leg wrap, her emotional pain was palpable, even though I had no idea what it was about. I felt a fierce need to take some of her pain away. I lost my head for a second and put my hand over hers.

She looked up at me, shocked, but didn't say anything. "Sarah, I'm sorry for bringing up something that caused you pain. I know family stuff can be hard, and I'm sorry it's hard for you right now."

There was some sort of electrical current flowing through our hands. My heart was pounding so loudly that I could hear it, and it only accelerated when she flipped her hand over and gave my hand a squeeze.

"Thank you, Mitch," she said simply, but I could tell by her face that something had changed, there was less strain on it. I hoped in some way I had helped just a little. She released my hand and finished taking off the wrap.

"Anytime, Sarah." And I really meant it.

CHAPTER 10

SARAH

"How was closing up the clinic?" Ethan asked me from across the dinner table after we'd started eating. As my boss, he often checked in on me, but since this was a meal with my friends, I knew he was asking about my day personally.

"Good," I responded softly, as my thoughts went to Mitch, yet again.

"Oh, it's like that," Ethan teased with a knowing smile.

"It's like what?" I asked, confused at why he seemed to know something I didn't.

"If I'm not mistaken, Mitch was your last patient today."

"You're not mistaken," I replied with my eyes on my food, refusing to look at him.

"I've sensed he has potential, too," he said in all seriousness.

My eyes snapped back up to him. "You have?" Could he read my feelings so well?

"In The Light, yeah."

"Oh, yes, in The Light," I smiled, a bit embarrassed.

"Yes, although, I don't think that's your only interest in him," he teased me again.

I looked over to see Nyiah giving me a knowing smile as well. They were my dearest friends, and they loved me; I could be honest with them.

"I do like him, as a friend, as someone with potential for The Light." I had to drop my gaze back to my food to say, "and maybe something more."

Nyiah touched my arm. "There's nothing wrong with that, Sarah."

"I know, but it feels almost wrong somehow."

"Why? Because he isn't part of the Eklesi yet?" She questioned.

"That's a big piece of it," I admitted.

"What's the other piece of it?" Nyiah pressed.

I took a deep breath, "My heart still feels taken." It was hard to admit that to them and to myself. I looked up at Nyiah and saw love and sympathy reflected back. She knew who I was referring to. Ethan and I had never talked about it, but he probably knew I was referring to Lucas.

"I know how you feel," Ethan broke in, bringing our eyes to him as he now focused on his plate.

"Your wife?" I prompted, not because I didn't know, but because he seemed like he needed to talk about it.

"Yeah," he looked up at me. "I can't see any other woman, because it still feels like my heart belongs to her."

"I'm so sorry, Ethan. I know you miss her a lot." I touched his arm resting on the table, consoling him.

"I do, but now I also know she's in the Land of The Light, and that gives me great comfort." He pushed his food around a bit.

"I'm so thankful Pneuma revealed that to you," I responded, giving his arm a squeeze.

"Remember, to me he's Ruah," he remarked with a smile, as his eyes came back up.

Nyiah laughed outright, "I'd actually forgotten that."

"What?" I asked, looking back and forth between the two of them.

"Ethan doesn't see Pneuma as a woman, he sees her as a man. Or I guess I should say 'him.'"

"Really?" I asked with interest, now that I could see they were being serious.

"Yes," Ethan continued the story, "Pneuma, or Ruah, takes the form of our gender."

"So Pneuma isn't a woman?"

"No, she isn't a man or a woman." Nyiah returned. "She is altogether something different. She just presents herself..."

"Or himself," Ethan chimed in.

"Or himself," Nyiah corrected, "in a way that makes sense to us. I'm not sure as humans that we could handle seeing Ruah in his full glory."

"Wow, it's amazing that I can learn new things about The Light every day," I responded in awe.

"I know, it's unbelievable," Ethan confirmed.

When I learned something new about The Light, often my thoughts would go to my sister. If I had known about The Light sooner, maybe, just maybe, things would be different.

I heard Ethan ask Nyiah, "Did you know that the word 'gender' wasn't used to describe your biological sex at birth until the 1950s?" But I wasn't really listening as my thoughts had drifted back to Amelia.

"No, what did we use instead?" Nyiah questioned Ethan.

"Just male and female, because that's all there truly is; the Father of Lights created them in His image, male and female he created them." I could hear Ethan's voice, but I felt like I was in a different place. "But now the Darkness has skewed that word to have all sorts of sexual connotations and the purity of male and female has been severely distorted."

"So, Mitch, huh?" Nyiah prompted, her change of subject drawing me back. After my last trip, I hadn't been the same. Talking with Lucas in the car had helped a lot, but I still grieved for my sister and thought of her all the time. Nyiah could usually sense when my mood darkened and tried to redirect me.

"Yeah, Mitch," I went with her pivot. "I like him."

"And?" she pressed me for more information.

"He's kind. He's letting his sister move in with him this weekend," I informed them. "And he's funny," I added, thinking back to his story about the co-worker. The story was terrible, but his humor and antics made me laugh.

I looked up to see both of my friends smiling at me. "What?" I asked as my cheeks turned red.

Ethan answered, "The blush looks good on you."

"I think you forgot something." Nyiah said.

"What?" I wasn't following.

"You forgot to mention his looks." She quickly followed, "I haven't met him yet, so I need details."

I laughed out loud at the double eyebrow raise she gave me, but I wanted to have a little fun of my own.

"Yes, Nyiah, he's very good looking... don't you agree Ethan?" I asked, which caused him to practically choke on his water.

Once he recovered, he said, "Oh yeah, he's really good looking," exaggerating every word, then adding a heart flutter with his hand on his chest, causing us all to laugh.

Since Nyiah knew about both our histories, we quickly turned the questioning to her previous crushes. It was a gift to have downtime with my friends who were more like my family. And it was good to remember there could be times of levity and joy in The Light, even with the Darkness that surrounded us. In that moment, it was just what I needed.

We wrapped up dinner together in the kitchen, cleaning and enjoying the easy friendship that had grown between us.

"Sarah, you're really glowing right now," Ethan commented, drying the last of the pans.

"It's tonight," I responded. "Our laughter and love for one another, it pushed the Darkness back. I can't help but let The Light shine," I was unable to contain my smile.

"I'm so glad," he said, returning my smile. "See, this is what I mean," he said, catching Nyiah's gaze.

"What?" Nyiah asked.

"There are two precious women of The Light standing right in front of me. I know The Light has more to offer me, but I just can't seem to move forward."

"Because of your wife?" she asked.

"Yes," he confirmed.

"Then, it's not yet time, Ethan," I responded. "You're still healing. When it's time to move on, you'll be able to embrace all The Light has for you."

"How do you know?" he questioned me.

"Not sure," I answered with a shoulder shrug. "Probably wisdom from Pneuma, but I feel it to be true."

"Well, that got deep fast," Ethan laughed, trying to lighten the moment. "Thank you, Sarah; I will take comfort in your wise words. And thank you, Nyiah, for cooking. It was delicious, as always," he said, tossing his dishtowel on the counter. "On that note, I'm gonna call it a night."

Together we walked Ethan to the door, both giving him hugs, and then watched as he walked out to his car. "Goodnight, Ethan," we yelled in unexpected unison, causing us both to laugh at ourselves.

"See ya," he called over his shoulder, smiling as he got into his car.

I watched him drive away, and then turned to find Nyiah looking at me, but almost through me.

"What?" I prompted, turning to look behind me.

"Why can't I see Ethan that way either?" she spoke softly.

"You mean as someone you could spend your life with?" We went back into the house, and I closed and locked our front door.

"Yes. It must be a great thing in The Light to have a lifelong partner who shares in both the delight and the calling that comes with it. I saw that in my parents' lives. Ethan should be my logical choice, but the lack of romantic interest is not just on his side. I don't see him like that either," she explained, slowly lowering herself onto the couch.

I sat next to her, taking hold of her hand to comfort her as she processed, but she didn't say anything more.

"Nyiah, you have more knowledge about this than I do, that's for sure. I know very little about dating, and even less about seeing parents live out their lives serving together in The Light. But you've known about The Light your whole life. I'm sure when the right person comes along, you'll feel it."

"But that's just it; even though we were joking about my crushes, I've kind of always felt like The Light was enough for me. I haven't actually pictured myself with a man forever. And now I'm wondering if there's something wrong with me." She seemed troubled at her admission.

"Whoa, no, there's nothing wrong with you. You've chosen to be single to have a singular focus on The Light; that's good and right," I paused, composing my thoughts. "And just because you're wondering about having a relationship with someone, doesn't mean you have to change. You keep doing what you're doing, and Pneuma will show you if there is a new direction."

"Is that what's happening with you and Mitch?" Nyiah asked.

"Pneuma talked to me about him," I confessed.

"She did?" Nyiah's eyebrows rose, matching the surprise in her voice.

I nodded to her question.

"Why didn't you tell me?" she asked; but she wasn't offended.

"It was during my last 'pond session,'" I answered.

A "pond session" was what we had begun affectionately calling my "better-than-therapy" sessions I had with Pneuma at the pond. "I shared so much with you, and Mitch seemed like the least important piece, especially since nothing can happen until he's awakened anyway."

"So, you can't date him until he's a Light Bearer or at least Awakened?"

"She didn't say anything about that, but I wouldn't want to, anyway. Unless he was in the Eklesi, he would never understand who I am or what I live for, much less the trips that I take." I felt very firm in my convictions.

"Will you still be taking trips?" Her question gave me pause.

"I don't know, probably not ones to look for Amelia. It seems very much like she'll be the one to come to me the next time." I felt the sadness wash over me. And then warmth spread up from my hand as Nyiah gave me an infusion of light. I took a deep breath and released it as I stared at my lap. I came back to her question. "We'll probably still travel sometimes to help others or to train Light Bearers."

"That's true, we will," she reassured me, giving my hand a squeeze and drawing my eyes up to hers. "I'm sorry I brought it up though."

"It's okay; it's my new reality, and I have to find a way to release her and not think about her all the time. I'm less effective that way, just like the Terrobah want," I commented, drawing conviction from my spoken words.

"Your glow has dimmed a little, and I hate that I did that." Nyiah sounded disappointed.

"You didn't do it," I argued, looking at her. "Besides, it's so much better for these feelings to come out at home instead of at the clinic."

"Did that happen?" There must have been something in my voice that gave her an indication that I wasn't speaking only in the hypothetical.

"Yes," I admitted, "Mitch asked me about Amelia, and it took me completely by surprise."

"What'd you do?"

"I answered as best I could, and he tried to make me feel better." I smiled.

"That's sweet." She smiled in return.

"It was. He felt really bad about it and told me he'd be there for me anytime."

Nyiah smiled at me and then leaned against me as I thought about what that meant for me, for Mitch, for us together, and for The Light.

* * *

MITCH

"Sir, where do you want this?" the next moving guy asked me. It hurt my ego a little bit to have to pay movers when I was fully capable of lifting and hauling all my own stuff. But I also didn't want to jeopardize my healing progress. Or my relationship with my physical therapist.

"In that bedroom there," I responded. We had spent the morning loading boxes at my old apartment, and now we were unloading them at our new apartment. She was already busy getting the kitchen put together, while I directed the movers.

Troy had not let up on making fun of me for moving in with my sister. Just when I thought he and I had become better friends, he became a jerk all over again. I'd even offered to pay two months' rent while he found a roommate, but that hadn't made him happy either. He seemed oddly more attached to me than I was to him. Needless to say, Sharon and I did not rent an apartment at the old complex with Troy. Instead, I found a place closer to Sharon's new job. And I gave my forwarding address to the old leasing office instead of Troy because of how poorly things had ended.

Sharon was in full agreement with that choice as Troy had always been rude and a bit creepy in her mind. She couldn't understand how I'd put up with him for as long as I did. I had to explain to her the complexities of men and how we all had our jerky moments. To which she commented that it seemed like Troy had more than filled his quota of jerkiness. We had a good laugh about that word choice and the fact that it was true.

In reality, Troy had gotten a lot worse over the previous few weeks. He seemed even more irritable after his impromptu hunting trip, which is the opposite of how most people felt after getting away for a few days. I never did find out what the deal was with his book of knives, which was probably for the best. Troy and his weirdness weren't my problem any longer, and that was a relief. Sharon and I didn't always get along perfectly, but she would definitely be a better roommate than Troy.

Sharon seemed so much happier already. She had quit her job and driven down from D.C. the previous week. I paid to have her stuff moved since I wasn't able to help her at all. She said I was spoiling her, but she'd been through so much already, and I was hoping things would start looking up for her in the near future.

"What about this one, sir?" another guy asked me, snapping me back to my present task.

After giving the box a quick glance, I answered, "That goes in the bedroom down the hall." I should have made color-coded stickers or something. This doorman-director thing was going to get really old, really fast.

I directed a few more boxes and then went to check on Sharon. She was humming as she organized her kitchen in her own particular way. That's right, her kitchen. I knew my place. I leaned against the door jamb, seeing all the changes she'd already made. When she turned to look at me, she was beaming. She shut the drawer she was working on and moved toward me for a hug.

"Thank you, Mitch," she said with a catch in her voice. "I know you did this all for me, and I'm so grateful."

"You're worth it, Sharon. I'm so glad you like the place."

"What's not to like?" she said, backing away and gesturing dramatically to all the kitchen's features. We could have found a cheaper place, but I knew how therapeutic cooking and baking were for Sharon. I went with an apartment that was high-end and had a fully equipped kitchen, complete with tall white cabinets and white granite countertops. She even had an island.

"Seriously Mitch, I'm so grateful." She teared up a bit.

"No more thank-yous. I'm happy, too. You're here, you're safe, and you're happy. That's all the thanks I need."

"I won't pester you with it too much, but I do know that it's not the coolest to move in with your sister," she acknowledged.

"Since when have I cared about being cool?" I asked, jokingly.

"Since forever," she said with an eyeroll.

"Shari, I'm good with this decision, too. You know what a nightmare Troy was."

"Yes, but you could have just moved out. You didn't have to move in with me just because I couldn't afford my own place. I don't want to cramp your style."

"What style?" I answered, laughing at just how true my words were.

"Oh, you know, ladies' man or whatever."

"I don't have a style, and I was never a ladies' man," I retorted. Her skeptical expression said it all. "Okay, maybe I was a ladies' man, but I'm not anymore. That whole scene of going out and hooking up just doesn't appeal to me anymore."

Her face brightened, and she asked, "This doesn't have anything to do with Sarah, does it?" Her voice was playful, matching her body language as she crossed her arms and looked knowingly at me.

"What? No!" I answered, dropping my gaze, but I knew the heat I felt in my neck was giving me away.

"I had a feeling," she replied as she raised one eyebrow at me.

"What?" I asked again, trying to cover. "What are you talking about? I barely even talk about her."

"Yes, but little brother, you've never talked to me about a woman before."

"That's not true," I protested.

"Well, maybe it's not completely true, but never more than just a quick mention. Honestly, I barely catch their names. With Sarah, I can just tell by the way you talk about her."

"She's my PT, and I barely talk about her." I protested again, perhaps too much.

"Maybe it's sisterly intuition; I can just tell."

She had me figured out, so why fight it? "Well, nothing can happen there anyway until I'm not her patient anymore. So maybe I should just go out and distract myself until I can actually ask her out."

"Is that what you want?" she questioned quietly, looking at me with her brown eyes.

Man, she doesn't miss a thing, does she?

I turned away from her and leaned on the countertop with my hands. I didn't answer right away as I thought about what I wanted regarding Sarah. "No," I finally answered softly.

"What?" she asked as though she couldn't hear me.

"No, that's not what I want." Sharon looked at me with understanding.

"What?" It was my turn to ask since she just kept looking at me.

"I like this you," she said with a smile.

"What me?" I asked in confusion.

"The you that lets me move in with him. The you that isn't chasing after every adventure and every fun night trying to forget. You're finding your true self, Mitch, and I really like this you."

"Now, don't get carried away. I may like Sarah, and I'm happy to have you here, but the rest is just my knee."

"We'll see," Sharon commented with a smug smile. "I can't wait to meet her." She gave me a pat on my shoulder.

"When are you going to meet her?"

"When I come with you to PT this week," she stated, her smile a little too cheerful for my comfort.

"I don't know about that," I returned.

"You know I won't say anything," she reassured me.

"But you might drop hints." I frowned at her.

"No, I promise I'll be on my best behavior. Sister's honor," she said as she saluted me. "Now get out of my kitchen so I can finish organizing."

"Yes, ma'am," I saluted in return and headed back to my post of directing the moving guys as I thought about what she'd said. Was I really changing that much? Did I want to change? No answers came to me other than telling the mover where to put the next box.

CHAPTER 11

SARAH

ETHAN WAS BUSY ON his laptop when I walked into his office on my break. "Ethan?" I called his name to get his attention.

"Hey, Sarah," he responded once his eyes met mine. "What can I do for you?"

I walked into his office and closed the door before I continued. "Letta canceled her appointment again," I stated softly, my concern evident.

"Again?" he repeated, the unease in his voice matching my own. "How long has it been since you've seen her?"

"Two weeks. I'd been somewhat concerned, but since I was still dealing with my own stuff, I didn't think on it too much. But today, with her cancelling again... it has an ominous feel to it."

"What do we need to do?"

"I don't know," I replied. "I guess I need to ask P about it."

"Okay, but you don't get a sense that we need to do something right now?" Ethan was a man of action, and I could see he was ready to go after her.

"I feel an urgency, but after my last great mistake, I don't want to just head over there, guns blazing and not knowing what we may be walking into."

"Okay, well, I'm here for you, whenever you're ready."

"I know and thank you." I turned to go back out to the clinic, but Ethan called my name, so I stopped before I opened the door.

"Are you going to be able to work or do you need me to stay and cover your patients?" he asked graciously. It was my night to close.

"Oh no, I feel better just having talked to you."

"Well, glad I could help," he said grinning at me, this time emanating some light.

I couldn't help but smile back as I turned and opened the door to step out.

"Sarah," I turned back again to see him standing, his arms open and waiting. I moved into them to get a hug and a small gift of light from him.

"Thanks," I beamed at him in return and turned to move out of his office. As I returned to the clinic, I almost ran into Mitch as he headed for the bike. He looked confused.

"Hey, Mitch!" I greeted him cheerily.

"Hey, Sarah," he returned my greeting, but not with his normal enthusiasm.

"How's the knee today?" I asked as I got the bike screen started for him.

"Good," he responded again, but I could tell he was bothered.

"You okay, Mitch?" I asked, trying to catch his eye.

He shook his head and focused on me. "No, yeah, I'm fine, long day, I think."

"You think?" I asked, grinning.

"No, I mean, I know it was a long day. I think that's what you're seeing on my face." His voice was still off, but I couldn't force him to tell me what he was thinking. Well, I could use The Light to persuade him a little, but I wouldn't do that since he clearly wanted to keep his thoughts to himself.

"Okay, well, I'll let you get to it and see you at the table in a few minutes."

THE DELIVERANCE

* * *

MITCH

I couldn't believe what I'd seen. Ethan and Sarah hugging, but not a platonic co-worker hug that I would have expected; it held something more. It took all my strength not to demand answers from Sarah. I thought she didn't date co-workers or patients, but it was clear that there was something going on between her and Ethan.

My exercises progressed with little restraint on my part. Leg pressing 300 pounds and running five miles was what I needed to get all the anger and energy out of me, but there I was curling 10 pounds with my hamstrings.

"Mitch, are you sure you're okay?" I heard Sarah ask. My face was buried in my arms on the table as I did my curls lying on my stomach.

"Yep, I'm fine," I said, not bothering to lift my head.

"The tech told me you wanted to go up on weight?"

It was clear she wanted to know why, but I wouldn't give her the satisfaction of knowing I wanted to feel some pain in my knee instead of my heart.

"It was getting too easy," I responded shortly, still not looking at her. I knew I was being a jerk to her, but I was too frustrated to reign myself in.

"It seems like you're doing okay with it. Are you having any pain?"

At the softness of her voice and the kindness it held, I wanted to tell her everything I was feeling, but of course, I didn't.

"Mitch?" she asked, touching her hand to my back. I felt a jolt of pleasant electricity and then her warmth. Feeling the warmth of her touch, I knew, as much as I wanted to, I couldn't lie to her.

"It's hurting now," I confessed.

"Let's stop with that one for the day then and let me have a look at your knee."

I rolled over to let her examine my knee but stayed flat on my back so I could stare at the ceiling.

"You're a bit swollen, so I want to hold you here. We won't go up on weight with anything else today."

"Okay," I agreed.

Somehow, I was able to back off and get through my next three exercises without aggravating my knee farther. When Ethan came to say goodbye to Sarah, he touched her arm and I was close enough that I heard his whisper, "Call me once you're home." When she smiled back at him and nodded, it was like a knife to my heart, and it took all I had not to order him outside.

"That's probably enough for today, Mitch. Let's go ahead and get some ice on you." The care in her voice should have softened me a bit, but instead I just felt worse.

"I'm not done with my exercises," I mumbled.

"I know, but right now your knee needs ice more than exercise."

"Fine," I muttered back like a little child.

Really mature, Mitch.

"What's going on with you today?" Sarah asked as she started working on my scar with massage cream.

I started to say nothing and that I was fine, but with her hands touching my knee and the warmth from that spreading through me, it was impossible for me to lie.

I closed my eyes so I wouldn't have to look at her. Since it was Monday, we weren't the only ones in the clinic, so I said softly, "I saw you with Ethan."

"You see me with Ethan all the time," she responded innocently, clearly not understanding why that would cause my weird behavior.

"Yeah, but today I *saw* you two. Hugging."

"Okay?" she asked slowly, still lost.

"I didn't realize you two were together," I stated, grinding my teeth. She was apparently going to make me spell it out.

"Together like boyfriend and girlfriend?" she asked.

"Yes."

"And that bothers you?"

"You know it does, Sarah." My eyes opened to meet hers. "You have to know that I like you by now."

"I like you too, Mitch, but..."

"But you don't date patients," I interrupted.

"Yes, that's also true."

"I don't have a problem with that. I was biding my time until I'm not your patient. But then, seeing you with Ethan hurt worse than I thought it would."

She was still looking at me with kindness in her eyes and some pink in her cheeks.

"I'm sorry, I'm embarrassing you."

Crap, Mitch, just shut up.

"It's okay. It's nice to be liked," she responded, looking down at my scar.

"But?" I prompted.

"But..." she trailed off and didn't finish her thought.

"So... how much longer do I have in my rehab?" I asked, causing her to laugh out loud. "I'm serious, Sarah."

"I know," she said smiling at me with a twinkle in her eyes, "And I'm not going anywhere."

"What about Ethan?" I floated the question out there, preparing myself for the worst.

Here it comes, Mitch. Just start getting over her now.

"Ethan is one of my closest friends. He's practically family to me. That was a brotherly hug you saw; he was trying to cheer me up."

I exhaled a rush of air, making me aware for the first time that I'd been holding my breath. I couldn't help but smile with the joy that burst through me, a fact I felt sure was showing on my face.

Sarah looked away, the color rising in her own cheeks as she got up to make a note in my chart. "Your scar is looking good and, with you distracted, I was able to get that knot out of your IT band. I better get that ice on you now so you're not too sore."

For the rest of my appointment, we talked only on safe subjects, just catching up on our weekends. She told me she wanted to meet Sharon, so I promised her that Sharon would come with me to a session soon. Since it wasn't Friday, I made my way out alone, which was for the best since I was feeling a little amped up. Who knew what I was capable of, like grabbing her in my arms to hug her or even kissing her? But I knew I would see her Wednesday; she told me she wasn't going anywhere, and that was enough for now.

* * *

"I like her a lot," Sharon whispered, as Sarah moved away to work with her other patient. As promised, Sharon came along with me to my Friday PT appointment to check out "my progress."

"Oh yeah?" I asked, as I continued with my exercise.

"She's so friendly and knowledgeable... and cute." She added an eyebrow wag with the last word.

"You don't have to convince me," I responded, focusing on my knee instead of being goaded by her teasing.

"I know. I'm just surprised," she whispered more forcefully.

"Surprised that I have good taste?" I asked in a conversational tone. If we kept whispering, we were going to draw attention to ourselves.

"Well, yeah," she said, matching the tone of my voice. Her sarcasm brought my eyes back up to hers and made us both smile.

"Let's ask her to go to dinner with us," she whispered again.

"What? No." I said a little too loudly. I quickly glanced around the clinic to make sure Sarah hadn't heard me.

"Why not?" She looked at me like I was missing the obvious. "You said you can't date her while you're a patient. So, we go to dinner, the three of us, then it's not a date. But... you get to spend time with her outside of the clinic."

The idea definitely had appeal.

"I guess so, but you have to ask her." I felt butterflies kick up in my stomach at the thought.

That made Sharon laugh and reply, "I've never known you to be scared to ask a woman out."

"I'm not scared." I was more nervous with excitement than scared. "I already told her I liked her. I just think she'll be more likely to accept if you ask. She may turn us down if I ask."

"Good point," Sharon agreed. "Okay, I'll ask," she lowered her voice as Sarah walked back over.

"Okay, Mitch, time for me to work on that knee," Sarah stated.

"Do you need me to move off the stool?" Sharon offered.

"Nope, I'll just grab this one right here," Sarah responded, pulling one from the other side of the half wall. She put on her gloves and got out the massage cream.

Sharon asked Sarah what the massage was accomplishing and once she found out, she asked how things were feeling to Sarah.

"Everything is progressing really nicely. Mitch does exactly what I ask, even though I think he was skeptical that he could follow instructions," she teased with a smile at me.

"Too true," I returned.

"Okay, let me grab the ice," Sarah said as she took off her gloves and headed to get the ice machine cart.

"I thought you were going to ask her to dinner," I whispered quickly.

"Anxious, are you?" she replied, smiling at our secret.

"A little," I admitted, not caring if I was teased about it later. I could handle some teasing if it meant I got to have dinner with Sarah.

"Don't worry, I won't forget," she said with a cheeky smile.

Sarah came back, wrapped my knee in the cuff, and started the ice machine.

"What do you have going on tonight, Sarah?" Sharon asked.

"No plans, just headed home," Sarah replied, as she moved behind her computer.

"Mitch and I were going to stop and grab a bite to eat at that new bistro on Elm. Would you like to join us?"

"Oh," Sarah said, caught off guard. She looked at Sharon as if really considering it, then answered, "Uh, sure." She didn't sound certain, though, so Sharon broke in quickly.

"No pressure or anything. I've just enjoyed our time together and since you have no plans...," Sharon trailed off.

"No, it's fine, great actually. I was just thinking about my roommate."

"She can come too."

"No that's not..." Sarah stopped typing on her computer.

"Or he?" Sharon said, making Sarah laugh.

"My roommate is a she. It's just that she normally makes me dinner on my late nights. I didn't want to stand her up, but I just remembered that she already had plans for tonight."

"Well, that's perfect, then!" Sharon beamed.

"Let me just finish up with my other patient and this troublemaker's note," Sarah responded, making a deliberate tilt of her head toward me.

"Yeah, you want to make sure that note is on point," I had to add. Sarah just rolled her eyes at me.

"Take your time; we're not in a hurry," Sharon added kindly.

"Okay, thank you." Sarah gave Sharon one of her genuine smiles that I had come to love as she moved back to her other patient.

"See, I told you I had it covered." Sharon winked as she came to stand next to where I sat on the table.

"Hmm, I thought you came across a little needy," I joked, making her laugh.

"I don't care. I am needy; my brother's happiness depends on it."

"It was definitely better coming from you. I don't want to scare her off before we even get to go on our first date." I offered her a stealthy fist bump. "You rock, Shari."

"I know," she said with a self-assurance I hadn't seen in her in a long time. This night was going to be good for both of us.

* * *

"What are y'all leaning toward?" Sharon asked, perusing her own menu. We were sitting around a four-top table, Sharon in the seat between Sarah and me.

"I was thinking the grilled shrimp looked good," Sarah answered, still looking at her menu.

Sharon's eyes immediately found mine, and I smiled. Sarah looked up since we hadn't responded and saw our smiles.

"What?"

"Nothing, we're just smiling because shrimp is my go-to at most restaurants. I'm a big shrimp fan," I added with a cocky tone of voice.

"Are you only a big shrimp fan or do you like the little ones as well?" Sarah quipped.

"I'm a fan of all shrimp, big, little, medium, I don't discriminate," I threw right back at her.

"That's good to know." Her eyes twinkled at me over the top of her menu before she dropped them back down to decide on her order.

"Well, I hate to be the odd man out, but I'm not going to join y'all on the shrimp boat. I like the look of the Mediterranean flatbread."

"It's nice to hear you got your 'y'alls' back," I said, smiling at Sharon.

"Well, I *am* a southern girl. Just because certain people found it annoying doesn't mean I should have changed to please them," she said, losing just a little bit of her luster.

"That's right," I affirmed at the same time Sarah said, "Who could have possibly found that annoying?"

Sharon answered Sarah's question, "My ex-fiancé didn't like my southern accent. He would get on me and call me a hick anytime I said 'y'all.'"

"Sharon, I'm sorry about the 'ex' part, but it sounds like you're better off now," Sarah stated, reaching to touch Sharon's arm.

"I am," she confirmed with a smile at Sarah. Normally, when Sharon talked about her ex, she got a little tearful and partially withdrew, but she seemed to be getting better.

"You deserve to be seen for who you truly are, not for who someone else wants you to be," Sarah encouraged.

"Thank you, Sarah, that means a lot."

"Obviously, I've only known you a short time, but I can already tell that you have great potential in just being who you were created to be."

"That makes me feel so much better," Sharon's smile returned in earnest.

"Good," Sarah affirmed, giving Sharon's arm a squeeze and then letting go, returning once again to her menu.

Sharon gave me a look that made it clear she adored Sarah for what she had just said.

Well, join the club. I already had feelings for Sarah, and they just increased as she encouraged my sister. I felt emotions clog my throat and knew I had to move in a different direction. I opted for humor, my usual distraction.

"Are you abandoning the shrimp boat?" I asked Sarah.

"No, why?" she asked, lowering her menu, a little confused.

"Because you're still giving that menu the stare down, and I thought you'd already decided to join me on the shrimp boat."

"I am still firmly on the shrimp boat," she said with a serious face, putting her menu down flat on the table.

"Good, because we on the shrimp boat take mutiny very seriously."

Sharon and Sarah laughed in unison. "You're ridiculous." Sharon said.

"I just like to make you two laugh," I admitted with a smile. To me, laughter was the best sound in the whole world.

"You're very good at it," Sarah agreed with a smile and, dare I hope, feelings in her eyes.

After dinner, we said goodbye to Sarah as we headed for our separate cars. I felt lighter than air, and it was almost impossible to stop smiling. Being with Sarah was better than any other sensation I'd ever experienced, and I was thrilled that this was just the beginning.

CHAPTER 12

SARAH

As Wednesday rolled around, I was still thinking about how much fun I'd had at dinner with Sharon and Mitch on Friday. I really enjoyed them as friends, and they had such potential in The Light as well. Sharon had texted me a couple of times with questions about moving back to the area that were better answered by a woman. She seemed to share her brother's humor, making me laugh with most of her texts.

I was thinking of Sharon and Mitch because I had just enjoyed a "pond session" with Pneuma. She had agreed that they both had potential in The Light, and she also said they would be forever special to me. That felt like a lot of pressure on Mitch's and my future, especially since my heart wasn't all the way there yet. I said as much to Pneuma, and she said they would forever be special to me no matter what future I chose with Mitch. That was more comforting.

Pneuma and I had covered so many topics as we sat by the pond in the early morning light. I had been a lot less anxious this time, unlike my previous visit when I was so consumed with thoughts of Amelia that I couldn't even rest in Pneuma's embrace. I had waited until the jewel of my necklace had filled fully with its brilliant ruby-red color so that I would have the longest possible time with

Pneuma. I couldn't call her if the stone was empty, and it took a few weeks to refill completely. It was either that or I was still a little nervous to see her face-to-face after disobeying her and almost dying due to my disobedience.

Nevertheless, I had called her, and she was extremely gracious and loving, as always. She reminded me that I had already asked for forgiveness, and it had been granted. She would remember the incident no more and counseled me to do the same.

My peace remained, even when we talked about Letta and my next steps with her. Pneuma informed me that it was time to rescue her. That was to be my next mission. Pneuma would send Owen to pick us up in a car, as usual. Ethan would join me, while Nyiah kept an eye on Letta's husband to make sure he wasn't sensing what we were doing. Just like I could protect my areas of influence, so could the Terrobah. They might have some sort of defenses that we could trigger without us even knowing it. I would obey Pneuma to the letter this time in order to save my great aunt and not alert the Terrobah to the Light Bearers who knew about her.

After Pneuma departed, I stayed sitting at the pond with my eyes fixed on the water while the sun climbed into the sky. I had more time this morning. It was Wednesday, so I didn't need to be at the clinic until 10 a.m., and I felt utterly calm and happy here in this space and time. Getting Letta out would be difficult and would take some planning, but I wasn't worried this time. I wouldn't be planning on my own, and I knew The Light would be fully with me. Pneuma explained that we needed to have some urgency and make the extraction this Friday.

We had no idea how Letta would take to the idea of leaving with three people whose voices and touch would most likely hurt her. Pneuma had given me a phrase in Noorha Lingua, or the Language of The Light, to say to her over and over if it were needed to break whatever curses and invisible chains held her. Pneuma had also encouraged me to sing her a song that her mother had sung over her and that my mother had sung over me. It would reach into the recesses of her mind that still held The Light. It was deeply buried, but Pneuma assured me that The Light was still there.

That was the only time I had asked her anything about Amelia. "Does Amelia still have The Light in the deep recesses of her mind?" I had asked quietly.

"Yes, my love, I know there is still light buried there."

"Do you still try to talk to her?" I was referring to how I heard Pneuma's voice throughout the day and in my sleep when she was reassuring me or giving me courage or encouraging me to stop when something might be harmful to me.

"Yes," Pneuma said, pausing. She paused so long that I lifted my head off her shoulder to look in her face. She seemed far off in her mind, but then she spoke, "I will never stop knocking on the door." I was assured in that moment, maybe more than ever before, that Pneuma's love for Amelia was far deeper even than my own, and she was in the best hands possible.

"Next time, bring Nyiah," Pneuma's invitation broke through my thoughts.

"I will," I accepted on Nyiah's behalf. "She would love to sit with us." To commune with Pneuma like I was able to do was a rare privilege. Most Light Bearers only met with her in their dreams. Nyiah had never even been to Ganheela. Pneuma embraced me one last time and turned, the electricity of her presence fading into the surrounding light of the rising sun.

It was time for me to move from this sacred place. I would let Ethan know we needed to meet tonight, but at the moment, the day was upon me, and I felt confident to walk it out.

✳ ✳ ✳

At the clinic that evening, as I was finishing with Mitch, I let him know that I would be gone for at least a few days. I wasn't sure I needed to, but I felt like it would be better coming from me, since both Ethan and I would be gone.

"Are you going on vacation?" Mitch asked.

"Not exactly." I said, grimacing a little, but reluctant to add more.

"Is it…" he trailed off before finishing his question, most likely thinking of my sister.

"It's not my sister. It's my great aunt."

"Oh," he said, seeming like he wasn't sure how to respond.

"She's really sick and needs to be moved from where she lives now to a place that can better care for her."

"And you're the only one that can do that?" Mitch asked curiously.

"Yes, though I will have other family with me," referring to Owen and Ethan. They weren't blood family, but they were my brothers in The Light. "But I will hopefully be able to bring comfort to my aunt that the others may not be able to bring."

"I'm sorry, that came out wrong. I'm glad you can help her. It just seemed like you were the only one to help your sister as well." He seemed genuinely concerned for me.

"I don't mind. My family is worth it to me, just as your family is worth it to you."

"That's true. It's just me and Sharon against the world, and I'd do anything for her."

I smiled at his understanding. "I'm not sure exactly what day I'll be back, but I hope it will be sooner rather than later."

"Is it okay to say I'm going to miss you?" Mitch asked softly.

"I think you just did," I replied with a smile. "And yes, it's okay." I couldn't meet his eyes as I said softly, "I'll miss you, too."

"What's that now?" he asked with a playful tone.

"You heard me," I responded louder. "Be good for Tim and Rose," referring to the two therapists who would be covering for me.

"Oh Tim," Mitch muttered like he was bummed out.

"What's wrong with Tim?" I questioned.

"He told me he asked you out one time. I see him as competition," Mitch bantered.

"Did he tell you I said no?" I replied softly, as I hid behind my computer. Mitch could still see me, but I felt the need to hide.

"Yes, he told me you said no." Mitch spoke with such a seriousness that my eyes rose to meet his. His gaze was so intense that, for a second, it reminded me of how Lucas looked at me, causing my heart to skip a beat.

Still looking at me, Mitch continued, "But you didn't say no to me."

"You're right," the sound of my voice came out breathless, "I didn't say no to you." My words were little more than a whisper, as my heart hammered in my chest.

"Well, okay then," Mitch smiled, the intensity leaving his eyes. I smiled in return. "But you'll be back?"

"Back?" I'd lost track of our conversation.

"From your trip?"

"Yes, of course, I'll be back. Why did you ask me that?" I inquired, curious for his answer.

"Because for some reason, I keep thinking you're going to leave my life as fast as you entered it, and I'm not sure I could handle that," he murmured, causing me to move closer.

"Mitch," I cautioned him, looking around to make sure no one heard. I didn't want additional questions.

"Sarah, I know, it's not the time to talk about us yet, but that's my reality."

"I can appreciate that," I said, moving away to finish my note.

Mitch was doing so well that he would be moving to twice a week starting the following week. I was mentally counting out the next phase of his rehab when he asked, "So how much longer do I have in PT?"

His question was so close to what I'd just been thinking that I burst out laughing. He knew what he was doing because he was sitting with a big grin and started chuckling himself. Our laughter was interrupted by the timer going off on the ice machine.

"I was literally counting out the next phase of your rehab when you asked that," I told him, still smiling. "Next week, you'll move down to twice a week, and then we're in the home stretch. We also get to move to more sports-specific activities."

He kept his smile in place as he raised an eyebrow at me and gave me a confident nod. He was clearly eager for our time as patient and therapist to come to an end. And while in this moment I felt some excitement for that time as well, I was glad we weren't there yet. I said goodbye to Mitch as he hopped off the table. He told me he would see me soon, but he posed it as a question yet again. I assured him that he would, and he left with a smile on his face.

I liked Mitch a lot, but I wasn't looking forward to him being done with PT. That meant a progression in our relationship, and we would have to have a conversation about The Light. I was still uncertain how he would take that. While he clearly liked me, he was also a numbers and facts kind of guy, and I wondered if he would think I was a little off my rocker. What we had right now was so nice, I could pretend it was just *boy-meets-girl*. But I couldn't be with someone who didn't understand the call of The Light on my life. It would hurt greatly if I let myself fall for him, and he rejected me because of The Light. I was not afraid of who I was and what dwelt within me, but I knew the same couldn't be said for so many around me.

I was finishing up my last note when Ethan came out of his office.

"Ready?" he asked.

"Almost done."

"Okay, I'll close up shop around here while you finish so that we can head that way ASAP."

"Thanks, Ethan." I was so grateful to The Light for Ethan. Having a Light Bearer as my boss was the best possible scenario I could imagine, and I hadn't even thought to ask for it.

"You bet," he said with a wink before he switched off the sound system and moved to turn off the exercise machines.

I finished up my note quickly so that we could get to dinner and planning. I was looking forward to it, feeling so thankful for my family in The Light. What we faced with my great aunt on Friday seemed less daunting knowing they had my back. We would be freeing someone who had been held by the Darkness for a long time. It would be a huge victory for us and for The Light to have her back on our side. While I felt confident about retrieving her, I had no idea what it would take to restore her fully to The Light.

✳ ✳ ✳

"Ethan's ready, right?" I asked Owen as he pulled out of my driveway.

"Yes," Owen responded confidently.

He glanced over at me and took my hand. "Ethan is one who fights for injustice. He just needed to be set free to fully embrace his identity in that."

"I know how strong he is; I just remember how scary the Terrobah can be the first time."

"Pneuma has shown him."

"Don't you mean Ruah?" I asked with a smile.

"Oh, you humans, I can't even see the difference that you speak of about Ruah or Pneuma. To me, Pneuma is life and breath and energy and power and beauty and all good things, the persona she shows you isn't even evident to our kind."

"So, there aren't females of your kind?" I asked but felt a pain in my heart thinking about Lucas settling down with a lady Mythreal.

"I guess not," Owen was laughing. "Am I male to you?" I knew he was joking because that was the form they all took. They were all in male form with humans because of their physical strength and their warrior mindset.

I laughed with him, but my thoughts returned to Ethan. I thought again about how this was his first time to really go against the Darkness. In becoming a Light Bearer, he had made that stand, but he'd yet to fight against them physically.

Owen pulled into Ethan's driveway, and I took a calming breath. Pneuma loved Ethan more than I ever could, and she was the one who would ultimately protect him, not me. Owen turned to me with a serious look on his face. I met his gaze, wondering what he would say, but he brushed my cheek with his thumb and simply said, "No fear."

"No fear," I repeated with a smile, taking a deep cleansing breath to release any lingering fear.

Ethan hopped in with a mixture of exuberance and anxiousness, which bubbled over into a million questions as we drove. But as we neared our destination, we fell into silence. I had closed my eyes thinking of the gifts of The Light and the joy that I held onto, not wanting to focus on what awaited us from the Darkness.

"Nyiah just texted again. She's still got eyes on Trevor," Ethan informed us from the backseat as we approached Letta's house.

There was no need to ask Ethan and Owen if they could feel what I could feel as we slowed to a stop in front of her house. The Darkness was tangibly thick all around the dilapidated townhome.

Her home sat in the middle of a row of similar houses but seemed to be marked with neglect. All the landscaping was dead, and it clearly needed a fresh coat of paint. One shutter hung by a single remaining hinge as if it, too, couldn't bear to stay.

"I don't sense any Terrobah at home, but there is someone inside," Owen commented as Ethan and I opened our cab doors.

"Go with The Light," Owen exhorted.

"We'll see you inside," I said to Owen, squeezing his hand for reassurance and an extra measure of light.

"Yep!" Owen said with a goofy grin, "Now get going." Though it was Owen's goofiness and charm that often put us all at ease, when the time came, there was never any doubt that he was a fierce protector.

Ethan and I stepped out of the cab and closed our doors, looking first at the house in front of us and then at one another. Ethan took my hand and pulled it through the crook of his arm as we walked up the sidewalk. By all appearances, we were a happy couple paying a visit.

When we reached the uneven steps of the shadowed house, we exchanged a quick glance. This was it. We had our shields up to guard us from the Terrobah's gaze because there was no way to know who or what might be watching.

I hoped, for Ethan's sake, that we wouldn't encounter any Terrobah, but there was no way to be sure. He'd trained with me for months, and I knew I needed to be confident in his abilities. If Pneuma said he was ready, he was prepared to at least defend himself.

"Ready?" I prompted.

"Yep," he said, and I felt his confidence. He wanted to help Letta and right this wrong. The Light was stronger in him than I had ever felt before, as he vibrated slightly, light pulsing through him.

I smiled at him and then turned to ring the doorbell. Even the chime of the doorbell sent a shiver down my back.

"Are you sensing anything?" Ethan questioned softly, so as not to break my concentration.

"Yes, it's that same feeling I got when I first met Letta; it feels close to a Terrobah but not quite, and that's all I sense." I left out the part about wondering if what I was sensing was a Terrobist and not Letta. No need to concern Ethan just yet.

I strained to feel or hear something that would give me a clue. We knew for sure that Trevor wasn't here because Nyiah was watching him at work. I heard moaning from inside the house.

"Wait," I squeezed his arm. The light was humming so strongly through me now that I felt no chill.

"What?" Ethan asked, as his arm squeezed mine even tighter.

"I heard something, like a moan."

His face was alarmed at that. "Is it Letta?" he whispered.

"I think so."

"Let's get in there," he said with increased strength in his voice.

I nodded in agreement as I reached out to try the handle. I was thrilled that the knob turned in my hand to open the door, but dread immediately overtook that feeling. *Why hadn't they bothered to lock the door for someone they had on strict lockdown?*

The hinges of the door protested loudly as I opened it, so I knew any Terrobah present would be alerted to our arrival.

"Shield up, helmet on, never let them drop," I whispered the reminders to Ethan as I released his arm, and he closed the door behind us.

I could see him glowing out of the corner of my eye and gave him a quick glance to confirm his helmet was on as well. My skin was crawling, causing me to instantly strengthen the light guard in and around me as we made our way down the dim hallway past the stairs.

"Ahh, Ahh, stop it, stop it!!" the screams stopped us in our tracks. It was Letta. I looked at Ethan, who nodded at me. I moved quickly, taking the lead and coming out of the hallway to face the screams and fight the enemy. There was only Letta; she was writhing on the ground screaming. Lowering my guard wasn't an option. Someone here was torturing her, I just couldn't see them.

CHAPTER 13

SARAH

"Ethan, do you see anything?" I called out, my eyes darting around, quickly taking in the dingy living room. Letta was lying on thick shag carpet in the fetal position as she continued to scream.

"No, there's nothing in the kitchen or out back. What's hurting her?" I could hear the strain in his voice even through her screams of agony.

In the glow of the light I was emitting, I could see dust floating through the air. It covered every surface of the outdated furniture and paneled wall. As I focused on one sparkling speck, it occurred to me.

"We are," I whispered, as I dropped the strength of my light. I kept my helmet on, and my light shield was still surrounding me, but at a lower strength. I had to fight my instincts to slow the power humming through me, and as I did, her screams subsided to moans.

"Ethan, keep your helmet on and shield up, but lower your intensity. Does that make sense?" I asked, even though I wasn't looking at him.

"Yes," he replied, and I knew he was doing as I asked because Letta's moans lowered to a whimper.

I withheld light from my voice before I said, "Letta. Letta Love."

"Momma?" she whispered like a small child.

I wanted to comfort her with my touch, but I knew at this point it wouldn't help her at all; it would only cause her more pain. My great aunt had been tortured enough, and I would do whatever it took to get her out of here.

"No, Letta, it's not your Momma, but a friend," I said softly, without injecting any light. She'd been facing away from me but turned her head to look at me as she continued to cry.

Her eyes were filled with tears, and her face was bruised from some sort of beating.

"We're here to help you," I barely got out the words as I saw the evidence of her torture and tried to hold back my tears.

Her eyes traveled past me to land on Ethan, and she started whimpering again. "No, no, no, you're the bad ones. Trevor said you would come for me some day, and you would hurt me even more than he ever has."

"Letta Love," I sing-songed again. It was a name her mother had called her, and it brought her comfort. Pneuma had told me to say it as much as possible, knowing she hadn't heard it in years, and it had the power to break through some of the lies in which she'd been imprisoned. I said it again, and her eyes came back to me.

"Do I know you?" she asked pitifully, as her face contorted.

"Yes, I'm your friend. I was your physical therapist at the clinic."

"I don't remember that," she said, whimpering again. "Trevor told me he would hurt me if I ever let one of you in here."

That reminded me about the door. "Letta Love," I said, her whimpering calmed again, "Why was the door unlocked?"

"I don't know," she answered, her eyes fixed on an unknown spot on the wall. "Trevor always locks it when he leaves . . . he doesn't know I have a key," she chuckled at her well-kept secret, then continued. "But I do, I do have a key," she whispered.

Ethan and I shared a look. Clearly Letta was not in her right mind. She turned her monologue toward me. "Did I, did I know you were coming?" Her eyes seemed brighter for just a moment.

"Yes, I think The Light let you know we were coming."

Her eyes darkened once again. "The Light, no, no, that doesn't sound right. Light is bad. We keep the curtains closed and the furniture dark, and I don't see people. I'm not allowed to sit in my garden. The Light is bad." She pushed herself up to sitting as she rambled, trying to make sense of her thoughts.

"Letta Love," I said to get her eyes to stop searching around frantically and come back to me.

"I know you," she responded.

"Yes, you do know me. And I'm here to help you."

"Okay. No. No. Okay?" She was so confused. Her mind was so trapped in the lies and the Darkness, and she had been tortured into knots, but it was clear she was still fighting for the truth. I couldn't let myself think about what they must have had to do to her on a regular basis to keep her here and keep her submissive.

"Okay. It's okay," I nodded.

"Okay?" she asked. I nodded back. I was still crouched in front of her on the floor.

"It's hard to look at you," she said, looking away.

"I know, but it'll get easier." I lowered my shield intensity just a bit more. "Will you come with me?" I asked very gently.

She took a quick intake of breath, "Oh no, no; I'm not allowed to leave. Trevor will be mad."

"That's why we'll leave before he returns. You'll come with us, and we'll keep you safe."

"No, no. I mustn't," she whimpered, shaking violently.

"Letta." She looked at me, but still she shook. "Letta Love," I softened. She looked at me, as if searching for meaning. I could see she was wondering if there was a different way than what she'd known for years.

"Would I go now?" she sounded like a wounded child.

"Yes, we should go now."

She started shaking her head again, so I pushed forward.

"Letta Love, I'm also part of your family."

"No, the only family I have is Trevor," she stated, shaking her head back and forth. She was sure of this fact.

"That's actually not true. I'm your great niece."

"I have siblings?" I hadn't expected that question and now was not the time to tell her that her siblings were no more.

"Yes, you had siblings," I couldn't lie to her, but I hoped she wouldn't catch my past tense in the reference to her siblings.

"No, no, it's only Trevor. No mom, no dad, no grandparents, no aunts and uncles, no brothers or sisters, only Trevor. Without him, I have nothing," she stammered out the lies repeated to her over the years.

"That's a lie; I'll show you that I'm family." It went against everything in me not to touch her and bring her some comfort, but I didn't want to lose the ground I had gained. I knew it was time, and so I began to sing,

"Beloved don't cry, you are being held tight
Feel the warmth, as you hide here in The Light.
Your tears are all counted, never one lost
Your fears are all conquered
You can't have a shadow without The Light
Rest in the assurance that you're safe from the fight."

"I remember! Momma, The Light, oh I remember!" Her face lost some of the fear, and I was overjoyed at her words. She was remembering.

"Yes! You remember. And now, we have to go."

The urgency in my voice seemed to change something in her. She went back to her childlike posture and said, "Okay, let's go. But, where? This is the only home I've ever known."

"That's what Trevor wants you to think. You had a home filled with light and love, but he took you from there."

"I don't remember any of that," she declared, the skepticism in her voice clear.

"Letta, you've been clouded by the Darkness for a while. We are here to take you somewhere safe." My voice was almost pleading with her to understand.

"Who are you again?" she asked.

Oh no, I thought. But I persisted.

"I'm Sarah. I was your physical therapist for your shoulder injury. I'm also your great niece."

"What? I don't have any family apart from Trevor," she repeated.

"That's not true." I felt the frustration with my light repressed.

"What?" she said, seemingly so out of it. It was like she was drugged and kept falling back into her old patterns of thinking. We didn't have time for any more explanations.

"Nyiah said he just left in a hurry," Ethan spoke quietly behind me.

"Letta, we have to go." But she was shaking her head again.

I started singing to her again, which calmed her greatly. My eyes met Ethan's. We needed Owen. At the same moment the thought entered my head, Owen was opening the back door and coming toward me. My feelings of relief at seeing him were in stark contrast to Letta's screams of agony at his presence. Ethan immediately took up his post outside the back door to keep watch in advance of our escape.

Owen walked right up to her and spoke, "Letta, it's time to sleep." He touched her forehead and said, "Peace," as Lucas had done to me numerous times. She was helpless against the calm that overtook her. She didn't go under quickly like I always did, so he repeated the word two more times as her eyes slowly fluttered and closed. Owen spoke, "Peace," one more time with such power that I got sleepy and thought I would slip into unconsciousness.

"Sorry," Owen apologized to me as I shook off the feeling, renewing my armor and light guard to full strength.

"That's okay," I responded, shaking my head once more. "I'm good," I assured him as he lifted a limp Letta off the floor with ease.

"They're coming; we must go," he stated with urgency.

We ran across the backyard, Ethan hot on my heels. I used my hands to vault over the waist-high chain link fence. Owen did the same thing with one hand while holding Letta. We ran on, vaulting over fence after fence to get to the end of the townhouse row.

As we rounded the last house, I saw our cab sitting there. Owen made it to the cab before me, but I was there quickly to open the door and slide in the backseat, turning to reach for Letta. She looked like a frail child in his arms, and that was really what she was at this point.

Ethan jumped into the front passenger seat, and Owen had the car moving in no time at all. He drove fast, but not so fast as to draw attention. I chanced a glance back through the yards and saw four Terrobah staring after us. They were in human form, but I could tell what they were.

"They know," I informed the guys, trying to keep the alarm at bay. I wasn't afraid to face the Terrobah, but I refused to let them have Letta back. Owen didn't acknowledge me, but I knew he'd heard.

Our shield was still up on the inside of the cab. The Terrobah would not be able to see us individually, but at this point, we couldn't be sure how much they knew.

Owen turned down an alley that cut behind some shops. He headed for the city, hoping we'd blend in. We didn't want to endanger anyone else, but we needed to throw the Terrobah off our track.

The impact from behind came so fast that we didn't even have time to brace ourselves. We were slammed forward in our seats, and it was all I could do to maintain my hold on Letta.

"I didn't see them coming. They're using a shield as well," Owen informed us. As we came out of the alley, he jerked the car quickly to the left, and our tires squealed as he accelerated across three lanes of traffic. The car had barely straightened out before another car slammed into the right side of us and the side windows shattered, raining glass throughout the cab.

"How are they finding us so fast?" Ethan asked, his voice a mixture of fear and anger. Another car slammed into the left side of us, crashing us back into the car on our right.

How were they finding us so fast?

"A tracker!" Owen yelled. "They must have masked it!" He slammed the accelerator to the floor, and we shot forward, but we were no match for their speed. Our cab was not built for outrunning the cars they were using.

"What do we do?" Ethan asked in alarm, turning to look at me.

"Owen, what do we do to get rid of them?" I asked. "We can't remove her tracker, can we?"

"No, it's probably a chip, so a doctor or Pneuma will have to do it," he explained, his voice was steady, assuring.

"Can you block it, like Lucas did for me when the Terrobah were close in the woods?" I asked.

"Yes, I can," Owen replied, "but I'm a little busy at the moment." Judging from his smirk, and knowing Owen like I did, he was probably enjoying the chase.

His smile slid to a frown as we were slammed into once again. I could feel my anger rising at the injustice of it all. I turned and blasted the car behind us with enough force to stun the driver. I knew it was effective as the car behind us swerved away.

"Ethan, your turn. Aim for the driver," I instructed. It was hard for me to fight and hold Letta at the same time.

While I saw his blast building, I gave a smaller blast to the car next to us, causing them to back off slightly.

We were weaving in and out of other cars while the one on our right stayed locked to our side. Ethan blasted, and it had little effect.

"Again!" I shouted.

He blasted again, this one larger.

"Ethan, pull from the energy within you. Focus it all on that car and push, hard." My words were assuring, encouraging, transferring all the confidence and light I could, just as Lucas and Owen had done for me during my first battle.

This time, he let a much more forceful blast come forth, and he didn't just stop at one. When Ethan's second blast hit, the car started fading back, its driver stunned. The engine suddenly burst into flames with the impact of his third blast.

"Now, Owen!" I shouted. As he slammed on the accelerator once more, the car to our left swerved into us. He sped up enough that they only caught our tail end, but it was enough to force us off course, skidding down the road. Owen looked like a movie stunt driver, handling the steering wheel of our car like a pro as we barreled down the busy street.

"Ethan, let's focus on our car now; emit light to try to help it straighten out," I shouted. Owen joined us, and the car righted itself, moving forward just as we felt another impact from behind.

I turned around as much as possible and let every bit of light I was feeling push forth. The car behind us didn't stand a chance as it was engulfed in light. I had focused on the electrical system, and judging from the way it slowed immediately, I knew I had succeeded in frying the circuits with too much energy.

"What did you do to it?" Ethan questioned me.

"I targeted the electrical components."

"Why didn't you suggest that to me?" He was upset. "Instead of letting me obliterate that car!"

"I didn't think of it until just now." I assured him. "I remembered how fancy Uncle's SUV had been. I knew that I could overload the electronics, and it would stop the car without harming people. Owen, do we need to go back and check on anyone?"

"No, Pneuma is sending a Light Bearer who is a firefighter. He'll be on the scene with his squad soon."

"Did I hurt anyone?" Ethan asked, his eyes begging me to say no.

"I don't know, Ethan," I answered him honestly. "But you were just following my orders. If someone is injured, the blame rests with me," I replied. "I'm honestly more concerned for the first one that I blasted backwards. I did it without thinking, and it was very abrupt."

"We need to switch cars," Owen said in his normal voice, clearly not concerned. If Owen wasn't concerned, then I didn't need to be either.

We had a car hidden just 20 minutes from where we'd gotten Letta, and that's where we were headed. "What about Letta's tracker? Won't they just be able to find her again?" Ethan asked Owen.

"Only if they're close enough," Owen responded. "Since we lost them back there, I've been trying to cloak Letta. They have to be near to access the tracker's location."

"How close?" Ethan asked.

"100 yards, give or take. Why?"

"I'm just trying to watch and see if we're being followed," Ethan responded.

I turned to look out the back window as well. It was hard to tell on these busy city streets. I thought about how our car was probably attracting attention and our hunters would be able to tell any other Terrobah to just look for the smashed cab.

"How close are we, Owen?" I asked.

"Two minutes." He wasn't wasting any time getting us there.

We made it to the parking garage with no sign that anyone was following us. There was only one car on the second level, parked in the back right corner. Owen pulled up right next to it, and the guys quickly piled out. As Owen reached in to take Letta from me, she started moaning. Once again, he whispered, "Peace," and she went limp in his arms, as he moved her over to our new car.

I was climbing in to sit on the bench seat from the other side when I heard tires squealing up the ramp.

"They found us," Owen stated, looking up into my eyes.

"We'll never get out of here if we don't fight."

"Agreed," Owen replied.

"Ethan?"

He was standing at my open door. "I'm ready," he said confidently.

I turned to Ethan and directed, "Shield up to full strength, helmet on. Never let either fall, even if it comes down to not having an offense." I quickly turned to face the two black SUVs coming at us.

Ethan didn't answer.

"Ethan, I need you to agree, or I'm going to lock you in this car with Letta," I demanded with a tone he'd never heard from me before.

"Agreed," he confirmed.

"Good."

Owen was securing the car behind us so they couldn't get Letta, no matter what the outcome. It was sealed with an almost metal-like, light substance. I had a flicker of recognition that the metal was like the quicksilver that had rolled off Lucas when he emerged from the furnace at Camp Tuano. I didn't have time to think about that now though.

For some strange reason, Trevor wasn't among the group of six Terrobah we found ourselves up against. Of course, he could be avoiding taking his normal human form, but I didn't sense that any of these Terrobah were strong enough to be him.

They didn't waste any time letting their arrows fly. As the battle raged, Ethan seemed like he was holding his own, and I never once saw his shield so much as quiver.

With all that was happening around the vehicle, Letta had woken from her sleep. "Where am I? Trevor, I'm sorry. Please don't hurt me! Help!" I could hear her screaming. She was hysterical now. I had to help her. We had almost all the Terrobah defeated anyway, and Owen was preparing the light ropes to bind them.

"I'm going to help her," I shouted to Owen and Ethan, without really waiting for their response.

I opened the door quickly, forgetting about the fact that once I released the seal, I wouldn't be a comfort to her either. She came out swinging and hit me in the face. "Letta Love," I practically shouted, trying to calm her, but it had no effect. I quickly tried to overpower her with my strength in The Light, but I hated that I was hurting her. I let my shield down slightly, and still she screamed. With a glance behind me, I lowered it completely. Letta calmed some, as I tried again to reason with her.

This time, however, instead of a fist to the face, I got a stabbing sensation in my right arm. I had enough time to glance down to see the arrow protruding from my arm before I dropped to the ground.

CHAPTER 14

MITCH

"Sarah," I spoke her name out as searing pain went through my right arm.

"What?" Sharon asked, looking up from her plate to meet my eyes.

"Sarah..."

"Did she text you or something?"

"No, I feel like something has happened to her," I replied, looking at my right arm where pain was now pulsating. My left hand came up to touch my arm as my eyes examined it. Upon inspection, there was no visible reason for the pain I had just experienced. Sarah had told me she had to help her aunt. Was she in danger?

"Do you think we should call her?" Sharon asked, the confusion and concern evident in her voice.

"No, what if what I'm feeling is wrong? She'll think I'm crazy. We don't even have a relationship where we text yet."

"But I do; I can text her and just ask if she's okay."

"She's okay," I stated, feeling confident that was true. My eyes met Sharon's confused gaze. I continued, "I think she's hurt, but she's not alone, so she's okay." I looked at Sharon in bewilderment. "How would I know that?" She had the same look on her face.

"I have no idea," she said slowly.

Sarah. Just thinking her name made my heart and lungs feel constricted.

"Maybe you guys have a deeper connection than you realize."

I wanted to deny it and tell her she was crazy, but my right arm was killing me. "Maybe," was all I could reply.

✳ ✳ ✳

SARAH

There was haziness all around when I opened my eyes. I could see Owen running in front of me. I turned my head and realized Ethan was carrying me as he, too, ran.

"Ethan," I breathed.

"We took care of them, Sarah. We're just trying to get somewhere safe before Owen gets the arrow out." His breath was ragged, his words coming in gasps, weighed down by the effort it took to carry me as he ran to safety. As my eyes drifted shut, I caught a glimpse of the arrow sticking out of my arm, which laid lifeless across my chest.

"Be careful," I breathed.

"You don't get to say that to me right now," his voice was filled with a mix of anger and concern.

"I'll be okay," I breathed, then succumbed to the effects of the poison-laced arrow.

When I was shot with an arrow before, I got very close to the Land of The Light, but this time, I just drifted in and out of consciousness as my friends worked to get the arrow out.

"Sarah, hold on, I'll get it out," Owen assured. My eyes weren't open, but I knew I was in good hands. I felt intense light enter my right arm as I slipped back under.

The next time I came to, I knew I was fine. My eyes opened, and I tried to figure out what I was seeing. A high metal ceiling came into focus above me.

"Where are we?" I asked Owen, whose face had moved into my line of sight.

"In an abandoned warehouse."

I started to sit up, and he helped me get all the way there. I felt a bout of dizziness, but I didn't show it. I knew Ethan would be struggling, and I wanted to be strong for him. I saw that my head had been resting on his leg.

"Where did it even come from?" I asked, looking down at my arm as if I hadn't just come close to death, again. In the brief glimpse I had of Ethan's face, it was etched with deep concern.

Owen knew I meant the arrow, "I don't know. I didn't even sense him, which meant he was only a Terrobist." I looked at Owen and saw deep sadness in his eyes. I knew the sadness meant he had taken the Terrobist down. Because Terrobists were human, there was still a chance they could be brought to The Light.

"Owen," I said, reaching to touch Owen's hand as it rested on my arm. His eyes came up to meet mine, the deep sadness still lingered there at destroying anything that could be saved. "It's okay," I said to comfort him, even though I knew it wasn't okay with either of us.

"What's a Terrobist again?" Ethan asked. I could tell he was trying to understand why we seemed disappointed about hurting any of them.

"Terrobists are humans that are trained in the Darkness by Terrobah. As Light Bearers, they are our equivalent," I explained.

"Aren't they still bad, then?" Ethan questioned, not under-standing.

"Yes, but we never like to hurt any creature, especially if they still have a chance to return to The Light."

"We're supposed to try to turn them back to The Light?" Ethan's frustration was evident. He was probably struggling with why we were talking about someone like this when that someone had just tried to kill me.

"The Father of Lights does not desire any creature to perish if they aren't headed to The Land of The Light," Owen answered. "As beings and followers of The Light, our desires grow to line up more with his. There is a small chance that we can turn Terrobists, and a part of me holds out hope to be able to turn each and every one of them to The Light."

Ethan's gaze moved to my right arm. The light Owen had used to remove the arrow was dissipating now, and I was left with no pain. I would, however, have a permanent scar from the poison-laced arrow. Thankfully, it hadn't been as powerful as the ones I had faced in my first battle. In the same way Ethan was just learning to harness his strength and weapons in The Light, clearly the Terrobist who shot me was just learning to harness the Darkness. The arrow was not deadly, and Owen had been able to heal me easily on his own.

"This arrow was mild. It wouldn't have killed me," I informed Ethan, trying to comfort him. "Even if I had been on my own, The Light would have eventually dispelled the poison and the arrow."

He jumped to his feet and started to pace. "It's still not okay with me, Sarah." He was almost shouting, his words laced with anger and frustration.

"I know, I'm sorry," I responded.

"What do you have to be sorry for?" Ethan asked, turning to look at me like I had lost my mind.

"It's all so hard to see. I wish I'd prepared you better."

"None of this is your fault," he railed. "They are the evil ones causing all this darkness. You just got shot, and yet, you mourn the one that shot you..."

"Ethan," I said firmly, the light in my voice immediately stopping his tirade. "Come here," I said more gently. He moved toward me and sat down beside me.

I grabbed his hand. "This was hard to see. This day has been intense for me as well, and I've already fought the Terrobah many times before. It's okay to feel the ugliness of it, just don't let the ugliness consume you."

He had been looking into my eyes, but he dropped them and said, "Sorry." I could hear his fatigue.

"What do you have to be sorry for?" I repeated the same question he'd asked me.

He looked at me with a small smile, seeing my attempt at humor. "It's a lot to take in."

"Yes, but you've done so well. You defended well. Fought well. And apparently, you proved you can run well."

"Owen offered to carry you, but he had his hands full with Letta."

"Letta!" I was bewildered that I'd forgotten about her. "Where is she?" I turned to look around and saw her on the ground, not moving.

"She's fine," Owen assured me. "She's just sleeping."

"What's the plan?" I asked, sure that something was already in motion for when we left the warehouse.

"Nyiah is coming with a new car and should be here any minute," Ethan reported. He was a leader, and it strengthened him to relay that information.

"Great. And then what?"

Owen answered, "Pneuma has asked me to bring Letta to her."

"She thinks that's necessary?" I asked.

"Yes. Letta is in a lot of pain with us and Pneuma thinks it will take her presence to bring Letta back to The Light."

"But Owen, won't Ganheela be much more painful for her?" I wasn't arguing, just curious. Ganheela was a place filled with light.

"Pneuma will tailor it to her just as she did for you. Don't worry, Sarah Joy, she'll be in good hands."

"The best hands," I said with a smile, but felt it fall almost immediately, as I realized I had failed yet again.

"What are you thinking right now?" Owen questioned me.

"What do you mean?" I asked, trying to cover my feelings.

"A shadow passed over you, and your smile fell after you said she would be in the best hands." I knew exactly what he meant, but I had wanted to cover my insufficiencies.

I didn't answer him, so he persisted, "Sarah?"

Owen loved me and was concerned; I knew I could be honest with him. "I failed again," I said, as tears welled up.

"You did not fail. How is it that you see this as a failure?"

"I couldn't help Letta. I couldn't free her." Both men grunted in disbelief.

"That's not true, Sarah," Owen countered. "Without you, we would not have been able to take Letta."

"What do you mean?" Owen had put her to sleep and carried her out; he hadn't needed me there.

"Sarah," Owen chided, "you know we can't bring people into The Light against their will. You convinced her enough that she was willing to come with us. Even though she fought against it, she still made a choice. That was through your words and your song, your patience and your gentleness."

"You even lowered your shield to spare her from pain," Ethan added.

"You've succeeded. Letta will be free. You set her on the path to freedom, and Pneuma will bring it to completion."

Owen's words allowed me to see the truth. My tears dried as the truth pierced my heart. I had succeeded. It didn't have to all be on my shoulders. I had done my part, and now it was time for another to continue with her. Owen would take Letta, and Pneuma would bring her fully back to The Light.

"Can I go with her?" I asked softly, as Ethan's phone buzzed.

"Nyiah's here," Ethan informed us, as Owen shook his head no in response to my question.

I felt the sting of failure again, but Owen was quick to break in. "It's not because of your performance here."

"Then why can't I go with her?"

"Because two humans can't exist in the same Ganheela simultaneously. If you went, you would be in your own Ganheela, like last time."

I stood up. "Oh, right. I thought it was maybe because I would hurt Letta's progress."

Owen moved to pick up Letta, but Ethan waved him off. "I've got her," he stated, scooping her up with ease. He carried her past me just as Nyiah peeked her head inside the door.

"Let's go guys. The coast is clear," she encouraged, waving us out. I trusted Nyiah's ability to sense any Terrobah that might be present.

"Can I still go with you to Ganheela?" I asked Owen, as we all hurried for the door of the warehouse.

"I think a time will come soon, but not today," he responded.

I nodded my understanding, but I longed to be in that place where pain and fear disappeared.

Once outside the warehouse, Nyiah opened the rear passenger door so that Ethan could slide easily into the seat, still carrying Letta. Nyiah then hurried around and slid into the backseat opposite them.

Owen jumped behind the wheel, and I quickly moved into the passenger seat. He adjusted the rearview mirror, then in typical

Owen fashion said, "Buckle up, folks! Safety first." We all chuckled at his goofy grin and breathed a deep, collective sigh of relief as we pulled out of the parking lot. For now, we were safe.

I could hear Nyiah and Ethan chatting in the backseat and smiled, thinking about our earlier conversation. Maybe there was a more serious relationship in their future. Only time would tell.

"Ethan will be going with me," Owen whispered, breaking into my thoughts.

"That's great," I said, and I meant it. My sadness lessened at knowing Ethan would get to experience Ganheela.

Owen turned down a gravel road, stirring up dust and fishtailing just a bit. He flashed that playful smile I'd come to know and love from him. Then, he continued in a whisper, "Ethan will come back stronger and more equipped to help you in future battles."

"What are you two whispering about?" Ethan piped up from the backseat.

"Why don't you tell him," Owen suggested.

I turned to try and face him in the backseat. "You're going to Ganheela."

"What? Really?" Ethan asked in excitement.

"Really," I affirmed.

He looked at Owen, "Really?"

"Really," Owen confirmed.

He looked at Nyiah, who sparkled a big smile at him and said, "Really," before he even had a chance to ask.

"What about Nyiah?" Ethan asked, even though his excitement didn't wane.

"I'll have my time someday, Ethan. Today is your time."

She said it so sincerely. I would have understood if she'd been a little jealous, but she didn't seem to be. She was completely happy for Ethan.

"I've driven far enough to feel confident we aren't being followed. Let's head back into the city and drop off the girls, then we'll be on our way," Owen said to Ethan.

"What about Letta's tracker?" I asked Owen.

"Once I put her back to sleep, I surrounded it with light. They can't find her now," Owen assured me.

"Won't it be painful for her to pass through the tunnel?" I questioned, still worried for my aunt's sake.

"It would be, yes. But I plan to keep her asleep, so she won't feel it."

"How will you keep her asleep if you're driving?" I gave him a knowing look.

"Ethan will drive us through."

"What?!" I responded in fake outrage. "He gets to go through the tunnel, *and* he gets to drive? No fair." Everyone laughed at my fake pouting, easing more of the tension from the day.

*　*　*

MITCH

"How's your aunt?" I asked as soon as I saw Sarah.

"She's actually my great aunt, and she's good," she responded with a smile. "They're taking very good care of her."

"Oh good, so everything went well, then?" Sarah was getting my screen going on the bike, but she turned her head to look at me. She really stared at me as if she was trying to read my thoughts.

"It was a bit rough, but all is well now."

"Good, I just know family stuff can be difficult sometimes," I said, trying to cover for my curiosity. I had eventually broken down and had Sharon text Sarah just to ask how she was doing. Sarah had replied she was doing the best she could, given the circumstances. That had done nothing to ease my worry. Sharon had pressed for details, but Sarah only shared that her great aunt had been reluctant to leave her home.

Sarah was still looking at me.

"What?" I asked.

"Nothing, just thinking," she said, still looking at me.

"Well, you're looking at me kind of funny." I played along.

"Well, you asked your question kind of funny."

"Did I?" She just smiled at me, clearly aware I was dodging her question.

I ramped my legs up to speed, and she didn't say anything else. I was a minute in before I spoke again. "I worry about you," I said softly, not looking at her.

"You don't need to worry about me," Sarah responded just as softly, as she increased the resistance on the bike.

"I'm not sure that's possible at this point." I could tell she was looking at me, but I didn't return her gaze.

"Hey Mitch, how are you today?" I looked up to see Ethan waiting for a response. I paused because he looked different, taller maybe?

"I'm doing well. Just two more weeks here before Sarah sets me loose."

"That's great, man. How's the knee feeling?"

"No pain, just having trouble trusting it will do its job."

"That's great about your pain. Sarah said you're doing more agility stuff this week that will help with that confidence as well."

I was trying to focus on my knee, but his appearance was just so different that I couldn't stop myself from saying, "Dude, I have to say, you look different."

Ethan laughed, "Good different or bad different?"

"Good, if that's not too weird to say. Did you go on a vacation that I missed or something?"

"I took a vacation of sorts over the weekend, and I've never felt better."

"Well, it shows, man."

"Thanks. Keep up the good work." He patted the bike and moved away. Sarah had moved to work with one of her other patients when Ethan had come up. As he left, I saw she was still working with that other person. From where I was on the bike, it looked like a back injury from the stretches she was doing.

Her right sleeve slipped up and I saw a bright red scar, right where my arm had hurt a few days ago.

"What in the world?" I whispered to myself.

"You ready, Mitch?" The PT tech had come up when the bike beeped and interrupted my thoughts.

"Yep, let's get to it." I said the right words, but my mind was on Sarah and the physical evidence of the connection we shared.

CHAPTER 15

SARAH

ETHAN HAD COME TO see Nyiah and me after he returned from Ganheela, and he was brilliant to behold. He didn't come to us immediately, but he came for dinner the next evening. A lot of his human hang-ups had fallen away, and he even seemed to walk taller.

He shared much of what he had learned with us, including that his wife had been Awakened, someone who had been made aware of The Light and chosen to believe, but did not hold the power to wield The Light as a Light Bearer. Ruah had shared with Ethan that she had been killed in a Terrobist attack. Ethan's only moment of sadness was over his revelation in Ganheela that the Terrobah had killed his wife to stop her from guiding him to The Light.

The Darkness had succeeded at silencing her on Earth, but not at stopping Ethan from finding The Light. The Darkness had not prevailed with Letta, either. Pneuma had relocated her to a house about eight hours away from us in another state. Even with her tracker removed, her Terrobah husband, Trevor, knew her scent better than any other human, and that meant she needed to move out of the area.

She was now living with the Johnsons, a family belonging to the Eklesi, the community of those who followed The Light. Not surprisingly, Letta hadn't been eager to live alone, and at Pneuma's leading, they had been happy to offer to take her in as their beloved aunt. I would now be a surrogate family member as well. A cousin, if anyone asked.

Aunt Letta was a short flight away from where I lived. So, at Nyiah's urging, I flew out to see her. But as I pulled my rental car up to the curb in front of her new house, I felt surprisingly nervous. Nyiah had flown out with me, but she thought I needed some time alone with Letta, so I didn't even have Nyiah's presence there for comfort.

Taking a deep breath, I climbed from the car and took in the lovely, blue, two-story Victorian house with a red front door. It was picturesque with two large oak trees in the front yard, seeming to stand guard on both sides of the brick walkway that led to the front porch. As I passed under them, I sensed The Light strongly and realized they were most definitely serving as an extra protection against any Terrobah that happened to be in the area.

Although I saw the doorbell, I still chose to knock on the door. It'd been a few weeks since I had seen Letta, and I was just apprehensive enough that I was okay if she didn't answer on the first knock.

That was not to be, as the door opened quickly and there my great aunt stood, radiating light, healthy and beautiful. She looked so different, with her gray and blond hair styled and shining, I almost thought she was someone else. But she had to be my great aunt Letta because the amount of light that she bore made it clear she was fresh from the healing waters of Ganheela.

"Sarah Joy," she greeted me, her voice thick with emotion, as both of our eyes filled with tears. She held her arms open to me, and I moved quickly into her embrace. All my anxiety and apprehension about this moment melted as soon as her arms surrounded me. I was slightly taller than her, but it still felt like she was holding me.

"Aunt Letta," I whispered back as I cried. What a gift it was to have a family member restored to me after losing so many. After a few minutes, we finally pulled back to look at each other, still holding onto each other's arms.

"You're so beautiful," she said slowly, her chin quivering and tears still glistening in her eyes. "Thank you, Sarah, for saving me."

"I'm so grateful we were able to free you," I responded, still not believing the changes my eyes were seeing in her. She was radiating light, and my touch no longer caused her to scream.

"Words aren't enough to express how thankful I am to you for freeing me. You ran toward danger to save a person that seemed to hate you. I'm eternally grateful."

Words failed me as well in that moment; I didn't know what to say to that. It seemed like the story of my life, but I didn't want to downplay what she'd been through. It had been horrific. I just nodded as emotion clogged my throat.

She closed the door and took hold of my right hand, drawing it into the crook of her left arm, pulling me close and leading me down the hallway.

"Where is everyone else?" I asked. My question was met with silence as we walked into the living room and sat down on the couch.

"The family thought it might be best for us to have this time alone. They'll join us for dinner later." She smiled as she pulled me to sit next to her on the couch and began to sing.

"Beloved don't cry, you are being held tight
Feel the warmth, as you hide here in The Light.
Your tears are all counted, never one lost
Your fears are all conquered
You can't have a shadow without The Light
Rest in the assurance that you're safe from the fight."

I joined her in singing the last two lines. Once we finished, we both laughed with joy through our tears. Letta handed me some tissues and took some for herself as we dried our eyes.

"I can't believe I have a great aunt. And she's a Light Bearer," I stated, feeling in awe of the gift that she was to me.

"I *can* believe that my niece is one of the strongest Light Bearers this world has ever seen!" She returned with a huge smile.

"Wait, did you say can or can't?" I asked, laughing.

"Can," she said, proudly beaming at me.

"You knew what I would be?" I asked.

"In a way. I knew that we would have a Light Bearer in our line that was stronger than any other we knew in our time. I didn't know it would be you specifically, as I was taken before you were born," she informed me, her eyes taking in my face as if she just couldn't see it enough.

"Wow," I said in shock. She'd been with a Terrobah for over 25 years. "That is such a long time for you to endure. And to endure like you did. You could've given up and moved into the Darkness, but you fought it every day." My words were drawn out as the reality of her experience settled in my mind.

"Every hour, love. And it was terrible." She closed her eyes and took a deep breath before opening them again. She continued, "But now, I'm back where I belong, and I have you!" She smiled so brightly at me that the tears threatened once again. "Okay, enough talk about that awful part of my past," she said, giving my hand an affectionate pat as she held it between her hands. We were still sitting on the edge of the couch, our knees touching. It was already as if we had known each other for years.

Letta offered me some lemonade, but I held off, wanting to stay present in this moment. "Could I ask you something, not about what you went through, but before that?"

"Of course," she replied, pouring herself a glass and making herself more comfortable on the couch.

"If you knew of me, did you also know of Amelia?"

"I knew someone in our family would wield the power of The Light like you, but no, I didn't know what you or Amelia would become. Many in our family have moved to the Darkness because of their thirst for power. The Terrobah entice people to use their power for themselves. They blind them from the beauty that is The Light. Even my own brother became a Terrobist."

"What?" I was shocked.

"Yes, George gave in to the lure of power. I was trying to save him when I was taken," she said softly, staring down into her lemonade glass, but not really seeing it.

"I'm so sorry." I paused, "Is he still with them?"

"No, he was killed." Her light was dimming somewhat.

"Can I ask why?"

"Because The Light used my capture to show him the error of his ways. George saw what the Terrobah were doing to me, torturing me, and trying to force me to become a Terrobist and use my power for the Darkness. He saw how much pain I was in as I tried to fight against them and their ways. I think he realized how much The Light meant to me, and that I would give my very life before I ever gave it up. George returned to The Light and tried to save me but was killed for his efforts."

"Oh, Aunt Letta, I'm so sorry."

"So am I, dear heart. I miss him still. Even after all of that, they couldn't strip George from me. Pneuma confirmed to me that he is in the Land of The Light, and I will see him again someday." Her glowing smile returned.

"That's wonderful," I agreed, momentarily caught up in the idea of all our dear family that we would one day see again. I took a breath and returned to the present, grateful for who was sitting right next to me. "I'm so thankful I have you," I said again, leaning into her for another hug which she gladly received and returned.

"And I, you, Sarah Joy," she replied as her voice broke with emotion. It was clear that she knew exactly how I felt about Amelia. It was a gift to me, to have someone understand that I would do almost anything to bring Amelia to The Light and free her from the wretched Terrobah. I said as much to Letta.

"I do understand, but with you, dear heart, there is so much more at stake." Her tone caught my attention.

"What do you mean? Do you mean with losing Amelia?"

"No, specifically with you," she paused, but then continued. "You're the strongest Light Bearer that has ever been seen."

Pneuma had told me this before, but I didn't know how to receive it. Plus, I still struggled with the fact that if I was the most powerful Light Bearer that anyone had ever seen, why couldn't I easily save my sister? I shared my thoughts with Letta.

"Amelia isn't your failure. She has made her choices, just like you did. Just like George did. What makes you strong and powerful isn't your perfection. It's your unwavering belief in The Light, in the power of The Light to do absolutely anything, and in the gift of knowing that anyone can change. And you wield The Light in that capacity."

I knew what she said was true; my friends had told me, Pneuma had told me, but I still didn't feel special. "The Light is what's special," I said, finishing my thought out loud.

"Of course, and because you believe that and only use your powers for The Light, and in a pure nature, you stay humble," Letta continued. "Anyone that you have Awakened has become a Light Bearer. That's not normal. And any Light Bearers that come about through you have other giftings, new powers and the same devotion to The Light that you have."

We talked for another two hours, never really leaving the deeper topics, but sharing our worlds with each other. Letta didn't share much of what she'd experienced in Ganheela, but she'd always wanted to go, and her dream had now been fulfilled. We were laughing over something I shared with her about Mitch when we both heard the door open. Her new "family" was home.

The Johnsons were wonderful and so welcoming. They encouraged me to text Nyiah and have her join us all for dinner. Nyiah graciously accepted, and when she arrived, Letta wrapped her in a long hug, also thanking her for the rescue. We had the best time together, all laughing and talking at the same time. It felt like we'd known each other forever. The Johnsons insisted we stay with them for the night, but we had to decline, explaining we had to catch a plane and get home for work the next day.

While we were sad to leave Letta and the Johnsons, Nyiah and I had such a great time and we talked about all that had happened during our visit on our way home. I knew we would be back to see them all again soon. I had true family, The Light was prevailing, and I was so thankful.

* * *

Where am I? I felt so cold, bitterly cold, as the wind whipped around me. I tried to get my bearings, but the inky blackness was oppressive. *Why is it so dark? Why am I not able to emit any light?* In my fear, I twisted but quickly realized my arms were bound behind me. With each movement, whatever I was tied to scraped my skin. I took a breath and tried again to bring forth light. Nothing, not even a flicker. I was shaking, from the cold, from the fear that gripped me. I didn't think there was anything that could dampen my powers in The Light like this.

I took another breath and squinted hard, peering in front of me. I could barely make out what looked to be tall trees around me. The trees somehow reminded me of Camp Tuano, and I sucked in a quick breath.

"Finally piecing it all together, Sis?" I heard a voice hiss right along with the wind.

My head jerked to the left, but I couldn't see her.

"Where are you, Amelia?" I called out.

"Right here." Her voice was eerily close, sending ice through my veins.

"Where? I don't see you. It's too dark." My sister was here, but I was bound, and I didn't have my powers. Did the Terrobah now have ropes like The Light did? Ropes that could limit the opposing powers? I felt breath on my neck and a violent shiver ran through me.

"I begged you to come for me, but the 'all-powerful Sarah' can't ever seem to find me." Her statement sounded like an accusation, filled with anger, laced with pain, sarcasm dripping from every word.

"I've done everything in my power to find you and free you," I returned, trying in vain to find a way out of the ropes that had my arms bound around the tree behind me.

"I'm *sure* you've tried your very best." More sarcasm hissed out of her, and she remained close as she continued. "I bet you wrote me off as soon as I came back from the bonfire."

"No," I shook my head violently, "you were so hurt, you were dying. I got Lucas, and he healed you."

"That's what you say, but I woke up from a great sleep to find my little sister had abandoned me. Run off with a guy in the woods. A guy I liked, I might mention." With that comment, she still sounded like my 17-year-old sister.

"Amelia, it's not like that at all. We were fleeing for our lives." I pleaded with her to understand.

"If there was enough danger for you to flee, then why didn't you take me?!" She shrieked with venom in her voice.

"You were unconscious. Please Amelia, let me see you. This darkness is terrible." She didn't respond, so I continued feeling the agony of leaving her behind radiate through me. "Leaving you behind was the worst mistake I ever made."

"Whatever." She was close and to my right. I tried with everything I could to see her.

Red eyes. A pair of red eyes met mine.

"Are you alone?" I asked quietly.

"I'm never alone." She growled and was suddenly in front of me. Her beautiful face appeared, with red eyes that dimmed after her growl tapered off. We were the same height. Looking into a face I knew, but eyes I didn't know at all, my heart dropped into my stomach.

"I wish it could've been me. I wish you were in The Light and I was the one that had been left behind." I spoke softly, trying to reach her, but my words had the opposite effect. Just like at the warehouse, my kind words seemed to anger her more.

"I doubt that," she responded with malice. "You're the enemy's little princess; everybody adores you. Sweet little Sarah Joy." She said my name in a sickeningly sweet voice, her disgust evident.

"It's true. I wish I was the one left behind," I shouted.

"Don't lie!" she screamed back at me.

"I'm not lying. That's what the Terrobah do," I said, feeling anger rise in me at my inability to get out of this situation. What power did I have outside of The Light?

"No, the Terrobah awakened me to the truth that having power over others is the only way to live." She spoke with such confidence, it was clear the words had literally been beaten into her.

"You really feel like you're living, being tortured so that your powers grow stronger? And for what? To bring more people to the wrong side?" I kept her talking while I was thinking. I had a strong urge to protect my mind from her words. Just that basic realization seemed to light a spark. Something was happening in my mind. I could feel it.

"No, little sister, I couldn't care less about other people." I felt the lie in her words. There were three people she cared about, three living people. But how did I know that?

Amelia continued, "I am being trained to destroy you, my sister, the Princess of Lies."

"I think that's *your* title," I retorted, and the words cut me as soon as I said them. It hurt me to wound her in anyway, but I had to keep her distracted while I thought my way out of this. The Terrobah wouldn't let her gloat much longer and would be upon me.

She laughed, a wicked, condescending laugh. "Maybe."

I was now feeling tingling in my back where my light armor had formed from my first battle against the Terrobah. They had pierced me with two highly poisonous arrows, but instead of killing me, the healing from The Light gave me armor to forever protect me from the Terrobah. I thought about the tingling in my back, willing the spots to come together as I slowly wiggled my hands up the tree, trying to get the ropes up where they would be in line with my armor.

"There's no 'maybe' about it, sister." This brought her to my face again.

"You're the one who is compromised here. I will destroy you." She turned to walk away.

"You can't," I stated, stopping her in her tracks. "You still care about me." I spoke slowly as I felt something changing in my hands. I could feel light pulsing there. My armor must have been doing something to the ropes. I felt the tingling move to other parts of my body. I tried to keep any light from coming out of me though. I didn't want to give away what was happening too early.

"I do not!" Her voice thundered.

"I know they're trying to remove your feelings for me by any means, and I'm so sorry if they hurt you more for this. I know you care about others, too. I don't know who they are, but I know you care deeply for them." I kept stalling, as I felt the restrictions on my wrists release. I heard in my head, *the twins*. Was that Amelia's thought? Pneuma? Had the ropes even restricted my connection to Pneuma? I hadn't heard her this whole time. But now light was pulsing strongly within me. I let it free at the same time Amelia responded.

"I care about no one," Amelia screamed, as a black tar-like substance burst forth from her hands and came straight at me. With my light now in full effect, I could see everything around me. It appeared to just be me and her in the middle of a vast forest. I launched a counterattack of light against the black tar coming at me. When the light coming from my blasts collided with her tar of darkness, there was a ground-shaking explosion that blew me backwards. And after a bone crushing fall, I felt nothing.

❋ ❋ ❋

I sat up quickly, breathing heavily, ready to launch another attack, but my surroundings had changed. There was warmth and light. Had I died? There were no trees, only walls. I wasn't on the frozen ground, but in my bed. My bed was beneath my hands, and my sheets and blanket were on my legs. I looked around, seeing the normalcy of my room around me, not the dark forest. I was glowing with light and had no trouble seeing.

Could that have been a dream? It had seemed much too real to be a dream. Also, when I had a dream with Pneuma, I usually knew it was a dream. Or if she showed me a vision, I was still very aware that it was from her.

In this "dream," I hadn't even thought about her. This "dream" ...

No, this is no dream. It's a nightmare.

This nightmare had not come from Pneuma. It had felt awful having my powers rendered useless. And I had willingly fought with my sister for my own survival.

* * *

"What're you thinking about?" Nyiah asked at dinner the next evening. Her question left me confused. I'd been so far away in my own thoughts that I had forgotten we were even eating dinner.

"What do you mean?" I returned, knowing she was referring to something specific she was seeing in me.

"I've been watching you stare out the window for the last fifteen minutes. I don't think you blinked for the last five," she said with wide eyes, trying to get me to laugh. When I didn't, her face fell. "Sarah, what is it?" She was worried.

A terribly uncomfortable feeling overcame me. I wanted to hide the nightmare from Nyiah, but I knew that was wrong. To decrease the power the nightmare seemed to have on me, I proceeded to tell her the whole thing, including the overwhelming sense I had that Amelia loved three living people. I also shared about the explosion at the end of the dream where it seemed like Amelia and I had ended each other.

When I finished, she was quiet for a while. Our food sat forgotten as the nightmare seemed to have a presence of its own in the room.

Finally, she spoke, "Have you talked to Pneuma about this?"

"No," I whispered.

"Sarah," she said in concern.

"I know I should, but I'm afraid of what it means," I confessed, having even avoided Pneuma when she beckoned in my mind.

"But nightmares only come from the Darkness. How did they gain access to your mind?" she questioned.

"I don't know. That's why I'm afraid." That and the fact that my sister and I had simultaneously destroyed each other.

"I think you need to see Pneuma now."

"But my stone is low," I said in return, grasping at anything to avoid confirming my fears.

"It will be enough time to talk about this."

I remained silent, my stomach churning, so she engaged again.

"They want you to fear; they want you to hide instead of taking this to Pneuma. By waiting, you're giving power to the Darkness."

I knew what she said was true. I had nothing to fear from Pneuma. But I still couldn't get myself to move.

"I'll come with you," she said, standing and offering me her hand. I took it and reluctantly followed her out the back door. The sun would set soon, and we would lose our chance to talk to Pneuma, but still, I didn't move to take off my necklace. I just stared at the water, seeing Amelia's eyes, or what her eyes had become, red and filled with hatred for me.

I felt Nyiah gently unclasping the necklace from my neck. She grabbed my hand again and led me to the water's edge. She must have been concerned that I would drop it because she wrapped it around my fingers twice and supported my hand with hers as we dipped the ruby into the water, beckoning Pneuma to come.

Pneuma appeared immediately and took me into her arms as my necklace suspended itself in the water, ticking down the time until Pneuma would vanish from physical form.

"Sarah," she said. Just speaking my name, I heard and felt her say that she was so sorry for my nightmare experience, and she was hurting for me as I was hurting.

"What was it?" I asked pitifully into her shoulder.

"It was a vision, but not from me, and not from the future. Somehow using Amelia, they passed that message to you. It was meant to wound and incapacitate you. But even in their message, you managed to summon The Light."

"And kill my sister."

"No, my love. You just broke free from their hold. Amelia still lives."

"How did they do it, Pneuma?" Nyiah asked from behind me. I didn't turn to look at her, but I felt Pneuma reach for her, while she somehow continued to hold me. We were both fully in her arms, neither feeling anything but her full presence and attention. I never ceased to be amazed by Pneuma's capacity to offer love. I didn't understand it, but I didn't need to.

My face was still buried in Pneuma's shoulder as she answered Nyiah's question, "There is a bond between Amelia and Sarah, a bond stronger than just sisterhood for what they endured together in losing their parents. It can never be severed." I turned my head just slightly so that my eyes were looking at Nyiah.

I saw fear pass over her face, fear immediately replaced with peace, most likely from Pneuma's touch.

"They can access Sarah at any time?" Nyiah wasn't wasting any time with her questions.

"No, it is nothing like that. They may not even know that they reached her. They were just trying to get to her through the parts of Amelia's mind that still care for Sarah."

"Is she okay?" I whispered.

"Yes. She was hurt, but she is recovering."

"Can I go to her yet?" I asked desperately, tears filling my eyes at the thought that Amelia was suffering all because of me.

"No, my love, and you must take a moment to breathe. For our time together in the flesh is very short."

I tried to obey as Pneuma used her hand to hold my entire face to her shoulder. We had somehow moved to the bench, and I was on her lap being cradled. Nyiah was still in her embrace as well but sitting beside her. My tears slowed and my breathing became more even, as I inhaled her peace and exhaled my pain.

"When can I go to her, Pneuma?"

"This is not the time. There is still more for you to do before you see her again. The time will be upon you before you know it."

"Is there anything Sarah can do to block them from trying this again?" Thank The Light for Nyiah, always looking out for me.

"There is another type of shield, like what she has on her back, that she will learn to wield, in time," Pneuma said, rubbing the very shield she spoke of on my back.

My head came up at that to look into her face. In my nightmare, I had used that very same shield to overcome the ropes which Amelia had used to bind me and take my powers. Pneuma gave me a nod at my understanding.

"I love you," she said, and it echoed into the very depths of me.

"I love you, too," I said at the same time I heard Nyiah say it. Nyiah had heard the *I love you* just for her and I had heard it just for me. There was always more than enough of Pneuma to go around.

All at once, Pneuma was gone. I sat on the bench as Nyiah went to retrieve my necklace. She fastened it around my neck and sat back against the bench.

"Well, I guess we have a new shield to learn," I stated, causing both of us to smile. We looked at each other, the relief we felt in Pneuma's presence and the mysteries revealed passing silently between us. Eventually, we stood and walked back into the house, arm-in-arm.

"What we thought was evil, was still actually good." Nyiah said in contemplation.

"What do you mean?" I questioned.

"Well, the Terrobah want to use the connection between you and Amelia to hurt you, but you were able to feel that Amelia is still capable of love. So, even though the Terrobah prompted the nightmare, maybe Amelia was still calling out to you."

Getting ready for bed that night, I pulled out Amelia's old fake ID as I had done many times before. It was my only picture of her. I pulled it out often to remember her as she was, young and carefree and full of life. Knowing my sister had called to me, I held her ID to my cheek just wanting her to be close. I couldn't go to Amelia yet, but I knew she was trying to reach me, just as I longed to reach her and that was enough.

CHAPTER 16

MITCH

Sitting on the table in the PT gym for the last time, I had a hard time not fidgeting. It was Wednesday night, and it was my last session with Sarah. I wanted to get down on my knees and beg Sarah to go out with me, but I had a bit too much pride to allow myself to do that. She was taking off the ice machine cuff when I got up the nerve to whisper, "Okay, so we're done with PT." She smiled at me knowingly. "So can I call you at the number my sister has?"

"Yes," she returned, not looking at me and blushing slightly.

"Just like that?"

"Just like that," she repeated, and a huge grin spread across my face.

I drove home, but waited a while before I called, just to be sure Sarah had time to get home, or so I told myself. I picked up a few items in the already-clean apartment and paced the living room before I plopped on the couch with a sigh. I proceeded to pick up my phone a few times, sliding my thumb across the face of the phone, then setting it back down.

Sharon finally exclaimed, "For goodness' sake, Mitch, just call the girl!"

I took a few deep breaths before I pressed "send" to call her.

"Hello?" she answered.

"Hey Sarah, it's Mitch."

"Hey Mitch. Not one to let any grass grow, are you?" She teased with a smile in her voice.

"I've had to wait four months (*and one hour*) for this, so I think there has been plenty of grass grown."

"True," she chuckled, but she didn't say anything else. She wasn't going to make this easy on me.

"Well, I was calling to ask you if you would go to dinner with me Friday evening."

"I would like that, but I need to be upfront about something," she said.

My excitement dipped just a bit at those words. "Okay, shoot."

"I haven't dated much, so I'm not really sure I'll be any good at this." She was so sweet.

"I have no expectations here except getting to spend some time with you," I assured her.

"Okay. Well, I work late Friday."

"I'm okay with that; I can just pick you up once you get home."

"Can we just meet at the restaurant?" She kept surprising me.

"Uh, sure." I got out, not exactly sure what was going on.

"I'm sorry, was that not an okay thing to ask?" She could clearly hear in my voice that I was a bit disappointed.

"No, it's fine. I had just hoped after all this time that you would feel comfortable around me." I felt like I was back in high school, trying to play it cool for the prettiest girl in class.

"I do, Mitch. This isn't really about that," she returned, but didn't offer anything further as to why she didn't want me to pick her up at her house.

"Okay, fair enough. Can you meet me at Morino's once you get off work? Or would you rather do it Saturday evening so it's not so late for you?"

"I already have plans for Saturday, so let's go with Friday."

"Okay, sounds good," I agreed with excitement, even though I felt a bit jealous over whomever she had plans with on Saturday.

"Thanks for the call and the invitation, Mitch," she said sweetly, it almost sounded like she was nervous as well.

"I'm looking forward to it."

"Me too, bye."

"Bye."

* * *

Over the past month, Sarah and I had been out on three dates. Each date was great; our personalities were clicking, and we never seemed to run out of things to talk about. I had gotten bold enough to kiss her on the cheek after we went out the last time, but that was as far as our physical relationship had gone.

I was working much slower with Sarah than my normal pace with other women. While the urges were still there, Sarah just seemed too special to rush into anything. I was treating her how I would want any guy to treat Sharon, with complete consideration and respect. Sarah was someone to be cherished.

With this new perspective, I felt guilty at how I had treated women in the past, because each one of those women was also someone to be cherished. I had just never seen it that way before.

Instead of trying to rush on to the next thing or force feelings by being physical, I was savoring each moment I had with her. I wasn't sure if it was from the long wait we had before we could start dating or if it was just Sarah and my feelings for her, but I liked this new me. I liked who I was becoming in order to be someone worthy of her.

Sarah was hesitant as well. I chalked it up to her inexperience in the dating world, but it felt like she was holding back something more. Except for the kiss on the cheek, our relationship remained much as it had been before. That didn't deter me, though. I could tell she liked me, and I would go at whatever pace she needed.

For tonight, I had asked Sarah to dinner and a movie, but she said she wanted us to meet at her work. I got out of my car in the parking lot and saw that she was waiting inside for me. She was watching for me and gestured toward the employee door at the side of the building. I followed the sidewalk to the door, and she met me there. It was eight o'clock on a Friday night. The clinic had been deserted for at least an hour.

She opened the door for me. "Hey Mitch." She greeted me, smiling so sweetly that my heart took an extra beat.

"Hey Sunshine." I felt almost breathless when I looked at her and the 'Sunshine' just slipped out.

"Sunshine," she pondered the name. "I like it," she concluded with a beautiful smile.

"You remind me of sunshine, so it just came out." I couldn't tell her how I would stare at sunbeams streaming through the clouds and think of her. How she was a ray of sunshine in my dreary life that I hadn't even realized was dreary until I met her.

"Well, I like it," she said warmly.

"Nickname, check," I joked, and she gave me a soft chuckle in return as she gestured for me to sit on a stool next to one of the treatment tables while she took the one next to it.

Once we sat down, I noticed Sarah seemed nervous as she studied her hands in her lap. My gut tightened. I'd been around the block enough times to know when a break-up was coming, even though she'd seemed happy to see me just moments before.

"As much as I loved spending time with you in this clinic, I wasn't super eager to have a date here," I joked, trying to get her to look at me. Suddenly, I felt as nervous as she seemed. My palms were sweaty, and I rubbed them across the tops of my thighs as I waited for her reply.

She finally looked up at me, but her gaze was serious.

"Why did we need to come here?" I asked. I wasn't sure why she would want to spend even more time at her work, but I got the feeling I wouldn't like the reason.

"Because we had to meet someplace safe," Sarah replied. Was she joking, why was work a safer place for her than somewhere else?

"Safe? What do you mean safe?" I inquired.

"It's not just that it's my work, but there are important safety measures in place here already, and I don't know you well enough yet to take you to my house."

Ouch. I nodded, even though I didn't really understand yet.

"Why did you want to meet someplace safe tonight as opposed to the places we've been going?" I asked, hoping that I hid the pain in my voice well.

"Because I have to talk to you about something important," she returned, her eyes brimming with an almost palpable sadness.

"Okay, I guess I'm ready," though the pounding of my heart said otherwise.

"I've been holding back with you, Mitch..." She trailed off.

"Sarah, it's okay. We don't need to rush anything." I comforted her, almost reaching out to touch her arm, but not following through in case she didn't want that.

"No, I've been holding back on pursuing this relationship with you. I had to make sure you were safe."

"That I was safe?" That comment threw me. "Well, I mean, yeah, I guess there are a lot of creeps out there, but I thought you got to see what a nice guy I was during all of our torture sessions." I'd been on my best behavior with Sarah, so I wasn't sure what she meant.

"You are a nice guy, but that isn't what makes you safe," she responded, still being annoyingly vague.

"Okay...so what makes me safe?" I asked, eager to get to the bottom of this.

"Some of your," she paused, "attributes."

"Attributes?" I was confused and a little hurt. "What are you..."

Sarah interrupted me to say, "Mitch, why did you want to be with me?" Though she asked the question, it seemed like she already knew the answer.

"I thought it was clear that I'm attracted to you and enjoy spending time with you," I said slowly, measuring my words. Was this some kind of test I suddenly had to pass?

"What attracted you to me?" she asked bluntly, but with that same look of certainty on her face.

"Umm, well, you're pretty... uh, you're, um, pretty unusual," I stammered. I didn't normally get flustered, so it was weird that she could sit across from me so calmly while I felt like a wreck on the inside.

She raised an eyebrow at my blundered comment, looking almost amused. I continued, "I don't mean that in a bad way. You're just different, less stressed, calm, peaceful no matter what is happening around you."

She smiled. So, I continued, "Like even now, I called you unusual, and you don't seem offended or even affected by it."

"Because what you say is true, I am different," Sarah responded, not elaborating.

After a pause, I jumped back in, hating the awkward silence while she didn't seem to be bothered by it. "Like meeting at your work, for instance. That's a new one for me."

"I know it's unusual, and I want to explain, but I would really like to hear why you were attracted to me," she pressed.

If it had been anyone but Sarah, I would have thought they were fishing for compliments, but Sarah wasn't that way. She wanted a serious answer. I realized we were at a pivotal point here, and I needed to be honest with her.

"I noticed you the first day you walked in; I couldn't stop staring at you." *Okay, maybe a little less honesty, Mitch.* "There was just something about you; you almost glowed with life." I gulped; this 'putting yourself out there' stuff was hard.

"Everyone was so excited to have you back, and it seemed like they all just enjoyed having you around." My eyes had fallen as I explained, so I raised them back up to her. "Then, I got to talk to you, and just talking with you made me feel better." My eyes dropped to the ground again. "I've never met anyone like you, and all I want to do is be around you."

I dreaded the pity I would see in her eyes when I looked back up, but to my surprise, none was there. Instead, her eyes were filled with tears, happy tears.

"Was that okay, to say all of that?" I asked, sure my neck was red with embarrassment.

"Of course that was okay to say. Thank you, Mitch, for your beautiful words."

"And when were you first attracted to me?" I asked sarcastically, trying to make her laugh. It worked and her tears seemed to come back under control.

"I noticed you right off as well, but maybe not in the same way." She gave me a half smile. "I notice people and normally get a read on everyone I meet. You, however, were a bit tougher to read."

"You mean you couldn't tell how I felt about you?"

"No, I could tell that," she said, a blush coloring her cheeks. "I just couldn't tell what you were about. What you were living for, exactly."

"I'm not sure I really knew that either," I confessed.

"You also changed a bit for the better, once you moved your sister down from D.C.," she continued.

"I think the change came before that, and that's why I let her live with me."

"Who was your roommate before that?"

"A guy named Troy."

"Were you close?"

"No, we were buddies, but we shared our apartment for convenience more than anything else. We did some stuff together but had very different lives. Why?"

"Just curious. You seem a lot different since you moved in with your sister. And who we hang out with says a lot about us," she said cryptically. "But I'm getting off topic."

"What is the topic, exactly? I'm still not understanding why we're here."

Sarah took a slow, deep breath before she continued. I could tell she was nervous, but I couldn't figure out why. She went on, "You're right, Mitch, I am different. I've been Awakened by The Light."

"What?" I asked, as numerous feelings washed over me at that statement.

"There are forces at work in the world around us. There is the side of The Light and the side of the Darkness."

"Good versus evil, it's pretty obvious, actually. They even make movies about it." I tried to make a joke, but it may have come across as annoyance.

"The good choices and bad choices of people are really obvious, but the forces at work behind them tend to be less so." She paused, but since my only thought on forces involved Jedi and lightsabers, I figured it was better to keep my mouth shut.

"I was just like you, living my life and completely unaware of what was really going on around me, until a few years ago when I was rescued. Through that experience, I was given eyes to truly see what was going on around me and I chose the side of The Light."

"We have to choose sides?" I was still confused. This was not at all what I'd expected.

"As humans, we choose sides everyday with our words and actions, but there is more to it. If you decide to choose The Light and your heart is sincere, you become Awakened with your eyes being opened to what's happening around you."

"What *is* happening around me?" Sarah was talking in riddles, and I could feel a sense of frustration growing inside me.

"A fierce battle over humanity," she said simply, like that was a phrase everyone used in normal conversation.

"And you're what, a warrior?" This was getting ridiculous.

"Yes," she said sincerely.

"I was being sarcastic, Sarah."

"I know, but it's the truth. I am a warrior for The Light."

"Are you trying to scare me off? Do you not want to date me anymore? Because this all seems a bit much. You can say you just want to be friends." The frustration in my voice was apparent.

"I very much enjoy your friendship, Mitch, and I hope that doesn't change, but I can't go any further with you in a romantic relationship without you being aware of who I am."

I couldn't even respond. This was the woman I was in love with, and as it turned out, she was seemingly out of touch with reality.

"The reason I am so attractive to you is because of The Light that dwells inside of me. You can see it in me and feel it in my touch."

"So, you've what, been using your powers on me?" I asked, my thoughts splintering in a thousand different directions. *I really thought I loved this girl. How could I have missed something as big as her being completely out of her mind?*

"No, no, it's not like that," she said, reaching for my hand, but I pulled it away.

I saw the pain of my rejection move across her face and my insides ached, but she was trying to drive me away. She was the one telling me crazy stories so I would leave.

"Sarah, I'm sorry. I don't want to hurt you, but this seems a little out there. You're telling me you're a warrior, for an unseen army, fighting an unseen enemy? And you say you had to make sure I was safe. Were you trying to see if I was the enemy?" It was hard to hide the pain I was feeling at her rejection.

"I knew you weren't one of them, but I did have to make sure that there weren't some around you, or that you weren't being pulled to their side." I could tell she was being sincere, but it wasn't helping.

"So, without this *light*, I'm not good enough for you?"

"It's not that either, Mitch. I have chosen my path, and you have the right to choose yours as well. I just want you to have all the facts."

"I thought I had chosen my path, with you, but now it seems like you're trying to get me to choose a different one." I was shaking a bit now.

"I can't be the only path you choose. One day everyone will have to choose The Light or the Darkness."

"But if I don't choose The Light, I can't be with you? Am I getting that part right?" I asked in anger.

"I guess that's true, but this is more about you, Mitch. You have tendencies toward The Light, or I wouldn't have been at-tracted to you. You pursue the right things and stand up for in-justice. Those are things of The Light." Her tone was comforting, but her words did not have the same effect.

"I'm not sure I want my eyes opened," I pushed back, still feeling the anger from her rejection. But was it really rejection if she said she was attracted to me as well?

"That's your choice," Sarah said, still giving me a steady gaze, but with saddened eyes.

"I'm not sure this is worth it," I said, letting my anger come out in my tone, as I gestured at her.

"You mean that I'm not worth it," she said, clearly hurt.

"No...yes...I don't know. This is not the conversation I thought we'd be having tonight. I can't just accept what you're saying without any proof. Surely you can see how this sounds?"

This afternoon, I thought Sarah and I were on the right track and maybe ready to keep moving ahead, but now I couldn't help but think: *Where do we go from here?*

CHAPTER 17

SARAH

SHOWING MITCH WAS RISKY because I wasn't sure where he stood with The Light. I really did want him to see me for who I was and to believe me, but with the others I had led to The Light, I had more assurance they were ready. Mitch seemed interested, but it was hard to tell if it was for me alone or for The Light as well. With others I had spoken to about The Light, it was easy to share with them because they'd had an awareness of The Light before I entered the picture. Mitch was the most unaware person I'd ever had this conversation with. And it wasn't going well.

"Okay, Mitch. Because I care about you, I don't want to hide this from you." I took a deep breath and forced some visible light to come out of my hand. I let it hover over my hand as I looked up at Mitch. His face was not filled with awe, but with panic.

"How did you do that?" he stammered, eyes wide with fear.

"Because I chose The Light, I can wield The Light that's inside of me." I created another ball in my other hand. "These are the weapons I carry, not guns."

"Is that what you used on me?" Mitch questioned, sounding more frantic as he stood from his stool and moved away from me. I let the light dissipate in my hands.

"What?" I asked, surprised by his question.

"Have you been using your powers on me to make me do what you want or whatever?" Mitch took another step backward, his eyes searching the room for the nearest exit.

"No, I don't use my powers for my own purposes," I responded, pain in my voice.

"So, you haven't used any of these light energies on me?"

"Not in the way you mean." *This is not going well at all.*

"In what way then, Sarah?" The anger in his voice was building.

I had never seen Mitch like this; he was furious with me. He didn't even give me a chance to respond before he repeated his question again, louder. He looked down on me with such anger in his eyes, he could have mirrored a Terrobah.

"I didn't use light on you except to help the healing in your knee," I answered more defensively than I intended.

"You have powers to *heal*?" he asked in a mix of anger and exasperation.

"Yes, I can help bodies heal faster with The Light."

"This is just too weird; I don't want anything to do with this voodoo, Sarah. I have to go," he said, shaking his head and backing away.

"It's not voodoo," I responded, trying to keep the hurt and anger from my voice. "But I understand if you need to leave, Mitch." I gave him a wide berth as I moved to unlock the door for him. "I would appreciate it if you wouldn't talk with anyone about this except for Sharon. It's for my safety and yours," I informed him, trying to keep the tears from falling.

"Okay," he said, seeming to calm a little at my words. "I'm sorry, I just..."

"Maybe I'll see you around," I said softly, interrupting whatever he was going to say next, lifting my chin, and swallowing the pain in my throat.

He paused on his way out to look at my face, "Sarah, I..." he paused, his voice was no longer angry but deeply hurt and confused. "Yeah, I don't know. . . maybe." he shrugged, then turned and walked into the night.

I had been wrong this time. As his car pulled away, I locked the door and leaned my forehead against its cool glass.

My thoughts moved to my discussion with Nyiah from a few days before....

* * *

"It almost feels like cheating," I said softly.

"Cheating. Why?" Nyiah looked at me like I'd gone a little crazy.

"Because when I touch him, I touch him with light. It's The Light he wants. He wants the feeling he gets from The Light. Not me." Was this self-pity or something else?

"That's just the most ridiculous thing I've ever heard," Nyiah said, in a rare display of anger.

I started to defend myself, but she continued, "Sarah Joy, you are The Light. The Light is what makes you, *you*. From your legacy, to accepting The Light, to choosing to walk as a Light Bearer. There is no separation of the two."

I raised my eyes to look at her, feeling tears threaten. What she said was true. The Light was such a part of me that you couldn't remove it without killing me. I couldn't withhold it in any relationship I had.

"When light pulses out of you as you touch him, that light is a gift. It is a gift of the purest form of love, real love." A tear trailed down my cheek.

Nyiah continued, "Mitch is attracted to The Light, but he is also very attracted to you, Sarah. You and The Light are one in the same."

I tried to wipe my cheeks with my palms, but I could tell my tears weren't done. I gave her a small smile.

"This isn't just about Mitch," Nyiah stated.

"What do you mean?"

"You're too hard on yourself, and you don't ever feel like you're enough." Her statement caused a gripping sensation in the vicinity of my heart. She continued, "I wish you could see yourself how I do, how Pneuma does, how Ethan does, how Owen does."

Another tear made its way down my cheek as the sensation in my heart grew even tighter with her words.

"Remember what Pneuma has told us: it is The Light within us that changes us; we cannot just fix ourselves. That is a treadmill marathon," she said. "We keep running and running, and we never get to the goal. Instead..."

"We have to stop and let The Light do its work," I finished for her. That truth resonated in my heart even as I said it aloud.

"Can I try something with you?" she asked me, with caution in her voice.

"Yes," I replied, still feeling tender and emotional.

"I've been practicing," she said softly, as she laid her palm on my forehead. She was standing in front of me, but suddenly, I couldn't see her anymore.

"Nyiah?" I asked in confusion.

"What do you see?" she asked, in a voice that sounded closer to Pneuma's than hers.

"A field."

"Describe it to me," she instructed.

"I see tall prairie grass across rolling hills." She didn't say anything, so I continued. "There are mountains in the background and fluffy clouds moving slowly across a bright blue sky."

"What do you feel?" she asked in the same voice.

I had practiced this kind of thing with Pneuma and knew to just let myself go to feel what Nyiah was showing me through this vision. I knew I was safe with Nyiah and her new gift, which seemed to come straight from Pneuma. "I feel warmer, lighter. I feel the heaviness falling away. I feel content. I feel joy."

Nyiah didn't speak and something was added to my vision. "There's a woman there now, dancing. Well, she's spinning in a circle raising up her arms."

Nyiah still didn't speak so I kept going. "She's so beautiful; she must be a Mythreal. She has so much light, and the joy is written all over her face. She doesn't have a care in the world. She has beautiful blond hair, so blond it's almost white. She's breathtaking."

"Sarah, look closer."

I obeyed and tried to focus in on the woman's face. I certainly recognized her now, "Oh, it's me?!" I realized and asked all at the same time.

"Yes, that is you," she confirmed, still sounding like Pneuma.

In my confusion, I pulled back from Nyiah's hand. "What . . . how is that me?" I asked, opening my eyes to the reality around me. Nyiah still had her hand extended toward my forehead. She slowly blinked and seemed to come back into focus on what was happening in the room around her.

We just stared at each other for a second or two, and then, we both started laughing.

"I have so many questions, but Nyiah, that was amazing! How did you do that?" The vision had filled me with peace.

"Pneuma is training me in imparting truths of The Light. I quite enjoyed it myself."

"Could you see what I was seeing?"

She nodded.

"Could you feel what I was feeling?"

She nodded again, as her smile grew.

"Did you make me see that?"

Her smile diminished a little as she shrugged. "I don't think I can make people see whatever I want them to. I think I make it so they can see the truth if they are willing."

"Well, that *clarifies* things." I teased her.

"It's confusing, but you did see yourself."

"I saw a version of myself," I clarified.

"The version of yourself that you saw is what the rest of us see in you all the time," she countered.

"But it seemed like that would be me if I were a full Mythreal or being of The Light."

"I think it's you, fully transformed by The Light," Nyiah reasoned.

"But that's not who I see in the mirror," I confessed.

"Because you don't see yourself as you are. You get caught up in fear and worry as we all do, but you see it as failure, not as something you learn and grow from."

"That sounds true," I admitted.

"I was hoping you would be able to see yourself as we see you. Did it help?" she asked, hopeful.

"It's just so hard to believe that I'm her."

"Do you trust me?"

"Of course, I do," I returned.

"Then that *is* you, my precious friend. Trust me in that. Let me believe it for you until you grow into believing it about yourself."

We just looked at each other until we caused each other to laugh again. As a friend and sister Light Bearer, Nyiah was so dear to me. "Thank you," I responded to her last comment.

"My pleasure, Sarah Joy." After another smile at each other, I grabbed her hand.

"Okay, tell me all about your gift: when did it start, how has it changed, who have you tried it on?" My flurry of questions caused Nyiah to laugh, and before I knew it, we were laughing hard.

Laughter was a gift from The Light, and we were overwhelmed by it, releasing all our cares and resting in the beauty of the moment.

* * *

There is no beauty in this moment. I thought, as I returned to the present, my forehead still leaning on the glass. I pulled away and stared at my reflection in the door. My blond hair shined brightly, The Light shining out even when I hadn't meant for it to do so. It was amazing how much I seemed to glow even though it felt like a part of me was dying.

Mitch's feelings for me must have overshadowed where he was with The Light. I hadn't dealt with this sort of thing before. I thought what I was sensing in him was an awakening, but maybe it had been his feelings of love.

I had made a mistake and hurt Mitch, but he had to learn at some point. Deflated as I was, I needed to head home. Nyiah and Ethan were waiting for me and Mitch, believing our conversation would go well, but Mitch would not be joining us tonight.

* * *

MITCH

What a sucky night.

I had just left Sarah behind at the clinic, and I missed her already. But what she told me, what she showed me was too much for anyone to take in. It seemed like she hadn't told many people, and I could see why.

My heart ached with the thought of how I had hurt her. She'd tried to prepare me by asking what attracted me to her. I was sure it hadn't been the light energy or whatever she described.

She glowed with life.

I'd had that very thought about her. All my thoughts about her were of light and life and love; I even called her Sunshine. Maybe this energy thing had played a part. But then, didn't that mean she'd manipulated me? No matter how I wrestled with it, I couldn't make any sense of this night.

I slowly got out of my car and made my way up the stairs to the apartment. Just as slowly, I put the key in the lock and opened the door.

Sharon was on the couch in the living room, watching some sort of sappy Hallmark movie. At least we all knew that guy would get his girl, and she most likely wouldn't have glowing balls of light coming out of her hands.

"You're home early." Sharon stated. I could barely force my eyes to look at her, but she still quickly noticed my mood.

"Mitch, what's wrong?" she asked, sitting up and starting to rise from the couch.

I stopped her by holding my hand up, palm out. "Don't get up, I'm okay."

"You're clearly not."

"Sarah just... wasn't who I thought she was." The disappointment rang in my words.

"What? What do you mean? What happened?" Sharon stood up, despite my objection, and took a step toward me.

"I can't explain it right now, I just...I ... I'll be in my room."

"Okay," she said, with concern written all over her face.

"We can talk tomorrow," I said, trying to soften the hurt I was causing her.

"You sure?" It was clear she didn't want to let me go.

I gave her a nod and headed to my room. She was probably so shocked by this turn of events. In her head, she only knew I was head-over-heels and nothing would stop me from being with Sarah. I had thought that was true as well. And now, I couldn't be with the woman I loved because of some stupid light and a crazy war. It all had to be made up. It had to be a trick. *Maybe she's a magician. No, that's ridiculous.* But everything she told me seemed ridiculous, too.

I walked into my room, not even bothering to turn on the light. I sat down hard on the edge of my bed and slowly took off my shoes. My curtains were open, allowing me to see into the dark of the night beyond the glass. Everything seemed so calm and settled out there. I envied that world, as I thought I might never be calm and settled again.

A streetlamp that I hadn't noticed flickered to life and my heart jumped. The rest of the streetlights were on and glowing, but this one seemed to be struggling.

I know the feeling, buddy.

I sat entranced, watching the streetlamp flicker, willing it to succeed, but it wasn't long before it went out completely. I felt the disappointment and darkness of the moment and thought back to Sarah, how her light had dimmed when I'd caused her pain, and how the flame of any potential relationship had been all but extinguished.

The next light I was aware of was the morning sunlight streaming through my window. I blinked at it and covered my eyes with my hand while I sat up. I stared at that streetlamp so long last night, willing it to relight, that I fell asleep on my bed with my clothes on.

Standing up, I made my way to the window to look at the streetlamp in the daylight. It remained dark, standing at attention alongside the row of other lamps, all likewise extinguished. My stomach turned at the thought of lights being dimmed and of my conversation with Sarah from the previous night.

Rubbing my hands over my face, I tried to erase my thoughts. I grabbed some fresh workout clothes and quickly got dressed to go for a run. When I stepped into the hall, I heard Sharon in her shower and felt relief. I could put off talking with her a little longer. I left her a quick note and headed out the door at full speed.

Now to put some miles between myself and these feelings, I thought as I took off at almost a full sprint.

* * *

Days later, after going for multiple runs and taking many cold showers, I still couldn't shake off the conversation with Sarah. Could I believe some of what she had said? I'd never known her to tell a lie, and she was always so genuine. This would have been a big lie, and to what end? If she hadn't wanted to date me, she could have just said so. No reason to make up an elaborate lie, complete with a light show. That wasn't what it had seemed like either; she liked me as well. She wanted to be with me, but she'd said that I needed to know about The Light first.

Since that night, I had neglected my knee exercises and icing in favoring of killing myself on runs, and I was paying for it. I'd talked to Sharon about all of it, and she seemed to believe Sarah was capable of anything. She'd been texting with Sarah often, as they were now friends and she hadn't found it too far-fetched to think about Sarah having supernatural abilities. In fact, she wanted to talk to Sarah about it, but out of my anger and feelings of betrayal, I begged her not to contact Sarah.

So, here I was on Wednesday morning, staring at my computer, unable to think about work. My knee was hurting, and my sister was mad at me. *What a mess.*

Without truly forming a plan, I drove to the clinic on my lunch break and sat in the parking lot, my eyes moving between the back door and her car. I knew her break was at 12:30 p.m., since we had texted before during that time. I was there by noon, eager to catch a glimpse of her. A fast-food hamburger was sitting next to me as my excuse for leaving the office even though I had a perfectly good lunch in the breakroom fridge.

At 12:32 p.m., Sarah came out the door, letting it close behind her as she lifted her face toward the sun with her eyes closed. A smile spread across her face, and my breath caught in my lungs. She was so beautiful.

The moment passed and she moved toward her car, the smile disappearing as she walked. I knew where she normally parked, so I was down the row a bit to avoid her seeing me. When she backed her car out, I pulled mine forward to follow.

She only drove a few miles and pulled into a park. I pulled in after her but saw that the park and its parking lot weren't nearly as crowded as I needed if I was going to stay hidden. I stopped right inside the entrance as her car drove all the way to the end. She got out and walked toward the lake with her back to me. I pulled into the first parking spot and got out. Sarah stopped and was just gazing out over the water, and I couldn't help but follow.

Dude, this is borderline stalkerish. My thoughts tried to derail me, but my feet seemed determined to go to her.

As I came up to the lake, I turned the corner to follow where she had headed down the path that hugged the shoreline. I stopped abruptly because she was right there, sitting on a bench, watching the water. She had her lunch beside her, but she wasn't eating.

"Hey Mitch," she said, without even looking at me. Just hearing her voice, I could barely speak.

"Is that an ability you have from the light or whatever?" I finally managed to get out.

"Does it matter?" she asked, her voice a mixture of sadness and hurt.

"I guess not."

She didn't say anything in return, just kept watching the water.

"Sarah, you know I care deeply about you," I started.

"Do you?" she asked, with an edge of doubt in her voice. "Do you really care about me?"

"Yes, of course, I do," I replied, sitting on the bench beside her, willing her to look at me.

"But not enough to see past this," she countered.

"It's a lot to see past," I returned a little too quickly, wanting to bite my tongue as soon as the words left my mouth. "But in my defense, Sarah, you've had a long time to come to terms with all of this. For me, it's just a few days old. And from my seat, surely you can see how it all seems just a little . . . out there."

"Yeah, it was probably too soon to tell you." She looked at me and the pain in her eyes pierced my heart. She continued, "I just didn't feel right about waiting any longer."

"Sarah, how am I supposed to believe in this battle I can't even see?" I was worried I would make her angry, but I was also fueled by an annoyance that I couldn't just have what she had. That thought took me off guard.

Wait, do I want what she has?

She was staring at the water, watching the subtle ripples as the wind danced across its surface. She didn't respond for about a minute, but then she spoke softly. "Do you believe in the wind?" she asked, still watching the water.

"Uh, yeah." I replied, not seeing where she was going with this.

"Well, we can't see the wind, but we know it's there. We can feel it on our skin and in our hair. We can see it moving the leaves of the trees. Just because you don't think you see something doesn't discount its reality or its effects. In the same way we see the wind, I can see The Light moving and affecting everything it touches."

"So, do you hate me because I'm questioning something you believe in so strongly?" I was being blunt, but I wanted to know where we stood.

"I don't just believe in it; I live it, every day." When she finally turned to look at me, her eyes had softened somewhat. "I don't hate you because you have questions. I'm just hurt, and I hurt for you in all the things you're missing out on."

"I didn't think I was missing out on anything until I met you." I admitted my confusion to her and myself at the same time.

Her face changed at that statement, and her eyes narrowed.

"What're you afraid of, Mitch?" She wasn't challenging me as much as she was leading me to think.

Now, it was my turn to break my gaze away and look out over the water.

"I used to say nothing, but now..." I paused, watching the water lap onto the sand in front of me. "But now... I'm afraid of losing you. I'm afraid that what you're telling me might be the truth. I'm afraid that you might be some sort of amateur magician," I joked, turning to smile at her. "And I'm afraid of snow skiing."

Sarah smiled at the magician part and chuckled at the skiing comment. I just couldn't keep it a hundred percent serious.

"I was afraid, too, Mitch," she confessed.

"Of skiing?" I deflected with humor once again.

"No," she smiled. "I was afraid of accepting what my mind knew couldn't possibly be true. I got to see the battle up close and personal four years ago. So, my mind could no longer deceive me about what was so obviously true. And in seeing the battle, seeing the alternative to The Light, the Darkness infiltrating all good things, there was only one choice for me."

"If I choose your side, will balls of light come out of my hands too?" I joked again, but I was also slightly curious.

"Not necessarily," she replied with a sly smile.

I couldn't help but return her smile even though we were discussing an unseen battle and light coming from our hands.

"You're one of my few assignments that wasn't already somewhat intrigued by The Light," she shared.

"Wait, what? Assignment?" I asked, taken aback once again.

"Assignment is a weird word, sorry. And you really weren't even one of my assignments." Her cheeks turned pink.

"Explain further, please." I kindly prompted. She just kept dropping bombs on me.

"I wasn't assigned to bring you to The Light or educate you on it. But since we became friends, I stepped into that role as well."

"Just friends, huh?" I inquired, feeling the disappointment keenly at what I'd lost.

"That's up to you, but it's not safe for you to be with me if you're undecided. I want to make sure I'm not putting you in danger."

"Danger from what?" I asked.

"The Darkness," she stated matter-of-factly. Was she talking about nightmares and the boogeyman?

"Can you be more specific? Do you see anything right now?" I asked, looking around.

"I don't see or sense anything right now, but that can change in a moment and it's not safe for me to speak further of these things here."

Fear gripped me at her comment. "Are you sure we're safe?" I questioned.

"Yes, but I need to get back to my patients." She stood up to leave.

"Can we talk again?" I asked, almost desperately.

She studied my face intently, as if trying to figure out exactly what I was wanting. "Sure, but it probably needs to be at the clinic. Don't try to follow me again." She warned with a small smile.

"Oh, you saw that, huh," I muttered, feeling embarrassed.

"I saw you parked at the clinic," she smirked and started to move past me.

"Sarah, wait." I touched her arm.

"What?" she responded at the same time I felt warmth spread into my hand and up my arm.

"Is that the light stuff?" I asked, in wonder at the sensation I felt in my arm.

"Yes, I could tell you felt fear. I was trying to help."

"Thank you," I replied softly, releasing her arm and watching her walk away. As she climbed into her Jeep, I raised my hand in farewell. She gave me a small smile and a wave in return, then pulled out of the parking lot. For the first time in days, I felt hope.

CHAPTER 18

MITCH

THE NEXT FRIDAY EVENING, Sarah and I met after the clinic closed so we could talk. I asked her a number of questions that had stuck with me since our last conversation. She shared with me more about her experience of choosing The Light, contrasted against her sister, Amelia, who had chosen the Darkness. At my prompting, she described in vivid detail the enemies of The Light, the warriors of the Darkness. As the conversation continued, the consequences of choosing the Darkness over The Light became much more apparent.

"Mitch, at some point, we all must choose sides; there's no escaping it. And if you continue walking down the road you're on, it will end in darkness."

After the lake I had felt peace, but this conversation had the opposite effect, breeding fear and even some anger.

I tossed and turned that night, thumping my pillow into submission, trying to get it to agree with me that sleep was what I needed to escape all of this. I knew after being with Sarah twice this week that I truly did love her. But I was still having a hard time with the rest of it— this whole underground-war-right-in-front-of-our-noses thing. Sarah explained that a lot of it was seen. All the wars, abuse, starvation, bullying, eating disorders, divorce, loneliness, her list went on and on. All of it was from the forces of the Darkness, their effects on the world and the humans that embraced and perpetuated that path.

To think I had helped horrible creatures tear someone down when I was mean to them or talked down to them. No. That couldn't be right. I was a good person. I lived with my adult sister, for goodness' sake. But the Mitch I was before meeting Sarah, I had to admit he was kind of a jerk. That Mitch looked out for himself, and for Sharon, and that was about it. I had wanted more, more, more; no success was ever enough. Even the apartments I'd lived in were luxurious by most standards. I could have had a nice house to go along with my nice car, but I hadn't wanted the upkeep.

Okay, maybe I could admit I did participate in some things that would be considered dark in order to get ahead. I felt deep fear in that moment. I didn't want to be something that Sarah would despise, someone who would purposefully harm someone. *I have to change*, I thought as I sat straight up in bed.

But wait, Sarah had told me I could never make myself better. I had to choose The Light, and then The Light would change me.

"Okay, Light, how do we do this?" I asked out loud to my room, hoping desperately for an answer from someone. I suddenly wished I'd asked Sarah more questions on this part, instead of asking questions trying to find a hole in her story.

When no answer came and the minutes ticked by, I laid back down feeling foolish. I'd thought in that moment of declaration I would see something, hear something, be changed somehow, but nothing happened. I rolled over and pounded my pillow again, just for something to do and to try to escape my feelings.

Lying on my side, I saw the same streetlamp out my window. Someone had fixed it so that it no longer flickered, but it was still a great reminder of Sarah and the other world she lived in, or rather the world we all lived in. I felt it in my gut then. This was real, and I wouldn't give up on finding out more about it just because I didn't get the answers I wanted right when I wanted them.

Flopping onto my back, I spoke in the direction of my ceiling, somehow knowing that someone was listening, "I'll wait as long as it takes. I know you're out there. I'll wait as long as it takes."

I said that phrase repeatedly. It echoed in my mind as I felt myself being pulled under into sleep...

"Thank you, Mitch."

"What, who said that?" I asked, startled, sitting straight up. I was still in my room, but it wasn't exactly my room, and I felt fear rise in me.

"I did, my son. Do not be afraid." I swung my head to the left toward my window and saw a man standing there. Seeing someone in my room should have increased my fear, but instead, I only felt relief. He had a soft glow of light around him, and I could see all of him and his features, even though my room was dark. He looked to be in his forties or early fifties, and he had dark brown hair and a beard. His outfit looked like it would have been in style centuries ago, when clothes draped all the way to the floor.

"It's you," I spoke in a soft whisper.

"Yes," he answered.

"Is this real?"

"Yes."

"Really?"

"Yes, Mitch. Your mind is very powerful. Your body still sleeps, but your mind is with me."

I wanted to ask all sorts of questions that I hadn't already peppered Sarah with, but I held back wanting to enjoy this moment more. It was strange; I almost felt like I was learning by just being with him.

"You are," he confirmed my unspoken thought.

"Who..." I started to ask who he was, but I just knew. He was The Light, and he had come to see me, so instead I asked, "What do I call you?"

"Ruah, my son."

"Ruah," I repeated. Just saying his name flooded me with peace.

"We have been waiting for you, Mitch."

"Who's been waiting, The Light?"

"Yes, we have watched and waited," he spoke quietly, but firmly.

"Why didn't you just shake me or slap me upside of the head? It would've gone a lot faster."

"That is not how I work," he said with a smile. "Nothing in The Light is ever forced onto someone, but once you choose to acknowledge The Light in whatever form that takes, we can make ourselves known to you."

"Did you plan for me to meet Sarah?" I was curious how this all worked.

"No, and then again, yes."

"That doesn't make sense." I quickly added, "To me," not wanting to offend him.

"May I sit?" Ruah asked, gesturing to my bed.

"Uh, yeah," I stuttered, never thinking I would sit on my bed with a divine being. I ran my hands through my hair and tried to straighten my shirt.

"Is your appearance bothering you?" Ruah inquired.

"I, uh, just didn't want it to bother or offend you." I was out of my element here.

"Mitch, I love you just the way you are. No need to clean up on my account." His declaration should have made me uncomfortable; I don't think a dude had ever told me he loved me before, and I hadn't even known my biological father. But again, this was just different. I loved to hear that he loved me, and somehow, I loved him as well.

"Should I say I love you, too?" I asked hesitantly.

He smirked and answered, "I think you just did."

I let out a puff of laughter and smiled back at him. He had a sense of humor; I guess I didn't expect that from an all-powerful whatever he was.

"Mitch, can I show you something?"

"Absolutely," I said, feeling excitement at the thought.

Ruah had been looking at me, but now he focused his eyes out the window toward my streetlamp.

"Was that you?" I asked, thinking back to how the flickering streetlamp mesmerized me and lulled me to sleep.

He gave me another smile. He didn't need to answer; of course, it was The Light, subtly trying to get my attention.

"Look with me, Mitch," he instructed, as he put his arm around my shoulders. A sensation like I had never felt before invaded my body. It was like warm honey started spreading from Ruah's touch to every other part of me. I was trying to be cool, but this was the most amazing sensation I'd ever experienced.

I looked at Ruah to tell him, but he wasn't looking at me. He was still looking out the window. I turned my head back to join him, but instead of seeing the darkened street and my streetlamp, I saw the most beautiful landscape I'd ever seen, framed by my window. The vision before me didn't seem real. I saw trees and bushes greener than any green, flowers with colors so vibrant they almost hurt my eyes, and the sweet sounds of nature filling my ears. It was like I was watching all of it on high-definition TV.

"What . . .?" I asked, not even able to finish my question to him because I was too overwhelmed by the feelings in my body and what I was seeing before me.

"Take a walk with me, Mitch."

I didn't even need to know where we were going before I agreed.

Ruah stood and pulled me up with his arm still around me. Together, we took a step toward the window. One more step and we were through the glass and amongst the vision I had seen before me. We didn't have to climb through or anything; in the moment of taking our step, our surroundings changed. I turned my head to look back, but we were surrounded by the lush trees and bushes. My apartment building was gone.

"Walk with me, my son," Ruah said, gently encouraging me with his arm, turning the way he wanted me to go. As we started walking down a path lined with fragrant shrubs, I noticed that his arm didn't feel heavy to me. It was as if the weight of it wasn't there, just the comfort. He was taller and broader than me, but he didn't make me feel small in any way.

Feeling utterly content, we continued in silence as the sounds of this otherworldly place made their way to my ears: the sound of trickling water, birds singing, and the leaves blowing in the gentle breeze. I could smell the heavenly scents from the flowering bushes that we passed. Everything around me was new and full of life.

"Ruah?"

"Yes."

"Where are we?"

"Ganheela, my son." I didn't know what Ganheela was, and he didn't elaborate, but still I was content.

"Am I part of The Light now?"

He smirked at me, but it wasn't condescending as it would have been if I had made the same face. It was comforting, like he was my buddy, and we could joke with each other at the same time we were being very serious.

"Do you want to be?" he asked.

"Of course, I do."

"Yes, Mitch, you are Awakened. You know the truth, and because you called to me, you are now a part of The Light. On Earth, you will be a part of the Eklesi."

"Does it last forever?" I asked softly, never wanting to be separated from Ruah.

"Yes. If you make the choice to follow The Light with all that you are, if your heart is true, it is forever." And then, he answered another unspoken thought, "You won't ever be separated from me."

I took a deep breath, letting that soak in, "So, I'm safe." And in that instant, I finally knew what Sarah meant by safe - not safe from harm, safe from the Darkness and safe from eternal death.

"Yes," he continued, "a part of you will be forever safe in The Light."

"What part of me isn't safe?" I questioned. I didn't feel alarm; I'm sure it had to do with Ruah being close and being in this place together, but I was still curious.

"You are human; your body can still die. But your Spirit, your mind, and your soul will remain safe forever in the Land of the Light."

I nodded, not quite understanding, but liking the sound of what he had said. Another thought occurred to me.

"Yes," Ruah said.

"What?" I asked aloud, since I wasn't sure what he was referring to.

"You were wondering if you were a Light Bearer, like Sarah."

"So, I am?"

"Yes, you are. Sarah and Ethan will see to your training, my son." I wasn't surprised at all that Ethan was also in The Light and that The Light had been their connection. I did feel a little disappointed that Ruah wouldn't be the one training me.

"My son," he said with a power that pulled my eyes to his. "I will be with you every step of the way."

* * *

Opening my eyes, I found I was lying on my left side in my own bed. Out my window, I saw the morning light was just starting to come over the horizon. I sat up on the side of my bed and thought about how Ruah had sat there beside me.

"Was that real?" I asked out loud with my gaze out the window. The streetlamp flickered and then went dark as all its companions did the same. Apparently, there was just enough sunlight for them to shut off for the day. A shudder of thrill ran through me, a good one, one where I felt like Ruah still had his arm around me, and the streetlamp confirmed it.

Normally, on a Saturday, I wouldn't bother getting up until the sun was fully up, but this morning was too wonderful, and I wanted to be out there as the sun rose. I was now a part of The Light. I had asked, and it had happened. I believed with everything in me that my experienced in that place between sleep and waking had changed me forever.

I wanted to call Sarah and talk to her about my dream, but I knew in my excited state, I would just trip over my words and sound like a goof. Sarah wouldn't care, but I knew I needed a run to blow off some energy and just take in all I had seen in my dream, or experience, or whatever it was that had happened to me.

The sun was just making its appearance through the trees as I entered the largest park in the city. It was two miles away from our apartment, but I was in the mood for a long run. I was familiar with that park because it was not far from my old apartment, and Troy and I had often worked out there. I was overwhelmed with the feelings inside me. Grateful and happy and filled with light, I had never felt that great on a run before.

Basking in the glow of the morning and those feelings, I was surprised when another feeling came over me as I crossed one of the many bridges in the park. A sudden unease descended on me as I tried to make out the shadows on the other side. I was so stunned that I came to a complete stop as I almost ran full speed into Troy at the end of the bridge.

"Dude, what's your problem?" I asked angrily. He had totally freaked me out. We hadn't seen each other in weeks, so it was crazy to run into him (almost literally) that morning of all mornings.

"Mitch, buddy. I've been looking for you!" His words sounded forced.

"What are you doing out here in the dark?" I asked, maintaining an angry tone, still on edge from him jumping out in front of me. Suddenly, his face contorted in anger.

"I knew something was different about you!" Troy shouted at me even though we weren't that far apart.

"What're you talking about?" I responded as a cold chill slid its way down my spine.

"You! You changed. I thought we were cool, and we had a good thing going," he said, still angry at me.

The sun was slightly over the tallest trees now, but we were still in shadows. This was bizarre, and I got the feeling Troy wasn't upset with me for leaving him without a roommate or for almost running into him. Something was very wrong about the whole situation.

"What're you talking about, Troy?" I was immediately on high alert.

It was clear Troy was trying to calm himself as he spoke.

"You had to mess it up by moving in with your sister. And now you're all screwed up. Your new friends are bad news, and they're feeding you lies."

Troy's words made my blood run cold. I knew he was lying. I remembered Sarah saying something about how the beings of the

Darkness, Tarobies or something like that, were masters of lying. Maybe Troy was one of those things. Knowing some of what they could do, I decided to play dumb.

"Dude, you're tripping." My words seemed to break through the remainder of his façade.

He cussed at me and spit at the ground. "Who led you to your Awakening?" he growled out.

I was completely caught off guard at this point. I had no idea that Troy would confront me like that. I decided to keep playing dumb. "Awakening? Dude, I have no idea what you're talking about. You're so weird. This is why I moved out in the first place," I said, matching his tone.

"Me, weird? No, man," he proceeded to call me several horrible names, "You're the weird one. Wanting anything to do with The Light." As he said light, he trailed off and his human features began to distort, changing like shadows rolling over one another. It was like his body couldn't make up its mind. With his eyes disturbingly red and focused on me, it was all I could do not to scream like a little girl.

I was frozen; I couldn't run, and I wouldn't give him the satisfaction of screaming. His body was still changing as he kept trying to find a form. Each human form he took was more horrifying than his previous one. Standing there, I knew my words wouldn't get me out of this one as they had so many times before. Could I use The Light that Sarah had shown me? Ruah had said I was a Light Bearer, but I hadn't had any of the training Ruah told me I would get from Sarah and Ethan.

I tried to focus on my palms and attempted to make a light appear. There was a spark in my right palm. I felt excitement but was immediately distracted by Troy. He now looked like my mother had looked as she lay dead on our low-rent apartment floor. It took everything in me to try to make the spark move toward him. As my dead mother's voice called to me, I made a last-ditch effort by turning my palm with the spark toward him and pushing with all that I had.

He was blasted back by light with a scream of agony. I couldn't believe my eyes. I'd done it!

"Mitch!" I turned at hearing Sarah's voice as she ran up behind me. "Are you okay?"

"Wait, was that light that knocked him back you?" I asked, turning to look at Troy writhing on the ground. Sarah raised her hand and shot another blast so that his grotesque form stilled.

"Yes," she said, breathing a little heavy.

"Thank you," I grinned, a little embarrassed that I thought I had blasted Troy, but also relieved she was here.

"My pleasure," she said with the most beautiful smile. I could stare at her forever.

"Wait, how did you know where I was?"

"A dream," she said simply without elaborating.

"You had a dream that I would be here?" I asked in disbelief.

"No, I had a dream that I needed to be here, and when The Light comes into my dreams, I always listen."

"So, Ruah sent you?"

"Yes," she said quickly, then looked at me with eyes filled with questions. "You met Pneuma?"

That threw me off a little. "I met Ruah," I corrected.

"Same thing, he appears as a man to men and a woman to women, for our comfort." She said all this really fast and then continued, "But he came to you?"

"Yes, in a dream or reality or something. It was very real. And Sarah, I'm in The Light."

"You're Awakened?" She asked, with tears welling up in her eyes.

"Yes, I am," I said, feeling overcome. "But it gets better." I barely got the words out with the emotions clogging my throat.

"What?" She asked when I didn't continue.

"I'm a Light Bearer."

* * *

"If people could just see those things, they would run to The Light right away," I said, sure I could never unsee Troy in that state.

"That's exactly why they don't show themselves to humans. It's not good for their cause," Sarah said with some humor in her voice. She had just finished tying Troy up in ropes that looked like they were made of light. When I asked what she was doing, she told me the light ropes would hold him until some of his own kind came to retrieve him. She then stood above him and aimed a light beam at his forehead while explaining this would erase his recent memories so that he wouldn't know to tell anyone about either one of us.

I helped Sarah move Troy off the path, and then she stood, sending gentle light in a beam toward him until he seemed to become almost translucent. I was staring at him intently as he all but disappeared before my eyes. Sarah looked at me and said, "Can't have any kiddos coming to the park and seeing him tied up like this."

"Did you just make him disappear?" I asked in awe.

"No, it's a trick of The Light. We can still see him because we're in The Light, but the light refraction blends him into his surroundings so that others can't seem him."

As we walked back down the path I had taken, I knew I had to say something.

"Sarah, I'm stunned by all that I've been blind to," I said in disbelief. She had come to save me even though I had pretty much called her crazy to her face. I had never stopped loving her, but what she'd said scared me. So instead of admitting my fear, I had tried to make her feel bad about being different.

"We're all blind for a time," she responded kindly.

"Sarah, I'm so sorry for how I talked to you. Can you ever forgive me?"

"I already have. I know that wasn't really you talking. Fear is a powerful thing," she explained.

"How did you know?" I asked without thinking. "The Light," I said to answer myself.

"Yes, and like you, I have been motivated by fear in the past as well."

"That's hard to believe."

"Well, believe it," she said with a soft laugh and some spunk. "So, tell me about this dream of yours."

We walked to her car outside the park while I told her about my dream.

"Do you want a ride?" she asked.

"If I say 'yes,' are you going to think I'm a scaredy cat?" I didn't want to admit it, but the run-in with Troy had spooked me.

"No. Terrobah are terrifying, and you haven't had any training yet. I can almost assure you, Mitch, that another one won't be attacking you anytime soon. But I understand not wanting to be alone after that."

"Then, yes, I would love a ride." She was right, I didn't want to be alone, but I also wanted to be with her.

"Thank you, again, for coming," I said, taking in her workout clothes and hair pulled back into a high ponytail once we were in the car.

"Mitch, you're welcome. Don't think any more of it," she responded as she pulled into traffic.

"How can I not? You came and fought Troy like he . . . like it was nothing."

She shrugged in response.

"It was nothing for you, wasn't it?" I had a lot to learn.

She took a deep breath.

"Don't worry. I won't scare off so easily this time," I assured her, sensing her apprehension to tell me more.

"Actually, I've faced Troy before. I just didn't know he was your roommate. It was in a cave I'd been led to where my sister had been held. He was there with a few other Terrobah when I arrived, only to discover that she'd already been moved. Even though Troy was the leader then, he's still one of the weaker Terrobah I've encountered."

"There was more than one?" I asked, raising my eyebrows and my voice in unison. I thought back to Troy's book of knives and shuddered.

"I've faced much stronger Terrobah and many at the same time." She said this with no apparent pride; she was just stating the facts.

"And here you are, which means you won." There was some pride in my voice for her.

"True, but I always have help."

"Ruah?"

"Yes, and many, many friends," she said with a smile.

"Ethan's one of those, huh?" I said more as a statement than a question. I finally understood her and Ethan's relationship.

"Yes," she confirmed, gifting me with one of her brilliant smiles.

I directed her to my apartment.

"Should we tell Sharon?" she asked me. She was literally glowing, and it took my breath away. She was being fully herself in front of me, and she was so beautiful. I had called her my sunshine before because of how she figuratively glowed with life. On this day, she was actually glowing.

Wait, what had she asked me?

"What?" I asked, feeling like a doofus.

"Should we tell Sharon?" she asked again.

"Tell her what?" I was still lost.

If it was possible, her smile grew even bigger, "Everything!"

CHAPTER 19

SARAH

"Are you doing okay, Sharon?" I asked her from my chair. I was across the living room from where she and Mitch were sitting on the couch. She'd been quite surprised to see me walk in following Mitch, but she had quickly recovered with a squeal as she ran out of the kitchen to come give me a hug.

"Yes," she responded, "it's all so much to take in, but it's beautiful and wondrous. There really aren't words to describe it all. I'm excited!" She said all this very quickly as she gently bounced on the couch.

I gave her a warm smile. My enthusiasm was just as strong as hers, but mine manifested in a different way. I was literally glowing while we discussed The Light, but neither Sharon nor Mitch seemed alarmed by it. I had safeguarded their apartment when we had come in so that we could talk freely about all things of The Light.

Mitch waited until I confirmed it was safe before telling Sharon about his dream. She responded by saying that she'd wanted The Light ever since he had told her about it; that was why she wanted to contact me. I could tell Mitch felt bad about keeping her from it, but she brushed it aside, excited that she could finally see me and talk to me about it now.

"So, I can be a part of The Light, too?" Sharon asked, pulling me back into the conversation.

"You're already Awakened, Sharon. I wouldn't be surprised if Pneuma came to see you soon to tell you that you're a Light Bearer."

"What?!" she gasped in excitement, "Really?"

"Really! You were already strong before and now, with The Light, you're even stronger."

Her excitement bubbled over causing her to jump up and down excitedly. I'd never seen this reaction in someone I had helped walk into The Light, and I couldn't help but laugh with joy. Mitch joined us, and it was a moment I would never forget.

"Let's go to my house! I want you to meet Nyiah, and I'll have Ethan meet us there as well."

Sharon squealed again, "Just when I thought it couldn't get any better!" She had pulled Mitch to his feet, and they were dancing around together.

"Can I just get a quick shower first?" Mitch asked. "I'm still a bit of a mess from the run."

"Oh, if you must." I rolled my eyes at him, but I was also overcome with tenderness for him as I saw The Light shining out through his eyes.

"It's a must," he assured me, winking as he passed me to walk down the hallway.

Sharon squealed again, drawing my attention back to her. "I'm so sorry about the middle-school-girl screams. I just can't seem to contain it."

"No need to apologize. I'm loving your response, Sharon. It's so fun, and I know Pneuma is loving it as well."

"I love Pneuma. I think I've heard her before. I feel stronger just getting to acknowledge all the stuff about The Light. I feel more . . . free. I'm know I'm in The Light forever; it's amazing!"

She had moved close to grab my hands, "So, does this mean you and Mitch are back together?" she asked conspiratorially.

It was such a contrast, her loud excited words and her quiet secretive voice. "I'm not sure," I whispered in return. "We haven't talked about us yet. It's just so great to see you both in The Light. A new relationship with The Light is a lot to take in, and I'm happy to wait while he enjoys it."

Again, she squealed, which caused both of us to resume laughing. She pulled me in for another hug, and I gladly returned it.

"Oh, I felt The Light! I love it!" Sharon squealed, and I laughed at her merriment. We released each other as she literally skipped down the hallway yelling over her shoulder, "Let me just get my stuff!"

"Thank you," I said out loud to Pneuma.

My pleasure, Sarah Joy, sounded in my head, and my smile literally stretched across my face.

✳ ✳ ✳

"So, Mitch," Ethan said, leaning back comfortably in his chair on the back patio. "Are you ready for some training?"

We had enjoyed the delicious feast that Nyiah had cooked up while we told our different stories. I loved getting to watch my four friends interact and grow to care so much about each other in the few short hours we'd been together. Mitch really enjoyed telling the story of that morning and how I had saved him. While he told it, his eyes often found mine. The depths of his feelings were so clear in his eyes that the blush still hadn't left my cheeks, even though we'd moved on to other topics.

"Yes!" Sharon squealed. "Sorry, I know I'm not a Light Bearer yet, but I would love to see it!"

Mitch added, "Absolutely. Sarah won't always be able to come to my rescue." The blush deepened.

Ethan sat up. "Excellent!" he exclaimed, rubbing his hands together. Since he'd returned from Ganheela, he was a force to be reckoned with, and I couldn't wait to see what he would show them first. "Sarah, would you please assist me?"

"It would be my honor," I said, returning his formal request with some formality of my own.

"Let's talk defense," Ethan instructed. In a flash, he had his helmet in place, his shield on his arm, and his forcefield glowing around him.

Mitch and Sharon's eyes lit up, and a gasp slipped out of Sharon's mouth. Back at their apartment, I had brought light into my palms to show her a little of what I could do with The Light, but this was something else entirely. Sharon didn't know it, but the fact that she could see Ethan's armor confirmed she was a Light Bearer. It wasn't my place to tell her though; Pneuma had that honor.

"A blast, if you please, Sarah, but take it easy on me," he said, with a wink and a smirk. Since he had trained in Ganheela, he didn't need me to take it easy on him, but he still liked to joke with me.

With a flourish, I brought light into my palm and then sent it in a ball toward Ethan. Since I was using light, it just absorbed into his shield, not causing him harm or exploding, but still giving Mitch and Sharon a general idea of how we could make the light behave.

"That was a little anticlimactic," Ethan said with a smirk.

"Well, I can't hurt you. Light versus light just makes more light."

"You could hurt me if you really wanted to." I looked at him trying to decipher the hidden message I knew he was sending me.

"But I don't want to," I said back, giving him an opening to explain.

"I know," he said simply. I rolled my eyes at him.

"Again?" I asked.

"Again," he confirmed.

We trained and snacked until it was late. It was one of the best days I'd had since returning from Ganheela. Mitch was able to produce his shield, but the pulses were still difficult for him. He was only able to generate a spark in his hand that dwindled quickly. A little defeated, he had grown quite embarrassed at his abilities until Ethan started telling stories about trying to chase his spark around when I'd been training him. We all ended up laughing together, and I was thankful for Ethan's intervention as I didn't have personal stories of my own like that to tell.

I'd gained proficiency with all the skills of a Light Bearer from the beginning. Even in Ganheela, Ethan hadn't improved as quickly and still wasn't at the level that I had attained. I knew I was special in that way and didn't want to make Mitch feel bad. Sharon had tried harnessing The Light as well. She could keep it in her arms so that they glowed, almost like her physical body was a light weapon. She didn't have to imagine a shield for it to form; her skin was her light shield.

By the time Nyiah and I walked the other three to the door, Sharon had calmed her squeals and was radiating The Light and beauty and walking more confidently than I'd ever seen her. We ended the evening by setting a time to get together the next day for more training.

"Well, that was fun," Nyiah said, plopping on the couch next to me.

"It really was," I agreed.

"And two more Light Bearers. That's thrilling!"

"I know, I'm so grateful," I replied, still overwhelmed by it all.

"It was because of you, you know."

"I don't know about that," I argued back.

"I do," she sassed, causing me to smile.

I was completely at peace in that moment. I leaned my head on my best friend's shoulder and just savored the gift.

* * *

MITCH

What a day! I was staring at my ceiling, replaying in my mind everything I had witnessed and been a part of in the last 24 hours. Was it just the previous night when I met Ruah in my dream? Was it just that morning when I found out Troy was a Terrobah? I mean I knew he was a messed-up ; I just didn't know how bad.

And Sarah, wow. She was everything I thought and more. We'd shared some sweet glances, and she had blushed more than once. I was getting everything I wanted and more, but I had this feeling that it wasn't my time with Sarah yet. I didn't like that feeling and I wanted to ignore it, but The Light called to me so strongly. I was nervous in front of her earlier that day, worrying about what she would think of me compared to Ethan, that I couldn't even perform the simplest of tasks.

I wasn't normally a nervous person, but everything since I had met Sarah was so far from normal, I couldn't even tell you what normal was anymore.

As we had walked out, Ethan offered to train with me on my own without the girls. "It might be easier for you to concentrate," he had said kindly. He was the bigger man. I had felt I was in a competition with Ethan in the past, but he was clearly on my side and wanted to help me improve. Maybe I should only focus on training and The Light for the time being.

I wanted to give up my job and all the other stuff that seemed like nonsense compared to what I knew in The Light, but Nyiah had explained that it was important for those around us to see us working at our jobs with good attitudes and treating others well so they might also experience The Light through us.

It was clear to me there were Terrobists and Terrobah everywhere, including at my work. The people I worked with, the people many of us worked with, were unaware of this battle between The Light and the Darkness. So even though it felt like we weren't really fighting the fight, we had to go about our daily lives, interacting with those who weren't yet Awakened. We were their best hope of finding The Light and not being overcome by the Darkness.

There were other ways, of course, that The Light could reach humans, but it was clear through my and Sharon's experience that encountering a person of The Light made all the difference.

I rolled to my side and saw that my clock showed 1:37 a.m. I groaned, stretching and rolling to my other side, feeling how desperately my body needed the rest, when my streetlamp caught my eye.

"Hey, Ruah," I said toward the streetlamp, knowing he could always hear me but wouldn't always respond. To my amusement, the streetlamp flickered, and I felt more than heard. *Rest, my son.*

* * *

The next morning, the sun, already high in the sky, woke me up to see I was missing out on the day. I was still lying on my left side and felt stiff, like I hadn't moved all night. I stretched, reaching my limbs to the four corners of my queen-sized bed, groaning at the good feelings as I worked out the kinks.

After using the bathroom and splashing some cold water on my face, my stomach growled its interest in the delicious smells coming from the kitchen, and I made my way there.

"Good morning, sleepy head," Sharon called to me.

"Good morning," I returned, my voice still rough from not being used. She was still overjoyed this morning, so I opened my arms, and she came in for a hug.

While we held each other, she whispered, "Did yesterday really happen?"

I laughed as I released her, "It sure did!"

"It's unreal."

"Yeah," I agreed.

I knew what I had heard and seen was real, yet an hour later I was texting Sarah the same question.

"Yes, Mitch, it's all real! Are you freaked out?" Came her text reply.

"No," I paused, trying to find the right words to describe what I was feeling. "I'm in awe."

Sarah texted back, "That's a good place to be."

"How long does it last?" I typed back to her.

"A while, then it comes and goes as circumstances change and hard things come up."

"What hard things have you faced?" I quickly replied, eager to know what might be in my future.

"Stuff with my family."

"Are they LBs?" I wasn't sure how much I should put in a text and if the Terrobah could somehow intercept it.

"Most were."

"Were?"

"I told you I didn't have much family."

"So, who's left?" Each text was taking longer and longer for her to send a reply.

"My aunt, we rescued her from the T two months ago. She's an LB."

Her reply confirmed I had made a good choice to use initials. "Anyone else?" I asked.

When she didn't respond for five minutes, I started to worry. She wasn't always great about responding to texts right away anyway so that normally wouldn't alarm me, but since we had been having a sensitive conversation, I felt the need to check.

"Sarah?" I pressed send, then saw those helpful bubbles appear to tell me she was typing.

"My sister," popped up on my screen, confirming my concerns.

"Where is she?" I pressed for more details.

The bubbles appeared, then vanished, then reappeared again. "With them."

* * *

Sarah's last text echoed in my head while I went about my morning. That afternoon and evening, all five of us trained together and shared dinner again, but I didn't say anything to Sarah about her sister, knowing she probably preferred if I didn't.

The next day, after work, I met up with Ethan for some training, just the two of us. His house was a lot like the girls' in the way of protection. It was smaller and clearly housed a single man, not many decorations, but still comfortable. He had something the girls didn't have in their house, though: a training room. He told me the girls always trained in their yard, but for some reason he liked the feel of working out and training in a gym. He taught me a lot and even told me about some of his time in Ganheela.

Even with all that new information, I still couldn't get Sarah's last text out of my head, "With them." Those two words had never stricken such fear and despair in me as they did when they appeared on my phone. We had signed off shortly after, with me saying a pitiful "I'm sorry," and her saying she had to go.

"Ethan, can I ask you something?"

He grinned at me. I'd been asking him one question after another the whole time we'd been training, so he was probably wondering why I had to ask if I could ask another one.

"It's about Sarah."

"Go ahead. I'll answer if I can," he said as he rigged up a training dummy.

"Where's her sister?"

His face fell and his posture slumped slightly. "We don't know."

"What?"

"We don't know where she is," he continued.

"But doesn't Ruah know all; can't he just tell you?"

"It doesn't really work like that. You can't just demand answers from Ruah."

"He answers most of the things I ask," I replied, not proudly, but more out of confusion.

"I know, and he delights to answer you, but this is tricky." He paused for a moment, collecting his thoughts. "The last time Ruah, or Pneuma in Sarah's case, told her where Amelia was, she disobeyed Pneuma and went alone. Sarah almost died. Ruah isn't governed by our wants or wishes but reveals information as it's needed. We can't force or demand things from Ruah. He shows us in the wisdom of his timing. In time, Pneuma will tell Sarah where her sister is."

"How long has Amelia been with them?" I pushed for more information.

"You can say Terrobah here, Mitch, we're safe."

"How long has she been with the, uh," I had to clear my throat. Ethan grinned. "The, uh... Terrobah." It was hard for me to say the word because of what it represented.

"Since Sarah became a Light Bearer, almost five years," he said with pain in his voice.

"What?! Wow, so she's a Terrobabist or whatever?"

"Terrobist, yes," Ethan corrected me.

"So that means we can still win her back?" I was feeling a little hope for Sarah's sister.

Nyiah had given Sharon and me a history lesson of sorts, explaining all the different forces and beings we were up against. The Darkness was against The Light. Ruah was The Light and then at the same time a separate being. (I didn't quite understand that part yet.) We were now part of a group called the Eklesi, and we were in a battle against the Terrobah. The Terrobah were supernatural beings on the same level as the Mythreal beings, whom I had yet to meet.

"We don't know," Ethan's whispered comment brought my eyes up from the mat to his.

"I thought Nyiah said that we could win them back," I quickly countered.

"There's always hope, but from what Sarah saw in her sister the last time they faced each other, it will take a whole lot of The Light and truth for us to win her back."

"What did she see?" My mind couldn't imagine what she might have seen to draw such a conclusion.

"That's probably all I should tell you without Sarah's permission."

"And Sarah almost died?" I kept pressing.

"Yes."

"I kind of felt like Sarah was indestructible."

"She's still human and as mortal as the rest of us, but from what I know from Ruah, she is the strongest Light Bearer that has ever been seen."

"Then how did she almost die?"

"At the hands of her sister." Ethan delivered the comment in such a way that I knew the conversation was over.

CHAPTER 20

MITCH

"Let's grab dinner out tonight," I suggested when Sharon answered my call on my way home on the following Friday. I was still having trouble with the fact that Sarah's sister had tried to kill her after Sarah had spent five years searching for her. It made me want to cherish the sister I had even more.

"You read my mind," she replied. "I've been so distracted these last few days that I forgot to go to the grocery." I could hear in her voice the constant smile that was on her face.

"Okay, let's meet at that little sushi place."

"Sounds great," she agreed. "I'll see you there!"

After we stuffed ourselves with delicious sushi, we left the restaurant and decided to walk for a bit before heading home.

"Are you going to keep training with Ethan by yourself?" she asked, continuing our conversation.

"I think I will, maybe not every time, but I've made a lot of progress with him. I was finally able to send a blast at a dummy last night. It fizzled before it reached him, but still. I even got to see some flashes of my sword," I said, looking at her with excitement. "It was so cool."

We laughed at my excitement.

"I can't wait to try again." Sharon returned, her voice filled with anticipation. "I'm wondering if it's only my arms, or if I can do the same thing with my legs and body. If I'm picked, I feel like I'm supposed to train in martial arts."

"Picked?"

"Well, P, you know, hasn't visited me like she did you, so I'm not sure I'm, you know, like the rest of you."

"You have to be, you can bear..."

"Hey guys." We were deep in conversation about whether Sharon was a Light Bearer, but our heads whipped up at that voice.

"Troy," I said, feeling a rock in my gut. "What's up, dude?" I asked, hoping my voice maintained a casual tone.

"Nothing much. Me and my bros were just having a night out on the town." He gestured to the two guys with him. The hair on the back of my neck stood on its end.

"Yeah, us too." I used that as an excuse to put my arm around Sharon's shoulders and pull her closer; I could feel her shaking.

"How's it going, living together?" he asked with a weird smile, I'm sure making fun of us. That was the least of my concerns at that moment.

"Good," I responded, giving Sharon another squeeze, but not taking my eyes off Troy. "Did you find a new roommate?" It was weird to talk to someone when he was twenty feet away, but neither one of us was willing to bridge the gap.

"Yep, one of my old buddies moved to town. I had an accident, and he came to help me get back on my feet." I knew exactly what he was talking about. Not even a week ago, Sarah had dropped him with one blast of light in the park near our old apartment. She'd said he would be tortured for failing. I never expected to see him standing in front of me only a week later. He was looking at me strangely as well. He had been friendly at first, but suddenly he was looking at me like he was confused.

"Oh, I hate to hear that," I said, trying to distract him, "Obviously, I know what it's like to be down, but you seem to be good now."

"Yeah," he agreed, but his eyes had narrowed to slits. I was guessing he could sense we had The Light.

"Well, we're actually running late to meet some of our friends. Why don't you text Ethan to let him know," I said to Sharon, who quickly reached for her purse. "Good to see you, buddy." I gave him a wave with my free hand as I turned us back up the sidewalk. All I could think about was getting away from him before he transformed and scared Sharon to death.

"Can't you stay a little longer, *buddy*?" he asked, and I could hear the sarcasm dripping from his words.

I looked around me, and as I turned back toward him, I shielded Sharon from his gaze by stepping in front of her. The street was deserted; we must have walked farther than I realized. "No, sorry, man. Our friends are expecting us, and we didn't realize what time it was. We were just going to head to the car when we ran into you."

"Really, Mitch, I insist you stay. We need to catch up." All the words were nice, but his tone made his evil intentions clear.

"Try to do the helmet," I whispered to Sharon. "No, we need to *go*." I said forcefully to Troy, which caused him and his buddies to flinch. In my mind, I saw them running away in fear, but instead it appeared that I'd only angered them as they started moving toward us.

"Go," I said to Sharon with a shove, and she started backing away from me with fear on her face. "Run," I said with force. She immediately turned and ran.

Troy and his goons were already on me. Troy had my throat and the other two had my arms.

"Leave us alone!" I thundered with my voice. They flinched again, but kept ahold of me, their touch searing my skin.

I screamed in pain.

"You *are* one of them," Troy ground out, half in astonishment and half in anger.

"What's the matter, Troy, having trouble with your memory?" I had no idea why I was trying to rile him up further. My arms were already in agony, but I just couldn't let him have the upper hand.

"What did you do to me?" Troy spat out.

"Nothing."

"Then, how do you know about my memory?" I thought about Sarah and how she had said the Terrobah hunted her. I resolved in that moment not to give him any more information in case it would lead back to Sarah. My silence enraged him even more as his face contorted and he slugged me in the stomach.

"Oh good, little sis is back," Troy commented in a way that made my skin crawl.

"Sharon," I whispered.

"She was easy to catch. I don't think she's one of them," one of Troy's friends said as he held her arms tightly behind her. Pain ran across Sharon's face at that. Even though she was a captive and very afraid, I knew she would rather be a Light Bearer than not.

Ruah, help us.

My silence sent Troy into a bigger rage, and I thought for sure he would transform right there just like he did in the park. But as he started to shift with the Darkness, I felt a surge of light come over me that made my captor scream in pain as my shield expanded around me. Mine was still more of a dome, a lot less form fitting than Sarah's and Ethan's, but it still made him let go.

"Turn that off or she dies," Troy growled out at me.

I didn't turn it off, knowing that Ruah would send help.

Troy nodded at the guy holding Sharon. In a flash, his arm changed to something grotesque with a claw that wrapped around Sharon's throat. I dropped my shield instantly, but he didn't release her.

"Let her go!" I demanded.

Troy's other friend's hands restrained me quickly as they, too, were exchanged for claws and securely locked onto my arms while Troy had his hands around my neck. They wouldn't allow me any movement toward her. Sharon's captor had now fully changed into a monster and was lifting Sharon by the throat with her feet dangling off the ground, her eyes filled with panic. I tried to summon The Light into my arms, but seeing Sharon like that and with the Terrobah in their other forms, my efforts seemed ineffective. That despicable creature was squeezing harder, and I could tell Sharon was struggling to breathe. I thrashed uselessly against my two captors. With Troy right in front of me, I felt a surge of The Light come through me once again.

"Sharon," I gasped out. "Don't let him win, fight…" was all I got out before Troy's hands tightened around my throat until no air could escape.

She closed her eyes and almost seemed to relax. Dark spots started dancing before my eyes, but I could still see her head and throat as they started to glow with a light so intense that her captor had to let go. Sharon turned and struck him with her glowing fist, knocking him backwards. Air rushed into my burning throat as Troy released me to move toward her. Sharon turned and delivered a left hook with light that sent him reeling to the ground. He got up quickly, though, and I saw The Light in her flicker a bit as fear replaced it. I couldn't let her fight him alone.

Feeling the coldness of the scales wrenching my arms, I focused on forming a pulse of light and sent it hard behind me, eliciting a scream of pain from my captor as he released me.

Troy was enraged, and the other two creatures were getting up. We'd gotten free, but we were so new at this I knew we couldn't possibly win.

"Help!" I screamed, and before the word made it all the way out of my mouth, I heard sirens wailing.

"We gotta get out of here," one of the goons said in disgust.

"Then run, little man. Run away." Again, I had no idea why I was trying to antagonize him.

"Don't...call...me...that...," he spat.

The other guys had returned to their human forms and were running. "I'll be seeing you again," I yelled out. Troy growled with a menacing glare and then turned and fled as the first cop pulled to a stop at the curb right where we were.

"Are you folks, okay?" he shouted as he quickly jumped out of his car.

"Yes, officer, but they're getting away," Sharon pointed after them, the fear still very much in her voice.

"The assailants have fled on foot," he spoke into the radio affixed to his shoulder. He gave our location and the direction Troy and the other Terrobah were headed. Then, we saw two more police cars fly past us on the road in hot pursuit.

The officer, and his partner who had gotten out of the car more slowly, came toward us.

"Are you sure you're okay?" He asked more toward Sharon than to me. She had tears streaming down her face. I moved to wrap her in my arms.

"I'm Officer Cory Tanner, and this is Officer Jacobs. Can you tell me what happened here? We got a report that a couple was being attacked by three men."

"That's true officer, except we aren't a couple. This is my sister," I responded. "Shh, Shari, it's okay, we're okay."

"Do you know what they wanted?" Officer Tanner continued.

I wasn't prepared for that question. "I think they were out for some fun, but they tried to take her, and when I wouldn't let them, it seemed like they were probably going to kill us both."

"Did you know any of them or was this random?"

"One man, sir, Troy Brown. He used to be my friend and roommate."

"So, he had feelings for your sister?"

"Yes," I said, immediately causing Sharon to look up at me. She was probably wondering if I was telling a lie. I wasn't. Troy had wanted to ask Sharon out, but I'd warned him off since I knew he was a player. It was now apparent that my reluctance stemmed from other reasons as well.

"Okay, well, an ambulance is on the way," Officer Tanner informed us.

"No, no, I'm fine, I don't need an ambulance," Sharon insisted, shaking her head and pushing away from my arms.

"Ma'am, it's protocol. You were attacked, and I'm not able to make the call that you're well enough to make your way home. You need a medical evaluation."

I watched as Sharon tried to pull herself together enough to convince this officer she was okay. She'd never feared the hospital or doctors before, so I wasn't sure why she was adamant about not going.

"But really, I'm okay physically." She lifted her eyes to find skeptical faces on both officers and me as well. "Really, I'm good." She took a steadying breath, nodding her head at me, wanting me to agree.

"Sharon," I started, but she cut me off.

"I just want to see Sarah," she said softly to me. I knew the officers could hear her, but she was talking softly so that I could understand her meaning behind it. She didn't want the help of mere humans when we had friends in The Light that would make sure she was okay after everything we had experienced.

I was initially in agreement with her, but then I saw the burns on her arms and neck. "Shari, we'll see Sarah soon, but maybe they can look you over just in case." She wasn't happy with me. I turned to the police officer. "Officers, is there any way we could sign off saying we refused care?"

Officer Tanner looked at me like I had gone crazy. "You clearly aren't okay, sir, and your sister is shaken up." I'm sure I looked like a mess, but Sharon was right, the best place for us was with our fellow Light Bearers.

"I know, you're right, we are, but we have a friend that's a doctor, and we would prefer to go see her."

He nodded, seeming to understand us a little better. "You can talk to the paramedics about that; they'll know better what to recommend," he tipped his head toward the sound of an approaching siren in the distance. "They'll have a form for you to sign if you still refuse treatment."

"Okay, we'll sign whatever they need us to sign and then go see our friend." I looked at Sharon to see if she agreed. She nodded her reply.

"Alright," the officer said, still looking at me a little funny. Clearly most people who had survived an assault didn't refuse care. "Let's talk more about what happened, and I'll need any details about Troy Brown that you can give me."

"Absolutely, sir." I agreed. "Thank you, officers, you just saved our lives. Please don't think we aren't extremely grateful."

"Yes, thank you so much, you got here just in time," Sharon said, her voice still shaky.

That seemed to ease some of the strained lines on his face, and he replied, "Glad we got here in time."

Tires screeched next to us and then we heard our names. It was Sarah, Nyiah, and Ethan all running toward us. Ethan made it to Sharon first and he wrapped her up in a hug. "I was so worried," he said into her hair.

I opened my arms for Sarah, and I felt her shaking. "I'm okay," I assured her. Ethan had released Sharon for Nyiah to move in, and he came to wrap both of us up in a hug. "We're okay," I told them both. "These officers arrived just in time."

✳ ✳ ✳

SARAH

Why hadn't Pneuma called me?

That question echoed repeatedly in my head as Mitch and Sharon refused treatment from the paramedics (the healing burns were hard to explain), retrieved their cars, and drove back to Nyiah's and my house.

We were now sitting in the living room after we'd healed what was left of their burns. But as I listened to Sharon and Mitch tell us about their evening of running into Troy and the two other Terrobah, I was angry. They'd barely found out about The Light, and from what they'd told me, they had faced some high-level Terrobah.

I was shocked that Troy was out and walking around so fast after I had disabled him and left him in the park. And he hadn't been able to transform, which meant what? That he was still being punished? They couldn't move outside of time, like creatures of The Light, and I knew there hadn't been enough time for any sort of punishment to take place at the Terrobah headquarters.

I got up to move around the room; I couldn't just sit when I was this agitated.

"Mitch," I said in the next moment of quiet, trying to get more questions answered.

"Yeah?"

"Where exactly were you guys walking?" He told me the name of the street and the sushi restaurant where they had eaten dinner.

"That's right by the park." I returned, as I paused my pacing to focus on the chilling realization growing in my mind.

"Yeah, it is, why does that matter?" he asked me, trying to discern the cause of my worry.

"They were trying to track us from the park," I stated, as I came to that realization.

"Is that even possible?" Mitch questioned.

"Yes, but once we were at my car, they would have lost the trail. It may have just been a coincidence and they were just patrolling that area, but it still concerns me."

"What are you thinking?" Ethan asked, coming to stand next to me with his arms crossed.

"I erased Troy's recent memories. There should have been no reason for him to feel threatened upon seeing Mitch and Sharon," I trailed off.

"But couldn't he have just picked up on The Light once he came across them?" Ethan questioned.

"I guess so." My thoughts consumed me.

"Sarah, what's really bothering you about all of this?" Ethan questioned.

"Why didn't she send one of us?" I blurted out, my eyes filling with tears. "They're newly Awakened and untrained. One of us should've been there."

"I've been wondering that myself," he agreed quietly. "Since Sharon sent me the text."

"I called for help," Mitch added, bringing my eyes to his, pain gripping my chest as I saw the bruises on his neck and thought about what they had faced alone. "I called for help, and it came."

"What?" I asked in confusion.

"As soon as I called for help, we heard the police sirens," Mitch responded.

"So, Ruah still sent someone," Ethan summed up.

"Yeah," Mitch agreed.

"He sent someone that would make them return to their form without giving any of us away," Ethan said, processing out loud.

"Pneuma was protecting all of us at the same time," Nyiah added.

I sat down hard on the couch, knowing what they said was true, but it still felt awful.

"Sarah, we're okay," Sharon consoled, moving to sit beside me and touch my hand. She was comforting me when it should have been the other way around.

"I know. I thank The Light for protecting you."

And I did. I was so very thankful, but maybe my pride had been wounded. When any sort of battle was going on in our general vicinity, I was called upon. I felt like the guardian of this area in a way, but I wasn't really. That was The Light's job. I knew all that, but I was also wrecked emotionally because I'd once again come close to losing people I cared about to the Terrobah.

"Sarah, are you okay?" Ethan asked, his eyes searching for the truth.

"Yeah, I'm just being enlightened to even more truths about myself and The Light," I said, dropping my gaze.

"What truths are those?" Nyiah asked.

"That The Light is still The Light, Pneuma is all powerful, and I'm... not." I didn't want to question Pneuma, that felt like Darkness, but she had always allowed me to ask my questions. I felt that I should be able to control my emotions by now, knowing that Pneuma always worked in good, in light, in truth. If she did something or didn't do something, that was right and good, no matter what my perception was.

"I may be new at this, but I kinda thought we already knew that?" Mitch teased, smirking at me.

I gave a small laugh, feeling some of the tension drain away, "We do. I do. But I sometimes have to learn the same truth repeatedly before it sticks."

"Don't we all," agreed Nyiah.

"Is that all, Sarah?" Ethan prompted.

"I'm just not sure I can take another loss," I whispered past the emotion in my throat, my eyes welling up again.

"Well, you don't have to. We're right here," Sharon assured me, still holding my hands as she sat beside me. I looked up to see Mitch's caring gaze on me.

I squeezed Sharon's hands and said, "I'm sorry, you guys. You came here for comfort, and I haven't been very comforting."

"Just being here is comforting," Sharon reassured me. My heart turned over at her sweetness, and I pulled her in for a hug, trying to give her as much of The Light as I could.

Ethan kept his eyes on me while the conversation continued in the room around Sharon and I. Sharon was so relaxed that I thought she had fallen asleep on my shoulder, when she suddenly gasped and sat straight up. Her eyes were open, but it was clear she wasn't seeing any of us or the room around her. I looked to Nyiah with a question in my eyes, but she wasn't looking at me. She was staring straight at Sharon with a look of concentration on her face.

Nyiah's concentration broke suddenly, and a huge smile came across her face. She turned her radiant face to me and spoke, "It's Pneuma; Sharon's a Light Bearer."

I was overjoyed for Sharon, and I couldn't help the happy tears that filled my eyes at another Light Bearer joining our ranks, especially one I already loved so dearly.

"I haven't ever seen or heard of it happening this way," Nyiah said, "but what a gift that we all get to share in it with her."

"What is that?!" Mitch asked in alarm, as we quickly looked at him and then followed his gaze back to his sister. There was light visibly flowing through her. It was pulsing down from her head in branches like blood vessels and nerves. She had a beautiful smile on her face, so we knew she wasn't in pain, but this was something none of us had witnessed before. We could even see The Light shining through her clothing as it continued pulsing over and over again.

"Her gift," Nyiah whispered, "I knew her arms were just the beginning."

"What is it, Nyiah?" Ethan asked in alarm.

"It's nothing to worry about, Ethan. The Light is bestowing an extra gift upon Sharon. I'm getting the sense that she was a protector from the time she was small." She looked to Mitch for confirmation.

"Yeah, she always protected me. From our mom's boyfriends and even when we entered the system. She's always fought for those who were weaker," he said, his voice breaking with emotion. "She changed though . . . with her fiancé. He had her all twisted up in lies and feeling small."

"Wow!" Sharon exclaimed as our eyes turned back to her. We'd all been so caught up in what Mitch was sharing, we didn't realize she'd come out of her vision and was focused back on the room. The electrical streams of light were no longer working their way down her body, but she was glowing.

"Wow is right," Ethan returned, in awe of her.

"Sharon, tell us what you saw." Nyiah encouraged, pulling Sharon to come and sit beside her on the couch.

"Well first of all, I'm a Light Bearer," she confirmed proudly and gave one of her signature squeals.

CHAPTER 21

SARAH

WEEKS PASSED WITHOUT ANY trace of Troy, even though Ethan and I had tried to track him like he'd tracked us. He wasn't at the apartment that he used to share with Mitch, and every other trail we followed went cold.

For an extra measure of protection, Sharon moved in with Nyiah and me, and Mitch moved in with Ethan. They hated to inconvenience us, but with Troy now knowing what they were, we just couldn't risk them returning home.

We trained Sharon and Mitch more than we had trained any other new Light Bearer before, not only because of their encounter with Troy, but also because Ethan, Nyiah, and I had felt a greater urgency to have them prepared for what was to come. All three of us had different dreams about a major battle, not a direct call from Pneuma to go and fight, but more like a foreshadowing of what was to come, so we could all be ready.

I even cut back on my bi-weekly visits to Aunt Letta. She understood why, and we still made it a priority to talk on the phone every week. In one of those calls, she told me she had a special visitor. A Mythreal named Brandon, whom she'd met in Ganheela, came as a tangible presence of The Light whenever the Darkness seemed to threaten her again. With the knowledge that she was struggling, I wanted to be with her, but I knew my place for the time being was with my friends, and Pneuma was taking care of her through Brandon.

Mitch was coming along at a good pace, but it was Sharon that really shone, literally. She was able to bring forth The Light in any capacity and at any time. She actually struggled more with concealing The Light than with bearing it. It was as hard for her to restrain it as it was for Mitch to bring it forth. But they were both advancing.

Mitch often commented that it was hard to go to work when there was real work to be done for a much greater good. He understood the reasons that we all had to continue in our normal lives but still seemed to struggle with not just chucking it all to hunt down Terrobah on a daily basis. We could all certainly empathize with that feeling, as we'd all been there many times, but we had to keep him reigned in just the same.

Every day, The Light gave us more insight into Sharon's gift. It seemed that she was constantly shielding. There seemed to be no part of her that a Terrobah's arrow would be able to penetrate. In addition, her shield would likely injure any Terrobah who touched her, just as it had the night of Troy's attack.

Sharon wanted to teach me the same constant shielding, having been led by a dream to do so. She knew at some point I wouldn't be able to maintain my light armor in battle and would need this protection to survive. I showed her that I already had it covering the upper half of my back, which led to me sharing with them about my first battle against the man I had once thought to be my uncle.

Our discussion also reminded me of my dream with Amelia and how I had used the armor to dissolve the ropes that bound me. When Sharon and I practiced, I had a tingling sensation that ran through my whole body, like a current of electricity traveling from my head to my feet. I had felt this same sensation in my dream and shared as much with Sharon, who confirmed she felt it as well. I had to really focus when I was trying to get my body to shield on its own. Sharon, on the other hand, did it without a thought. It took much more concentration than my normal shield did, so I didn't really see the benefit of it. But since we all took our dreams seriously, I continued to practice.

One Saturday, we were all together at Ethan's house, training and talking. The others had moved to the kitchen to grab some lunch while I stretched on the floor. Mitch remained in the room, and I looked up to find him staring at me.

"What's up, Mitch?" I could tell he had something on his mind.

"Are we okay?"

"What do you mean?"

"Well, you and I were headed somewhere, like in a relationship, and then all this stuff about The Light came up, and that became our focus."

"I know. I think we're okay for now."

"We're okay, but now it doesn't seem like we're headed anywhere," he commented.

"I wanted to let you have this time with The Light. It's important, and now it feels like our focus must be on The Light because of what we all feel is coming."

"I get that, but is there still an *us* to consider in the future?" he asked hesitantly.

"I hope so," I returned with a smile.

"Well, that's good to hear." His face relaxed into an easy smile, but his voice wasn't as convincing.

"Have I given any impression there wouldn't be an *us*?" I asked, since he still seemed unsure.

"Not really. You just treat me the same as you do Ethan, and everyone else, for that matter."

"I wasn't trying to seem like I didn't care. I was trying to give you the space to be with The Light and with Ruah without me distracting you," I explained.

"Well, Sarah, you distract me no matter what's going on," he replied with a mischievous grin, causing me to laugh.

"It's true," Mitch said, joining in my laughter.

"Thank you," I said and kept stretching as I thought the conversation was over. But Mitch cleared his throat and then sat on the floor beside me.

"Something else on your mind?" I prompted.

He had to clear his throat another time or two before he could speak again. "I gotta say, I'm really starting to feel intimidated by this Lucas. You refer to him with such awe and reverence." He tried to joke about it, but I could tell it was a real struggle for him.

"He's everything wonderful," I stated. I wasn't trying to hurt Mitch. I was just speaking the truth.

"Are you in love with him?" he asked, not able to hide his hurt as his gaze returned to the floor.

"Mitch, it's not like that," I replied, touching his arm. His eyes returned to mine with doubt. "I may have thought myself in love with him at one point," I admitted, suddenly needing to drop my eyes as the intensity of the feelings I had felt for Lucas resurfaced. "Okay, I was in love with him, but that's not what The Light had for us." I had to continue so that Mitch would understand that Lucas would always be a part of me, but my words seemed to fail me. "We'll always have a deep connection." Those words didn't begin to describe the relationship I had with Lucas, but it was all I could formulate at the moment. Apparently, they were the wrong words to use with Mitch since he grew angry.

"You mean you and he . . . you had . . .?"

His distaste and the nature of his question caught me so off guard I laughed out loud. His face looked so hurt, but the idea of Lucas and I being physically intimate was just so absurd. "No, we never had …" I finally managed to get out, even though I was still chuckling.

"Then, what was the deeper connection? And why is that question so funny?" His frustration and pain pierced each word, quickly sobering me.

"I'm sorry; I really don't want to hurt you, and I'm sorry that I was laughing. The thought of it was just so silly. I promise I'm not laughing at you. It's just that the thought has never even crossed my mind."

"Well, then what did you mean by a connection?" He was truly trying to understand.

I had to take a breath as my eyes looked up toward the ceiling. *Pneuma*. Before I could even think, *give me the words*, the answer had already formed in my mind.

"How do you feel when you're with Ruah?" I asked him.

He paused. "I can't describe it," he admitted.

"Exactly, that's how it is with me and Lucas as well. We went through an experience together that bonded us forever."

"But you're not in love with him anymore?"

"Mitch. I don't think that's it either. I will always feel for Lucas as I do now. But that doesn't mean I don't have a great capacity to love…" I paused, "to love others in the same way, or in a more romantic way."

I watched as his Adam's apple moved up and down, like he was swallowing hard to gain control of his own feelings. "Okay," he started, but paused to clear his throat again, "I'm sorry, I got so heavy there. I just felt like I had to know."

"It's okay. I'm glad you felt comfortable enough to talk to me about all of this." I had been a little hurt that he seemed to go to Ethan for everything now—talking, questions, and training. I said as much to him, trying to be as transparent as possible.

He laughed, which I found ironic since that was what I did when he bared his heart and concerns about Lucas.

"What's so funny?" I asked, curious but not angry.

"Well, since we're being truthful..." He leaned back on his hands with his legs stretched out in front of him. "I work with Ethan because I'm too nervous in front of you."

"Why are you nervous?" I asked, hiding a smile.

"I guess I just don't want to disappoint you with my inability."

"Mitch, you're doing great, really."

He made a face at my comment like he didn't believe me.

"Seriously, Nyiah and I have trained many other Light Bearers during our time together, and you are moving along faster than any of them. . . even in front of me," I added with a wink.

"Really?"

"Yes, really, especially after you faced Troy. But now I'm curious of your abilities when I'm not around if you think you're doing poorly in front of me," I said, feeling so stirred in my heart by the look that crossed Mitch's face at my affirmation.

"Sarah, can I give you a hug?"

His schoolboy smile made me blush. "Yes, please," I returned, feeling shy for the first time in a long while.

He stood up and offered me his hand, pulling me up quickly in front of him as I felt heat creep into my cheeks. He pulled me close, and I could feel my heart beating faster. This was a hug where I was giving just as much as I was receiving. Mitch now bore The Light and it felt incredible to be hugged by him. It was very reminiscent of the feeling of "home" that I got when Lucas or Pneuma hugged me. But Mitch was human and a Light Bearer; I could be with him. I let myself breath in and out, enjoying the experience not just as a Light Bearer and friend, but as a woman.

He squeezed me and stepped back. While I felt peaceful, he seemed more amped up. I tilted my head at him in question.

"Yeah, uh, that was pretty great," he said with a big smile and something else altogether alight in his eyes.

"For me too, Mitch," I replied with a smile that covered my entire face. "For me too."

* * *

MITCH

"Mitch, what's with you today?" Ethan asked with an edge to his voice.

"I don't know, man. I just feel off," I confessed panting with my hands on my knees, trying to catch my breath. I glared up at the faceless dummy still mocking me from its standing position. I'd managed to knock down two but had lost my weapons as I tried to get through the third. This was one of my poorer performances, and I understood Ethan's frustration. Frequently, I defeated a whole row without losing my shield and sword, but this time even my forcefield had fallen.

"Is this about Sarah?"

"I don't know. Sort of. I knew this life as a Light Bearer wasn't going to be easy, but this just makes me want to chuck it all and watch some football." Man, those were the days when I was oblivious to what was going on around me. But then again, were those the days? I was stuck in a battle I hadn't even seen, numb to things around me, all while pursuing the American dream. Besides Sharon, I hadn't had any real relationships. Now, I had true friendships and a purpose.

"You can still watch football," he quipped.

"I know. I don't know why I said that."

Ethan was standing there with his arms crossed and a look on his face that I knew meant we weren't moving on until we hashed this out.

"Sarah's on my mind a lot," I admitted, dragging my hands though my hair and moving around a bit, trying to clear my head. "I think it's still all this crap in the world and I feel like it's distracting me from getting all of my training right."

"It's not about perfection, Mitch. We can't achieve that on our own anyway," Ethan explained.

Still circling the room, I shook my head, trying to escape the weight that plagued me. What he said was true, I was still very much human, but all this stuff in the world was just distracting me. I said as much to him.

"The world isn't a distraction, it's our purpose. If we focus solely on The Light, then we miss those who need it," he repeated. This wasn't news to me. In fact, it was a conversation we'd had many times. Apparently, I needed to hear it a lot. Maybe it wasn't the distractions that were the problem. I still wanted to push to be better, push to be enough...

"Maybe it is about Sarah," I said quietly

"What specifically is it about Sarah?" Ethan asked, seeing I was homing in on what was bothering me.

"I want to be enough to protect her."

"You want to be more than enough," Ethan summed up.

"Yeah."

"And who are you comparing yourself to? Sarah herself?"

"No. Yes. Maybe. I don't know."

"Mitch, I have fought alongside her, and it's unreal. She doesn't have any protection other than The Light, and she doesn't need any other protection."

"But I've heard the stories; I know that Lucas had to save her."

"So now you're trying to compete with Lucas? Dude, you do know he's not human, right?" he said, smiling at me like I was crazy. "He's a Mythreal. We can't compete with that."

"I know, and I don't think it's like a man-competing-against-Superman kind of thing. I know I'm not in his league.

At all. But…" I didn't continue; I was again seeing the same vision of Sarah and me fighting side by side. I felt like I was so far from being able to fill that role, much less protect her from whatever the Terrobah wanted to inflict upon her.

"But what?" Ethan prodded.

"But I can't help but feel like I'm supposed to be in a protector role with Sarah." I was looking down at the floor mat, hoping he wouldn't press for more. The visions of Sarah and me together, battling or just living life seemed almost too personal to share.

"I get it, man." My eyes shot up to him at that.

He held his hands up, palms out, "Probably not in the exact way that you mean. But I have felt driven to protect her and Nyiah since I first knew of The Light. I think The Light puts that protective instinct into us as men."

"I feel it for Nyiah and Sharon as well, but not as strongly as I do for Sarah," I confessed.

"Brother, what are you thinking about now? I can see the storm clouds rolling across your face."

"I am so far from being worthy of her." Just speaking those words over myself made me feel deflated.

"None of us are worthy, but The Light chooses us anyway," Ethan countered. "Why would you want to throw away what The Light offers you? You're saying that what The Light has done in and through you isn't good enough, and that's just not true."

"You don't ever seem to struggle with anger and jealousy, while I seem to struggle with it all the time."

Ethan laughed out loud. "Dude, I'm not a Mythreal either," he said, still laughing. "I have human emotions and everything, just like you do. Just like Sarah and Nyiah. We're all still completely human, just set apart because we've been called to something higher. A lot of my hang-ups disappeared while I was in Ganheela, and I came back different. I realized a lot of my worries had been fruitless.

It's not about the things of this world and the circumstances. It's about the people in the world and their need for The Light."

I had no response, but one wasn't needed as he continued.

"We only have this one life to give to The Light. To be a Light Bearer, you're having to let go of a lot of the things that tied you down. You're already farther along than you know. I learned in Ganheela that people can know of The Light, experience The Light, and even be Awakened to The Light, but unless you're fully surrendered to The Light, and your intentions for The Light are pure, you cannot bear The Light to others. And clearly, dude, you can bear The Light."

I felt my chest swell at his words. I could feel The Light flowing through me, just from his encouragement. I *was* a Light Bearer. I was growing. I already looked much different than how I had behaved and acted before being Awakened to The Light. I had moved way beyond giving in to what everyone else thought I should do or say. My focus had shifted off myself to others and to The Light. In my flesh, I felt the weight of that responsibility and vowed once again to not make any more mistakes.

"It's not about not making mistakes," Ethan remarked.

Surprise flooded over me as my eyes met Ethan's. "Maybe you are a Mythreal. How did you know what I was thinking?"

"I didn't hear your thoughts. I took an educated guess at what you were thinking because I know you and your perfectionist nature. If we could make ourselves perfect and pure, what need would we have for The Light?"

His comment made me pause. I was already a Light Bearer. Sarah had hinted that we could be more than just the friends we had been for so long. She had friend-zoned me from the beginning, and I could admit I needed to go there. I thought I was a "good guy," but I'd been far from it, completely living for myself and what would make me feel good. So now that I was different and walking differently and seeing the world differently, there was a difference in her as well. A softening in her toward me.

Sarah had told me that to align myself with her brought with it a heavy burden. She was from a long line of Light Bearers, and she was constantly targeted, even by her own sister. My head swam with all the thoughts of what could be and what couldn't be.

In the end, she was worth it. Any suffering that would come from being with her wasn't as bad as it would be to be apart from her.

"Now can we get back to work?" Ethan's question and his joyful demeanor quickly snapped me back to the moment at hand.

"Yes," I declared, holding my hands in a battle-ready position. "We've got a lot to do to be prepared for whatever's headed our way."

CHAPTER 22

SARAH

Awake, rise, Beloved!

It was the early hours of the morning, but as I sat up in bed, I knew it was time. I knew where I would see Amelia again. She was calling me to come to her, and Pneuma was giving me permission to answer. I saw each of my friends gathered around me. Nyiah, Ethan, Sharon, Mitch, Lucas, Owen, and others I had met throughout the last few years. I even saw Aunt Letta, and that concerned me. Was she even strong enough to fight? And would her ex-husband, Trevor, be there?

I saw Amelia as well; she was so fierce and so very dark.

Pneuma, I'm weak when it comes to her. She's the only one I've ever given up my shield for.

Immediately, I heard, *My power is made perfect in weakness*, as Pneuma's words reverberated in my heart.

Pneuma had said that to me many times. I knew I had to be emptied of my worries and fear and to let go of any imaginary control I thought I had in regard to Amelia. The Light would be my strength. The more the enemy could see The Light and the more my friends could see The Light, the more powerful we all would be.

"Amelia, I'm coming," I said to the dark room. She couldn't hear me, just like I couldn't hear an audible call from her. But our lives were forever intertwined, and it seemed like our destinies as well. I would see my beloved sister again soon. That very night, it looked like from my dream, and at the same docks outside the warehouse where I had faced off with her the last time.

It was fitting that the battle would happen in a dark and abandoned place like that. From what I saw in my dream, even the sky would be overcast. There would be no earthly light even from the moon and stars. And the lights on the decrepit dock had long since burnt out.

Preparing to go, I remembered Pneuma's last words from my dream, "Today, it will be finished. Be of great courage, my love." Either Amelia or I would see our last day, maybe both. Pneuma always knew the outcome, but she did not share the future with those who could still make decisions to change it.

Outside my bedroom window, the sun's rays were just starting to glisten off the water of the pond. I took a deep, cleansing breath as I texted my friends, "It's time. Please come to our house so that we can travel together."

* * *

On the plane, I sat between Nyiah and Sharon. Mitch and Ethan were across the aisle from us. They had been talking most of the flight, but I couldn't really hear what they were saying. Nyiah and Sharon had mostly remained silent. I suspected that neither one of them wanted to add to my already swirling thoughts. They were like quiet soldiers guarding me on both sides, which was a little amusing since I was taller than both of them.

In a bout of anxiety, I had already glowed outwardly in the waiting area of our terminal gate. Thankfully, no one seemed to notice, maybe just assuming it was a light beam streaming in through one of the windows. Ethan had grabbed my arm and whispered, "Easy, Sarah." That had helped me focus on my breathing, and I drew my light back.

It wasn't just my thoughts of Amelia causing anxiety. My thoughts lingered on who was coming with me. Pneuma had given permission for so many to join me in this battle. She knew the Terrobah's numbers would be quite large, and I would be facing my two greatest adversaries. I hadn't seen Uncle in my dream, but I had a strong feeling he would be there as well.

Sharon and Mitch, who were still very new to The Light, would be fighting for me. My Aunt Letta, who had endured so much, would at least be in the general vicinity, but I hoped to keep her out of the battle. The father of the family she was staying with, Mark Johnson, would be coming with a group of Light Bearers that he knew. Of course, Brandon, the Mythreal who kept watch over my great aunt, would also be traveling with them to join in the fight.

In addition, Owen had texted me that he would be meeting us there with other Mythreal that were already on earthly assignments. I had seen Lucas in my dream and knew he would be coming as well.

All these precious people and Mythreal were gathering with me to fight on my behalf. I couldn't bear the thought of losing even one. I wanted to call this whole thing off, but Amelia was such a strong pull for me, and Pneuma had told me to go. This was my last chance to reach my sister, my last chance to save her, but what if someone else died for me?

"It wouldn't be just for you. It would be to honor The Light," I heard out loud, to my right. I turned at what I thought was Pneuma's voice but realized Nyiah had spoken.

"What was that?" I asked.

"I heard that and knew you needed to hear it, too." She regarded my huge eyes. "I wasn't trying to hear your thoughts. Pneuma shared it with me, and I knew I was supposed to say it to you."

"That's different," I said, making a silly face to cover my shock.

"I know, but she's had us speak to each other before."

"Not quite like that."

"True." She kept looking at me, searching. I looked away, feeling a bit raw and exposed.

"Sarah, you can't bear this burden alone." She entwined her hand into mine. She dropped her voice to a whisper, "Each one of us has chosen to come and fight the Darkness. You are a part of that, but we are each coming as warriors of The Light to fight in this battle for which we've all been trained and to which we've all been called."

"It's true, Sarah," Sharon said from my other side, pulling my gaze toward her. "I love you, and I'm coming to support you, but you weren't the only one who had a dream last night. Mitch and I were both called to this fight as well."

"Really?" I turned my head to look at Nyiah on the other side, "Did you have a dream?"

"Yes, and so did Ethan." Nyiah confirmed. "Gavin said that he had one as well."

"Gavin, from Colorado?" I was overwhelmed.

"Yes. I know you trained him, but I don't think he would fly all that way to Miami without Pneuma calling him to do it," Nyiah stated matter-of-factly.

I took a deep breath. Everyone had been called by The Light just as much as I had been. This was bigger than me getting my sister back. The Light was taking a stand against the Darkness, and the Eklesi had been called together to accomplish that.

"Do you think Light Bearers are coming that we've never even met?" I asked out loud to no one in particular.

"Yes," Nyiah answered. I turned my head to look at her.

"Wow, I was only thinking of myself and Amelia, but this is so much bigger than that."

"There's no doubt that you two are the major pieces leading to this confrontation, but yes. I think this is much bigger than that," Nyiah said with no shame in her voice.

Sharon spoke next, bringing my gaze to her. "Ethan was telling me that the Darkness hasn't taken a stand like this in about 2,000 years. They don't dare come against The Light in full force like this because The Light always wins."

"How does Ethan know that?"

"There were history books in his version of Ganheela."

"Of course, there were," I replied, knowing how much Ethan enjoyed history.

All this conversation had taken place in low whispers. We had placed a shield around us when we sat down, but it was still weird to be so close to other people and talk about any of these things at full voice. We had sensed some Awakened on the plane, but no Terrobah. Many were still undecided, and as a number of people were leaning more toward the Darkness, we had to be careful.

Sharon felt this the most and had been drawn to speak to many of them as she walked by, but we cautioned her that if they were leaning to the Darkness, her touch and her voice might hurt them instead. They would see her as a threat instead of someone wanting to help them.

I took a deep breath and rolled my shoulders.

"Feeling better?" Nyiah asked.

"Yes," I leaned my head back against the headrest, then rolled it toward her. "I can't carry everyone," I said out loud, though not quite believing I had fully surrendered that burden.

"We all have to focus on our own part of the fight," Nyiah seconded my statement, but this time didn't address my thoughts.

"Yes, we're all bound together by something much greater than ourselves," I agreed.

"You're a little excited now, aren't you?" Nyiah squeezed my hand.

"This many Light Bearers and Mythreal gathered together? Yeah, I'm excited," I whispered. But then in a much stronger voice I declared, "And the Darkness doesn't stand a chance."

✳ ✳ ✳

At the Miami airport, Ethan and Mitch rented a large van, which we sat in outside of baggage claim, waiting for the others. I was watching the automatic doors when I saw my Aunt Letta walk out. I couldn't help but climb out of the van and give her a huge hug. I pulled back quickly, looking at her face. "Are you sure about this, Aunt Letta?"

"I had to come, sweet Sarah," she replied, caressing my cheek.

"I'm just not sure it's safe for you here," I remarked, searching her eyes.

"I've been through hell here on earth, and I have to admit, I was frightened, but I cannot let that fear determine my actions for another minute of my life. If I do, then I remain their slave."

"But what if Trevor is here?" I whispered.

"I'm quite sure he will be, but so are you, and so is Amelia. My girls are going to war, and I'm walking in the power of my freedom to be here as well."

I let her pull me close once again. There was really nothing I could say to that. She had the full power of The Light, and she had clearly been called here to fight as well. We held each other for what felt like an eternity, oblivious to the world around us.

"All aboard," the Mythreal who had accompanied Letta and Mark said quietly behind us. We turned to see him gesturing to the van.

"Hi, Brandon, is it?" I asked as I tried to smile, moving out of Letta's embrace to hold her hand.

"Hi, Sarah," he said with a knowing grin. "It's nice to meet you."

"Same here," I said, still trying to smile back. "I guess I need to introduce everyone."

"Nyiah took care of that for you," he quietly assured me. He had the great presence of a Mythreal, but he was more soft-spoken than any I had met before.

"Oh, good," I said in return, my face falling.

"What is it, Sarah?" Letta asked in concern.

I took a moment to swallow the lump in my throat and push back the tears that threatened. "I guess I just wish you all were here for the same reason as all the families around us." I said, looking around at the loading zone. "I wish we were all piling into this van to head to the beach for our family vacation. That we were going to eat and catch up, not going to fight, or..." I tapered off.

"I know, Dear Heart," Aunt Letta said, bringing me in for another hug. "Someday, we will have that time as one big, happy family."

"But, for now," Brandon said and gestured to the van.

"He's such a taskmaster," Letta chuckled as she moved past him to climb into the van.

"Thank you for coming, Brandon," I said quietly.

He put his hand on my shoulder and spoke without any further prompting from me, "She is ready; The Light is strong within her. She may falter at seeing him, but not for more than a moment." Brandon's hand on my shoulder brought me peace, and he passed light into me. "The Light will prevail no matter what."

"Okay, then," I responded with a nod. Looking at his peaceful face one last time, I climbed into the van.

CHAPTER 23

SARAH

OUR VAN SLOWED TO a crawl as we reached our destination. While I had been to this place before, the atmosphere had changed. Sliding the van door open, I stepped out, illuminating the area around me. They hadn't arrived yet. When I had been there before, my eyes had taken in the seeming lack of life at these abandoned docks. Now my gaze took in the shadows that surrounded them. There was still a dim light from the sun that had nearly set, but even that had been obscured by clouds. There was a haze hovering in the air. I wasn't sure if it was humidity, dust, fog, or a combination of the three, but it was clear this was an environment that the Terrobah would thrive in and nightfall was coming quickly.

Once we all had exited the van, our light spread much farther. Even with just our small group, we brought with us a warmth that seemed to transform our squalid surroundings from a place you would avoid at all costs into a place where you would want to come hang out.

The Mythreal had given instructions for the rest of the Eklesi to initially stay at a nearby rest stop of the highway. We didn't want to tip our hand as to how many we had by gathering too early. The rest of the group would stay at our meetup location with the other Mythreal until Owen called for them. When we had arrived at the rest stop, Owen was already there waiting, and I walked straight into his arms. He hugged all of us, having some sort of connection to each one. Mitch seemed a little taken aback by the Mythreal at first, but now, at the docks, he was laughing at something Owen had said. It was so like Owen to bring some levity to the moment.

I didn't have the heart to ask where Lucas was in front of Mitch. I'd seen him in my dream, so I trusted he would come, and hopefully this time, he came a little before I was knocking on death's door. I had wanted Mitch and Sharon to stay back while some of the stronger fighters came, but they moved forward with the first group like they knew that was their place. What could I say without making them feel like they were lacking something?

Sharon was talking to Ethan, and I saw him hug her from the side. The sweet smiles they were sharing gave me pause. Had I been so distracted lately that I hadn't seen their connection until this moment? I knew that Ethan had been in awe of her giftings, but apparently it was something more. I watched as Sharon touched his chest, the golden covering she normally wore spread out through her hand to protect his heart.

I turned away from the tender moment and concentrated on my inner defense, feeling the electricity surge through my body until I was covered from head to toe. I flexed and moved in my light armor that still felt a little unnatural except on my back.

As I looked at my beloved friends and family gathered around, I knew we were as ready as we could be. We had done everything we could to prepare, and we just had to wait until the Terrobah, and my sister, arrived.

They didn't make us wait long. When the sun finally gave up and all the light was gone from the sky, only a breath passed before we heard a terrible screeching sound, like nails across a chalkboard. It was coming from overhead.

"Helmets!" "Shields!" Brandon and Owen shouted simultaneously. There was no need for this warning as we all had them up and ready.

"How is the sound coming from overhead?" Ethan shouted back. We were clustered close together, but he still had to shout to be heard over the screeching. In our helmets, it wasn't painful, but we could still hear it.

"Helicopters!" someone shouted.

We needed more light. I closed my eyes and focused on gaining more light so we could see what was above us. The word "flare" popped into my head. I immediately shot bursts of light up into the sky just like flares. They burst above the helicopters, making it clear we were outnumbered, by a lot. I had seen at least ten helicopters above us; all filled with ten plus soldiers.

Owen had seen them too. "I've called the others," he said firmly. "All of them."

We had planned to come in waves to continue overwhelming them, but we weren't left that choice.

The Terrobah repelled down their ropes from the helicopters onto the warehouse rooftops and right into the midst of us. Light blasts were going everywhere as military-clad bodies transformed to shadow and nightmarish forms.

"Formation!" Owen yelled.

We tried to move toward each other, so at least we would have our backs protected, but the Terrobah were everywhere. It was hard to find each other and fight at the same time. I had barely taken in the onslaught around us before I was fighting three Terrobah: one in the form of Uncle, but who was too weak to possibly be him; one as a sickening sea creature; and the other in the form of my mother, hurting and bleeding. These images didn't even slow me down, knowing the tricks they were capable of, so I concentrated on The Light bringing us all together. I felt a pull at my back and slowly took one step at a time backwards until the pull stopped. I glanced behind me and could see Owen, Brandon, Ethan, Mitch, Nyiah, and Sharon.

Arrows were coming at us from all directions. It seemed like bombs were going off as well. If we didn't have The Light uniting us, it would have been chaos. It was full-on war, the likes of which I had only seen in a movie. Arrows were even coming at us from above, most likely where the Terrobists were hiding out. The Mythreal had placed a dome of light above us so that we were protected from all sides. With The Light, what could man do to us?

The rest of the Eklesi arrived much faster than I thought they would; they must have already been on their way when Owen called. They seemed to understand the same thought I had, and as they came onto the scene, they grouped up and allowed The Light to hold them together.

Terrobah after Terrobah came at me, and each one ended up lying smoldering on the ground. They kept changing into Uncle, or my mom, or my dad, or some scary monster. I was growing tired of their game, to the point that I blasted one of my Terrobah enemies before I even noticed he was coming at me. I wrapped light around the throat of another one imitating Uncle so that he had to focus more on his breath than on transforming.

"Where's Amelia?" I questioned my captive, not wasting any time getting to the heart of the matter.

"Dead," came the strangled voice. His word had no effect on me.

"Where is Amelia?" I gave him another chance, pulling him toward me with the light as he grasped at the choke hold around his neck, trying to free himself from my grip.

"I'm only going to ask you this one last time, and then you'll have to face your own form of punishment," his neck was smoking where my light was bound around it. "Where is my sister?"

"Right here!" My head jerked to the left as my shield brightened at the venom in her words. She'd already sent arrows flying at me. She was unleashing a torrent of arrows at my entire group of beloved friends. Instead of just one sword, I came out with two and crossed them. A pulse of light came out so strong that it shattered the arrows where they flew and the pieces fell to the ground.

I moved away from my family as Amelia and I continued sending light and arrows at each other. Her with the intention to kill, me in self-defense and to slow her down. Not one single pulse held its full energy; but I knew at some point, to incapacitate her, I would have to use something stronger. I moved away to protect those I loved. I could sense her power was much stronger this time with the Darkness pulsing through her. With her red eyes glowing out at me from a face so twisted in rage that I barely recognized her, I knew she wouldn't hesitate to hurt and kill every person that I loved.

It was then that I realized the fighting we were doing at that point seemed more like a tiff between siblings. I felt the venom in her arrows, but she was not giving it her all. Her red eyes started to flicker, and confusion was coming in waves across her face.

"Amelia, come with us. We can help you." I tried to get through to her.

I saw a flicker of something in her eyes, and then the red blaze returned. "Help me? Help me? You abandoned me, and they took me in. You, Sister, are the enemy."

"No, Ames, I didn't have a choice. I never would have left you if I had a choice. Please believe me." Some strange part of me wanted to take my helmet off. I wanted her to be able to hear my thoughts so that she could know I only spoke the truth.

"You saw me as damaged goods long before that day, and you left to be free of me." She cursed me with her red eyes blazing.

"You were never damaged goods. Is that what they told you? They did horrible things to you, and I found Lucas who healed you."

"Lucas?" She questioned with the red blaze dimming in her eyes. "No, he was the one that hurt me and got you to leave me behind."

"No, precious sister. Lucas saved your life after Ben and his friends almost killed you." I was still sending out light bursts to block her arrows, but even those had slowed in her confusion. I tried again. "Please, Amelia, I'm here to help you."

I wasn't sure why, but that seemed to anger her even more. "Help me? Help me?!" Now she was shrieking at me. "You aren't here to help me. You're here to steal my power!"

"I don't want to take anything from you, except for the darkness they have tortured you with." I knew now I couldn't use the word 'help' with her; it was somehow a trigger word that incited her to pain and rage.

"The Darkness is what gives me my power," she continued, shrieking as the black tar that had almost killed me once before poured forth from her with me as its target.

"You can have a beautiful power in The Light as well," I proclaimed at full voice. She shouted in pain, even bringing her hands up to cover her ears. I hated to hurt her, but I thought maybe I was getting through to her. The Light poured forth in my voice as I shouted over the battle raging around us. "The Eklesi is your true family. Please, let me show you the way." I moved a step toward her and reached out my hand. I couldn't stand the pain she was in.

Pneuma, help her, help me, please!

The confusion was written on her face. I could see she was fighting the forces that waged in her head. Darkness battled The Light in the space between her ears.

"Amelia, you matter to The Light. You are loved. You can come home with me." I shouted truths over her, trying to win against the voices that tormented her.

The confusion and pain washed over her face in waves. "Sarah," her voice came through, pleading, and her form shifted so that I could see my sister as I remembered her. "Help me." The blackness began its retreat toward her.

I had been prepared for her words filled with venom, but I hadn't been prepared for her pleading. As her words found their mark and I started moving quickly toward her, I realized I had let my helmet slip, and I was stunned that I was unable to renew the helmet. I was almost paralyzed. I looked down and found the source of my paralysis, the black tar had its fingers wrapped around my ankles.

"Amelia, release me, let me come to you." I felt fear clawing at me without my helmet; I couldn't seem to bring it back. I had felt the need to let it fall, but that wasn't of The Light; it had been a scheme of the enemy. Amelia didn't have the power to hear my thoughts, only Pneuma did. I looked back up to see that Amelia's eyes were flaming red. I knew then it had all been a trick, even her pleading was meant to disarm me. It hadn't been real.

She shrieked and arrows flew from her straight at me as the black tar rendered me completely incapable of any movement. I could feel its effects creeping up my body as it continued to paralyze me.

At almost the same moment, I heard "Sarah!" screamed as a light shield was suddenly in front of me, dissolving the arrows as they flew toward me. In my next breath, Mitch was in front of me and blasting Amelia with light. I still couldn't move and feared an attack from my back. I was worthless. All my friends were going to die. I'd been wrong to move toward The Light; Darkness was where I belonged. Dying was what I deserved.

Was that right? No. Yes. I left Amelia. I deserve to die.

The life was being pulled from me, and I was okay with it, I deserved it. I was choking on my own failures. But something was squeezing me. It felt good, but in the wrong way.

Who am I? I'm an orphan. No one loves me. Warmth was spreading through me, that was right, that was good. *No, death is what I deserve.*

I heard a faint echo in my head, *Errah.* I was hearing a foreign language. It sounded wrong to me. I didn't know it. Or did I? I was in a foggy tunnel that seemed so long, but I wanted to move toward that voice, and the light at the end of it.

Errah, Errah, wake, wake up, wake up, Sarah Joy. It came louder and louder and became clearer. There were explosions around me, shrieks, screaming. I was in the middle of a war zone.

"I deserve to die." My voice came out in a croaking whisper.

I heard someone whispering in my ear, "You are Sarah Joy. You are much loved. You have the strength of The Light."

"I deserve to die," I said, but I no longer felt that way.

The voice continued getting louder. "You could not have prevented what happened to Amelia. You tried repeatedly. You have salvation in The Light. Embrace The Light, sister." I knew that voice. Nyiah's voice. That voice was truth. She had her arms around me.

"Sarah Joy, you are deeply loved. You are beloved in The Light. You have power and purpose. Come back to The Light." I saw myself again on the hill, twirling in pure joy and light. Light, Light, Light! I could once again feel The Light surging through me.

Nyiah still had her arms around me, but my hands held my helmet made of pure light. I was being given the choice yet again to choose to put it on. Was I going to believe The Light or the Darkness, no matter what form that Darkness came in? I put my helmet on with a finality that it wouldn't leave me for the rest of the battle.

As quickly as I had started leaning toward the Darkness, I was reunited with The Light. Nyiah helped me get to my feet even though I didn't need it. I took in my surroundings. There was a group around us shielding us from the battle that was still raging. There were many Terrobah on the ground, but still so many more fighting.

Nyiah let go and I turned to her. "Thank you," I said fiercely as I hugged her, and tears streamed down my cheeks. Nyiah was my sister as well, and she spoke truth, not the lies and pleadings that had been uttered by my birth sister. My shield was up and around both of us now as I released her.

"You're brilliant in The Light," Nyiah said with a fierceness I had never heard from her. I looked down and I was glowing just as brightly as ever. What the enemy had meant for evil was being used for good.

I saw the Mythreal, Brandon, and a few other Light Bearers battling Amelia alongside Mitch. I could tell they weren't giving it their all. They were waiting for me to resume my position. I had known all along that it would be Amelia and me in the end.

"How do they keep coming?" Nyiah asked, searching the surrounding area with her eyes.

There was no need to respond. Nyiah knew the inner workings of the Terrobah as well as I did. Standing side by side, we sent a strong electrical pulse at each of the helicopters overhead, causing their electrical systems to fry and forcing them to land.

Mitch was tiring and was only shielding at this point, trying to hold up against Amelia. Love surged in me for this man. He was out here fighting for the very first time in defense of *me*. Without looking at Amelia, because I just couldn't, I blasted in her direction as hard as I could. I glanced at her to see it had caused her to stumble and stop her onslaught against Mitch. Pain tore at my heart as I blasted her again.

"Behind!" I shouted and blasted a Terrobah coming up fast behind us. It only took one blast over Mitch's shoulder and the creature was flat on its back.

I turned back to my sister. Owen was the only Mythreal to remain beside me, and he turned to be my rear guard.

Amelia was not slowing, and my blasts seemed to have only angered her further. Her earlier confusion was all a ploy to get inside my head. Her red eyes no longer wavered. She'd been taking on a different form of herself to incapacitate me; that was the twisted mind of the Terrobah. The truth was I now had to incapacitate Amelia in order to take her.

Love for her surged in me. Knocking her out would be merciful. Then, she could come with us and stop enduring the torture and brain washing of the enemy, if her true self was even still in there. I raised my hand toward Amelia, emitting a pulse of light that continued until she was flat on her back, the black tar nowhere to be seen.

I heard a rumbling overhead and then a bright light. At first, I thought Lucas had come as the light was so bright, but instead, what I saw was a spotlight on one of the helicopters.

And then a voice spoke slowly over the loudspeaker, "Ah, my little Sarah." It was a voice that still haunted me and sent chills straight through me. I reacted without thinking, sending a fierce blast of light straight at the helicopter. It hit its mark, and the helicopter caught fire.

"Sarah, stop," Owen shouted. "We don't know if there are humans on board."

"It's Uncle," I shouted back. "I have to stop him, or he'll take her again." I blasted the helicopter once more.

"That's not your decision, and that is not who you are," Owen shouted over the noise, using force as he made me physically lower my hands.

"He can't have her again." I shouted back.

"If it's at all within my power, he won't leave with her today." Owen's calming voice got through to me.

My blast had damaged the helicopter, forcing it to land. I tried to take a step toward it, wanting to be between Uncle and my friends, but I was unable to move again. I checked to find my helmet was still glowing, but my forcefield was down and as my eyes took in the scene around me, I realized that the black tar was around my ankles again. I was still able to turn my head, and I looked to where Amelia had been lying on the ground. She was on her knees, but back to battling.

"Sarah, you're not using your shield!" I heard Sharon shout. I knew from our many practice sessions that meant the one I could project within my body, my light armor. It still felt uncomfortable to achieve a full body covering, but I closed my eyes and asked The Light to do just that. I felt it radiating through my body at the same time the tar released, and I could hear Amelia shrieking in pain. I opened my eyes and looked down to see my whole body completely covered in gold. It was even shining through my clothes; my internal, impenetrable shield.

The battle sounds had ceased around me because everyone was looking at me. I could hear Amelia, but her screech had no effect on me. I looked around and most of the Terrobah were cowering and trying to hide themselves from The Light coming out of me. The Mythreal were also golden, and I saw Sharon completely glowing as well. Many of the Eklesi were moving around, quickly making ropes to tie up the distracted Terrobah.

"ENOUGH!!" I heard Uncle roar. I turned to look at him as he moved toward us out of the wreckage of the now smoldering helicopter. My golden skin never so much as flickered, even at the power of his words.

"Enough?!" I shouted back in question, not believing that he thought he got to be in control of this situation. He also had the black tar coming out from his feet in all directions. "You don't get to say '*enough.*' The Light says '*Enough*' to you!" At my words the tar retreated.

"Oh, Sarah," he snarled, his voice dripping with disgust. "Do you actually think your pathetic little words have any power over me?"

Why was I even dialoguing with this maniac? Without further hesitation, I blasted him with the fury I had felt inside of me for the last five years. He would not take Amelia, and I would end him if necessary in order to keep her from his clutches. He staggered a bit, but that only increased his fury. I kept blasting and Owen joined me. Uncle was different than the last time we'd faced him. He was much stronger and he could tolerate The Light in ways that I had never seen in a Terrobah before.

"He's received more of the Darkness," Owen said gravely.

"He's a Terrobah. How could he get any darker?" I asked as my blasting continued.

"He has agreed with the Darkness to no longer be any of himself. He has given himself over fully. He no longer fears or feels pain. He can no longer selfishly decide to run away. I'm not sure what other power he possesses."

"Then how do we defeat him?"

Owen didn't answer, but I looked to my right as Brandon joined us. *Together. We would defeat him together.*

We were touching shoulder-to-shoulder as we sent light in his direction. It reminded me of my first battle, side-by-side with Owen and Lucas and how powerful we were together as a unit. I felt fatigue in that battle, but in this one, I felt only strength and the pulse of The Light.

Uncle was smoking, but black tar still rolled out from him. It wasn't getting through our shields, but neither was it stopping. Many Terrobah were getting up around us to join Uncle, which made our jobs even more difficult. My heart dropped a little when I heard more helicopters coming overhead.

"How long can we keep this up?" I asked Owen. "Most of the Eklesi are human and they will fatigue."

"We'll go as long as we have to," Owen replied, and I knew he was right. The onslaught wasn't slowing, and I could see members of the Eklesi tiring with stumbling steps and flickering shields.

"I have to go help them."

"Go," Owen replied, knowing I meant my friends. "We'll hold him."

It was perfect timing for me to move away; I turned just in time to see Trevor battling my Aunt Letta. I didn't know for sure that it was him. Another Terrobah could have taken on his form, but whoever it was, it looked like my great aunt was losing.

Feeling as light as air as I moved about with my golden skin armor, I blasted as many pulses as I could at Terrobah as I passed by, running to stand between Aunt Letta and Trevor. I blasted him back. It really was him, and he came hard at me with another snarl. He clearly had an axe to grind with me. I had taken something very valuable from him, and he was holding nothing back. Channeling my feelings of what my poor aunt had been through for decades, I sent a continuous blast into him with such strength and power that within seconds he was flat on the ground, smoldering. I didn't stop until his twitching did. I hadn't reduced him to ashes, but he wouldn't be getting up anytime soon.

I turned to Letta to check on her. She was pale but still had her shield up. "Are you okay?"

"Yes, love. I'm just fine, thanks to you." She had been looking at Trevor's still form, which had returned to smoking shadows, seeing him yet again as he really was. But she looked up at me as she finished and moved toward me, reaching out to touch my cheek with great sadness in her eyes. "Don't you have a battle to finish?"

Amelia.

I turned to see that she had Mitch kneeling on the ground, black tar surrounding his lower legs. Sharon and Ethan were blasting at her, but it didn't seem to have any effect. I ran to stand in between Amelia and Mitch, also giving him my shield, as a sickening question came to the forefront of my mind. Had she also given herself fully over to the Darkness? Was there anything left of her that I could save?

Yes. I heard from Pneuma. I heard Pneuma numerous times throughout the battle, but her voice sounded almost audible this time.

I blasted Amelia back hard, so I could have some space to take in what was happening around me, when behind me, a scream tore through the air. I didn't even have to turn to know that it was Owen. I had heard him scream one time before when an arrow had pierced his side. I turned to see Uncle had ahold of him, and it looked like he had sunk his claws into his chest.

"No!" I screamed. I blasted Amelia until she was flat on her back. Then, I turned to sprint across to Owen, blasting at Uncle as I ran. Brandon was blasting him too, but it only seemed to jostle Owen about like a rag doll in Uncle's grip.

"Pneuma help!!!" I screamed louder than I ever had before as I jumped on Uncle's back, grabbing him around the throat and using my second skin as a branding iron, blazing as hot as I could manage. There was a brilliant white light that blazed overhead, and I saw Owen fall, comforted by the fact that Uncle's claws had released him. Most of the Eklesi were helping us, still trying to defend as they got Owen to safety. Brandon was still trying to help me as others shielded Micah, another Mythreal, while he carried Owen away.

I felt Uncle start to stumble and I let go to jump away from him before he fell. I continued to blast as he tried to get up. He was up faster than I'd expected, and I doubled my swords up to cross in front of me and shatter the onslaught of his arrows. I swiped down and the tar he was sending forth was cut off in its path.

We continued to battle. Brandon was helping me gain the upper hand, but I was the one that captured Uncle's gaze. We were equally matched, and at times, he seemed to be winning. He was nothing like I had ever fought before, even ten Terrobah at a time. My arms were weakening, and exhaustion was starting to take over when a voice that was sweeter than any other called my name.

"Sarah, this is not why you came," he said. *Lucas is here.* I dared not turn my head, but I felt his presence come up beside me.

"I have to stop him!" I shouted.

"No, you don't," Lucas said calmly in return, his hand on my shoulder, filling me with light and resuscitating my body.

"How's Owen?" I asked.

"He's recovering." Lucas was shielding but sending no light toward Uncle.

"Lucas, why won't you stop Uncle?" I questioned, finally looking at him.

"That is not why I was sent." His gaze was not indifferent. He would have taken out Uncle if he could.

"I can't stop," I said as a sob tore through me. Lucas knew what Uncle had done to me, to my parents, what he'd done to Amelia, and probably so many before us. This world would be a better place without him.

"You have to let go." He didn't mean anything in the physical sense.

"You're asking too much of me. I can't." Another sob tore through me.

"You can," he assured, returning my gaze with a confidence I didn't deserve.

I shook my head violently at him as I continued to sob. After everything Uncle had done, he didn't deserve forgiveness. He deserved death.

"That is true Sarah Joy, but you will not be the one to deliver it." Pneuma was talking audibly to me, and as I turned to look at her, the war zone around me faded away. I continued to turn as the scene in real time gave way to the beauty that was Ganheela. My sobbing had ceased; I could breathe fully and the brilliant light of Ganheela warmed me all the way through.

Pneuma had brought me to Ganheela when the pain and agony of everything I had lost at the hands of Uncle threatened to tear me in two.

"I can't let him get away again," I said to her. "I can't let him hurt anyone else that I love." I felt peace here, much more than I had only a few moments before, but my thoughts hadn't left me.

"You must let go of him. Your anger and bitterness toward him are an aid to the Darkness and block The Light from covering you completely." Pneuma moved to face me and grasp my hands.

"How can I forgive everything he has done?" I asked her in disbelief.

"It is a choice you make. You choose to forgive, and all the ties he has used to ensnare you are gone forever."

"So, he just gets away with everything?" I asked, hurt.

"No, his time is coming to an end, but it does not come at your hands. All the Darkness has a finite number of days and will be eradicated. Today though, dear one, you can truly be free of him."

I liked the sound of that a lot, but for five years I thought I would be the one to end his tyranny. I held onto that in the moments when I didn't think I could go on. He didn't deserve forgiveness.

"That is true, but then again, neither did you." Pneuma answered my unspoken thought.

"What?"

"In order to come into The Light, you needed forgiveness as well. You were granted forgiveness and a life guaranteed after this earth without ever having earned it. While Uncle cannot be brought to The Light, you need to forgive him for your journey to continue fully."

She was right. What had I ever done to deserve The Light and the gifts it bestowed upon me? Pneuma was asking me to forgive, which meant it was for my good, even if I couldn't see it. But could I do it?

"You have been in the process of forgiving him for years. All it takes is saying the words. You do not have to feel it. That will come in time. It does not mean you forget everything he has done. It just means you are severing the hold your unforgiveness has allowed him to have on you."

"Okay," I responded, nodding at her.

"Okay," she said calmly, matching my words and giving me a brilliant smile as I moved to hug her tightly.

Before I could form another thought, I was back. My absence hadn't been noticed since Ganheela was outside of time, but even in that space outside of time, Lucas had moved between Uncle and me as another form of protection while my mind was elsewhere. I felt as if I stepped back inside of my body, but I wasn't feeling the fatigue of the battle anymore.

Sensing I was back, Lucas turned to look at me. I stepped up beside him, continuing to fight Uncle all the while. I released all feelings I still had for him into The Light. My anger and bitterness hadn't hurt him anyway, but they had been like a poison inside of me that I hadn't or couldn't see until this moment. I wanted the poison to be eradicated, just like he would be eventually.

"I forgive you," I shouted to Uncle. He was standing there still battling with everything he had. While my words seemed to only anger him, they brought great peace to me.

"Sarah," said Lucas in a breath, tears in his eyes and pride shining forth. "Let's quiet him for a while, shall we?" I nodded.

With Lucas on one side of me and Brandon on the other, I felt the pulse building within and between us before we released it. When he was reduced to a still shadow on the ground, I turned my back on Uncle to look across the dock at my family, the Eklesi.

Some were still locked in battle; some were helping those who were wounded.

Himiza.

At Pneuma's encouragement, I shouted, "Beloved, arise, we no longer fight their war. We fight for love, life, beauty, and truth. These creatures have chosen darkness and death. As we stand united, they will fall! Eklesi, with all that you are, call upon The Light!"

CHAPTER 24

MITCH

My arms were shaking with exhaustion, and my clothes were soaked through with sweat. The battle had been nothing like I could've ever imagined, and it didn't seem like it was coming to an end. I had been knocked on my butt more times than I cared to count and by Sarah's sister, of all people. Not only that, but I constantly had to keep myself in check because I was so enthralled with watching Sarah fight. She seemed to grow in power even as the battle raged on, but I was forced to refocus when horrible shadow creatures with red eyes would transform into a bloody mess right in front of me.

As Sarah stood with her back to her greatest enemy, exhorting us not to stoop to their level, the strength of her voice alone caused the shadowy shapeshifters all around to shriek as they fell to their knees. When others started to raise their voices in praise, light suddenly poured forth from the sky. Across from me, Amelia stumbled backwards, debilitated by the sudden brightness. At the same time, it filled me with a deep warmth, and I felt my strength returning.

Next to me, I heard Sharon say, "Thank you, Pneuma!" All around me, shouts of praise broke out, and I could see all the Eklesi shouting and cheering, even those who'd been wounded.

The Light had come in full force. Those of us who were a part of it were healed and restored, while those who came against it were screaming on the ground in agony. It was strange because I couldn't really hear their screams, but I could see them writhing in pain.

My focus returned to the battle at hand, taking note that Amelia was incapacitated on the ground, while Sarah was sandwiched between two Mythreal. Her attention remained on the Terrobah I knew to be Uncle. They had him on the ground, but he was somehow still fighting. As if on cue, I saw Micah and Owen join them to confront him.

"Let's get to work," Ethan said, suddenly at my side making a light rope in his hands.

As we bound the Terrobah, light was still pouring forth from the sky, brighter than the brightest noonday sun. It didn't hurt my eyes at all, but instead, comforted me and restored everything I had given in the fight. I made a light rope as well and moved to tie up Amelia, feeling a little scared to get so close. This chick was crazy and creepier than any nightmare I'd ever had. She struggled in vain to escape the brilliant light coming from the sky. I wanted to hate her, but I knew how much Sarah loved her. Amelia was one of the main reasons we were here, and it was clear to see that the Darkness had her deeply ensnared.

It was with mercy that I bound her hands and feet in as much light rope as I could manage, rendering her completely still. If Sarah's sister was still in there somewhere, I would help to bring her back. With that thought, I moved to the next Terrobah as the outpouring of light from the sky slowly faded, like the setting sun.

I looked again to where I'd last seen Sarah, but she had moved on while Uncle was being bound by a Mythreal named Josh and another Mythreal that I hadn't met yet. Looking for gold, I spotted Sarah across the dock, helping to tie up more Terrobah. She stood up and looked over at me in that moment, smiling. I returned her smile as I moved to the only remaining Terrobah that wasn't bound, bending down to tie him up as I finished making my light rope. It occurred to me a little too late that he wasn't smoking and since the light had completely faded from the sky, I was now at his mercy.

∗ ∗ ∗

SARAH

The tides turned swiftly once we, as a group, had called upon The Light. The Father of Light had emphatically answered; the battle was almost done. Terrobah were either blowing away as dust in the breeze or they were being bound. Lucas and Josh were binding Uncle after we delivered a devastating blast of light. I had moved away because I knew they would take care of him, and I no longer needed to see him defeated to feel that all was right in the world.

The knots now finished on the Terrobah I had bound, I rose and looked up to see Mitch across the huge dock. Just to the right of him, Amelia was down and bound with light ropes of her own. It ripped at my heart to see her like that, but she was finally in the hands of The Light, no longer the Darkness. I smiled at Mitch so he would know I didn't hold his defeat of my sister against him.

Mitch smiled back and then bent down to tie another Terrobah. Something wasn't right, though. I knew it in an instant and started sprinting toward them, sending light toward the Terrobah that now had Mitch by the throat. *Tristan.* Could it possibly be one of the Terrobah from Camp Tuano? One of Uncle's most trusted minions.

"Stop right there, Sarah," he sneered at me. By his smile, he clearly knew I wouldn't. I slowed but still moved decidedly toward them.

"I would stop if I were you," I heard to my left, a bored voice that belonged to someone I thought was dead.

"Steve," I acknowledged him as I turned to see that he had Letta by the throat. When I escaped his clutches at Camp Tuano, I was certain they would have killed him for such a mistake.

"Don't make us hurt these pitiful humans more than you already have," another familiar voice mocked me.

Carson. The other enforcer from camp. I hadn't seen these Terrobah since Camp Tuano and had dismissed them from my mind, but here they were, as real as ever. They'd been able not only to withstand the light ropes but had gotten out of them. I didn't think that was possible, but another Terrobah jumped up and grabbed Sharon. What was going on? It was then that I saw it. The black tar was slowly oozing out of the still forms of Amelia and Uncle, wrapping around the light ropes and disintegrating them.

For one moment, I felt defeated and overwhelmed, but then remembered the power of The Light we'd seen just minutes before. The Light would prevail here today. My thoughts were affirmed as I saw Lucas, Josh, Brandon, Owen, Micah, and other Mythreal I had not yet met take aim at each of the freed Terrobah. With one simultaneous blast of light, each Terrobah that had been freed was dropped. The Mythreal ran to those that had been held captive, but I ran to Amelia to stop the tar. As I passed Uncle, I blasted him as hard as I could, causing his tar to retreat. Another Light Bearer saw what I did and started making a circular pattern around Uncle with light.

Using light pulses to stop the tar seeping out from Amelia, I saw her light ropes were almost gone. I moved toward her to re-tie them, but before I could even start the light rope formation, she was on her feet and firing arrows at me with possibly the worst shriek I had heard out of her yet. Again, I brought up two light swords. When they touched, she was blown backwards by the force, but not even five seconds passed before she was coming at me again.

Amelia was fighting with everything in her for something she believed in, just like I was. My beloved sister had been pulled into the Darkness, and she was fighting to dispel The Light from me. I couldn't reach her with my words or my touch, and my most precious gift, The Light, was like poison to her, just as the seeping tar was to me.

Confusion was rolling across her face again as her eyes flickered, but I could sense that this time the confusion was real. The Darkness was being defeated and whatever part of my sister was still in there was trying to get out.

Free her, my love, I heard in my mind.

I looked at my sister as her eyes began to clear. It seemed like her eyes were almost pleading with me to help her. *Free her? How?* I thought back.

Show her the way.

My heart leapt at the thought. If I could show her the way, that meant she was coming into The Light.

She is crying out to me, asking to come to The Light, asking to be free from the Darkness.

All of this was happening in my mind as I held Amelia at bay. The Darkness in her was still battling The Light.

She has made her choice to follow The Light.

Pain and hate were emanating out of her to destroy me, but I could see the separation now. It was as if that body had ahold of my sister, and she was trying to get out. I caught glimpses of fear on her heavily scarred but still beautiful face.

"Ames!" I shouted, using my name for her from our childhood. "It's time. You've made the choice for The Light. Stop fighting so we can help you break completely free from the Darkness!"

The war inside her was weakening her, possibly even tearing her apart. I could see it from my position just twenty feet from her. I started moving slowly toward her, only defending, not sending any light her way to increase her urge to fight.

"Ames, I'm here."

The struggle inside her was painful to watch. Shots of light would come out from unseen places, and then tar would follow. I was afraid if it continued much longer, she would be torn apart from the inside out.

"Ahoova-te lah geh shay." The words came forth from my mouth of their own volition. It was the key to calling Pneuma, and it was the key to calling the Amelia of The Light back to me.

Her body went rigid as her face cleared. She slowly lowered her arms to her sides as if fighting herself to get them there.

"Ames, Ahoova-te lah geh shay. You are free in The Light, reject the remaining Darkness." I held my hands out, palms up, showing her I meant no harm. I was only about six feet away from her as her face transformed from clear to pained. Her eyes, however, remained brown, never going back into the Darkness enough to turn red.

"Well done, Sarah Joy," Lucas's voice reached out to encourage me as he walked toward me. The battle had finished around Amelia and me. He was emanating such brilliant light as he walked through the dust of defeated Terrobah all around. The beauty of The Light within him almost drowned out the shrieks of the bound Terrobah lying on the ground.

"Lucas?" I asked, feeling every emotion roll through my body. His words told me my part in this was done. He smiled at me and laid a hand on my shoulder, then turned to focus on Amelia, closing the remaining gap between them.

He took her head in his hands and whispered, "Tetelestai."

All at once, a shadowy figure shot up and out of Amelia, shrieking as it left her body. It shot straight for me, but it couldn't get through my golden skin armor.

"Shields up!" I shouted as I turned to the rest of the Eklesi. I saw shields immediately glowing. Once again, the shadowy figure shrieked, then disappeared into the ground. When I turned back, Amelia and Lucas were embracing.

A sob rose up in my throat and broke free, causing both of them to turn toward me. I lunged for Amelia, wrapping her up in a hug that had been inside of me for years.

"Thank you, Sarah. Thank you for never giving up on me," she whispered fiercely.

"I love you, Amelia, so much."

"I love you, too," she said as a sob broke in her throat, and she joined me in tears.

We pulled back a bit only to look at each other. Her eyes were clear and shining with light.

My eyes narrowed on her neck and the brands she wore there, undoubtedly punishment for any weakness or compassion she'd previously shown. My training had been done in love; hers in misery. The tears continued down my face as I felt the depth of the pain she'd endured.

"Sarah, I'm so sorry for everything. For not telling you about The Light, for trying to lead you to the Darkness." I cut her off by pulling her in for another hug.

"Amelia, I forgive you. Can you forgive me for not getting to you sooner?"

"That's not your fault. I had to stay . . . for them." I pulled back to look at her again.

"Them? The Terrobah?"

"No, my..." Suddenly, she gasped in pain. Her face was set in alarm, and I couldn't figure out why. She was suddenly ripped from my grasp and pulled like a rag doll 20 feet away from me.

The source of her pain, initially invisible to my eyes, slowly became a shadow and then changed again into a man. He looked like a Mythreal, so glorious and beautiful. I would have been taken in by him if I hadn't seen the tar coming out the front of Amelia's body. Clearly, he was the one hurting her.

"Let go of her!!" I screamed, then targeted him with every bit of strength that I had and fired light at him. He smiled a cruel smile, and did just as I asked, sending Amelia crumpling to the ground.

"Amelia!" I cried out as I ran for her. I should have been afraid of this new enemy, but my sister was my only focus. Light was surging all around me, so I knew the Eklesi wouldn't let him get away. I dropped to my knees and pulled my sister to me, trying to infuse her with as much of The Light as possible.

As I held her unconscious body, I could see the extent of her wounds. He had been holding her with a massive claw and when he released her, blood flowed freely from the wounds. I wasn't healing her fast enough.

"Lucas!" I screamed. Amelia's eyes fluttered opened to meet mine as Lucas pulled her into his arms and flooded her with light.

"Sarah," she gasped out. Her voice was filled with pain, and she was losing her fight for life in our world. I pressed against the wounds on her abdomen, pushing light in with everything I had.

"I'm here, Ames," I assured her through my sobs, kneeling beside them.

"I'm sorry, but I had to stay for them. Please, find them," she rasped out as her lungs no longer seemed to be working.

"Find who?" I asked desperately, as I knew I was losing her.

"My sons." Tears were streaming down her cheeks and mine. We had Mythreal all around us, but still it wasn't enough to heal her.

"Your sons?" I questioned, begging her for more information.

"That's why I had to stay with Uncle." She barely got his name out over the duress her body was under. All these years, she'd stayed for sons I didn't even know existed.

"Martha . . ." Amelia choked out her name.

"Martha?" I asked, desperate for more details.

"The...the twins," she barely whispered. "Save... them," she labored out, "like... you... saved me."

So, I had heard her correctly in my dream. "The twins," I said out loud.

Amelia had two sons. She didn't respond. She was slipping away. "Of course, I'll find them," I confirmed. Her eyes slipped closed as her final breath escaped her lips, a peaceful smile confirming to me that she was finally free. "I promise you I *will* find them. I love you, Ames."

"Lucas!" I cried. "There has to be another way to save her," I pleaded with him.

"If there were, Pneuma would give it to us," he reminded me. The Mythreal were all trying to infuse her with The Light but nothing was working.

I saw the pain of it on Lucas's face. Amelia was special to him as well. Some of the small fragments of The Light that had returned her to us had come through Lucas when he saved her way back at Camp Tuano.

As if they were given a signal, one by one, the Mythreal stepped back while Lucas still held Amelia.

"What are you doing?" I was frantic.

"She's home," Lucas whispered, looking up at me, and then he wept.

"No, no, no, no!" I had just gotten her back, and she was gone. I felt hands on me and The Light around me, but in my grief, I wanted to push it all away. This wasn't fair; this wasn't how it was supposed to end.

This is not the end, my child, not for Amelia or for you.

I almost felt betrayal as I heard Pneuma's voice, but The Light surrounding me wouldn't let it linger. Pneuma had wanted Amelia back from the Darkness even more than I had. Amelia was in the Land of The Light. How could I want her to come back from there? I continued to weep as my feelings warred with The Light. I felt like I would break into a thousand pieces at the sheer agony of my grief.

The Light can take your anger, your hurt, all your feelings. We will not let you break.

I had arms all around me, but I reached for Amelia. Lucas set her gently beside me and I took ahold of her.

I sobbed as I cradled her in my arms, rocking back and forth in my grief, telling her how much I loved her. She had the most peaceful expression on her face, a look I'd thought I would never see again. The sun crested the broken-down buildings as I released my beautiful, beloved Amelia to The Light.

Gentle hands touched my head, my back, and my shoulders as I wept over my sister. Gut-wrenching grief and sadness at my loss hung heavy over me, but my friends would not let it overcome me.

*　*　*

MITCH

It just about killed me to watch Sarah sobbing over her sister. It was harder than anything else I had faced that day. We all just stood around her, touching her, lending her our light and strength.

The night hadn't turned out how any of us expected, and the ending seemed to be the worst part of it all, Amelia dying after only just returning to The Light.

While Lucas and Sarah worked to try to save Amelia, the rest of us had joined together to fight the fake Mythreal, but he had some type of shield up and just smiled at us from behind it. He called Uncle and three other Terrobah to him, and together, they all disappeared.

I didn't even know who he was, but I would kill him for all the hurt and pain he had caused Sarah.

Lucas looked up at me from where he was holding Sarah and tilted his head as if to try to figure out my expression. I tried to conceal my feelings as he stared at me, but I don't think I was successful. He rose and nodded his head at me as if he wanted me to follow. I shook my head at him.

"Mitch." His voice came to me, but it didn't look like anyone else really noticed. I felt compelled to move toward him as he opened his arms for a hug.

"Uh, I'm good, thanks." Did he really believe I was going to hug him? I gave a slight exhale that was kind of like a laugh.

"Mitch." Lucas said again, still holding out his arms. And this time I couldn't tear myself away from his gaze. The look I saw in his eyes could not be described as anything other than love. It was as though he understood everything about me, including the depth of my feelings for Sarah, and yet he still loved me. I felt tears forming in my eyes. I shook my head to break the power he seemed to have over me, clearing my throat to try to get rid of the emotional lump that had formed there.

I took a deep breath, feeling like every kind of fool as I moved to hug Lucas. What I thought was going to be an extremely awkward encounter, instead turned into a defining moment of my life. As soon as he embraced me, I was filled with peace, breathing in that feeling of home like I had experienced with Ruah. What was going to be a quick step in, step out on my part turned into me hugging him back. A being I had almost thought of as my enemy was now my brother.

Remembering that we weren't alone, I cleared my throat and stepped away from Lucas. Sarah gently laid Amelia on the ground and turned to our friends to be hugged. I looked back at Lucas who also had his eyes on Sarah. He had more Ruah in him than any of the other Mythreal, not that I went around hugging them. He was just on another level.

"Not all of you sense that," Lucas said, cutting his gaze to me like I had figured out some big secret.

"Are you a Mythreal or something else?"

"Yes," he said flatly.

"Well, that's helpful…" I trailed off, my attention turning to Sarah as she walked toward us, our friends parting to make way for her as she approached.

"Lucas, who was that?" Sarah asked, tears still in her eyes. He pulled her into his embrace.

"Enfiero," Lucas responded.

Just that one word sent terror racing through me, and it seemed to have the same effect on all the Eklesi around me.

"He is the Leader of the Terrobah," Lucas answered, anticipating our next question.

Silence hung thick in the air.

Sarah stepped back away from Lucas and nodded her head as though she fully understood who he was talking about. She wrapped her arms across her chest and shifted her feet as though some kind of chill had come over her.

"Where do we start looking?" She questioned Lucas, her voice filled with a sudden determination.

"What are we looking for?" I asked, trying to keep up.

She looked at me and answered, "Amelia stayed with the Terrobah because they had her twin sons. She asked me to find them and save them."

"So, she *was* aware of The Light before today?" I asked, feeling a sense of relief.

Sarah nodded, "I think maybe she felt like she couldn't move toward it without losing her sons. I just wish she could have trusted The Light sooner."

"So, where do we start looking?" It was my turn to question Lucas and the other Mythreal who were standing beside him, but Sarah cut back in.

"Martha, she was our housekeeper when we lived with Uncle. Amelia mentioned her name. She must know something. But where do we even begin to look?" Her question was posed to Lucas.

"I've already been assigned to the search," he assured her. "We'll ask Pneuma."

"Yes, okay," Sarah returned. I saw the determination etched on her face once more. This was next on her path. Our time had not yet come. The twins and her promise to her sister would now be the driving force of her life, right behind serving The Light with everything she had.

"Sarah, you'll come with me," Lucas instructed with a small smile.

"Really?" she asked with surprise in her voice. I felt a sharp pain in my chest.

Lucas nodded and said, "Yes, we'll search together. Josh will join us, and Letta will search with Brandon."

Sarah was leaving. It was hard for me to even comprehend what life would look like without her. The sadness must have shown on my face because Sarah quickly crossed the space between us and drew me into a hug. "I'm sorry, Mitch," she said, "I had no idea it would end like this."

"I understand," I replied, feeling like I was choking on my own words. "But I'm also here to help you, Sarah. Anytime. Anywhere." I had to lean on The Light now more than ever.

"As am I," Ethan said.

"And me too," Sharon seconded, as many other voices joined in.

"Thank you, my friends... my family," Sarah smiled through tear-filled eyes, reaching her hand out to mine, passing me The Light she knew I needed.

* * *

SARAH

What had happened in that battle? I couldn't get my mind around all of it. I had known deep down that most likely either Amelia or I would not be leaving those docks alive, but I think I still held out hope that Amelia and I would continue on together. I knew she was in the best and most wonderful place she could be and that The Light would take care of her. But The Light had chosen for me to stay.

I was to remain on Earth and find Amelia's sons. She hadn't said it, but I suspected Ben was involved. The fact that Enfiero had come to silence her meant that most of the Terrobah would try to interfere with me finding my nephews. That didn't intimidate me though, because The Light knew where they were, and Light Bearers and Mythreal would be looking for the twins as well.

I looked at all the faces that were surrounding me. "I thought this was an ending, but it appears to just be the beginning of something else."

Nyiah spoke up, "This is a time of mourning and sadness, but with the dawning of a new day, it will be a time of hope as well." Nyiah's words were comforting as she wrapped me in a warm, light-filled hug.

The task ahead of me didn't seem as daunting with my family and friends gathered around me. I looked over at Amelia's still form, wanting to gather strength from seeing her sacrifice, but her body was gone. In her place was a flower, growing through the concrete. I gasped at its beauty. That it was a flower from Ganheela or even the Land of The Light could not be mistaken. I immediately moved toward it, being drawn in by its magnificence.

Bending down to touch it, I heard Nyiah say softly beside me, "It looks like a rose, only like no rose I've ever seen here on Earth."

At my touch, the flowering plant changed and shifted and grew, producing many more of the same brilliant flowers. They were blue and purple and pink and seemed to glow with light from within. Just the touch of the flower petals was pure bliss. The brilliant flowers warmed my insides. Amelia had been delivered from this life and from the Darkness. She was free forever.

"Goodbye for now, my precious sister," I said softly, reaching down to take one flower as they continued to multiply, a memory of my sister's sacrifice. "I have a promise to keep."

I stood with my flower in hand and looked at the docks and the clean-up that had already started taking place. Then, I turned back to all those who were gathered around me. We had lost two Eklesi humans and many Terrobists in the battle, and we would mourn them. The Terrobah, of course, were never really gone, even though many had been reduced to dust.

I looked around at all the beloved faces surrounding me. I was thankful, even in my grief, for what I had. This was my family. "It won't be easy," I said, "but through it all, the Eklesi will stand together."

"TOGETHER!"

Acknowledgements

The Deliverance has been a long time coming. Thank you, readers, for your patience and grace as I labored in love to get this book into your hands. Thank you for continuing to see the Light Bearer series as a great read and worthy of your attention. I know your time is precious, and I'm thankful you decided to spend it here.

Thank you, to my husband. Without you, *The Deliverance* would still be held hostage on my computer. You're my prayer support, my encouragement, my grammar guru, my proofreader, my IT guy, my business manager, my best friend, the best Daddy to our boys, and you're the one who truly gets me. You have never wavered in seeing how these books could bless so many. I would have given up long ago if I hadn't had your encouragement and understanding. Our first 21 years have had their highs and lows, but the last five years have been heaven sent. I'm very much looking forward to the next 21+ years with you and what God calls us to together.

Thank you to my oldest son, Cooper, my tender-hearted leader. Thank you for not only reading and helping with my books, but thank you for being a fan! I couldn't do what God has called me to do without your encouragement and tech support! Thank you for learning how to use the audio software, recording/editing/posting my podcasts, and for doing your own proofread through *The Deliverance*. Thank you for not getting exasperated with me when we have to record the same sentence over and over; I couldn't record the audiobooks without you and your support!

Thank you to my middle son, Paxton, my peace-bringer. You're quick to pray for me when I'm in pain, help me with all sorts of tasks, and you come in for hugs and cuddles at just the right time. Thank you for understanding the time these books take and for cheering me on! You're so excited to read this book; don't worry, your day is coming!

Thank you to my youngest son, Theo, my gift from God. You bring me joy and cuddles when the edits feel overwhelming. Thank you for understanding when Momma needs the house quiet for recording and when I say, "Just one more paragraph and then I'll get you lunch." Even your little waves through my office door encourage me as I remember that these books are also about the discipleship they bring.

Thank you, Carol, my editor, for continuing with me in the Light Bearer Series. We worked together on this project 3 years ago, but I still remember it being a fun time of fellowship. You added polish to a dream and helped the story continue!

Thank you, Cat, for being my first fan. Those moments that you would sit outside your mom's office trying to hear parts of this story encouraged me to carry on when being an author was hard. Your love of these stories reminds me that these books will be cherished because of where they came from.

Thank you, Amanda S., for always being there for me! You have encouraged me, grounded me, proofread for me, and even let me borrow your closet for recording sessions when I didn't have a closet to record in. I'm grateful to have you as a friend for life!

Thank you, Taylor J., for being my sounding board, my prayer support, an aunt to my boys, and a great friend to me. You have been a behind-the-scenes supporter of this book ministry and I know I wouldn't be where I am without you.

Thank you, Heather B., for finding *The Awakening* on Amazon and being obedient to the Lord to reach out and encourage me. Eighteen months ago, we didn't know each other and now, I'm not sure where I would be without your emails and texts of encouragement.

Thank you to the Stone family for backing this book and the ministry the Lord has called me too. Thank you Lauren S. for continuing to ground me, calling me to more in my relationship with the Lord, and loving me as a sister despite my quirks.

Thank you to the Saunders family, without whose generosity and land, I would not have been able to accomplish the Kickstarter or finishing *The Deliverance*.

Thank you to the Rodden family for opening your home to us when we didn't have one of our own. In fact, I'm typing this "thank you" from your home as I get *The Deliverance* ready to go out!

Thank you to those of you who have prayed for me and been my rearguard. God knows your name and I'm so thankful for you. Whenever I think of you, my prayer people, I see an army of angels. You have prayed for me, for my family, and for this ministry and I am eternally grateful.

Thank you to my friends. I am beyond blessed to have so many friends that love and support me that I cannot list them all here, but I had to say thank you. Thank you for your prayers and your support of me and this ministry. I am thinking of your many faces as I type this and saying a prayer for each of you.

Thank you, Candi, for loving me and supporting me with these books and short stories. You have read each of the stories more times than anyone, second only to me. You have cheered me on, proofread, prayed for me, and blessed me.

Thank you to my mom, for your support even with your physical pain and through your grief. I have been encouraged to press on through my own physical pain.

Thank you to my dad, for supporting me no matter what the Lord has me doing. I'm always grateful you're only a phone call away.

Thank you to my entire family for continuing to support me in my writing and ministry. To the Clarks, Grubbs, Hites, and Odells, these books are part of our family legacies. Our faith comes from many who are already in Heaven, but their legacies live on.

Thank you, my Heavenly Father, for the dream in May 2018 and for all of the beautiful visions and words that have followed. Thank you for keeping the words flowing and how you grow and heal me as I write. SDG.

* * *

Finally, to all my Kickstarter Backers, *The Deliverance* wouldn't be here without you! Thank you...

Adelynn Post * Alexis Flint * Alli * Angela Miles * Barb Owens * C.J. Milacci * Caitlin Proulx * Callie Thomas * Candi and Darl Hite * Carol Jones * Caroline Roberts * Cori Davidson * Dad * Darlene N. Böcek * Dawn Adams * Dawn Blair * Dianna Kovach * Dominique Henriquez * Donna Kelley * Dustin Hite * Elisabeth Proffen * Erica Reinfeld * Esther Wong * Florentina * Friend of Jill Briscoe * Genelle * Gina Webster *Giselle T * Grace * Heather B * Heather Lamarche * Hilary Anderson * Isabel Fernandes * J. A. Webb * Jacob Williams * Jamie * Judy Nelson * Kamee * Kandi J Wyatt * Karen Martha Odell * Kathy Brasby * KL Wagoner * Kraig Cox * Kristin Hite * Kristin Flanagan * Laurie Christine * Linda Clark * Lindsay * Liv Viengar * Lorelai * MadiJoy * Mandy Crussel * Melissa B * Michael S * Michelle Bleess * Morgan Adkins * Mrs D Ford * Natascha Vogel * Olivia * Pamela Hart * Paula Dover * Rachael Ritchey * Rachel @ McBee-Moore Realty Inc * Rachel Wirtz * Robert Pritchard * Seana Johnson * Shanna Brown

The Bogun Family * The Cox Family * The Johnson Family *
The Matt Clark Family * The Rodden Family * The Saunders
Family *The Schreiner Family * The Stokes Family * Tiffany W *
Wheatcrofts * Will * William, Wyatt, and Weston

* * *

"The night is far gone; the day is at hand. So then let us cast off the
works of darkness, and put on the armor of light." Romans 13:12

From the Author

Thank you for reading *The Deliverance*. I'm sorry that it took so many years to get this second book out, but I'm grateful to you for your patience and grace. This book was harder to write, as it deals with painful family dynamics and deep emotions. I spent many scenes crying as I typed, crying for my characters' pain and for the wounds the Lord was healing in me. I hope and pray that you are blessed by these stories on a deeper level as well!

In the third installment of the Light Bearer Series, *The Reckoning,* we will find Sarah searching for her nephews. She is helped by Mythreals and friends, both new and old. We will also see more of Enfiero in his element.

While reading this book, if you were stirred to hope and want to learn more about The Light, please visit this page:

https://mindyhite.com/the-light/

If you want to stay connected with me, head over to my webpage

https://mindyhite.com, where you can find my newsletter, devotional podcast, blog, and other resources.

I love you, dear readers, and hope to be with you in the pages of my next book again really soon.

You are seen. You matter. You are loved!
Mindy

P.S. Read on to start *The Reckoning...*

The Reckoning

PROLOGUE

"It doesn't matter what I try, the dumb kid won't adapt to the Darkness." The dark-haired, younger man growled out angrily.

Another man, taller and darker, glared across the room at the boy sleeping in the corner on a dirty cot. The boy glowed with light.

"See," the younger man let out a string of cuss words. "The more I try to turn him, the more he glows." He kept cursing until the taller man interrupted.

"Make it stop!" The tall man shouted with such force and evil that I shook in terror even though he wasn't talking to me.

A small woman made her way to the sleeping boy and tried to wake him. "I, I don't know how to make him stop," she said, clearly afraid of what would come next for her.

"Make him stop!" The older man roared as he closed in on her, and I shut my eyes, afraid of what else he might do.

I heard a scuffle and a cry of pain as the woman pleaded, "Please, I've tried everything." She was crying now.

"We may have to face the fact that he's a lost cause. Your beauty queen had more light in her than we ever realized. You took her too soon!" his voice boomed.

My eyes came open, afraid he was talking to me. Thankfully, he wasn't.

"I did what I was told; I followed orders!" the younger man shouted back.

"You stretched those orders and you know it. If I'd had more time with Sarah, we wouldn't be where we are!" the older man thundered in return.

"You had ten years with her and it didn't help!" There were so many cruel words flying around that I had trouble keeping up.

The woman was trying to muffle her soft crying as the boy was startled awake, his glow remaining.

"STOP IT!" the taller man screamed in rage.

While the woman and I both cowered, the boy on the cot just sat up and looked at the screaming man. The man's voice seemed to have no effect on him.

"You have one more day to get control of him," he declared through gritted teeth, glaring at the woman. "And then I kill him." She lifted a shaky hand to touch the glowing boy, but nodded that she understood.

"Now, get him out of here! I can't stand his filthy light!" He uttered more cuss words as he yelled at the women. She picked up the boy, paused for just a moment to look at me, and then practically ran down a dark hallway as fast as she could.

The taller man turned to look at the young man, who was following her with his eyes, a cruel smile on his face. "We need to focus our full attention on the other one," said the tall man. *What other one was he talking about?*

I immediately got my answer as his red eyes landed on me, and an evil grin formed on his face. I was the other one.

CHAPTER 1

SARAH

"Our destination is just five miles up ahead," Lucas said as he slowed down from a jog to a walk and paused to look at me. "Are you doing okay, Sarah?"

"I'm good, just ready to find them." He wrapped his arms around me, giving me light and love. My heart swelled at his touch, and I felt at home even in this desert wasteland. Lucas's hug was the closest thing to hugging Pneuma; not even the other Mythreals could make me feel like Lucas could.

He was my original rescuer and still one of the most important people or beings to me. My sister, Amelia, had recently died at the hands of the Terrobah. Only with the help of two powerful Mythreals could I continue on in the wake of my devastating grief.

Lucas released me in time to see Josh stepping to my side. "I have a strong feeling we're right where we need to be," Josh added with his British accent. He had offered to "transform" enough to eliminate the accent as he was no longer on an assignment in Europe, where he needed it. I had asked him to keep it because I found British accents to be very comforting. Josh wrapped his arm around my shoulder, giving me a smile and a nod; that was enough to bring about my agreement.

"Me too," I responded, smiling at him while my breath returned to normal. We had already run for over five miles, but I ran and trained all the time for missions just like this. We'd been searching for the twins for the last two months.

Just like when Amelia was with the Terrobah, we had to wait for Pneuma to reveal information about my nephews to us in her time. Unfortunately, the few other places we had been sent to showed only the evidence that the boys presence there before, not the boys themselves.

Both Lucas and Josh had heard from Pnuema at the same time about this new location. While we were eager to find them, there was also an underlying concern. It was clear that the Terrobah had the boys, but in what condition would we find them.

"Let's go," I said with a nod and a smile at both of them, and off we went again.

I kept having flashbacks of the last time Lucas and I had run with urgency together. The setting was different, as we were in the middle of the desert during the day instead of a dense forest. It was blazing hot, but the sunshine added its own feeling of comfort. The Terrobah didn't like to operate during the day and any light was good for us. The feelings that accompanied this time together were also different because we weren't fleeing. Instead, we were the aggressors coming to take back what was ours.

Amelia's final request to me before she passed into the Land of the Light was that I find her twin sons. With Lucas and The Light on our side, I knew we would find them. I was determined to return them to where they belonged and raise them in The Light, to one day be reunited with their mother.

To continue reading *The Reckoning* visit:
https://mindyhite.com/books/

www.ingramcontent.com/pod-product-compliance
Lightning Source LLC
Chambersburg PA
CBHW051216190726
48288CB00006B/1984